Bible Quest

Bible Quest

A Novel

JC
DAMIEN

Straus Simon & Morrow Publishing, Ltd.

New York   London   Toronto   Sydney

PUBLISHED BY STRAUS SIMON & MORROW PUBLISHING, LTD., an imprint, headquartered in London, England.

www.strausandsimonandmorrowpublishing.com

www.thequestnovelseries.com

www.biblequestthenovel.com

Straus Simon & Morrow Publishing, Ltd. and the portrayal of sails and star with the SSM monogram are registered trademarks of Straus, Simon, and Morrow Publishing House, a private limited company. Original logo, SSM monogram overlaid with the Paternoster Row image, is a registered trademark of Straus, Simon, and Morrow Publishing House.

The cataloging-in-publication data is on file with the Library of Congress.

ISBN 979-8-9856552-1-6

December 2021

First Edition

10 9 8 7 6 5 4 3 2 1

FOR THOSE WITH A DREAM. DREAM.
FOR THE LAST OF THE L' ENTITA.
YOU KNOW WHO YOU ARE.

Acknowledgments

For those who encouraged me, who believed in me, who fostered confidence. And for those who didn't. Thank you for the motivation to achieve in the face of adversity.

Thank you, mom, for everything. Thank you, brother, for showing me that even in the most difficult of circumstances, one's need to create art is achievable. Thank you, Allen, for your expertise. Thank you, Tim, for your hard work behind the scenes. Thank you, Adrian, for your support. Thank you, Robin, for being there with everything over the years. Thank you, Dan, my freshman high school English teacher. You were the first to encourage me to write. Thank you, Jeff, my other high school English teacher, who helped me believe in myself, and the writing workshop group you provided.

Thank you all for your time.

BIBLE

QUEST

Coincidence. That's an explanation used by fools and liars.
—Lionel Luthor

For those who watch with their mind, here is a
riddle worthy of such rare wisdom:
Points to B, S, A. Below is above. 180. Now, eye.
Time is key.
If you unlock its secret, send your answer to claim
your prize:
biblequest@thequestnovelseries.com
(one prize per person)
Best of luck

enidrac sutro silos a solis ortus cardine

Prologue

*T*he earthquake hit without remorse or justification....

Malta has long been an enchanted tapestry of history, woven from the golden threads of mystery. To follow this silken road, with rapturous whispers tugging at your feet, skin, and heart, is a seduction of the soul. Come, for a silent song of color will wrap poetry across the senses most divine....

The fishing village of Tarxien, Malta, thrashed in the early morning. Buildings convulsed and stones shattered to the streets. Windows burst from their storefronts. Electricity shot free as power lines snapped and hissed. In the harbor, angry blue waves toppled hand-painted fishing boats. Then, as abruptly as it had all begun, the violent shaking found its end....

Cries of car alarms and frenzied dogs filled the air as the chaos softened. They gave way to emergency sirens. First responders surged through the once picturesque community. At the center of town, firefighters led the disoriented shoppers and employees out of Carters Supermarket. Arturo and Gorg were the last of these firefighters to exit the store, ensuring none succumbed to abandonment.

"Did you hear that?" Gorg asked. "Sounds like a child."

"There—there's your child," said Arturo.

A tabby kitten cried and clung to the side of a shopping

cart. A howl built within the kitten. Just as the howl climaxed, an aftershock hit, toppling the men. Before them, the parking lot tore open into a chasm wide enough to consume a house.

The shopping cart teetered on the edge. The kitten held on for dear life, eyes widening as the cart started to tip. They scrambled to their feet—the kitten and cart fell into the black abyss.... They shined their flashlights in this seemingly bottomless pit.

"Holy hell," Gorg said.

Arturo lifted the crucifix from under his jacket and pressed it to his lips. "Straight to the fiery inferno itself."

His flashlight beam found the shopping cart, complete with kitten snagged on a protruding rock about fifteen feet down. Swiftly, he removed the climbing harness from his equipment bag and pulled it on. Securing a line, Gorg helped lower him.

The flashlight now clipped to Arturo's jacket illuminated the terrified tabby. The shopping cart slipped free. Arturo's hand lunged for the kitten, but the cart broke away, plunging from sight.

"Christ!" he yelled.

Gorg watched from atop the chasm. "You lost him?"

Arturo's flashlight revealed the kitten clinging to his leg. He winced as the kitten's claws sank in, proceeding to climb up his body. By the scruff of its neck, he peeled the kitten off and tucked it within his jacket.

"Get me out of here."

Gorg began pulling him up.

Something reflected off the beam from Arturo's flashlight. "Stop!"

"Make up your mind!"

Arturo pivoted himself to get a better view, though still not quite seeing it. "Lower."

Gorg lowered him.

"Stop." Coming into focus now was a ten-foot cross crafted from a metal he'd never seen. Somehow, it'd been emblazoned into the sheer rock face. The design appeared as, or similar to the ancient Celtic style with a cross-haired circle at its center.

His flashlight followed past the edges of the massive cross to reveal the arched doorway a few feet away. The open doorway lead into a long corridor of blackness. He shifted the light on the doorway's arch, carved directly from the rock. Inlaid upon the arch were symbols with the same unknown metal, in a language entirely otherworldly.

Above the arch was more inlaid metal. It formed a symbol not witnessed in over two-thousand years. Before him was an inverted pyramid with an all-seeing eye at its center, perfectly framed within a pentagram. This symbol was about four feet across by four feet tall, by his best estimates.

Gorg tugged on the line. "You get lost?"

"Give me a minute." The kitten, nestled against his heart, began to purr. Carefully, he removed his phone and took photos.

"Okay!" he shouted. Gorg pulled him to the surface.

With the first glimpse of morning daylight, the kitten launched itself out of Arturo's jacket, disappearing into the disarrayed parking lot.

"Hey little guy—some gratitude," Gorg said, helping Arturo to his feet.

Arturo caught his breath. "We've got to call somebody."

"Who?"

"The Church..."

Gorg gave him a puzzled look, then turned and gazed deeply into the chasm full of darkness. A coldness, not from the earth, but from somewhere else, deeper, wafted up, chilling his skin. He shivered. "Whatever this place is, it's malevolent. Of death..."

Body Bags

*T*he Moroccan sunrise blossomed across the vast Port of Casablanca. Light melted away the shadow, canvassing the cargo and naval ships and tugboats, spreading over the uniquely azure water, moving on to the sprawling concrete docks brimmed with shipping containers. A gentlest wind, salty and aired, flowed past the pigeon-lined rooftops as the light continued on, illuminating into the heart of the city.

Not far from port was a place free of any romanticized notions. The shadows here lingered, as if to resist the hope a new day could beckon. In front of the signature giant green doors and stone walls adorned in razor wire was a sign proclaiming, 'Prison Oukacha'.

Deep within this concrete tomb, in a cell all his own, a shirtless man finished up his last set of pushups. The lone tattoo upon his right bicep, a Jolly Roger flag, seemed to ripple in a nonexistent breeze as the muscles below the skin pulsated. The array of various scars across his toned frame filled in the otherwise blank canvas of his body. He pulled himself up onto the metal slab, the deliberately poor representation of a bed it was. Using a tattered T-shirt for a towel, he wiped the sweat from his face.

Swift bootsteps ominously echoed through the cellblock. El Hani, the guard captain, stopped in front of the cell. He compared the mugshot photo in his hand to the matching face staring back at him through the bars.

"Howard Lyon?" he asked.

Howie gave the slightest of nods. Looking over the guard's immaculate uniform, there was only one thing and one thing alone out of place. The guard's holster was unsnapped. His gun protruded slightly up from the holster, revealing the safety was off.

Tucking away the photo, El Hani unlocked the cell door and entered.

Howie's grip instinctually tightened on the T-shirt in his hands, his only weapon against what was about to happen... "Teresi sent you...?" he asked, noticing the guard's name badge, "Guard... El Hani?"

"*Captain* El Hani." He glanced around to make sure there were no witnesses, then quickly offered a scrap of paper. Howie read it, then immediately stuffed the paper into his mouth and swallowed.

"Stop, prisoner!" El Hani shouted.

The yell drew the eyes of the inmates from the nearby cells. El Hani pulled his gun and aimed for Howie's chest.

Howie's eyes widened—the shot rang out. Howie gripped his chest, gasped, then fell face-first to the concrete floor. Keeping his gun aimed on the crumpled body, El Hani used his foot to turn Howie over. Howie stared vacantly toward the ceiling at nothing in particular.

El Hani crouched down and checked for a pulse. Getting blood on his hands from it now pooled upon the floor, he wiped his palms on the prison-issue T-shirt still in Howie's grip. He glanced at his watch just as four guards rushed into the open cell.

"Dead," El Hani told them, holstering his weapon. "Went for my gun." He got to his feet. "Bring a stretcher." They quickly exited the cell.

"And hurry!"

Dark silence entombed the prison morgue. On the cold metal table was a sheet with the distinct contour of a body beneath. The sound of a lock as it turned disrupted the deathly quiet.

A door opened. Fluorescent tubes flickered on, bathing the morgue in an ashen hue most grim. Footsteps approached. The sheet was pulled back, revealing Howie.

"Forgive the theatrics," El Hani said, releasing the sheet. "Best that could be done on short notice." He removed the small glass tube from his pocket, with just a little blood remaining within, having dumped the rest upon the floor of Howie's prison cell. He tossed the glass tube into the trash. "Well, come on then, climb on," he said, pointing to the pallet jack.

Howie turned... Two body bags, *filled* body bags laid limply across the pallet jack's twin metal prongs, as if forsaken sacrifices to this unholy place.

"Don't worry about them. They're dead. Can't bite now." El Hani unfolded a fresh body bag and handed it over.

Howie silently read the name label attached to the bag, 'Howard Lyon'.

"See," El Hani said, "I've made a breathing hole here in the side."

More than reluctantly, Howie climbed into the body bag. He hated—loathed tight spaces, and a body bag, airhole be damned, was a damn tight space. Though in no position to resist, he cocooned himself inside this PVC skin of death.

El Hani helped stack Howie onto the pallet jack. Proudly surveying his work, he quickly switched around each of the bags' name labels. More than a bit OCD in doing so, he shuffled the labels all around again, having thoroughly lost track of who was who. At the far end of the morgue, the light for the loading bay began to flash.

"Right on time."

The Fixer and the Spy

*B*eyond Vatican City's fortified thirty-nine-foot-high wall, past the countless and hidden security cameras, heat sensors, and motion detectors, away from the ever-familiar monuments and landmarks, in the northernmost corner, laid a place unknown. Here, within a cubby, lined on three sides by the perimeter wall, towering stone pines stood sentry. Their thick umbrella-shaped branches cast permanent shadow on the lone and most unremarkable building beneath them. Unlike all other locations within Vatican City, there was nothing declaring what this structure was.

In fact, it was so plain that if one were to take notice, they'd realize it possessed no doors or windows of any kind amongst its dull brown walls. Located innocent enough behind the greenhouses at the far end of the Vatican Gardens, a simple six-foot-high chain-link fence separated it from the rest of Vatican City. What gave this falsely humble building away was the state-of-the-art communications array on its rooftop. Even the elite Swiss Guard weren't allowed here within the confines of the Vatican's very classified-to-even-exist, very ancient, and very enigmatic intelligence agency, the Santa Alleanza.

Next to the chain-link fence, two Mercedes S-Classes, empty, sat neatly parked, with Vatican Government license plates. Displayed upon the doors were the seal and title of the Roman Curia, Vatican City's chief administrative agency. In designer Italian suits, six Roman Curia security agents situated themselves alongside the two Mercedes.

A short distance away, several more security detail patrolled the area. However, these security officers, not agents of the Roman Curia, but the Vatican's classified private defense firm, Giuseppe Security International, in their paramilitary uniforms, and Berretta XR9 rifles slung across their chests, stood in stark contrast to the agents of the Roman Curia.

They guarded the entrance to the unassuming, at least in appearance, Santa Alleanza security booth. Inside the booth, at the far end of the structure, numerous Giuseppe security officers repositioned themselves in front of a vault-like door just as it finished closing. Its massive internal bolts locked back into place with a great metallic snap, echoing an unchallenged authority.

On the other side of this immense door, a circular platform began down through a vast stainless steel tube sloped in a subterranean trajectory. This gradual and oblique movement created the sensation as if traveling in slow motion within an enclosed tube-shaped slide. Upon the platform, a man and woman in tailored and designer suits, stood.

Beneath the man's suit, excessively bulked and sculpted muscles bulged. Alongside the man and woman were two Giuseppe security officers. No one held any expression of any kind, and they could have just as easily been androids for all anyone could have known of them, or of this place.

The platform traveled several stories deep before stopping. The elevator-style doors at the end of the tube opened. Before them was the headquarters of the Santa Alleanza. The security officers escorted them and rapidly so down the bare concrete hallway. Abruptly, they stopped at the first doorway they came to.

The dual stainless steel doors slid open, and the well-dressed man and woman entered the large room there. Not a moment passed upon stepping inside and the doors sealed shut. Of concrete, the room was empty of everything, except for a glass table encompassed by office chairs, as well a small aluminum waste bin. And that was all.

A man, in most likely his fifties, stood there at the table in a suit not proclaiming a designer flair like theirs, but entirely professional. Displayed upon the photo keycard clipped to his suit, it stated in a serious and clear font, 'Domenico Favignana, Sovereign Padrino of the Santa Alleanza'.

Closing the distance, he offered his hand to the woman. "The one and only, Dr. Vaccaro, Prefect of the Roman Curia's Committee for Risk Assessment." He smiled, sincerely but coldly. "An honor."

She shook his hand. "Call me Lucia. Or... the Vatican's Fixer..." She shrugged. "Everyone else does. And, Mr. Favignana, the honor's mine, being the first member of the Roman Curia granted access inside the ever-furtive walls of the Santa Alleanza."

His frigid demeanor iced over completely. "Yes, well, don't confuse the fact fate has taken an immense shit upon both our agencies, ergo this moment of congeniality, for a voluntary invitation of friendship. Fixer." For her, he was impossibly ambiguous, untranslatable if he was being literal or cynical. Whichever, he was serious, deadly so. For him, he'd hoped his sudden candor would catch her, as well her as muscle-bound cohort, off balance. If it had, they revealed nothing.

She smiled a smile equally cold and gave him a mouthful in return. "If you mean the only reason I'm standing here is because my office per chance ended up with photos of whatever's been discovered after that earthquake in Malta, then, yes, I'm quite aware why we're having this conversation. So, thank you for your clarity." She watched his eyes, his muscles, his breathing, but saw no reaction, no change to his being. "We both know I hold no desire to be dealing in relics, of *any* kind, even as charming as your bedside manner clearly is, Mr. Favignana, *the one and only* Sovereign Padrino of the Santa Alleanza."

"Domenico," he said, offering her all the casualness she hadn't afforded him. His eyes narrowed. "All will be well, free

9

from hell, just as long as we stick to the same page." He turned to the man beside her, took his hand, and gripped strongly. "And, will just Oliver, do?"

"Certainly," Oliver answered, mirroring the solid grip.

"Your reputation precedes you," said Domenico. "Imperviously loyal... *Assistant*... To the Fixer." He released his hand. "Now, one last verification."

In conditioned response by this point, Lucia presented her ID. "Respectfully, I realize the emphasis on security here, but our IDs have been checked three times already."

"I don't need your IDs."

"Then?"

"Your blood."

"Excuse me," she said, and did so having finally been caught off guard.

He held out a device slightly larger than a cellphone. "It's a DNA scanner. Essentially." Pressing a button upon it, a small needle slid out, glimmering in the gently recessed lighting from overhead. "I need your blood. See, even the most sophisticated credentials and security protocol are not without vulnerability. But DNA, that cannot tell a lie."

Stepping forward, Oliver placed his finger on the needle and it sank in. Domenico set the scanner on the table. Immediately, the glass tabletop lit up, revealing itself to be a kind of electronic smart table. Oliver's information, in its entirety, digitally cascaded across the table's surface. Before them, and swiftly so, the interactive surface of the table confirmed his identification.

Ejecting the needle, Domenico tossed it into the waste bin, and another needle slid out from the DNA scanner, taking its place. Lucia punctured her skin with it. Her information displayed on the tabletop. It matched, at least according to the scanner, verifying her to be nothing short of exactly herself.

"Please," Domenico said, gesturing to the table.

Now seated, he turned his chair toward theirs. "For the sake of brevity, I'm going to keep this meeting as, well, brief as possible. First things first, has the site in Malta been secured?"

"Yes," she answered. "A mutual *understanding* has been reached with local law enforcement."

"Lovely. Ever the Fixer. Now, I've dispatched a Rapid Intervention Team. They'll relieve your people, already in the field there, by tonight, Lucia. From you, I need an inclusive list of everyone who saw the Tarxien photos before they landed on your desk. And I mean *inclusive.*"

"Done." She leaned forward. "See, Domenico, we both want the same thing here. Damage control."

"Sure. We just have different ways of obtaining that. So, don't confuse your allegiance to the Roman Curia, and ergo, to the Vatican, with that of my duty to the Santa Alleanza, and thus to the best interests of the Holy See itself. Please, realize, see, and know the difference." He sensed her hesitation. "Simply, Lucia, popes come and go, but the Santa Alleanza, and shall we say, its *hidden* mechanisms are here to stay."

He removed his cellphone, unlocking the screen. Setting it on the smart table, large digitized photos spilled out on the electronic smart glass, consuming the table's surface. Before them, vividly displayed were the photos taken by the Maltese firefighter of the archaic and symbol-laden chasm.

Domenico carefully measured his words before continuing. "Respectfully, and here's the thing, Lucia, this isn't an abuse or embezzlement case, or whatever scandal-of-the-week you're used to sweeping away beneath the marble-lined doormat."

Getting up, he paced around the table as he spoke, circling them like some kind of shark who'd evolved to tread freely wherever he pleased. "The Santa Alleanza is the most effective intelligence agency on the planet due precisely to the fact it operates *invisible* to the rest of the world. *Invisible.* There's never been a movie, news story, or book even to mention us, not *ever.* But, the bear's out of the trap on this, and no less, from inception. Hence, our obligatory reciprocity, here and now. And the ripple effects... Well, they've already begun across the Holy See, and during the worst of times, when our Holy See is already navigating multiple storms."

"Without robbing me of my plausible deniability," Lucia asked, "what is the nature of this latent catastrophe, so far, far away in Malta?"

Domenico returned to his chair, quite satisfied he'd sufficiently marked his territory with lapping around the table several times over. "Skeletons in the closet." He drew his hands along the tabletop, arranging the digitized photos neatly in a row. He zoomed in on a single photo. After magnifying this picture of the inverted all-seeing eye, he slid the digitized photo across the electronic glass surface to her. "Lucia, two of your degrees relate to history, with a third in religion. So, any idea what this is?"

She shook her head. "I've never seen anything like this."

He glanced at Oliver.

"Don't look at me," Oliver said. "I'm no academic."

"No, of course not—no one's seen this symbol. At least, no one living. It's called, Praesidio Autem Veritas."

Lucia tapped her finger upon the image, zooming in on the eye at its center. "Yet, whatever this fossil is, this... Praesidio..."

"Praesidio Autem Veritas."

"Yes, this thing, it's demanding your complete attention. Question is, Domenico, do you know enough about this, to effectively avert it?"

"I know this is a meteorite with Church extinction written all over it. How's that for knowing enough?" He let that sink in. "Oh, before I forget, thank you both for suppressing your curiosity, as I know you'll resist asking for any further context."

A relief in his words washed over her, for she knew not what this was, but she knew enough to know it was something to be avoided. *At all costs.* It would not end well.

"When maneuvering the mine fields of politics," she said, "the less I know, the better."

"Spoken like a true believer," he said. "So, while you manage the political mines and political minds, I'll tend to the intelligence side of things. Oliver, here, well, he'll be our liaison. How about it, Oliver?"

"As in, in the field?" she asked.

"Yes. That's why I invited him here today. Oliver, you can make up your own mind. Can't you?"

Oliver nodded, accepting. "I could do for a stretch outside the office."

"Good," Domenico said, eager to test out this bulking youth full of... *New blood.* "A bit of brawn always helps the medicine go down." Domenico focused upon his own hand, well-manicured, though laced with scars... *"Especially* so in the field." He leaned back in his chair. "In the morning, Oliver, be at the heliport at zero-five-hundred. Gear will be waiting for you. You'll be briefed accordingly on the flight over."

They followed Domenico's lead, and stood, drifting away from the table, misleadingly simple in appearance that it was... Like so many things were of this place.

"Now, dear Lucia," Domenico said, "go calm the waves, and I'll do what I can to walk on water." He bowed deeply. "In the mouth of the wolf."

"May the wolf die," she answered, completing the ancient phrase of their homeland.

Gently, he touched a button on his phone's screen and the office doors slid open. Security officers waited there. And they escorted Lucia and Oliver down the hallway of concrete, out of this place from which they didn't belong, back to where they'd come from.

Inside the meeting room, Domenico placed a call. It was one he never believed he'd have to make, but he knew now there was a glaring possibility the world was going to burn. For it was enthusiastically clawing at reality's doorstep...

Loan Sharks and Traffic

*H*owie came to a jolting halt in the back of the mortuary van. Laying headfirst on the metal stretcher, he gripped the side handles to keep his body from torpedoing into the rear doors. The frantic symphony culminated by Casablanca's morning traffic swirled all around the van's windowless interior.

Sunlight streamed modestly through the grated divider behind the van's driver seat. With the driver entirely focused on the traffic, Howie hoped more than anything Captain El Hani had possessed the foresight to ensure the rear doors remained unlocked after he'd loaded the van. Howie pulled down on the door handle—the van lunged forward in the stop-and-go traffic.

The doors swung open, and before he knew it, he was riding the stretcher out the rear of the mortuary van. A bus full of truly mortified tourists stared back at him as the stretcher rolled past. Yanking a phone out of a motorcyclist's hand in mid-conversation as he bounced by, he placed a call. Building speed, the stretcher barreled for the intersection dead ahead....

~~ ~~

Within Prison Oukacha, the guard stood in front of the meticulously organized desk. From the open desk drawer, he removed a box of bullets... *Blank* firing bullets. Upon the desk, the oak and brass nameplate, which gleamed, 'Captain El Hani', glared back at him, judgingly. The guard turned away, hitting the call button on his cellphone.

This call traveled one thousand miles to a truly breathtaking villa in Monaco. As molten diamonds, the bay of the French Riviera gleamed in the background. From the villa's rooftop terrace, a very, very large man, in terms of both height and obesity, laid facedown on a custom massage table of a scale grand enough to accommodate such a man. The masseuse ground her elbow into his lumbar as the impatient rings of a phone grew ever louder....

Proudly branded across the man's back, shoulder blade to shoulder blade, was the vividly bright yellow and red flag of Sicily with its signature three-legged Medusa head. A well-built man delivered a gold tray with a dozen high-end cellphones. Taking his time in selecting the ringing phone off the tray, the large man, not so much rolling but incrementally wiggling so, made his way onto his back. The masseuse shifted her focus to his bulging calves.

The large man answered, rather annoyed, this call from the Casablanca prison. "Yes?"

"Mr. Teresi?"

"Yes, yes, this is interrupting my quiet time, so..."

"Apologies. Though, that tenant you asked me to keep an eye on, seems this morning, he terminated his lease early."

"No forwarding address?"

"Not at all. His departure was quite abrupt in nature."

"I see. Thank you. Your gratuity will be provided in the normal fashion." He set the phone with the others upon the tray. With some effort, he turned on his side. "Richie."

On an identical massage table parallel his own, Richie, noticeably larger than even himself, muscle instead of pure mass, lazily looked up. "What is it now, Rino?"

"We're taking a trip. Appears our business associate, Mr. Lyon, has left the safe confines of prison, and so, we can finally inquire with him as to why he hasn't yet repaid the one-hundred and thirteen million dollars he owes us. Remind me, Richie, what was the interest rate we were charging Mr. Lyon?"

"What difference does the interest rate make? He doesn't have the money, inconsiderately forcing us have to end our business relationship with him."

"Richie, as businessmen of fair and ethical practice, it's our duty to first give Mr. Lyon the benefit of the doubt."

"In that case, let her finish my feet first."

Richie's masseuse pulled the sheet up from his legs and began to work on his deeply tan and exceptionally plump toes.

Skeletons

*D*omenico stepped out of the restroom connected to his office. The unauthorized individual, a woman, dressed as ordinarily and unremarkable as could be, stood there in wait, beside his desk. Her plain attire didn't, however, mask her remarkable attractiveness.

Her eyes were impossibly blue. They were bluer than any he'd ever seen. Though pale and richly so, they were both alluring and... *Yes*, haunting. That, when she looked at him, those eyes didn't just absorb the light, interpreting imagery, but devoured what they saw, analyzing it in ways beyond the realms of sight.

Holding a calm within his voice, Domenico asked, "How did you get in?" He casually moved for the closest desk drawer, beside her.

"Your firearm in that drawer no longer contains projectiles," the woman said.

He stopped midstep. "You have my attention. Whoever you are."

She pointed to herself. "Famke."

"Gosh, that explains everything."

Famke didn't exactly walk, but seemed to drift closer. "Your recent acquaintance, Lucia Vaccaro, there is an object you'll need her to retrieve. Beneath the place now designated for the Roman Curia, is their secret archives vault. Within it, is a space concealed. A room. Therein lays the object. Have her bring it here, to you."

"What and why?"

"It's the gateway to your answers, Domenico."

"How is me doing this for you providing me answers?"

"It's not for us."

"Us?"

"It's for you."

"And how's that, Famke?"

"Within your phone, we've placed a map to the object."

Domenico's eyes shot to the now empty place upon his desk where he'd left his cellphone. "If you're capable of the impossible—of accessing my office, you're more than capable to do the same at the Roman Curia."

"Consider it an act of goodwill," Famke said. "As well, your right to answers. Call it... manifest reciprocity."

Reciprocity was a word *he* used... *Had this woman and whoever she worked for listened somehow to his conversation with Lucia?* If so... *They weren't hiding their unprecedented propensities for espionage.*

Famke held up his DNA scanner, which she'd also taken from his desk... From within his biometrically *locked* desk drawer.

"Your technology, it's capable to store blood for a later time for analysis?"

"Of course...," he answered.

She slid out the needle and let it draw her blood. "Obtain what we ask, and you will find your understanding."

Domenico now saw his cellphone was in her hand. The phone's screen, locked by a biometric password only encoded to him, had been unlocked. She touched the button displayed on the screen, which opened the doors to his office.

She locked the screen and returned the phone to him, along with the DNA scanner. "Your phone can be unlocked in a few minutes. Until then, please don't attempt to stop my departure. I wish not to have to bring anyone harm."

He watched her leave. The doors closed. He stood there,

alone, the entirety of his being vexed in a conflictingly tranquil way. Unexplainably, he grew dizzy, and fixated upon the empty wall before him... Awaking from this momentary trance, he analyzed her blood sample now contained within the DNA scanner.

'No Records Found', displayed across the screen. He reran the sample, producing the same empty result. Again, he tried. Still, it came up the same.

Impossible. The scanner linked directly to the largest database of human DNA samples the world had ever known. Virtually *everyone* had been, at some point, entered into this database. He drew in a deep breath, and made the on-screen selection, 'Preserve sample'.

He dropped into the chair. His eyes now saw it there on his desk for the first time. He took it in his hand and examined the skeleton key. It was fashioned from bone.

"Skeletons," he said aloud. Holding it close, he wrapped his fingers tightly around the ancient and ghostly whiteness of the key.

Blue Sky, Blue Ocean

*T*he *Monotony Bay*, as if an immense rusted egg, this aged container ship, entirely void of all shipping containers and cargo of any kind, bobbed in crisply blue waves at an undisclosed distance from the Moroccan coast, in the Alboran Sea. In the equally blue sky, a helicopter hovered off the ship's stern. New and sleek, the AS365 Dauphine model chopper starkly contrasted with the peeling, bloated corrosion of the container ship.

On the horizon, a second helicopter broke into view. The Vietnam Era AH-1 Cobra helicopter, complete with sneering shark's mouth, closed in on the *Monotony Bay*. Cramped inside the Cobra's two-person cockpit, Howie focused on the ocean below. The cockpit's narrow tandem seating was more than stress testing his claustrophobia. Which, had diverted a prior though entirely prevalent concern. The teenage boy masquerading as the Cobra's pilot was young enough to look like he'd skipped school for the day.

While debating with himself whether to hit the eject button or try to hold out the last half mile to the *Monotony Bay*, Howie noticed a modern salvage vessel agleam in the sunlight. Decked out with sophisticated equipment, it screamed professional wealth and success. Spotting the extravagant ship was a double-edged sword. It caused him to forget about his claustrophobia, in lieu of a greater agitation.

He spoke into his headset. "Whatever's the lowest legal flyover distance you can do without losing your license... Do it over that bastard."

"What license," said the pilot.

Before Howie could respond to this disturbingly adolescent voice, the Cobra rapidly plummeted, swooping alongside the modern salvage ship. Howie immediately regretted his instruction. Parallel with the ship, they were now close enough to see the name stenciled on its hull, 'Great White Recovery'. Howie glared back at the shocked crew staring out at him from the ship's bridge.

"Onward," he told the pilot.

Quickly reaching the *Monotony Bay*, the pilot set down on its more than makeshift helipad. Howie climbed out, immediately greeted by his friend and colleague, Tom, who had a packed duffel bag strapped over his shoulder. Neither friend nor colleague changed the fact Howie had a bone to pick, and thoroughly so.

Tom's red hair, boyishly long, blew freely amidst the roar of the Cobra's rotors. He tucked his thumbs on either side of his large Western-style belt buckle. Hanging from Tom's belt was a quick draw holster, and nestled within, a genuine Colt Single Action Army revolver.

"You look... irregular," Tom said, his accent very heavy and very Irish.

"It's been an irregular morning, Tom." Howie realized he must've looked exceptionally terrible by now, everything considered. "The sharks are already circling, I see."

They turned to the modern salvage vessel half a mile out.

"Right," said Tom, grabbing his radio. "Almost forgot." He yelled into the radio over the throaty growl of the Cobra. "Avast, ye scallywags of a crew, attention! Captain Lyon, who's just arrived, gives his salutations and love, as it were. And being the ever-neglectful skipper his is, is abandoning ye once again. As I'll be joining him on this new and precarious journey of his, please enjoy the free-for-all that will undoubtedly ensue in our absence. However, during your rum-induced stupors, if those SOBs off the starboard-side out there get within shooting distance... Shoot! Carry on!" He lowered his radio.

The Cobra lifted off, departing into the sky most blue. In its place, the Dauphine helicopter set down.

Howie moved away from the roar of the helipad. "Tom, you've really got to convey your sarcasm to the crew better. Otherwise, those boys, they'll actually shoot."

"Sarcasm?" asked Tom, ever innocently.

"Look, as much as I dislike Jager White and his insatiable crew of leeches, shooting them out here in the ocean isn't entirely legal, international waters or not."

Tom grinned. "As long as it's partially legal."

"Got enough on my plate, Tom." Howie waved at the Dauphine. "An AS365? Friends of yours? And what's this of you going somewhere?"

"Aye, fastest civilian chopper in the world. Just catching a ride." Tom steered him back toward the helipad. "*We're* going somewhere."

"Where?"

"Up." Tom yanked open the door on the Dauphine and climbed in. Howie peered inside, deeply hoping the pilot was at least of an acceptable age. He couldn't tell from this angle. Maybe it was best he knew nothing when it came to Tom's choice of pilots.

"Fine," he said, turning back for the ship. "But first, a shower and a change of clothes."

Tom grabbed his hand and pulled him with impressive strength into the Dauphine's cabin. "Change on the way."

Seated across from each other, they strapped in and slipped on their headsets.

Howie looked to him, his friend, his business partner, whom he increasingly wanted to strangle. "Tom, just a rule of thumb when it comes aviation, one chooses an older pilot and a younger aircraft. *Not* the other way around." In the background, the pilot less than halfheartedly breezed through his preflight checklist.

Tom unzipped his duffel bag and tossed Howie some clothes. "What's the problem? You're alive aren't you."

Howie unbuckled from the flight harness and peeled off the mess of tattered rags he'd been wearing for far too long. "He looked twelve, Tom."

"Seventeen," Tom matter-of-factly answered, while watching out his window as they took flight. "The minimum legal age for piloting."

"*If* he had a license, which he didn't."

"Splittin' hairs, splittin' hairs, as always. Got you here didn't he."

Howie pulled on the fresh clothes. "And now you've got me on another chopper, headed for god knows where."

Tom leaned over, giving him a patronizing pat on the head. "Prison's made you picky."

The mention of prison brought Howie back to his original course of anger with Tom. "Speaking of, what about the *Sussex?* You know... that shipwreck of sunken gold directly under the water below us. Correct me if I'm wrong, Tom, and not that I'm not grateful to be out of that penal hellhole, but we had a really, really simple plan... I mean, really. I stayed relatively safe behind bars until you pulled up the *Sussex's* hull of gold, and paid off the Teresi brothers. *Then*, you spring me."

"Something came up." Unfolding a sheet of paper, he offered it to Howie.

"Oh, okay, something more important than my survival. Never mind then." Howie crossed arms. "That was sarcasm, by the way."

"As a matter-of-fact, yes, more important than the two of us."

Howie grabbed the paper. It was a printed photo from within the chasm in Malta of the Praesidio Autem Veritas symbol. It took a moment to register what was staring back at him.

He rolled his eyes. "Please... They're a myth. The L' Entita are a *myth*." He looked hard at Tom. "At best." Focusing in on the subterranean surroundings in the photo, he said, "Not that I'm buying into it, but where'd you get this?"

Tom grinned broadly. "That's the best part..."

The pilot, and thankfully with a voice of an actual adult, started to speak. "We'll be arriving in Malta in just under four hours. As we know, you have a very limited choice when it comes to chartering illegal flights. So, I'd like to take this time to thank you for flying, *No Flight Plan Airways.*"

Howie released a sigh and focused on the blue ocean below.

Blood

"*H*ere." Lucia plopped the leather-bound canister on Domenico's desk.

"I owe you," he said, taking the eight-inch canister.

"You bet you do. You're aware how many violations I committed against the Roman Curia, the agency I've only dedicated my entire life to, in order to get whatever that is. It stinks. I mean, it literally smells abysmal."

"There's not going to be a Vatican, let alone a Roman Curia if we don't get this opened."

"If I ask how you knew any of the information leading me to this thing, I'd be completely wasting my time, wouldn't I?"

"There's considerably more pressing questions."

"That answers that." She took a seat on the edge of his desk. "What the hell is this—you don't even know do you."

Domenico examined the canister. A keyhole was on one end. "I have a suspicion." He slid the skeleton key of bone into the hole. There was a soft click. Without even having to turn the key, a seam formed upon the seamless face of the canister, and spread out in each direction, until a small window had opened at its center.

He carefully removed the metal vial from inside. "It's airtight."

"Maybe it's the bubonic plague."

"We're not that lucky." Pressing on the button along the side of it, he slid out a metal two-inch needle from the vial.

"That scanner." She grabbed the DNA scanner off his desk and handed it to him. Studying the vial's needle, he was at a loss in how to retrieve whatever was contained within.

"May I?" He gave her both the needle and the scanner.

"The scanner's own needle slides from this slot here?" she asked.

"Yes, just use that button on the side."

Instead, she tried to fit the needle from the vial into the scanner's slot. It locked in, as if perfectly designed to do so.

"What's the chances of that," she said.

"Really good or really bad. Hit that blue button on the screen."

She did, and a large hologram projected up into the air from the DNA scanner's display. A three-dimensional double helix floated before them, flickering slightly as she ran her fingers through it. The helix transitioned in pastel colors as the scanner processed the DNA sample. Completed, the double helix faded, giving way to a full-scale hologram of a woman.

"Holy christ mother," he gasped, exposing a rare lack of emotional control. Beneath her image, the woman's name materialized, 'Ameci'. Though she was a different woman than that Famke who'd brought all of this to be now, there was a definite similarity... The *eyes.*

Activating the camera on his phone, he placed the coat of arms hanging on his office wall into the camera's viewfinder. He touched a button on the phone's screen. And like a door, the coat of arms swung out from the wall by hidden hinges, revealing the safe behind it. Scanning his palm to the safe's biometric display, it opened. He removed a wooden case, the solitary object within.

"Take it this somehow correlates to the Malta site?" she asked.

"Oh yes." He lifted the lid on the simple box, setting its contents from inside onto his desk. His fingertips rested upon the archaic book there. Inlaid with gold leaf on the front of the book was, and rather beautifully so, the Praesidio Autem Veritas. The ancient leather stretched over the book was so frail that pieces broke off when he opened it, despite doing so quite gently. The deep crimson on the yellowing paper seemed not as ink but blood.

Some of the book's symbols felt freshly familiar to Lucia as she watched him softly turn the pages. "That's the language found in the Tarxien cavern."

He stepped back from the book. On the page before them was a drawing of the woman in the hologram.

"Who is she, Domenico?"

He brought up Famke's blood sample on the DNA scanner's display. "Fourth time's a charm." The scanner quickly processed her sample. The woman known as Ameci within the hologram transitioned to a double helix of Famke's DNA. Exquisitely, it rotated around and around in lush detail. With the tap of a button, he expanded the three-dimensional image, nearly filling his office. The helix became a likeness of Famke, with her name etching across the open air.

She morphed. In her place, columns of numerous holographic individuals populated, depicting Famke's lineage in its entirety. Their names appeared below each. Swiftly, Lucia and Domenico became surrounded by these life-sized holographic people, ghosts of Famke's past, a woman most mysterious and most capable.

An automated female voice came from the DNA scanner. "Base match confirmed."

Suddenly, all the holograms merged into a single three-dimensional image of a woman. With her face not fully rendered, she raced straight at the two of them standing there at his desk. This woman of light incarnate came to freeze in the fraction of a second before smashing into them. There, with living precision, was Ameci, the woman originally manifested within the projection from the DNA scanner. They could see now there was no mistaking her, for she undeniably was the same one drawn upon the page in that archaic book.

Lucia reached out to touch this incredibly realistic hologram. "Have you ever seen such haunting blue eyes?"

Haunting was exactly how he'd describe those eyes. Ameci, this most distant ancestor of Famke's, didn't just have similar eyes. They were the *same* eyes. Skirting her question, he pointed to the surname now displayed beneath the image, 'Praesidio'.

"Like the symbol," she said.

With a tap of the scanner's screen, he dissolved the eerily lifelike image into thin air.

"Can I assume this Famke is who informed you of the canister?" she asked.

He coolly looked up at her. "Lucia, perhaps consider trading your pen in for a gun." He retracted the needle back into the metal vial. "I couldn't get a readout of Famke's genetic information earlier. I needed DNA from her lineage in order to first establish a baseline for the scanner. As to even have anything for it to process from."

"Meaning?"

"Meaning this *entire* bloodline has somehow managed to avoid entry into any database. Ever. That's not something that just happens by chance."

"Until now..."

"Until now." The perplexity of it begged a thousand questions for them both. Though, only one stood out as most pressing in the moment.

"Domenico... Why would she provide you with this information?"

Lowering himself into the chair behind his desk, and using a reserved tenderness, he closed the book before him bearing the Praesidio Autem Veritas. "I surely don't know. And surely, we're going to find out." He laid each of his palms upon the book's deteriorating leather face. "*Very* soon." Receiving a call, he checked the name on his phone's screen, 'Camorra'.

"I must take this." With his phone, he unlocked the double doors to his office. She nodded and left, to be promptly met by two security officers. Unnoticed by anyone, as Lucia was escorted away, a man watched from within his office doorway. His door, cracked ever thinly, was enough to bear witness that Lucia Vaccaro, the Prefect of the Roman Curia, had just been present within the walls of the Santa Alleanza.

The photo keycard clipped to this man's suit showed his name was, 'Simon, Deputy Director of the Santa Alleanza Intelligence Agency'. He was remarkably youthful for such a senior position. Quickly, he placed a call on his phone, slipping back inside his office, silent as a shadow....

Voodoo and Coffee

*R*oom windows of Hotel Tarxien that weren't broken out by the earthquake now sat open, drawing welcomed breaths of air into the building. A silent sea breeze stalked the encroachment of twilight, gently lapping upon the linen curtain of a fifth-story window. The curtain folded in the breeze, revealing a woman's face. Exotic, with features most different from each other, she was beautiful by every measure. Her richly bronzed skin was in sharp contrast to the powerful blue held within her eyes. As the breeze passed, the curtain fell back, and she was lost from view.

Slipping inside, through her window, could be seen the flicker of dozens of candles, all shapes and sizes which bathed her hotel room. On the bed laid a large triangular mirror. Cross-legged, she positioned herself in front of it.

Upon the mirror were piles of different colored powder arranged amongst black, unlit candles. Elongated fingers of light and dark danced across the walls as she ignited these candles of a most black. Their flames burned different from the rest, shifting in shades of lush plum and indigo.

She poured thick liquid out of a bottle onto one of the heaps of powder, and using her fingers, created a bright white paste. With it she then covered her face. Her eyelids closed, and with one hand she scooped a pile of yellow powder. Her other hand took from a pile of red powder.

Raising her hands high above the candles, the powder spiraled down, blending together into serpent-like forms that feverously hissed as the flames below consumed them. This helix aflame sparkled in her eyes. With each hiss, sparks burst forth. Hairline bolts of energy flowed from these bursts, and floating upwards, these thin electric serpents illuminated the stark white paste which covered her face.

Taking the bottle of thick liquid, she drank what remained, then blew upon these narrow bolts of energy. They turned to smoke. Flowing not as smoke should behave in a dissipating way, but as a heavy fog, it wrapped itself around her arms, torso, legs, and neck, until the entirety of her body became encased.

It was impossible to tell if it was her body that swayed now to the rhythm of the candlelight or if it was the candlelight that mimicked her. Then, as if from some electrical charge, her auburn hair began to rise. Suddenly, a single gust blew inside, extinguishing nearly all the candles.

Her eyes opened to see a light come on for one of the first-floor rooms overlooked by her window. She took the spotting scope lying next to her on the bed, and through it, zoomed in on the alit room. There was a man there. He checked a flashlight, ensuring the batteries contained much life, then put it inside a backpack, carefully zipping it up all the way.

Lowering the scope, she placed a call on her cellphone. With a distinct Haitian accent, she said, "Daniel, it's time."

Within seconds, the adjoining door between her room and the next opened.

Daniel, a fit man, and most clean-shaven, cringed upon seeing her in the white paste. "Warn me, Ingrid."

"Oh, sorry." Ingrid grabbed a towel and wiped her face. After pulling on her boots and jacket, Daniel handed her the custom Walther CCP M2 handgun. Releasing the magazine, she saw it to be loaded. With a fluid ease only gained by much experience, she snapped the magazine back into place.

He noticed the full pot of coffee on the counter. "Smells

good... Not powdered monkey brains? I hope."

Tucking the Walther into the holster under her jacket, she poured a cup. "Just coffee." She took a gulp. "See."

He drank. "That's fantastic!"

"Takes a witch's touch." She smiled. "Do me a favor and put the rest of these out." Her fingers pinched the wick on one of the candles, killing the flame. "Don't want to burn the place down. It survived the earthquake for a reason now."

He hugged her. An unspoken intimacy transferred, loudly declaring itself in their short and silent embrace.

"Be careful," he said, his voice asking rather than telling her.

"You know me." She aimed the scope down at the first-floor window once more.

"That's the problem."

Through the scope, she spotted the man there, just as he left, jumping the short distance from his window to the ground. He darted across the dark parking lot.

"Well, here we go." She slid on a backpack, nodded slightly to Daniel in doing so, then lowered a nylon rope out her window, and rappelled down.

He watched as she followed that man through the shadows. And he blew her a kiss she'd never see, then pulled up the rope. Noticing the hardcover book laying there near the windowsill, his eyes revealed an immediate and shocked recognition of the author's name. He quickly flipped the book over. The photo on the dust jacket was of the very same man who Ingrid now followed through darkness of night.

"Shit."

There was a loud, three-consecutive rapped knock. It wasn't upon the door to her room. A touch more distant, it'd come from his adjoining room.

"Shit!" He grabbed the pot of coffee as he hurried through the open doorway, entering back into his own room, kicking the adjoining door closed. There was another knock. With his free hand, he fumbled with the old-style chain lock, and pulled open the front door to his hotel room. Howie and Tom stood there. He yanked them inside.

"Here." He poured coffee, pushing cups into their hands.

"Thanks, Daniel," said Howie, "I surely need it." He tried the coffee. "Oh my god... That's the best coffee I've ever had." He stared into the murky black liquid. "No dairy, no sugar, but... Tom, you've *got* to try this coffee."

"Okay." Tom took a drink from his cup. He savored it for as long as he possibly could, then swallowed. "That's the best coffee I've ever had."

"Isn't it though," Howie said, grinning.

Daniel dropped two full backpacks at their feet. "Got all you asked for."

Howie glanced at Tom.

"Oh, right," said Tom. Digging out a roll of money from his pocket, he handed it over.

Daniel took the money, not counting it. "Everything's ready for you boys at the place we'd discussed over the phone." He pointed through his window, down at the unlit parking lot. "Now's the time to go. Power's still knocked out there, so it's not getting any darker."

They gazed upon the parking lot shared with the adjacent businesses. The area was lifeless as a graveyard amidst the witching hour. Which it was at this hour. There was only the faint hum from a generator at the far end of the lot. Lights run by the generator illuminated the 'Carters Supermarket' sign there.

Plastic and massive, a tent covered the chasm-like hole in front of the store. A grim glow cast across the new chain-link fence securing the tent's perimeter. Silhouettes of guards wielding automatic weapons behind the fence shown through.

"Man, the Vatican don't mess around do they," Tom said.

Howie gave one of the backpacks to Tom and took the other for himself. "Not the Vatican, per se. It's the agencies within, as well above them."

"Oh, okay," Tom answered, shrugging.

Howie slipped on the pack. "We should go."

They headed for the door.

Daniel reached for them. "Wait, there's something you should—" The door slammed closed and Howie and Tom were gone.

"Know..." Daniel sighed, pouring a cup of coffee. "Soon enough..." He downed the devilishly delicious coffee.

Ambition and the Assassin: Things Eternal

*W*ithin this very hotel, behind curtains drawn, doors locked, voices hushed, lights low, and souls blackened, a meeting most sinister took place.

"Call it fate, deus ex machina, fortuitous chance. Whatever it is, this is *it*. The opportunity each of us has eternally sought." Simon, Santa Alleanza's deputy director, spoke in what he believed to be perfect secrecy to the three other men in the room.

Each of them wore a photo keycard identifying themselves. And, no less, they each held vital positions of upper management within the Santa Alleanza.

"What of Domenico?" Piero, chief of field operations, and like Simon, unusually young for his senior position, asked.

Simon nodded. "My hubris isn't so lofty to consider Domenico anything but chillingly formidable... To say the least. Albeit, to answer your question, Piero, by the time what is done is done, what Domenico knows or doesn't will not matter."

"Which is?" asked one of the other men.

Simon felt himself rapidly growing annoyed. "As I just said, it would be folly to speak of such things now. All will be shown within the chamber. Let us not forget, at this juncture, everyone here has wedded, and did so long ago, their fate to the man next to him. That mutual consequence, good or bad, ensures our alliance. And through that alliance, we *will* succeed."

"You really believe it possible this society has survived, unseen, for so long?" another of them asked.

Simon tried not to reveal too much in answering. "What matters is their secrets have survived." He moved closer to them, to the center of this dim and grimly plain hotel room.

"What secrets?" Piero asked.

"The eternally damning kind," said Simon, sharply elevating his voice. He held not the temperament for management. And he was certain they could sense it easily enough. "Secrets with the power to bring the Church to its knees. And beyond... Albeit, we will harness this power. With it, we'll transform not just the very face of the Church, but the world over. What religion is and what it means to the people will be drawn by our will, through a vision divine."

~~ ~~

Well-lit, but not brightly so, by both the surrounding decorative street-style lamps and recessed lights nested amongst the grass, upon a bench encompassed by the beautiful and meticulous Vatican Gardens, sat Domenico. The tiny device within his ear transmitted in real-time every word with precise clarity being spoken at Simon's traitorous meeting in Malta.

Domenico shook his head. "Simon, Simon, Simon. Simple... Simon." The muscles along the side of his jaw pulsated as the silent fury built from within. "'Thou shall not commit adultery', Simon."

He lowered the transmitter's volume as someone, a man, approached from the path. This man stopped in front of the bench. He was not particularly remarkable. He was not strikingly handsome, though wasn't sinister in appearance or hard to look at either.

At average height, what did catch the eye, if anything, he appeared quite fit. This was an athletic fitness, a conditioning of his body for endurance. His muscles weren't augmented and exaggerated to the point as to draw attention, though just to that perfect place to perform thoroughly and effectively when called upon. And for his eyes, dark, watchful, and quiet, they took in everything while revealing nothing. They calculated all things. Dead or alive, it made no difference.

"Domenico," he said, with a sterile familiarity.

"It's been too long," Domenico responded. "When you change, you certainly change. Shall I now know you as... Camorra?"

Camorra nodded. "In title, and in way." Within his mind, he calculated the perfect distance that should be kept between Domenico and himself, as he did with all things. For the world was not of life, but of numbers. All, small and large, and in between, were governed by these numbers. He sat and held out his arm as if on cue.

Domenico used his DNA scanner to confirm Camorra's identity. "Can't be too careful, even amongst old allies."

"Especially so."

Tucking away the DNA scanner, Domenico said, "Yes, truly volatile times we exist in. Example of which, the space between a few hours ago, when I'd asked for you, and now, with your arrival, has altered the very reasons for you coming here." He removed the small device from his ear and placed it inside his pocket. "Seems a coup d'état is fermenting within my own house."

"I left barely two years ago," Camorra said, "and this is what the Santa Alleanza's become?"

Gesturing to Camorra's unkempt appearance, Domenico said, "What two years' difference it's been. Your suit's been replaced by... What do you call that?"

"Sweats."

"Sweats... Dirt covered sweats. And your hair... And no shave?"

"Sand. The beach."

"What?"

"Sand. Not dirt."

"Sand is all you have to say?"

"My gun's maintained. That's why you've called me here."

"Indeed."

"Pray tell, Domenico, so I can provide you my answer."

"There's a site in Tarxien, Malta, I need you to, and from a discerned distance, observe. Whatever's found there, if anything, personally deliver back to me. If that's not possible, then destroy it. With prejudice."

"And?"

"And... appears my deputy director, Simon, along with some select department heads, hold most deviating intentions, for whatever's to be found in Tarxien." He took a phone from his pocket along with a Santa Alleanza keycard and gave both to Camorra. "Card will grant you access to anywhere within Vatican City. Use the phone to provide me with field reports, daily. I'll now upload the dossiers on each of my, shall we call them, turncoats." With his own phone, he sent Camorra the information.

Camorra glanced through the employee files on his phone, his mind instantly analyzing every detail. He didn't memorize it, as there was no need. His brain literally scanned a perfectly replicated image of it all with an ease and swiftness as if a camera taking a photo.

Lowering the phone, he asked, "Am I to provide early retirement?"

"Securing what's at the Tarxien site, if anything, is your first directive. We'll address Simon's severance package once that's been achieved."

On the phone's screen, Camorra enlarged Simon's photo. The unbridled confidence radiating out from Simon's eyes was clear. "The ambition of youth... Nothing contaminates faster."

"Yes, unfortunately, Simon's aptitude has eclipsed his value. Be that as it may, he was once a brilliant field agent. A man like that, without a master, well, is truly dangerous. I'm uploading one more dossier. And Camorra, this one's not to be harmed. Listen, this man's to be shielded."

Camorra brought up Piero's boyish-picture on screen. "Another kid? I'm seeing a pattern emerging here regarding your present troubles, Domenico." He set aside the phone. "A child's caretaker, I am not."

Domenico leaned over and whispered something to him, something truly worth shielding, a secret of blood to be held within the confines of silence.

Camorra considered the words. "That *does* change things."

"To the extent it doesn't impede your first directive," Domenico said. "There is another. Oliver is his name. I dispatched him to the site this morning."

"And is he compromised as well?"

"Such cynicism." Domenico sent Oliver's file to Camorra's phone. "No. This one's on loan from the Roman Curia. To be returned. *Intact.* Again, to the extent it doesn't impede your first directive, Camorra, be a guardian."

Camorra reviewed the photo of Oliver. "Healthy fellow."

"And entirely inexperienced to the field."

"I'll hold out a wing on each arm." Camorra shrugged. "No promises though. You know."

"I know." Domenico slid his phone back inside his pocket. "I also know compensation is on your mind."

"And I know the Vatican's coffers are tapped out. Not to mention, but to mention, that recent embezzlement incident, concerning the Vatican's *infallible* bank. However..." His slender lips released something almost a smile, but not quite. "Looking past all of that, Domenico, the Vatican's *well*-invested in real estate."

"You're asking for what? A beach house?"

Camorra held up the phone. "This has internet?"

"Of course."

On screen, Camorra quickly produced a photograph of a sprawling Tuscan estate. "*The Eternal Heart of Florence.*"

"That's not even on the market."

"It's one of those *unlisted* Vatican assets. That's what I want. So, if you're having *me* do this, jingle the strings of your great web."

Domenico, well aware the futility of trying to change Camorra's mind once it'd been set, hadn't much choice. "As you desire."

"Before we go any further, Domenico, understand, this contract between us, it will be dissolved if it comes to conflict with the Oath of the Camorra."

"Yes. Understood."

"Then, let us consecrate our word."

Upon his palm, Camorra displayed an archaic coin. Pinching the coin at a certain place along its edges released a hidden mechanism. A small point of metal protruded out from the center on both sides.

Each man positioned his thumb on the protruding points, then simultaneously drew blood against the sharp metal. Veins carved into either side of the coin captured their blood. These veins led the blood of each man to a path of intersection, unifying it. Camorra activated another mechanism on the coin. The grooved veins closed, locking their blood inside, preserving it there to be held as a secret concealed.

Camorra gave the coin to Domenico. "Keep it upon your body at all times until our contract's dissolution."

Domenico read the words etched on it. "Ora pro venandi... Pray for the hunter? A pun?"

"A certainty."

At that very moment, the breeze kicked up, sending a bee, having lost himself in the sweet evening air, to circle Domenico. Reflexively, he swatted at it, repeatedly missing. The bee moved on to Camorra.

It landed on Camorra's arm. With an unsurpassed grace, he positioned his index finger and thumb at just the right place to pinch the bee while avoiding its stinger. He held up the small yet potentially painful creature with enough force to imprison it, though without bringing it harm. Then, fully extending his arm, he released the bee to be carried off by the wind now building up all around them.

"There's a G700 fueled, awaiting you, Camorra. You know the place."

Camorra looked to the storm clouds brewing above Vatican City, forebodingly illuminated by the lights of Rome, not far, just across the Tiber River. In silence, he left Domenico, heading back down the path, into darkness.

A Sewer

*I*n the alley behind Carters Supermarket, Howie and Tom, with great effort, finished sliding away the manhole cover.

"Heavier than they look," Howie, out of breath, said.

Tom wiped away the sweat on his face. "Yeah, two-hundred and forty-nine pounds tends to do that."

"Since when are you an expert?"

"It's not my first time crawling into the crapper." Tom shined his flashlight inside the sewer. "Shall we?"

"Let's just get this part over with."

They climbed down and dropped into the chunky, ankle-deep and grayish water. Tom held out his arms, easily spanning the concave tunnel of brick.

Howie felt his claustrophobia creeping up. "Narrower than I was picturing." He removed a map of the sewer system from his pocket. "It's this direction," he said, pushing past the dangling tree roots. "Watch your head." They made their way through the sludge as it sucked greedily at their feet.

"Never actually been in a sewer before," said Howie.

"Be sure to add it to your list of achievements." Tom admired the ancient brickwork as they trudged on. "You know, this isn't that bad. As far as sewers go, I mean."

"Sprung from prison just so I can climb into a sewer."

"Yep," Tom said proudly. "Just like *Shawshank*."

"Tom, that's the opposite of *Shawshank*." They continue down the tunnel as it curved around to the left.

"Rather be in prison?" asked Tom.

"I'd rather not have a retired mafia captain hunting me," Howie said, climbing over the large, congealed mass of all things unholy in front of them. "Watch your step."

"Shouldn't have borrowed all that money then." Tom grinned, maneuvering across the hardened waste. "Fatberg."

"Fatberg?"

"Yeah, the oil and fat harden with—"

"I get the picture," Howie said, as he reached the end of the fatberg and dropped down into the water again. "And whose idea was it to borrow the money to begin with, *Tom*." He pulled back a knot of roots blocking their way. The tunnel branched out into two paths in the near distance.

"Shouldn't have listened to me," Tom said. "I mean, hey, honestly, I wouldn't have listened to me. But the upside—"

"Upside?"

"Yeah—you owe them so much, so they can't afford to actually kill you. Because, then how would they ever get paid? Nope, you're in much better position with owing so much."

"Your positivity, Tom, is a real downer sometimes."

"Glad to help. We're in the same boat on this one. The Teresi brothers want both our blood."

"Maybe if we were back on the right *boat*, you know, where we should be right now, pulling up that gold, we could actually pay them off and keep our blood for ourselves."

"Oh... forgot to tell you."

"Tell me what?"

"Spain put an injunction on the claim."

With Howie's next step, he sank up to his knees. "Spain, as in the country?"

"Yes... Spain the country. They're saying it's not the HMS *Sussex*, but one of their galleons, because, you know, it's not off Gibraltar where everyone thinks the *Sussex* sank."

"That's because everyone's wrong." Howie shivered. "This crap's colder than I was thinking." The water grew deeper as they pushed on.

"More various than you envisioned as well?" asked Tom.

"Various alright," Howie said, pinching his nose. "And don't change the subject, Tom. Why are you just now telling me this?" The water rose to their shoulders as the ground sloped steeper and steeper down.

"You already had a lot on your plate, as you'd said, with... your fashion model wife..."

"There's a couple 'exes' in there."

"Sorry, I mean *ex*-model *ex*-wife leaving you for your direct business competitor, and the *ex*-mobsters, AKA your *ex*-business partners chasing you, and being bankrupt because you're now an *ex*-multimillionaire. Did I miss any 'exes'?"

Just as Tom had spoken the question into being, a large Maltese cross came into view on the wall. The crimson-colored cross contrasted with the wall's dark gray. It stared Howie sharply in the face like a giant 'X'. He checked the map. The claustrophobia clawing at his mind provided him with a not-so-sweet escape from the thoroughly depressing reality of what Tom had just said.

"And now that we're waist-deep in waste, Tom, and headed headfirst into a subterranean cave full of guys with guns, with no exit, *this* seemed like a good time to tell me that my one hope of getting us out of this mess is going to be tied up for years in some international court?"

"Well... You make it sound really bad putting it like that, man." They came to a stop at the place where the tunnel branched.

"Maybe because it is really bad. Just maybe, Tom." Howie double-checked his map. "Set the app on your phone."

"Twenty-three feet?"

"*Exactly* twenty-three feet." Tom programmed the distance into his phone, and they followed briefly along the tunnel's left branch.

"Okay," Tom said, "should put us directly parallel with the cavern."

Unzipping the pack on Tom's back, Howie selectively pulled out pieces of equipment.

"What'd Daniel conjure up for us this time?"

"Real cocktail of a potion." Howie slipped on safety glasses. "Man's a certifiable wizard." He gave Tom a pair of glasses. "Safety first."

"Yes, safety... Theory being," asked Tom, "the tunnel survived the earthquake so it'll survive a blast?"

"As not reassuring as that theory is, Tom, we're going with a non-explosive demolition agent."

"Won't that take too long?"

"Hence the cocktail part of Daniel's concoction." Howie locked in the bit on a portable hammer drill, then quickly punched a series of angled-down holes deep into the tunnel's brick wall. He stepped back from the large circular pattern of holes now drilled into the side of the tunnel. "Finishing touch," he said, popping in two more holes at the center of the pattern.

Tom opened a plastic container and looked inside at the gray powder. "Dexpan?"

Howie took the container. "ECOBUST. With a few other savory ingredients," he said, mixing a bottle of water with the powder. He funneled the mix inside the holes, while leaving the two center holes empty. Almost instantly, loud crackling pops echoed out down the tunnel as the gray powder immediately hardened and expanded within the wall. Deep cracks spiderwebbed across the face of the bricks, then through the solid rock behind it.

"Now for the real magic," Howie said. "Throw me that aluminum and nitrite." Tom tossed him a quart-sized bag of rust-colored powder. Catching it, Howie quickly poured the powder into the two remaining holes at the center of his work, leaving each hole halfway filled.

"Chlorite and sugar?" asked Tom, holding up another bag

45

of equal size. Howie nodded, stepping back.

Tom packed in the second bag of powder and fit a metal fuse into the two holes, twisting the fuse ends together. "Ready?"

"Ready."

With a pocket torch, Tom ignited the ends. Not wasting time, they moved several feet away—the entire section of wall bloomed into a blinding white fireball. The mortar, then the brick, liquified. As a molten puddle, it oozed out into the sewage water. The resulting cloud of steam rapidly engulfed the tunnel, sending the cloud roaring right at them.

"Huh," Howie said. "Didn't account for the steam."

"Certifiable shitstorm, as it were," said Tom.

Coughing, they grasped at their noses, taking refuge from the horrific odor, retreating back behind where the tunnel branched.

"Now, that was various," Tom managed to gasp.

The fireball along the face of the wall fizzled out. Able to breathe again, they returned to the spot and surveyed their work, finding the brick entirely gone and the rock behind it badly fractured. They broke away the remaining rock to expose the empty cavern on the other side. The milky and murky sewage water flooded down into the opening, manifesting the most disturbing waterfall one could imagine.

Howie shined his flashlight inside. "*What* the hell's going on..."

Rats and a Ducati

O utside the tent covering the chasm, Piero whispered, hissing into his phone as quietly as he could. "I didn't sign up for this. What do I mean— being some kind of... Internal rat. Yes—yes, but a spy spying on the rest of the world—not on our own agency. Yes. Yes, I understand. No, no, that's not necessary, Domenico."

Inside the tent, causally seated on a foldout chair, Simon listened in on Piero's private conversation with Domenico. Attached to the top of Simon's cellphone was a small spherical device which snatched up the encrypted conversation in midair, and decrypting it, channeled his coworkers' words into his ear.

The call ended, and Simon leaned back in his chair. "And I was just beginning to like you, Piero." He lowered the phone and removed the spherical device from it, and looking at it, said, "Speaking of rats, I'll really have to thank our American friends at the DSA for you, little guy."

His eyes drifted to the bustle of numerous personnel scurrying about inside the tent, so busy with their tasks. Installed now was an electric lift that could travel up and down the chasm. Workers finished loading equipment crates onto the lift, and it started its descent. Someone plugged in an immense power cord, sending electricity racing through it, leading over the edge of the chasm.

This cord followed down the sheer rock face for twenty

feet. The Praesidio Autem Veritas symbol unnaturally gleamed above the arched doorway carved into the rock there. The power cord bent sharply, going through the archaic entrance.

It continued along the passage, now aglow from hanging lights, and led into the expansive and naturally occurring cavern at the passage's end. From the outcrop there overlooking the cavern, the vast and towering rock walls hummed from the rush of an underground river, having carved its path eons ago through the cavern's bedrock floor. The base of the circular cavern, encompassed by this slender yet vigorous river, was an immense subterranean island, at several hundred feet across.

On the outcrop, overlooking the rushing water thirty feet below, the Roman Curia's muscle-bound Oliver aimed his gun. With her back to him, hands on her head, Ingrid faced the cliff's edge. It was a possibility, given her abilities, to leap off and hit the rather narrow swath of shadow-laden water there, three stories down. However, escaping without first resting her eyes and heart upon what she'd come for wasn't a possibility.

"Alone. Without a weapon," Oliver said.

She shrugged. "Haven't been afraid of the dark since I was five."

"We'll see." With his freehand, he took his radio and spoke into it. "Simon? Yes, we have a pest problem." He looked Ingrid over as he continued to speak into the radio. "Rather pretty, actually. And alone. Okay." He clipped the radio to his belt. "Taking a trip, mystery girl. And keep those pretty hands on your head." At gunpoint, he led her back up the passage toward the lift.

~~ ~~

Topside, inside the tent, Simon lowered his radio just as Piero entered. He casually waved Piero over to the lift.

"We have a pest problem," said Simon.

"What do you mean?"

"I mean, seems dark places can't help but attract rodents."

With a small wooden case, Simon stepped onto the lift. He tightly guarded the case to his chest, as if it contained his own heart, or perhaps soul, if he indeed had one. He stared hard at Piero. "So. Let us descend into the dark."

~ ~ ~ ~

The deep purr of a motorcycle engine emanated from the Gulfstream G700 as its door swung down—a Ducati 1199 Panigale R roared out of the plane, launching through the air before even the door completed opening. As the bike skidded to a halt, a gloved hand slid up the tinted visor on the rider's helmet, revealing Domenico's ever-alert eyes.

A suited man stood next to a Mercedes there inside the hanger. "From Rome in under forty minutes," the man said. "Must be a record, sir."

"Tonight, speed is the least of our obstacles," Domenico told him.

The man laid a large case on the hood of the Mercedes. Domenico opened the case and removed two FN SCAR-L rifles, along with a set of filled-out tactical vests. He placed the vests into the bike's storage compartment. By their straps, Domenico slipped a rifle over each shoulder and straddled the bike. He tore out of one of the many identical appearing hangars bordering Malta International Airport. Pulling onto the tarmac, he exited the airport.

The word 'Skeletons' projected on his visor's head-up display, and he accepted the call coming in on the helmet's built-in speaker system from Famke, that woman of mystery.

"Famke, I'm en route. Yes, I'm here—had a change of plans. Simon? No—listen, whatever Simon's told you—no—just wait for me—" The call went dead. Speeding the Ducati through the streets of Tarxien, he attempted to call Piero. There was no answer.

"Map." Immediately, a map materialized across his visor,

automatically routing the fastest path to the site. Tilting almost completely over, the bike nearly scraped across the ground. Domenico darted sharply around a barricade, and onto a street deeply severed by a rift from the earthquake. Jumping the rift, then over the curb, he roared down the precariously steep hillside there. Carters Supermarket awaited at the bottom. The Ducati's 1,098-cubic-centimeter engine screamed as it shifted into the next gear. Domenico placed another call....

Fatal Relief

"*That's* no way to treat a guest," said Simon, exiting the lift with Piero. Oliver had Ingrid pressed face-first against the passage's rock wall. The lift automatically ascended back to the surface.

"Allow me," said Simon. He grabbed Ingrid's arm and twisted, ratcheting it hard against her back. "Got to make sure the grip is nice and tight." He yanked up Ingrid's sleeve. With his other hand, he set the wooden case down, clamping it safely between his tactical boots, then removed a DNA scanner from his jacket. The needle slid out from the scanner, awaiting blood.

"What's that?" she asked, trying to maintain a false calm in her voice.

"Checking the only ID you brought with you."

"Good luck with that," she said.

He sank the needle in. The scanner's screen displayed, 'No Signal Available'.

"Have to go topside and connect to the network," Piero said, finding the excuse he needed in order to get back to the surface to call Domenico for help.

"We'll have to wait to ID her," Simon responded, glancing at his watch. "We have guests arriving."

"Who?" demanded Piero. "No one's supposed to be down here without Domenico's authorization."

Simon's hand silently moved to the gun holstered at his

side. "Being Domenico's off sitting in his office, and last time I checked, I *am* the deputy director, so I took the liberty. If, of course, that's okay with you, Piero."

Piero shifted to Simon's flank, bringing his hand to his own holstered gun. Oliver, still holding Ingrid against the wall, watched, entirely uncertain what would happen, but certain the result would be entirely not good. An electric motor kicked on, disrupting their standoff, as the lift lowered from the surface.

"Speak of Lucifer," said Simon. "Or, I should say... Much worse."

Famke, leading five others with equally piercing blue eyes, stepped from the lift as it came to a stop.

Using a key, Simon shut off the lift, ensuring no one would be able to use it to gain access from above. "One of yours?" he asked Famke, nodding in Ingrid's direction.

Even though Ingrid's eyes had never actually seen Famke or any of the other L' Entita, there was no doubt who and what they were. She'd spent—dedicated her entire life to seeking them out. And now, at last, her life's pursuit was over. And quite possibly, her very life as well.

"She is not us," Famke flatly stated.

"Okay," said Simon. "Then you won't mind her fate."

"We are only here, in deviation of our arrangement with Domenico," Famke said, "due to your message's claim to have found something, that which belongs to us."

"Then, by all means, this way," said Simon. Moving past Oliver, he whispered, "Adjourn with our mystery woman at the outcrop, while I accommodate our guests in the cave."

He led down the passage for the cavern below. Oliver escorted Ingrid at gunpoint behind the others. In front of them, Piero kept his hand close to his gun, knowing fully well he'd have no chance whatsoever if the timing wasn't absolutely ideal when he made his move against Simon.

Judging by what he'd witnessed thus far, there was no limit to what Simon was capable of. He was on his own, alone, here, underground, with no way to reach Domenico. And Oliver, an outsider, a glorified bagman for the Roman Curia, certainly couldn't be trusted.

Upon reaching the outcrop, a sharp nudge from Oliver's gun into Ingrid's back brought her to a halt. As subtly as possible, she scanned the rocks along the ledge. Her custom Walther was there, somewhere, having hidden it moments before she'd first been caught by Oliver.

From their elevated position, Ingrid and Oliver watched Simon as he descended with the others on the steep path along the cliff wall to where it leveled out into the cavern below. There were numerous tunnels there, each with unknown symbols carved above their entrances. Though none of these routes into the cold unknown, wrapped in darkness, were their intended destination.

Arriving at the river, Simon took them across the carbon fiber beam placed there, bridging over the rushing water to the island on the other side. The floodlights positioned along the island's perimeter cast shadows across their solemn faces. They passed the many equipment crates stacked beside the path to the island's center.

And at the exact center of this subterranean island, they came to a simple enough appearing stone table. Carved from the plateauing rock upon which they stood, the table was clearly quite old. Simon set the wooden case he'd brought with him onto this table of stone. Unlocking the case, he removed the ancient book contained within.

Silently, for only his own self, he read what was etched upon its decaying cover. For he dared not speak the words aloud. '*Nascita Dalla Morte*'. Carefully, Simon cupped the book in both hands and held it up before them all. "The only writings of the L' Entita not encoded into their native language."

Famke immediately recognized the book, knowing it for what it was, a true Pandora's Box. "*This* was not taken from this place."

The reproach in her tone rang clear. It was the inevitable precursor to what Simon had expected, yet wished to avoid. He held his silence, while his instinct to attack screamed beneath his skin.

"Where was this obtained?" Famke demanded. She had forsaken all diplomacy. Such was pointless when it came to this book of hell incarnate.

The resolve driving Simon held no more tolerance for such irrelevance. "What matters is we have it." He raised the book high. "That we know its instruction."

From their position above, at the outcrop, though Ingrid and Oliver could not hear every word being spoken, the conflict which played out was quite evident. For Oliver, he certainly understood what the book in Simon's hands was. It was his true purpose for being here. And why both the Roman Curia and Lucia had allowed him to be taken under Domenico's dark wing... Not for this book, but what it contained... He prayed for the best. That, maybe everyone down there would kill each other, and he could simply claim the book after the fatal fallout.

"It is madness," said Famke. With her lead, the five other L' Entita encircled Simon and Piero.

Simon began to sweat, defying the coldness of his surroundings. Here it was, the unavoidable tragedy he'd long dreaded, but nonetheless would embrace, and do so feverishly. Having correctly anticipated this rebuke didn't change the culminating fury of it now seizing him.

"Then this is madness decreed by the L' Entita's own oath," he said, "sworn upon these very pages." His unyielding eyes dared her to make her next move. He wanted her to, to end it all. It'd be a closure written in blood only the legendary L' Entita could author.

Obscured within his palm was a small laser. He shined it into one of the many tunnel entrances connecting along the cavern. Immediately, his twelve-man team concealed there, stepped into the light. Famke and her fellow L' Entita were utterly unphased by this, and held their ground, encircled around Simon and Piero. Their focus remained solely on that book.

"Possessing the *Nascita Dalla Morte*," Famke said, "means you also know that what it contains is the very reason our collective was indefinitely severed in half so long ago."

Simon smiled. *What I know is I'm in control.* "Yes. I'm quite aware, Famke, the contract this book contains. After all this time, it still binds you and your so-called collective to its fateful promise." Holding the book out, he pressed it against her chest, to her heart. "And once that blood's dried, literally, upon the page here, the L' Entita cannot break an oath. *Any* oath."

She pulled away from the book, somehow feeling its eternal nefariousness internally locked within, seeping into her very being. "You do not get to cherry-pick the rules, young Simon. The oath you speak of, it was dissolved with the divergence of our collective."

He pushed forward, holding out the book, repelling back their circle. "That didn't stop your ancestors from trying. The Dark Ages. The Plague—"

"Destroying religions is not what we do," she said, sharply.

"Don't delude yourselves, Famke. For every religion the L' Entita created, how many others were undeniably destroyed in its wake?"

"You're talking the end of Judaism... and its seventeen and a half million members. And Islam... With nearly two billion."

"From time to time, natural section needs a push," he said. "Religion is a plague. And the world demands a savior who loves life enough to sever the infected from the healthy."

"No, Simon—what you desire is a purge of life unlike humanity has ever experienced."

"No, no one murders more so than nature herself... In her hands, life is but death's shadow."

She shook her head. "No—Christianity cannot be allowed

to monopolize such power. To exist as the only Abrahamic religion, the Vatican would be nothing more than... A cartel with a crucifix."

"They already are!" He exhaled, with his frustration brimming up and spilling out. "What I desire, Famke, is unity." His desire, one in fact for power, swelled within him, feeling the goal for it closing in... *So close now...* "You people must understand *that!*" His voice resonated throughout the cavern. Drawing in a deep breath, he closed his eyes, centering himself. "I'm offering the solution for you and your broken collective to be whole again."

She inched forward, with her small collective doing so as well, moving as an extension of her, tightening their noose.

"We do not expect you to understand our ways," she said. "We accepted the reaping of our past so long ago. That's ours, and ours alone to bear."

Within this subterranean tomb, the uneven lighting sharply contrasting the light and dark which gripped each of them, Simon gazed upon the L' Entita, or more so, the remnants of what they once were. He knew now they couldn't do what he asked, even if they wanted to. They were shadows of something that no longer was. He found himself unexpectedly at the center of a calm with this realization. Their will was unmovable, while his own commitment, unstoppable. The intersection of the two would be something else entirely. That was absolute.

As if in a trance, the words flowed from his lips. They weren't at Famke or even to her collective, but as an affirmation for the universe at large. "Echoes of the past, phantoms wrapped with shadow, adrift within a limbo of your own authorship, go now. Anchor yourself to what end you may find. Let be whatever it may be."

She recognized the madness in his eyes, that lust for Armageddon, and the multitude of mushroom clouds proclaiming its arrival. There would be no silver lining. Lead of bullets and lining alike would pale to that power, withering so, melting as paper aflame. This chorus of searing screams would be the end branded with damnation without end, even for the Church... *Particularly so.*

Her mind churned with a spiral of terror. He'd tasted the power the book had to offer. There was no return from that. It was a one-way ticket... Straight to the same all-corrupting palpable zest of horror that'd brought her ancestors their own ruin.

This madman, wielding the book which could summon the end of all things, without a doubt, had crossed a line into the eternal wastelands of true volatility. It took all she had to keep her legs from betraying her, from pulling her to her knees. He had the book, and his men outnumbered her own, and those men held the guns. While hers, held none. But then, this madman, Simon, he did something entirely unexpected, unexpected indeed.

He followed her gaze to his men's guns. "Give your weapons to our guests."

His men stared at him, shocked as Famke and her L' Entita were by the words. Nonetheless, they did as ordered, then stepped back. Simon gestured to the correct tunnel which led to the place that would end the L' Entita's epic journey.

"How do you plan to open the chamber's behemoth of a door?" he asked.

"Leave that to us," she answered, trying to find reason for his actions. He was mad. And there was not a map in existence which could chart the mind of such a man.

The L' Entita awkwardly, though effectively, held the guns. These tools, which could end life, felt foreign, unnatural, and in diametric opposition to their nonviolent nature they'd each sworn themselves to long ago. Of course, and due to the tightrope they were forced to walk from time to time, they did utilize certain tools which existed within the gray areas of life. But not like this, and never so directly. Like the swords their ancestors knew all too well, these guns for them weren't devices to kill. They were shields to preserve their own lives and the lives of so many others.

As the leader of what little remained of the L' Entita, Famke had to be sure. This man, Simon, before her, either had truly lost his mind, or he'd painted a maze of uncertainty with it even he no longer held bearing of. And yet there was a simple solution to this question.

Switching off the gun's safety, she aimed. The single shot struck the rock wall at the farthest end of the cavern, precisely where she'd aimed. The guns they gripped indeed contained live rounds. Piero, in reflex, drew his sidearm and rolled behind one of the many equipment crates stacked there, taking cover.

"Secure your weapon, Piero!" Simon shouted. "Everyone else, stand down."

His men moved further back, giving the L' Entita more space. By any measure, this wasn't an ideal time, though, with Simon's men unarmed, it was ideal enough. Piero chambered a round, then faced Simon.

"You can't simply allow this decrepit cult of mystics, motivated only by pure contempt for the Church, to roam freely, here of all places... To take whatever they wish and use it for certain destruction. No, Simon, I won't let you. What you're doing, it's the highest treason of our pledge to the Santa Alleanza and to the Holy See," Piero said.

Simon leveled his gun. "Piero, you're so far in over your head that if you open your mouth again, you'll certainly fucking drown on your own words." He embraced the moment of mutual hatred with Piero, glaring back at him. "Now, you little shit, drop your gun." He held his eyes and aim on Piero. "Famke, go."

"Give me your men," she said.

"Hostages?" he asked, his focus still wholly upon Piero.

"Insurance."

Without another thought to it, he ordered his men, "Go, and do as she asks of you."

While he and Piero remained unmoving in their standoff,

Famke led the other L' Entita, along with Simon's unarmed men, toward the tunnel entrance at the edge of the cavern. As they entered the tunnel, Simon smiled at Piero, for he knew something neither Piero, nor anyone else in that fraction of a second knew. Of tangible flesh and blood, his men would be a steep sacrifice, but a necessary one. His free hand entered his pocket. Finding what it contained, he slowly removed the remote detonator, holding it up for Piero to see.

Forty feet inside the dimly lit tunnel, the single charge of brick-orange explosive awaited along the rock ceiling. Famke, spearheading her L' Entita and Simon's men, was the first to see the blinking green light of the receiver attached to the Semtex plastic explosive charge directly above her... *Well, Simon, that was why.*

She'd committed the cardinal sin of history. *Never dare underestimate the effectiveness of a madman.* Her eyes closed. With the entirety of her being, she welcomed this small flashing green light and the fatal relief it beckoned...

Simon's thumb plunged down on the detonator. Instantaneously, the signal transmitted through the air to the receiver upon the lone explosive charge inside the tunnel. As his thumb released, he knew, as with all things in his life, he'd chosen the best. This was no different.

Semtex was exclusively a rich man's plastic explosive. As a more than capable field agent, his mind floated full with the intimate details of what was taking place in this blink of a moment. The brick-orange substance which formed the Semtex was comprised of pentaerythritol tetranitrate.

This PETN, as it was abbreviated, served as the explosive filler. It had been bonded quite rapturously on the chemical level by a plasticizer, which in itself was nonexplosive. The two together, however gloriously so, they'd culminated in a truly wonderful crescendo...

Fallout

*A*s if a mist of bone, a ghostly plume flowed from the mouth of the tunnel. In twisting, disjointed knots, it spiraled forth, blossoming out into the cavern's vast expanse. And despite his expertise in all things explosive, the fallout was more than Simon had intended.

A brilliant rattling roar, instantly pursued by a shock wave, released. Within the tunnel, the air was no more. The rock was no more. And the lives therein, they were no more.

Ingrid knew the L' Entita's fate, but her brain refused to register what all had just taken place. Her eyes saw it. Her ears heard it. Her body felt it. And certainly, she understood it. The complete loss of the L' Entita simply could not be accepted.

To have dedicated her life to searching them out, to have come so close, only to witness them all die nearly right before her, was soul-crushing. That was the least of it. What it meant for the world was something of much greater and horrifying magnitude.

The L' Entita's matriarch, Famke, she should have known not to enter there, to have never trusted a single utterance from that man from the Vatican. The L' Entita's elevated state of being, that level of intuition should have alerted them... *Should have.* Otherwise, what good was being such... She, herself, should have done something.

It hit her. *Was this regret?* It wasn't something she'd felt before. It was a... Terribly consuming thing, this emotion. They weren't meant to die. They were supposed to tell—give her the answers to the questions she needed. Those answers she'd never know now. Those answers were dead as the L' Entita were... It *couldn't* be. It just couldn't... She deserved her answers... This was guilt. That she knew, for it was familiar.

And how could she have such a selfish feeling at this moment? It was wrong, explicitly so. Nonetheless, this guilt seeping up inside her didn't diminish her anger of not having received her answers before they'd all died. She should have said something—*anything* to Famke upon first seeing her.

She stepped closer to the outcrop's edge for a better view. With the tug of war of emotions within her, she'd completely forgotten the fact this man behind her had a gun to her back. Oliver's gun barrel jamming against her was a quick reminder.

At the center of the chamber, Piero and Simon continued their armed standoff. Each man's unflinching state forced the other not to yield. The explosion's pale plume reached them, swallowing the space all around. Not so much white now, but increasingly gray, it deeply diminished visibility.

"You really believe you're going to get away with this, Simon? Without Domenico finding out?"

Simon tossed the detonator. "What's done is done—" The mouth of the smoking tunnel suddenly collapsed with a great crumbling sigh, sending forth one final billowing cloud. Simon squinted as the cloud of smoke, wrapped in dust, rushed right at them. With the cloud to Simon's back, Piero waited until visibility had reached its worst. He dropped flat to the floor of the cavern, where the cloud was thickest— Simon rapidly fired. Rounds struck hatefully close to Piero as he rolled out of the way, leaped to his feet, and ran for higher ground. He sprinted up the steep and narrow path leading out of the cavern, back toward the lift.

Emptying his magazine at Piero, with one fluid motion, Simon swiftly reloaded, continuing to fire. Gaining distance, though placing himself into clearer visibility, Piero broke through the cloud, rising above it as he scaled the path upwards. Simon used one of the equipment crates to stabilize himself in preparing for the shot.

Making sure to align his sights not where Piero, in full sprint, was, but where he'd be in the next fraction of an instant... He squeezed the trigger, taking the long shot across the cavern. Piero, reaching the outcrop at the path's highest point, could see the passage leading to the lift—the bullet hit through the center of the shoulder blades. In the next moment, it exited his chest. He looked to the gaping cavity, the grisly surreality somehow eclipsing the pain. He toppled over the cliffside. Tumbling toward the ground, his body bounced off the uneven rocks protruding along the cliff's face.

Oliver, pressing his gun between Ingrid's own shoulder blades, pushed her forward to the sheer edge. *There*— amongst the rocky shadows directly at her feet, was her Walther she'd stashed. Remaining focused upon this woman, Oliver could feel Simon's icy gaze from below.

The inevitable moment had arrived. Oliver's eyes drifted downwards... The two men made eye contact. And both men tried to impossibly discern the other's next move...

It was the first time since her capture that Oliver's eyes weren't exclusively focused on her. Ingrid thrust herself backwards into Oliver. Using Oliver's own gun against him, her body drove the gun's handle into his stomach.

In one seamless movement, she dove, landing a razor's edge along the outcrop's ledge, scooping up her Walther, and somersaulted to cover amongst the formations of long, jagged rocks there. They protruded up from the edge of the outcrop like great stone fangs. Oliver fired a series of bursts. She fired back, striking quite close, revealing a skill level he hadn't at all expected. She fired again, deliberately so, nearly hitting his groin.

"Jesus!" He leapt for cover, away from her well-fortified position.

Each depleting their magazines at the other, reloaded, and both wondered what Simon was waiting for. They arrived at the same conclusion... Simon was simply letting the enemy of his enemy weaken each other before striking. Ingrid peered over the edge, surveying the distance between her and the slender, rushing river far below. Thirty feet down, and at the cavern's center, Simon tore the lid off the equipment crate in front of him, retrieving one of the XM84 bullpup rifles neatly packed within....

~~ ~~

Inside the sewer, having been watching the entire time through the opening they'd created in the cavern's wall, Howie couldn't accept complacency any longer. He grabbed an explosive charge from his backpack.

"What the hell are you doing?" demanded Tom.

Howie guesstimated the distance to that madman, Simon, below. The charge wouldn't reach him, though the resulting fallout would at least buy the girl trapped down there a chance.

"Not going to stand by and watch her die," he said.

"And what about everyone just blown to hell in that tunnel?" Tom asked.

"Can't help them," Howie said, preparing the charge, "but she's still alive."

~~ ~~

Simon took aim, leaning his elbows on the crate. He zoomed in on Oliver as well, whoever the female intruder was. Who she was mattered not, as both would be dead soon enough. *Two rodents...* He grinned fiendishly as he flipped the gun's selector switch, readying its grenade launcher. *One grenade...*

Their heat signatures, framed within the rifle's thermal scope, gleamed before him in lush hues and vivid clarity. He squeezed the trigger. This thirty-millimeter grenade now racing, spiraling so up through the air at Ingrid, wasn't something she'd anticipated. Likewise, for Oliver, seeing this unescapable death headed for him too, robbed him of all contingency...

The grenade, overshooting, hit several feet above the outcrop, exploding against the cliff face. A rain shower of shrapnel and rock sprayed down, blanketing the cavern. The impact fractured the face of the cliff, sending a rapidly widening rift straight for Howie and Tom, there above.... The entire cliff face split—collapsing the sewer's tunnel, where they stood.

"Aim for the water!" shouted Howie.

"Thanks for the advice!" Tom yelled, as the ground instantly dissolved underfoot.

They rode the half-avalanche, half-waterfall of rock and sewage flooding downwards. Ingrid and Oliver, reengaged in heated gunfire, dually shared a truly curious flash of eye contact with Howie and Tom, these two men, who, in that dire moment, seemed to have manifested from thin air, then wildly so plummeted through that very air. Continuing to fire, Ingrid swore she saw one of these men, the redheaded one, wink at her as he tumbled past.

Tom and Howie hit the ungodly cold river. Fighting the current, they managed to pull themselves up long enough for a lungful before being swept inside the narrow cave-like fissure where the river vanished into the base of the cliff.

"Why not," Ingrid said under her breath, firing her last round. Pocketing her empty Walther and dodging Simon's manic spray of bullets, she dove over the edge of the outcrop. Her body sliced deep into the narrow ribbon of water below.

Simon shifted his onslaught entirely on Oliver. Oliver dropped to his stomach, crawling behind the cluster of fang-like rocks at the outcrop. Sliding out his magazine, he only had three bullets left. As rounds struck all around, Simon had him pinned. Retreat down the passage for the lift wasn't a possibility, not without being shot through the back like Piero. This was his last stand. Outgunned, nearly out of ammo, whatever he was going to do, he'd have to do it perfectly.

He'd hold his cover and wait. There'd be a brief window in the automatic fire when Simon would have to remove the

XM84's massive and cumbersome four-hundred round magazine in order to load another. Even a man as skilled as Simon, that would take three or four seconds. The relentless shower of bullets stopped. *Now!* Oliver bolted up from behind the rock, sights aligned down upon Simon—the shot rang out from the *second* XM84 in Simon's other hand.

The bullet didn't hit Oliver's forehead where'd he intended, as perfect aim was rather difficult on full-auto. Even so, it obliterated the top of Oliver's shoulder. Oliver glanced at the devastating wound, folded over the rock where he stood, and fell headfirst to the bottom of the cavern. He landed eerily close to where Piero's lifeless body laid, crumpled into a mangled pretzel of torn flesh and shattered bone.

Simon recovered his radio from the ground. Catching his breath, he spoke into it. "Auxiliary Team, where in holy christ are you? Yes—*now* would be a good time!"

Wiping the sweat from his face, he licked his lips and tossed the radio, flipping it through the air. Catching the radio, he clipped it to his belt. *You're doing it, Simon. You're truly doing it... By inferno's blaze, baptize the world. Raze the Holy See. Capsize it in a sea of fire. Arise, to raise the earth anew.* The words he'd long memorized from the *Nascita Dalla Morte* didn't just echo in his mind... They sang.

Taking one of the rifles laying on the equipment crate, he reloaded it, then eagerly jogged up the path leading to the outcrop. He'd no sooner stepped foot inside the passage, going for the lift, when all the lights overhead went dead, releasing a deep darkness to pass over him. *Ah. Yes.* There was no doubt whose calling card this was.

And he should've anticipated Domenico would've played this card, with drawing in his legendary agent, who'd since retired. *So...* The time had finally come to see who was the greater warrior. Would he be the one to slay the mighty giant, the man more myth than man, the one now known simply as Camorra...

The Assassin and the Spy Part I:
Death and Darkness

*U*nder the cover of darkness, Camorra and Domenico repelled down, slipping past the lift, where it was suspended by thick cables within the chasm. Their boot heels brought them to a silent stop as they reached the arched doorway leading into the passage. The echoes from Simon and his twelve-man team rushing up the tunnel resonated along the rock face as Domenico and Camorra hung by their rappelling lines on either side of the doorway.

Simon held up his hand. His team slowed their pace as the flashlights attached to their guns illuminated the arched doorway fifteen feet away. He signaled again and they took tactical formation. Separating into two-man groups, they cautiously closed in on the end of the passage and the lift there within the dark chasm.

Simon knew Camorra was there, somewhere in the shadows. He could feel it. He shouted down the passage, "Even for you, Camorra, you're outnumbered!"

Unseen, with one hand gripping their rappelling lines, Camorra and Domenico raised the FN SCAR-L rifles strapped across their chests and swung, entering the arched doorway. Their rifles' night vision scopes outlined everything in a glow of electric emerald. And their movements, fluid, effortless, were a pure lethal elegance as they commenced their ballet of wrath.

Momentary flashes of light peppered the dark as the two men fired suppressed shots in three-round bursts. With both terrifying accuracy and speed, the bullets struck, snapping back the heads of Simon's men one after the other, who collapsed lifelessly. Domenico and Camorra released their rappelling lines at the apex of their swing. The momentum carried them overhead as they continued to take out Simon's men below, who blindly shot straight into the blackness before them.

Gravity found Domenico and Camorra and their feet made contact with the ground. They appeared more specters than flesh and blood with the seamless grace of their footwork, as if afloat on some unseen mist. Unlike Simon's men who kept the buttstocks of their rifles flush against their shoulders, Camorra and Domenico held theirs tucked under their chins, enabling them to fire centerline from their bodies, shooting with a far superior speed and precision. Side by side, Camorra and Domenico cleared the passage of any remaining targets. From their guns, orange-inflamed streaks spearheaded by silent bullets sliced the surrounding blackness.

As the sonata of gunfire played out through the muzzle bursts and erratically swung flashlight beams, Simon caught a fleeting glimpse of Domenico. Simon's blood froze. He now realized his gross misjudgment of the situation. *Well played indeed, Domenico.*

Within six seconds of having entered the passage, Camorra and Domenico had eradicated all Simon's men. And Simon could do the math. In that aftermath's sudden quiet, there was only one result for this equation. His men, all of them, were dead.

Camorra spoke, shrouded in the shadows. "Seems you're the one who's alone."

Simon did the only thing he knew to do... The only thing

he could. He pivoted and ran, emptying his gun's magazine into the dark behind him as he fled. Standing perfectly still, Camorra aligned his sights with the back of Simon's head. He felt Domenico's hand set upon his shoulder. Camorra stepped aside.

Through his rifle's night vision scope, Domenico locked the crosshairs on Simon, who was in full sprint. Domenico breathed in and held the air inside his lungs. Gently, his finger squeezed the trigger. The bolt of the gun clicked as the suppressed round discharged. Traveling at 2,870-feet-per-second, the bullet sank into Simon's back, directly dead center of his shoulder blades, with a fire and force matching the malice Domenico felt in that moment.

Simon's body thrust forward at the point of impact just as he reached the outcrop there at the passage's end overlooking the well-lit cavern below. His chest burst open as the bullet exited, continuing on. He fell over the edge of the cliff, tumbling through open space, and with a crackling thump, landed alongside the bodies of Piero and Oliver. The three of them, there, strewn in twisted ways, laid now in some fateful line of death upon those cold rocks.

From the outcrop, Domenico and Camorra looked down on the three bodies. Bathed in the yellow of the cavern's floodlights, Domenico saw Piero there, thirty feet below, lifeless. Camorra followed Domenico down the steep path to the place at the bottom of the cavern. They came to a stop in front of Piero's body.

Camorra removed his tactical vest, then his jacket from underneath. He gave the jacket to Domenico. Domenico knew this was Camorra's way of saying he was sorry for his loss, for the death of Piero.

Struggled breaths escaped from Simon, apparently still alive a few feet away. Domenico set the jacket aside. He'd wait to place it upon Piero's body. He wanted... No—he *needed* Simon to see, with his last breath, the body. Camorra moved out of earshot, providing privacy, as Domenico leaned down to Simon, and did so very close.

"You stated it best," Domenico said.

The life in Simon's eyes faded fast as they searched for context from Domenico's face, void of all expression.

Domenico would oblige him. "'Chillingly formable... To say the least.'"

"Your rat told you everything then," Simon managed.

"Piero *was* my nephew."

Simon's breathing was very shallow now.

"I'll share a gem before you go, Simon. That thing reflecting back in your soon to be empty eyes, that's fear. I've taken a lot of lives throughout my career. And those that lay dying, who'd made real human connections with others in their lives before that moment, regardless who that may be, always reflect back perceivably less fear in their eyes. I chalk it up to something along the lines of human connection cancels out regret of some kind, or some shit, when our end arrives." He got down eye to eye with Simon. "Piero was my human connection. And, Simon... All I see in your eyes is fear."

He stood before Simon could finish his last breath. Something caught Domenico's eye. He retrieved it, the DNA scanner which laid next to Oliver, evidently having fallen from his pocket when his body had hit the ground. Even with a cracked screen, it showed the DNA sample held within still safely preserved. About to slip the scanner into his pocket, he saw the dried blood upon his palm.

There was no way to know if it was Simon's or Piero's—reality hit him. He turned back to Piero's lifeless body among the rocks... The rocks, their shape narrow, each arched along their tops. Somehow, through a complex set of conditions, they'd grown to resemble tombstones. Of the right size, smooth and simple, they'd become unmarked ironies written by time. He stood there amongst these natural tombstones seeking solace.

Though he was familiar with taking life, when necessary, he

hadn't much experience, perhaps none, with the business of revenge. It had never been personal. Even now, he was rather certain the circumstances should disqualify this notation. His actions causing Simon's death occurred after the fact of having seen his nephew, Piero, there, dead.

Yes, he'd his suspicions... fear. And maybe, even, the instinct to suspect such an embittered act from Simon. Though it was only with seeing for himself, Piero's eyes brimmed with their eternal emptiness, that his death was a certainty. Piero wasn't his son, but he'd been the closest thing to being.

Now that it had happened, he couldn't suppress the grief in the same the way he'd witnessed others do in the past, by channeling it into a vendetta against the cause. That cause, being Simon, was dead out the gate. This left himself to blame for the death. And why shouldn't he. He'd allowed the situation. That was the only logical course for where to assign blame, and thus, guilt, from this point going forward.

There was an order, a sense of reason to be gleaned from holding himself, at least in part, accountable. None of this shifted the reality from Piero being dead to alive again. Piero was dead. And no one could dispute the absolute nature of death.

In his world of espionage, that eclipsed realm where fatal secrets extinguished life in any caliber, death was the only constant. This was true just as much for the dead as it was for the living. Neither, he held no illusions. He wasn't so arrogant to maintain he knew what happened to those who died. He dealt in absolutes. What he did know with resounding absoluteness was the dead lived on in memory by whom they'd held connection.

Therein, he'd be forced to face that grief. He'd have to delay doing so until after he'd preserved the cause for which Piero sacrificed himself. This commitment he'd shackle alongside his oaths to the Church and its clandestine knights, the Santa Alleanza. He drew the strength to be found within this new conviction. Clarity presented itself, and he knew he'd prevail because his damnation would be his redemption.

He could feel Camorra held his eye upon him, not directly, but with a reserved delicacy only Camorra could manifest. Even now, he knew Camorra was quietly calculating the impact of Piero's loss into some convoluted algorithm in order to determine how field-worthy it'd render him, or not render him. Making eye contact, he wondered how long they'd both been standing there in the cavern, lost in diverging worlds destined only to intersect again, now in this awkward moment.

With the jacket, Domenico covered Piero's body. He joined Camorra before the table of stone at the cavern's center. Domenico took the ancient book Simon had left there. It was familiar, not in the personal sense, but familiar in the way when one falls through the ice and the freezing water first seizes, then drains all energy. It was the second volume to that which rested within his office safe. Now he held the power of the L' Entita in its entirety. In silence, for himself, he recited the title, '*Nascita Dalla Morte*'. Simon's ambition may have brought his own ruin, but the depth in which he'd penetrated the realm of forbidden history was astonishing, even by Domenico's standards.

Holding the *Nascita Dalla Morte* was like reversed channeling. It sucked the energy and very essence from one's soul and being, leaving a void barren even of emptiness. Before it could leach any further, Domenico placed the book inside its wooden case. Closing the case, he knew this arcane evil had already spilled over from its pages of long ago into the present. It'd started and now was spreading, starved and infectious as the plague it had surely summoned.

"Smell that," said Camorra. "Plastic explosive." He pointed to the mouth of the rubble-filled tunnel. "Assume that was the way to the chamber?"

Domenico was well aware it was the main tunnel which led to the chamber. He also knew it had proven to be a dead end.

"According to the initial survey, that one was already collapsed near its midpoint. Either by the earthquake or by time."

Venturing to the rubble-filled mouth of the tunnel, Camorra grabbed one of the fragments of freshly broken rock. "Why demolition it then?"

Domenico scanned the area, not seeing the bodies of the L' Entita. "To kill who was inside at the time." He went to the river's edge and rubbed away the dried blood on his palm. Cleansed now, he brought up a schematic of the surrounding tunnel system on his phone. "There's another route. One which goes all the way."

Snapping new magazines into their rifles, they stepped through the shadowy entrance of one of the tunnels....

Intersection

*V*iolently launched from the underwater tunnel, Howie and Tom landed with a flailing splash into the shallow pool several feet below. An amber phosphorescent glow covering the rock walls all around them softly illuminated the space. The surrounding rock, perfectly smooth, rose far above, disappearing into unknown blackness.

"I was expecting at least a waterfall," Tom said, borderline disappointed. They got to their feet finding the pool was only waist-deep.

Howie spit a mouthful of water. "What do you call that?"

Tom looked to the tunnel feeding the pool ten feet above them. "That, that's more a cascade. Definite difference."

"Someday, please do fill me in on that difference..." Howie trailed off, focusing on the glow now coating his fingertips.

Where the pool met the walls, the phosphorescent film bled into the water, leaving a liquefied surface of light most graceful and golden. In a way only the thoroughly lost could, they took in their surroundings. Wherever it was they were, this was a place for intersection to a time of enchantment and mysteries lost. It'd been long abandoned for today's realm spellbound for a congestion of disconnection.

Elevated from the water in the middle of the pool was a great stone. Masterfully crafted, it tapered seven feet up, carved in the shape of a goblet. And beyond, all along the pool's rocky edge, as one giant and continuous ring, was a guardrail which stood, perhaps, three feet tall.

Like the goblet, this too was carved from the naturally occurring rock, not ornately, but beautifully so. It fully encircled the expansive, cylinder-shaped area, with the pool where they were at the center. On the other side of this guardrail were passages spaced out 360 degrees. Just as in the cavern, carved above the mouths of these dark passages, were unknown symbols.

"What do you think's causing that light on the rock?" Howie asked.

"Nuclear-charged algae. Flesh-eating amoebas. Magic."

"Sure," said Howie, "given this place, nothing would surprise me—" He stared, utterly surprised, wide-eyed, as that mysterious woman expelled from the mouth of the tunnel, landing in the pool near the base of the stone. Before either could move, this woman directly at their feet now had a gun drawn on them.

"Uh... hi," Tom managed. She moved back, keeping them in her sights.

"Should we raise our hands?" asked Howie.

"That'd be advisable," she answered. They raised their hands.

She sized them up. "You're not with the Vatican, so who are you?"

"Lyon Recovery and Discovery," said Howie.

His answer, though seemingly sincere, proved absolutely useless to her. "Lion?" she asked.

"No. L-Y-O-N. It's... my last name."

"Recovery and discovery done with a roar. *Roarrrr*," Tom said, humming out their company's jingle.

Howie glared at him. "Treasure hunters."

"You're archeologists?" she asked.

Howie frowned at her misconstruing of terms. It happened often, though he'd never grown used to the mistake. "Well..."

"Explorers," Tom said, trying to manage the situation. He

inched forward. "As it were."

"Treasure hunter-explorers, set your packs down and move away," she commanded. Although, her gun, resolutely aimed at them, did most the talking. They slid off their packs and left them at the base of the large stone.

Aiming with one hand, she searched the two packs. She removed Tom's Colt .45 and tucked it into her waistband. Then, finding the photo of the Praesidio Autem Veritas, she held it up.

"Explain," she said.

Hearing the echo of boots running down one of the surrounding passages, Howie said, "In the interest of all our survival, we really need to postpone this conversation."

Pressing her hand to the stone, Ingrid found the pulse from the echoes. Though each set of footsteps was quite similar in cadence, there were two pursuers. To herself, she quickly calculated the intervals of the echoes and estimated their arrival time.

"We have a couple minutes," she said.

In no position to question her questionable assessment, Howie resisted doing so, but still had to ask, "We can get the hell out of here then?" Ingrid leapt with unnatural height and speed. They watched as she somehow scaled the stone goblet's slick surface with an ease only to be described as an agile defilement of gravity and of physics at large.

Tom whispered to Howie, "Who the hell is she?"

Howie was beset with the same wonderment. " *What* the hell is she?"

Ingrid peered over the goblet's brim. Just as she believed, there were countless crystals, diverse by every measure of size, color, shape, kind, as one ever had gazed upon. And placing her hand, palm-up, not quite touching these crystals, though nearly so, she closed her eyes and waited. For what, she was not certain. It wasn't something one could know as it was to be felt, to be experienced in the gentlest of increments until one's soul accepted, then raptured with an understanding void of knowledge.

When it happened, the best her brain could interpret it to be was a sensation of magnetism. Though this pull wasn't an attraction between two separate objects, so to bring them together through closing a distance. It was a harmonization, and one which merged their very borders, blending their separation into a single, unified thing. It came in waves. That place between sight and sound, it was and always had been broadcasting, so very much compatible with the body, though long tuned out by the senses. This was the lost frequency she'd found, or more correctly, rediscovered.

Wherever its origin, it had always been there, not just in her, but all around. As one's first encounter with the pain of heat as a child burning their skin, or of cotton candy melting into sweet nothingness within the confines of the mouth, this too would be forever engrained upon memory and essence. Its intensity became overwhelming. Lacking an understanding for the emotion, panic began to spread within her. Quickly transitioning to fear, she tried to open her eyes, but couldn't. She demanded they open, though they would not.

Unseen by any of them, obscured to Howie and Tom at ground level, and Ingrid, eyes fastened shut, a single shard of crystal began to emit light within the goblet. It was not great in intensity or glorious in the milky hue that it was. It was enough to be, and it simply was. Unable to know in a knowable way if it had been the shard which drew her hand or her hand which drew the shard, contact was made, and not by touch but by something much more certain. Conceding, her eyelids finally opened and she removed the crystal shard from the rest, though no longer aglow.

When she dropped back down onto the base of the stone, Howie said with a forced authority he didn't actually possess, "We're going with or without you."

"With is preferable," said Tom. "Given, you're the only one who seems to know their way around."

The echoes of the running bootsteps sounded nearly upon

them now. Ingrid scanned the symbols carved above the passages. Watching her closely, Howie took note she very much appeared to be able to read this unreadable language. Tossing them back their packs, she scaled the guardrail of stone. Flashlights in hand, this unlikely trio indeed vanished into the most cherished of all the passages....

Pursuit

*C*amorra and Domenico switched their night vision scopes off and flashlights on for their rifles. They spotted the three sets of wet footprints leading into the passage. Whoever their intruders were, at least one of them knew the impossible, the location of the secret chamber.

~ ~ ~ ~

Howie and Tom struggled to keep up with Ingrid's full-out sprint through the darkness. Lungs aflame, certain they couldn't push much further, they reached a dead end.

"Now what?" Howie asked between gasps.

"Now we see if we die or we enter," she said.

"Uh... Enter where?" asked Tom.

"Into that which is pursued," she answered. Her flashlight beam revealed the rather subtle series of markings along the wall. Not knowing, but feeling, somewhere between intuition and hope, she chose a place on the smooth rock. She blew off the dust, revealing a hairline crack, just as flashlights behind them came into view not more than twenty feet away.

Taking the shard of crystal in her left hand, she clenched, letting its serrated edges draw blood. The shard began to resonate. Rapidly intensifying, it glowed translucently milky. Pressing her hand to the hairline crack, her warm and rich blood seeped. Without a sound, a section of the wall, four feet across, moved back, not in a sliding fashion, but as if floating in reverse.

"Stop—we won't harm you!" shouted Domenico, lowering his rifle.

Camorra followed Domenico's lead, laying his rifle on the ground. Unarmed and eye to eye, they faced these three who'd managed to infiltrate the site, locate the chamber, and open its invisible door which contained no apparent handle or lock. Ingrid slipped through the opening. Domenico offered his hand to Howie to Tom. In the genesis of considering Domenico's offer, Ingrid pulled them inside. Domenico lunged for the opening—the section of wall immediately melted seamlessly back into place—Camorra yanked Domenico away, saving his fingers from being severed by the sudden closure.

~~ ~~

The three of them, for a moment, remained in perfect darkness, having each somehow lost their flashlights upon entering. Locating hers, Ingrid switched it on. Her beam stripped away the shadows, exposing what was before them. And despite the impressive sum of each of their extraordinary journeys in life up until that point, they found themselves rendered utterly speechless, capable of only gazing in awe, most silently....

The Maltese Chamber

*B*lack blood oozed from the hairline crack on the wall.

Camorra touched the liquified darkness with his fingertips. "Blood. The cells are dead—decayed, as if been there for days, or longer..."

"It's their key." Domenico drew a sample of the blood with the DNA scanner. "Only the L' Entita's blood can open the chamber." He compared the sample to the one in the scanner's storage. "It's the same. Now we know *what* our intruders are. One anyway."

Camorra removed several flares from his tactical vest. "Can use the blood from the scanner to open the door?"

"Wish it were that easy. It must be of the body's temperature." Domenico checked his watch. "Our reinforcements should have arrived at the surface by now. I'll get the demolitions."

Activating the flares, Camorra tossed them, forming a half radius around the section of wall. "I'll wait here." Sensing Domenico's hesitation, he said, "Alive. I know. So, do know, I'm bound to the Oath of the Camorra. I cannot take life unless it is to preserve the oath."

"And if they bear you harm?" Domenico asked, "being an oath holder, are you not by that measure, in part, the oath itself?" He saw he'd caught Camorra off guard by his rather intimate knowledge of this deeply safeguarded oath. "I do run the Santa Alleanza, my friend."

"My way is to sustain the parameters of governance, not to bend or break them out of personal convenience. If, or when possible."

Domenico had little choice but accept Camorra's less than reassuring reassurance, and entrust this former assassin, now of the Camorra Order, not to assassinate the very last of this most secret bloodline. "No mortal wounds, Camorra." He turned, heading back down the passage.

~ ~   ~ ~

Inside the chamber, as moths powerless to a flame's hypnotic pulse, the three of them remained transfixed along the wall, taking in their surroundings. What laid before them, had, for the moment, suspended all memory of what laid behind them. Fear, regret, apprehension, was no more.

Howie and Tom turned on their flashlights, and adding their beams to Ingrid's, took aim. Dwarfing them in scale, the chamber brazenly proclaimed itself through its enormity as well engineering. There was archaic technology here, but vastly superior to anything modernity could offer.

The immensity which now contained them was a pyramid of exact proportions, artfully crafted from pure, negative space. Its four geometrically identical walls sloped inward from their base along the floor, and at the ceiling's summit, met, forming a great, pointed dome. Though it was the material comprising the pyramid that was the most intoxicating, as well perplexing of its genius. Top to bottom, each side seamlessly connected to the next, fashioned entirely of a substance most diamond-like. The surface of which consisted of countless layers, paper thin, compacted together, both reflective yet transparent.

Ingrid took the crystal shard from her pocket. "Light, please."

They shined their flashlights on her hand as she cut her

skin, drawing blood once more. Along the wall, where'd they entered from, she placed her bleeding palm. The glassy surface was mildly cool. On contact with the wall, she felt the slightest give inwards. Maybe she'd imagined it, as now it seemed solid.

She saw the small crack there, which could have just appeared before her eyes, or she'd not paid it notice before. It didn't take long to fill with her blood. Alongside the crack, a triangular section of the wall, each side not more than six inches in length, illuminated. From its quality and color, this glow could have been daylight, if not for the fact they were deep underground.

Spaced out, one by one, more triangular shaped sections came aglow. They did so faster and faster, spreading across the chamber, until thousands of them emitted light. And equally so, from the floor, ceiling, and walls. Now they could see the chamber's surface wasn't seamlessly smooth. Its diamond-like skin was the product of tens of millions of triangular facets end to end, corner to corner, culminating in a honeycombed plane of true brilliance.

With the increase in lighting, so did the chamber's reflective quality, becoming nearly as a mirror. Howie waved to his refection in the wall, staring back at him. There was a noticeable lag between his movements and that of his reflection. Sporadic in just how much, from a fraction to a few seconds, they each experienced this.

"That might be the weirdest thing I've ever seen," said Howie. "Which is saying a lot."

"Particularly, for today," Tom said.

The trio moved toward the chamber's center. Their boots made no sound against the surface as they went. Stranger, there was an ever-subtle elasticity to the floor, as if walking softly across a trampoline laden with a thin layer of snow. It was the same sensation she'd had upon touching the wall. She hadn't imagined it after all. Neither were any of them imagining the ripples of light radiating out across the facets on the floor with each step.

"How's this light thing happening?" Howie asked. "I mean, if it's not too much to explain. If you know..."

Ingrid did know, in a sense, at least the general principle behind the science. The L' Entita had been beyond their own time, far beyond. They were beyond the now as well. That was their true achievement, a spell for the ages. Regardless the decade or century, millennium, by any measure, the L' Entita remained mesmerizing, as much they were mystifying. Like with anything divulging of this archaic guild of mystery, the little her mind's eye held was due entirely to her grandfather, of his stories, of his and hers shadowed past.

As they neared the center of the chamber, Howie's forced throat clearing pulled her from her thoughts.

"Any input," he pressed.

"Light waves have memory," she said.

"And?" he asked. An illuminated facet on the floor larger than all the others marked the chamber's center.

"Solar panels store light as energy, right," she said, searching for some obvious or even less than so thing to press or activate in order to summon up the chamber's altar. *It should have been here. Where was it?*

"Right...," he said, no closer to understanding in the least bit.

She tried tapping her foot to the central facet on the floor. It had no effect. "So, this is the same thing. Just, the light these panels have stored, remained as light. Simple, right?" On her knees now, she searched the facet's surface for any indication of what to do.

Conceding to the futility of his own ignorance, he accepted not being able to understand. "Right." He sighed, joining her on the floor. "Uh, what are we looking for?"

Her palms ran across the facets surrounding them. "The central altar."

"Of course..." He really needed to stop asking questions, if he wanted to keep from exasperating his present pace into the starved quicksand of bafflement. "Why not give it blood. Like, how you did before?"

It was a good thought, and one she'd originally had, but how could she? "There's no opening for it to enter." She pointed to the central facet. "Look—no fracture there."

"Neither is there on any other altar. You just place the offering on it."

Right. It was so obvious. She hadn't even considered such a standard approach. With the crystal shard clenched in her grasp, she let her blood drip out. The swelled droplets struck upon the facet on the floor, bursting into splattered, flattened versions of what they'd just been a moment before. And noticing how quiet it was, they now both realized Tom was gone.

"Tom," cupping his hands at the edges of his mouth, Howie called out. There was no echo of his voice as there should have been against the walls, which sloped inward all around.

"Tom!" Again, instead of his voice rebounding off the chamber's surface, it was thoroughly and utterly absorbed.

Ingrid stood at the chamber's center, joining Howie in sweeping the vast space with the beams of their flashlights. Without realizing it, she still gripped the crystal shard in her freehand. The blood continued to fall, droplet by droplet, running into the creases which framed the central facet.

From the facet itself, or a place contained from underneath, bloomed forth roots as that of a tree. They were of the chamber's same glassy material. And instead of reaching into the earth, these roots reached up for the chamber's gleaming pyramidal ceiling.

The abnormal sight now before them stood at rather normal table height. Like a great, upside-down chandelier, the transparent roots dangled upwards. They began to glow with the color of natural daylight, just as that of the illuminated facets.

"What a trip," Tom said. "This place really pushes one's

own faculties... Wouldn't want to do it alone. There'd be no way to know if you're completely losing your mind."

He was standing beside them. Though, for how long, neither of them could say. They stared questioningly at him.

"What?" he asked.

"Where the hell were you?" Howie demanded, both annoyed and relieved, and not sure in which order.

"You guys ditched me," Tom said. He held up his cellphone. "I've been documenting this head-bender of a cave."

"*We* ditched you," said Howie. His frustration with Tom immediately fell away, as a mist started to emanate from those glassy diamond-like roots. Tom continued recording with his phone.

"Hot or cold?" asked Howie.

Ingrid touched her hand to the mist, causing her to immediately yank away. The resulting shiver provided his answer.

"Sounds like water...," she said. "You hear it too?"

"Yeah. Down there." Howie pointed to the small hole a few feet away now formed in the floor. It was no larger than a silver dollar.

From Ingrid's flashlight, they managed a glimpse of the water coursing beneath the floor. By impulse, based purely upon the size, she removed the crystal from her pocket and tried placing it in the hole. It locked into place like a transparent finger pointing to the honeycombed heavens above. Symbols from the unknown language of the L' Entita glowed to life, appearing, not upon, but within the surface of the walls. Multiple layers deep in the chamber's glassy skin, these symbols, known only to her to form actual words or perhaps something greater, radiated in the richest indigo any of them had seen or would ever again.

Ingrid studied each of the glowing markings. Then, casting self-doubt upon her interpretation, reread them to herself. Not that she wasn't fluent enough in the symbols' meanings, it was the message, or more so the instruction they rendered, that'd left her to question.

Howie, unable to contain his wonderment a second longer, asked, "So?"

"Life's fluid."

He squinted at the large illuminated symbols along the walls. They looked as alien as if they'd been written by aliens themselves. "All that for two words?"

She shrugged. "Yeah, life's fluid, or, fluid of life." She sat down cross-legged in front of the little crystal shard locked into the softly illuminated floor. He joined her. While Tom, remaining standing, recorded.

"What's that have to do with the crystal?" Howie asked. Unmoving, she sat, transfixed, waiting. Her eyes closed.

It was clear she had no answers for either of them, and he'd need to find his own. Somehow, having missed it before, he saw the faintest outline several inches out from the crystal. Maybe five inches away, there was a ring around the entire thing. Extremely thin, less than that of a piece of paper, but there was definitely a tiny black line encircling the crystal shard.

"Water!" she shouted, eyes still closed.

She was right. *The fluid of life.* It was glaringly obvious. Grabbing the crystal, he tried to pull it from the floor. With both hands wrapped around it, still it wouldn't budge. He might as well have been attempting to free the Excalibur. Remembering the ring around the crystal, he pointed to it.

"Let go," she told him.

The pain hit him when he released the crystal, seeing it'd lacerated both his palms. Estimating the necessary amount, she ground the side of her arm down into the tip of the shard, cutting rather deep. Howie turned away, unable to watch. It disturbed him, not just the gore of it, but by her dispassion for the certain pain, without hesitation, she'd caused herself.

She squeezed forth the blood into the ring which encircled the crystal shard. The droplets collected, spreading out in either direction, following the curvature, until the diverging streams came full circle, completely encompassing the crystal. Quickly, Howie tore a strip from his shirt and helped her tie off the wound.

"Shall I?" he asked, moving for the shard, now knowing its purpose was that of a handle. He took hold and the entire ringed section lifted up and out freely from the rest of the floor. It was surprisingly lightweight.

Setting the section aside, he joined her near the hole in the floor. A few inches down, they could see it clearly now, the water rushing underneath the chamber. He followed her lead, and removing his jacket, used it to soak up the water.

"Do you mind, Tom," he said.

"Mind what?" Tom asked.

"Making yourself useful."

A bit crestfallen, Tom propped up the kickstand on the back of his phone and positioned it on the floor, letting it continue to record. He submerged his jacket into the rushing water. Ingrid wrung the water from her jacket onto the cluster of roots that reached up from the floor's central facet.

On contact, the water froze, spreading out over the top of the roots, flat, like a table. Some of the roots still protruded, sticking through the surface. Howie and Tom squeezed the water from their jackets. The water instantly became as a sheet of ice, creating a perfectly flat tabletop for the altar now before them.

With a simple touch of her hand, Ingrid freed the small shard of crystal from the section of floor Howie had set aside. She knew this was the final step to awaking the altar, to summoning its secrets, most hidden and forgotten. She pulled back the fabric binding her wound and let her blood fall upon the altar of ice. The warm fluid made connection with the frozen surface. What happened next was far, far beyond what they'd witnessed thus far....

The Compass Piece

*D*omenico returned to the bowels of the earth, armed not only with his team of reinforcements, but with a newfound urgency to penetrate the chamber. The lift took them deeper into the chasm. With a jolt, it delivered them at the arched doorway, to the mouth of that subterranean labyrinth built with walls of stone and secrets latent in fearful dread and cherished reveal alike.

There was movement at the far end of the passage. Domenico raised his rifle. Through his scope, Camorra came into focus, there, at the cusp of the outcrop. What was in his hand was undiscernible at this distance.

The sudden unannounced explosion made clear what Camorra grasped, a detonator. Domenico's men immediately crouched into tactical formation, guns at their ready. Domenico held up his fist, signaling his men to stand down.

Camorra turned, entirely aware there was an audience now to face. Domenico lowered his rifle, knowing whatever Camorra had just committed action to was out of initiative. He led his men, joining Camorra at the outcrop.

"I helped myself to some of the contents within the crates," Camorra said.

He moved aside to let his work speak for itself. The dust settled in the cavern below, flowing out from a tunnel. It ran parallel to the one already collapsed.

"Clever. You made an access into the tunnel Simon had destroyed," said Domenico.

Camorra started swiftly down the path for the cavern. "The blood from the L' Entita's bodies contained there may yet still be warm enough."

~ ~ ~ ~

At the chamber's altar, Ingrid, Howie, and Tom watched, not at all understanding what they were seeing. Ingrid, who herself knew what the altar ultimately contained, couldn't say any more than they. Her knowledge existed in theory, being legends passed down by her grandfather. How the sum of that lore would manifest itself in reality, that was anyone's guess.

The heat of her blood cut into the frozen surface. It etched across like veins, altering the altar's face. Crimson lines crisscrossing, weaving both inward and outward, it traced, filling this canvas most cold, ancient, beyond old.

The illuminated symbols on the chamber walls transformed, morphing to display in real-time what was taking form upon the altar. An unplaced familiarity began to solidify in this otherwise random ensemble of linking shapes and outlines before them. What it was, was on the tip of their minds.

"What is this?" asked Howie.

"Whatever it is," Ingrid said, "is being reconstructed from the memory contained within my DNA." The process completed, leaving the surface of the altar entirely covered in an entangled mosaic written of her blood.

What was this? Howie knew, but he couldn't quite get his brain to make the connection... "It's your DNA, so, your memories, yet, you don't know?"

"No—yes, I mean, it is my blood," she said, "but the DNA itself is a *composite* of the entire linage before me."

"So, what *do* you know," asked Howie, "aside from, you know, getting us sealed in this place?"

Tom could see it a mile off, and he knew just how quickly

Howie's diplomacy could completely unravel during these moments of frustration. And so, he did what he'd learned through years of trial, and mostly error, the single thing that wouldn't accelerate Howie's present condition. He kept quiet.

"I know if you put more energy into helping instead of just slowing me down with your slew of questions, we could actually make some progress," she said.

Really resisting the urge to do the natural thing and jump in, Tom instead fully focused upon the image carved on the altar. After a moment of non-resolute staring, he tilted his head. Somehow, the new perspective seemed to help. Tuning Howie and Ingrid out, he quietly moved to the opposite side of the altar for a better angle.

"To be clear then, light has memory. Blood has memory. Does everything have memory," Howie asked, "excluding remembering to leave yourself an exit when being cornered?"

She stuck her finger in his face. "Listen—"

"We've been looking at it upside down," Tom said, speaking over them. They joined him at the other end of the altar. In less than subtle form, there it was. Upon the ice was a map of the world drawn in blood. Lacking labels, lines dividing countries, and scale here and there not exactly in how they knew, they now knew it to be the earth. Or, at least, one's depiction of it from a time long ago.

The symbols displayed on the walls transitioned, becoming new symbols. Ingrid removed an electronic tablet from her backpack. On it, she quickly yet carefully translated the symbols into English.

"It's a riddle—unlocks what's concealed within the altar." She set down the tablet bearing the translation. Anticipating their next question, she simply told them, "It's a compass piece, that serves as both key and map to what the Vatican desires."

The trio read silently the words there before them on the tablet which had not been spoken nor seen in over two millennia....

Jewel of the earth veiled in Muse's breast
Naught of earthly worth, abreast caged fire sailed to sky's
crest
Sought by flame's enraged ire, spark bitten yet prevailed   upon
phoenix's long wing
Ablaze feathers ethereal as paper the fowl did sing a song
unwritten

"Solving the riddle is proving one's rite of passage to obtain this compass piece?" asked Howie.

"Yes," she said. "Basically."

Howie glanced at Tom, who was recording with his phone. "Tom, there are guys outside who blow stuff up. We need to be collectively dedicated to getting out of here."

Tom propped his phone on the altar, letting it record. "Any idea what this 'jewel' is?"

"I don't think it's a literal jewel," she answered. "Treasure, something of greatest value, that sort of thing. The L' Entita, they had many treasures over the centuries."

"Naught of earthly value narrows it down," Howie said, placing his finger under the line on the tablet. "Tell me, pretending our lives kind of depended on it right now, if you had one guess, what did your ancestors value most?"

"Power," Tom blurted out.

Ingrid shook her head. "No. They... They valued information. Which was their power."

"Okay," Howie said, "so, was there a particularly significant fire at some point that threatened or implicated this knowledge of theirs?"

She took the tablet, rereading the lines to herself. At a loss, she said, "No, I mean, I don't know."

"Out of any of those words in those lines, does anything trigger anything in anyone's memory, or stand out?" Howie asked. "Whatsoever?"

"Well...," Tom said.

"Yes—what?" asked Howie.

"Why muse?" Tom asked. "Why did they choose that

particular word. It's really precise. Right?"

Wishing she was of more help, Ingrid offered the only knowledge she could, and, as usual, doubted her usefulness in doing so. "Maybe deconstructing the word... You know, reverse engineering the thing."

"Muse," said Tom. "Not a word used much in today's world."

"Yeah," she said, "it's evolved, evolved from its base word, 'museum'."

"So, replace it with that, then and see how it impacts the passage's context," Howie suggested. "And, while we're at it, let's change 'jewel' to 'information'."

"'Knowledge'," she said.

He nodded. "Even better."

She made the changes, and they reviewed the riddle.

Knowledge of the earth veiled in Museum's breast
Naught of earthly worth, abreast caged fire sailed to   sky's crest
Sought by flame's enraged ire, spark bitten yet prevailed   upon phoenix's long wing
Ablaze feathers ethereal as paper the fowl did sing a song unwritten

"That makes 'breast' stand out," said Tom. "I mean, further—more so than it was."

"Okay, lets... set that on the shelf for the moment, until it makes more sense," Howie said.

"'Knowledge' and 'museum' clearly go to together," said Tom.

Ingrid highlighted the line on the screen. "But museum in the context of back then..."

"Books—they were the sole form of knowledge at the time this was written," Howie said.

They all looked to each other and at the same time said, "A library."

Powerless, but to be nothing less than thoroughly enchanted at this point by these archaic poetics woven in riddle form, Howie grinned. "Yeah... A *great* library."

"The greatest," she said.

"Jewel inside the breast, being the *heart* of the Muse—the Museum," said Tom. "The center of which?"

"The Library of Alexandria," she answered. "Now the fire references seem rather obvious."

As if the translation had itself been entirely translated yet again, every word, and thus, every line, became wholly clear to them in an instant. Truly, it had taken on a new context.

"'Abreast caged fire sailed to sky's crest'," Tom said. "Alexandria's legendary lighthouse... It paralleled the city's library in both location and time of construction."

"Lighthouse. 'Caged fire', nice," Howie said. "That's rather adroit, Tom."

Tom focused completely on the single word there, staring back at him within the passage. He said it aloud. "'Fire'.... Uh, not to state the obvious, but everyone knows the library burned to the ground, destroying whatever earth-shattering secrets it may have contained. So... exactly *why* does the Vatican perceive this as a threat to their very existence?"

"Well... That may not be entirely accurate," Howie answered. "There was word of a journal reportedly found by a Roman soldier. This journal made mention that at least part of the library was salvaged. I think the inscription's whole 'phoenix' reference might very well be this alleged salvaging of the library."

"And did this journal happen to say where these rescued books were taken?" Tom asked.

"No," Howie answered, sheepishly, "the second half of the journal was illegible from the burn marks upon it."

"Well, that's ironic," Tom said.

"Yeah, quite," said Howie.

They just now noticed Ingrid was no longer with them there at the altar. Though she soon returned with the crystal shard.

She held out the shard. "We only get one shot, with

unlocking the compass piece."

"Why's that?" Howie asked.

"Because the resonance coming off this crystal is going to completely shatter the altar's surface." She handed him the shard. "One shot."

Howie gripped the crystal. "Right. One shot."

The crystal had begun to vibrate so violently that it caused both his arm and shoulder to convulse. The temperature of it grew with the vibration, becoming increasingly hotter. He struggled to keep hold.

She rested her hands at the edge of the map of ice and blood. "Stand the crystal shard on end where modern day Alexandria is."

It was burning his skin now, and he tossed the shard rapidly back and forth between his hands while scanning the old-world map. He located Africa, and hovered the shard over the general area of where he was guessing Egypt was meant to be. The hiss of his skin being melted from his palm wafted a most troubling odor through the air.

The shard's resonance became nearly uncontrollable. He forced himself to squeeze the crystal as tightly as he could in order to not drop it. For the first time, and at the worst time, they heard noise come from behind the sealed door where they'd entered the chamber from....

"Choose a place!" Ingrid shouted.

Howie hesitated—Tom yanked the crystal from his hand and slammed it upon the spot on the map. For a fraction of a second, the entire altar resonated in perfect pitch with the crystal. Then, silence, and all at once, the altar's frozen surface became liquid. The liquid became vapor. The vapor was swallowed into the air, as wholly gone from existence as if it had never been there.

Before them, nested in the diamond-like roots was what could only be the compass piece. Crafted from the L' Entita's unknown metal, it was a pyramid small enough to rest within a palm. About an inch down from its point, there was a razor-thin groove which went horizontally all the way around the end of the pyramid there. It must have been for something to lock upon and over its point, as a kind of detachable capstone. Whatever function it served, or had in the past, there were no other objects visible within the diamond-like roots of the altar.

Depending on the light, the pyramid's glassy skin shifted between any number of hues. It was golden for her. From his position, it appeared a glossy charcoal for Howie. For Tom, it seemed more of a tan, with a gentlest tinge of crimson.

Without touching it, Ingrid held her hand over this pyramidal compass piece. It rose up from the roots. With sitting freely there, they could see its base was perfectly square, a true pyramid. Each of the four sides of its base was about three inches long. There were no visible markings on its smooth, gleaming finish from what they could discern.

"It's beautiful," she said.

"We just might have a chance at outwitting the Vatican after all," said Tom.

"Outwitting isn't my concern," said Howie. "Their access to unlimited resources is."

Immediately replacing their trio's moment of success, Domenico and Camorra successfully opened the chamber's door. Spearheading their heavily armed team of men, they flooded in....

Family Reunion

*C*amorra bolted across the chamber at a brilliantly disturbing pace. In one gracefully blurring motion, Ingrid shed her backpack, grabbed the compass piece, tucked her arms to her sides and dropped through the hole in the floor. With no time to think, Howie and Tom did the same. Camorra's outstretched fingers scraped against Tom's long red hair as he plunged, vanishing into the dark waters.

At the diamond-like roots of the altar, Camorra examined the triangular empty space that'd held the compass piece. "The female removed something."

"Something to guide them to the next chamber," Domenico said.

Camorra stripped down to his pants. "I can go alone from here. I'm aware of your reservations for water."

"This woman's proven of particular value, Camorra."

Camorra sized up the hole in the chamber's floor. "Alive, I know." He took in a final breath, then squeezed his body through the hole into the freezing water below.

Domenico turned to his men, mesmerized by their surroundings. "I want this area secured. And for god's name, don't touch anything." As he'd said it, one of the men reached out to his reflection along the wall. With a bizarrely lagged response, his image reached back—the sharp bang of

Domenico's rifle against the altar reeled in his men's attention.

"*Anything!*" he shouted.

~ ~ ~ ~

Wrapped within the fury of the current, Ingrid, Howie, and Tom fought to keep their heads above water. They did their best to dodge the ever-changing height of the rock ceiling mere inches above blazing past. Like a rogue rollercoaster, the subterranean river rushed them along its course, spinning, jolting, and throwing their bodies deeper, further, blindly into the unknown.

The chilling water pushed the trio to the brink of hypothermia. With their beings thoroughly saturated with numbness and fear, things abruptly became a beautifully horrible waterfall, spewing them into an open abyss of certain death. Launching over the edge, Tom grabbed hold of the only thing there was to, a slender beam of rock bridging the chasm before him.

Catching his breath, he dangled there, watching down on the abyss patiently awaiting to swallow him. By mindless reflex more than thought, he caught Howie by the arm as he'd begun to tumble over the waterfall. Ingrid was next, snagging hold of the beam. Pulling themselves onto the slender and dreadfully slippery piece of rock, they could now see the pathway on either side of this chasm.

"Happy now?" gasped Howie. "Got your waterfall."

"When you're about to fall over one, waterfalls are suddenly overrated," Tom said.

Without asking them, Ingrid chose which side of the chasm to take. They inched their way behind her as she followed along the narrow rock beam to the left. As they reached the end, a mossy film which covered the rock all around them started to emit the gentlest turquois glow. Climbing off of the beam and onto the ledge brimming the cliffside, they faced another choice in which way to take.

"Right or left?" Howie asked. Ingrid started for the right side.

"Not big on conversation is she," Tom said, clinging precariously to the sheer rock.

There was a noise behind them. And very much not wanting to see what it was, they forced themselves to turn. Camorra was there, on the other side of the rock beam that bridged the chasm. Dripping wet, his eyes held an intensity none of them had ever witnessed from another human being. His eyes were, in this way, even more intimidating than the gun he now aimed at them.

Not that it stopped Tom from saying what he did in that moment, because it didn't. "Your bullets are soggy." He didn't really believe his own claim, but couldn't help himself.

Howie glanced at Tom. Even if he'd wanted to say something, through his intense shivers brought on by the cold water having drained him of all energy, he was at a loss for words. Camorra raised his gun—a well-aimed boulder crashed down from the partial plateau above them. Someone stepped out from where the boulder had been perched a second before. The boulder hit, severing the narrow rock beam bridging the impassible chasm, snapping it in two as if a dry twig. Boulder and beam together tumbled into the abyss below.

Camorra's gun fell, inhaled by the darkness, as he leaped to the cliff face to his right. He dangled by his fingertips, gripping nothing more than the thinnest of depressions in the moist, moss-kissed rock. And yet, he had begun to do the impossible. He'd started to scale that perfectly vertical rock wall with his bare hands.

Howie, seeing this, felt an icy shudder trace up his body, not from the cold, but from this creature, who only appeared as a man. "Glad he's on that side."

Shaking out the water, Howie removed his flashlight from his pocket and illuminated the shadowy figure atop the plateau, revealing his face to them all.... Seeing him, Ingrid knew him to be the same man she'd tailed from the hotel.

"What the hell?" Howie shouted, seeing the last person in the world he'd expected to—the entire side of the rock face behind the man started to give way, spewing forth an avalanche. Where he stood at the top of the plateau, it tapered out sharply toward them, leaving a much shorter distance to their side than that of the impassible expanse below. With only one way to go, he jumped for their side just as the avalanche tore away the place that he'd been standing.

Nearly making the distance, but not quite close enough, he hung from the edge along the narrow pathway there. His fingers broke free of the rock—Ingrid grabbed his hand. With surprising strength, she reeled him up.

High upon the cliff, Camorra watched as the avalanche of rock now raced his direction. Leaping off the cliff at the last second, he fell through the air. And in midair, he took hold of the adjacent cliff face as he fell past. The avalanche collapsed, then swallowed the entire cliffside where he'd just been. This mountain of shattered rock showered, flowing into the infinite abyss below like a colossus timer of sand destined to do so for all eternity.

Howie completely ignored all of this, going straight to the man Ingrid had just saved. "What are you doing here, Mike?" He pressed a finger to Mike's chest.

"You're welcome," Mike said.

Tom tried to step between them. "Thank you for saving our necks just now, Mike." He turned to Howie. "Isn't that what you meant, Howie."

"No," Howie said bluntly as he possibly could.

"You know each other?" Ingrid asked.

"Only one way to say this," said Tom. "Mike's Howie's father."

"*Estranged* father," Howie corrected.

"Glad to see you survived," Mike said to Ingrid.

"*You* two know each other?" asked Howie.

In the background, Camorra finished scaling the next cliff.

Atop this great underground mountainous slope, he calculated the distance through the expanse of open air to the other side, where his prey, *all* of his prey, now were. Taking into account the pitch of the summit where he stood, he'd decided the odds of success were in his favor. Ingrid watched across the chasm as Camorra moved back along the ridge of the great rock hilltop, preparing for his jump.

"The family reunion's going to have to wait," she said.

Camorra broke into full sprint, aiming straight for the edge of the cliffside before him, launching his body through the open air....

Knights and Morning Mass

*N*ot waiting to see if he'd landed successfully on their side of the chasm, they gave chase after Ingrid up the harrowingly narrow path along the cliff's face. Behind them, quite gracefully making the thirty-foot leap with a few feet to spare, Camorra landed on the heels of his boots. Without breaking stride, he somersaulted, returned to his feet and ran at full speed.

With him gaining on them, their team of now four reached the arched double doors of unknown metal at the path's end. Not locked, the doors pushed inward, allowing them to enter. In joint effort, Howie, Tom, and Mike rolled one of the large rocks along the passageway, jamming it against the doors. Taking all the will they had, they tried to catch up with Ingrid. She tore through the passageway at a breakneck pace, holding no regard for her three male colleagues struggling to keep up.

"Do you get the feeling we're just along for the ride," Howie managed between gasps.

"It's been flight at first sight with her," said Tom, equally out of breath.

Their flashlight beams wildly bounced off the ever-narrowing rock walls. Suddenly, Ingrid brought them to a halt. Partly caved in directly before them, the walls of the passageway leaned against each other, fragilely steepled.

"From the earthquake?" asked Tom.

Mike grabbed a handful of the dry dirt from the debris pile that blocked their way. "No, this happened long ago."

They dug quickly through the debris.

"Hey, Howie," Tom said.

"Yeah..."

"You're doing well with your whole claustrophobia thing, I mean, considering we're in a tiny underground hole that could collapse, burying us alive at any moment."

Howie wiped the grime clung to his face. "Tom, next time you get the urge to pay me a compliment that involves drawing attention to the peril of our situation... Don't." Grabbing what he thought was just another rock obscured within the dirt, something sliced into his palm. This new pain compounded on top of the burns and laceration caused by that crystal shard back in the chamber. Ignoring the pain best as he could, he pulled free whatever this object was.

Shaking off the dirt, there was a sword complete with the skeletal hand of its former owner still wrapped around the handle. He peeled away these clutching fingers of bone. And in typical fashion, his father, Mike, always having had to overshadow him, removed an entire skeleton from the debris. Howie glared as Mike's find came with sword *and* shield. They each now found several skeletons, dressed in knight's armor, dumping them in a rather grisly, though charming pile of their own out away from the debris. This left them with an opening at the passageway's center, hopefully large enough.

"Templars," said Tom.

"Knights of Malta," Ingrid said, correcting him. "See, their breastplates. The colors are reversed to those of the Templars."

"Malta. Guess that makes sense," Tom said.

The distinct sound of running echoed down the passageway behind them. Before any of them could say another word, Ingrid had already pushed herself through the other side of the narrow gap at the center of the collapsed walls. Compelled to take the knight's broadsword with him, Howie followed behind the others, wrenching himself through the space.

As the two precariously tilted rocks, of several tons each,

pressed upon his body, he'd started to see the upside in being pursued by something that was pure predator. Not ideal, though it was entirely effective motivation for facing his claustrophobia, and literally so head-on. Having broken through to the other side, he joined Tom and Mike, channeling all their strength to keep Ingrid in sight as they ran.

"Seriously," said Mike, glancing at the broadsword Howie still held at his side.

"Got to agree," Tom said between breaths. "You're not supposed to run with a sword."

Howie wiped away the dirt pasted to his face. "Don't worry, that's scissors."

"I'm not worried, just excessively concerned," said Tom.

Howie immediately dropped the sword, nearly impaling the others in front of him within the narrow tunnel. Ingrid, leading, had again abruptly come to a halt. Being the only one of them not out of breath, she swept the darkness all around with her flashlight.

Howie leaned over, palms to his knees, lungs aflame. "Don't tell me."

"Dead end," said Tom.

Heat flooded up Ingrid's thigh. It seemed to radiate from the pocket where'd she'd place the compass piece. She slipped the pyramid-shaped device from her pocket. All around its base glowed most golden an inscription written in the L' Entita's secret language. Quietly, she returned the compass piece to her pocket.

"Who builds a tunnel that doesn't go anywhere," Tom said, more criticizing than asking.

"There's got to be a way," Mike said.

"Tell that to the wall of granite in front of us," said Howie.

Camorra came into view behind them. Only fifty feet of shadowy tunnel stood between him and his prey... With the entirety of his being, he launched himself at full speed.

"Up. Look up," said Mike.

Their flashlights collectively illuminated badly aged floorboards where a rock ceiling should have been, but most gratefully wasn't. The broad, sagging and rotted floorboards were just out of their reach. Camorra was close, very close....

Howie retrieved the sword and thrust it into the weakest looking board. He repeatedly thrust as hard and as fast as he could, smashing out the splintering wood. The hole there above them now was no wider, and perhaps a little smaller than the gap they'd faced with the collapsed walls. With that unstoppable man, that *thing*, barreling down upon them, it'd have to do.

Tossing the sword up through the hole, Howie jumped. His fingers wrapped around the edge of the wooden floor. Cringing, he could add the generous amount of splinters that'd just sank in to the ever-accumulating afflictions of his hand. Sucking in his sides, he pulled himself up. He helped Ingrid, then Mike through.

Last, Tom reached out for Howie. Holding his dying flashlight, and compelled to do so by a force unseen, Tom turned to see how close their pursuer was.... Camorra was within arm's reach. In the flashlight's last breaths, a primal fear washed over Tom. He stared this predator in the eyes. In those eyes he saw hate or something worse. Hypnotized by his own dread, he could only stare at this beast guised as a man. It reached for him with fingers clenched as talons....

Thrusting his hand down, Howie grabbed Tom's arm, still extended up at the ceiling, breaking Tom from his spell. Camorra lunged, smelling Tom's fear—Howie yanked Tom upwards. Tom's feet dangled. Camorra crouched and leapt. His hand took hold, ratcheting around Tom's right boot. For both prey and hunter, they knew this clutch, embittered and steely, couldn't be broken. With an immutable strength, Camorra methodically dragged Tom back down inch by inch.

Howie's fingers fumbled at the sheath on his belt. He released the knife, trying to slip it to Tom. Though both of Tom's hands held tightly upon Howie. The frenzied attempt failed, and the knife fell. Still gripping Howie, Tom released one of his hands, grabbing the knife blade-first a moment before becoming lost. It sank in, biting into his palm. Camorra thrust his other hand up, clawing for Tom. Quickly flipping his hold on the knife, Tom sliced through his boot's laces. With Camorra's fierce grip pulling down on the boot, it slipped free—still clenching the boot, now entirely off Tom's foot, Camorra tumbled backwards, slamming against the rock wall behind him.

Howie drew Tom up, finding themselves in a basement filled with everything old, forgotten, and discarded. Working together, Howie, Tom, and Mike tipped over the massive oak chest along the wall. Crashing down on impact with the sagging floorboards, the chest seemed it might have decided to break through the floor. But with a crunching and heavy sigh, it came to rest over the hole.

They ran up the decaying staircase to the old wooden door at the top breathing light in from beneath it. Wielding the broadsword, Howie pulled open the creaking door and peered out. There was a simple and well-lit hallway. They rushed down its short length and in a less than graceful way, burst through the next door.

The four of them found themselves staring back at a most shocked congregation in the middle of Mass. Directly behind the wide-eyed priest at his pulpit, Howie, layered in dried sewage water, dirt, dust, and sweat, lowered the sword in his hand.

Tom graciously bowed to the onlookers. "You may continue."

With Ingrid in the lead, they ran down the center aisle and out the front doors of the church. Immediately, sunlight blinded them.

"Really is Sunday," Tom said, squinting onto the quiet, though disheveled street.

Sections of the sidewalk were badly lopsided. Their surroundings, strewn with signs of destruction, brazenly reminded them of the earthquake which had fatefully drawn them all together. Ingrid scanned the area, seeking anything familiar from which she could regain her bearings.

Howie said to Tom, "Great way of not drawing unnecessary attention back there."

"You're the one holding a sword," Tom responded.

Howie proudly held up the broadsword. "Yeah. The same sword that saved us all."

Mike frowned. "A god with a crane no doubt must've lowered it down to keep you so humble."

"If a god were real, perhaps. But no, a god isn't," Howie said, artfully twirling the sword. "Dumb luck, smartly used." He twirled the sword again, almost dropping it. Mike rolled his eyes.

Ingrid sprinted across the street. The three of them forced their entirely worn and weary legs to try to do the same. On the other side of the street, she darted through the empty lot there, then across the next street. Finally catching up, they joined her in a back-alley parking lot behind Carters Supermarket.

She pulled open the unlocked driver side door on the older model Range Rover Discovery parked there, and looked squarely at Tom. "You drive." Before he could ask why him, she grabbed his hand and guided it to grip the steering wheel. He climbed into the driver seat. The others opened the passenger doors, about to jump in. Camorra came into their field of view, stepping between them and the only way to exit this small, boxed in parking lot.

"Wherever we're going, we need to do it faster," Howie said. They piled inside, while Camorra took a runner's pose only a few car lengths away. Low to the pavement, he launched himself. Every muscle in his body in perfect unison, fully dedicated to a single objective, as he coursed through the air at them, impossibly fast, cheetah-like.

"Where the hell's the car keys?" Tom asked, sending them into a frantic search....

The Sound of Blood

"*W*here?" exasperated, Tom demanded, canvassing all around the driver seat.

"They should be there," Ingrid said, emptying her pockets.

Tom looked behind the visor to no avail. Camorra grew larger in the rearview mirror, racing down the heart of the parking lot.

Ingrid *knew* she'd left them in the vehicle. But if she did... *Then they'd be here.* "The floor?"

"Is that a question?" asked Tom, running his hand across the floor mat.

"I don't know—just check."

"I am!"

Camorra was nearly upon them, almost able to reach out and touch... In the back, Howie and Mike simultaneously slammed down the locks on their doors. Camorra lunged for the latch on the rear of the Range Rover. Tom hit the button along his armrest, locking the hatch.

Camorra yanked on the latch. It wouldn't budge. He crashed his fist into the hatch's glass. It spiderwebbed, bulging deeply in, though held, barely so.

Not wanting to spill blood, but having not much choice faced with this predator brimming with wrath, Ingrid drew her Walther, chambering a round. Spinning around in the front passenger seat, she tried desperately to align Camorra in her sights. Despite her training holding her nerves steady, she couldn't find a clear shot.

Between her and Camorra, who thrashed his now bloody fists through the rear glass, were Howie and Mike seated in the back, entirely in the way. The glass gave way, caving in as one blood-splattered piece, thoroughly mangled and fractured. Howie climbed over the backseat, thrusting wildly with the broadsword at their attacker.

Camorra balled a fist dripping most crimson and punched the sword with his bare hand, knocking away the blade right before it pierced his eye. He breathed not like a man should by this point, not out of breath, but steady, uninterrupted. The same primal fear laced in terror that'd seized Tom back in the passageway, took hold of Howie. He froze, unable to look away.

Camorra pulled himself through the now glassless hatch, slithering his body inside. In the next moment, his hand sprang out in a blur, twisting and taking away the sword from Howie's grip. Mike swung with both fists for Camorra, who gracefully dodged the double swing. Camorra positioned the tip of the broadsword to pointedly kiss the center of Mike's throat, pressing him back.

Tom continued to scour through the front for the keys. Tight in Ingrid's grip, her gun continued to follow Camorra's movements, attempting to lock in for a clear shot. And Howie, he continued to remain frozen.

Holding back Mike by the sword's blade, Camorra's free hand found Howie's neck. His iron fingers constricted around Howie's throat, extinguishing any hope for oxygen. Howie's eyes started to bulge as water generously swelled, welling from them.

Camorra nearly aligned himself within Ingrid's sights... Her finger tightened around the trigger. Camorra yanked Howie toward him by the throat—Howie's head came perfectly in line with her aim—she immediately released the trigger.

Her skin along her thigh burned horribly now where the compass piece rested inside her pocket. She resisted the pain, keeping her gun aimed. Howie's complexion had begun to shift to a bit of a light blue. He gasped, his hands and arms flailing, utterly desperate, despairingly.

Why the hell was it burning? Ingrid yanked the compass piece from her pocket and shoved it into the glove box. Then, swinging back around, and thrusting her body and gun between the heads of Howie and Mike, took aim upon Camorra's forehead. In that brief breath, she knew the shot would be devastating for Mike and Howie's eardrums, tightly bookending both sides of her Walther.

A fate with fatal hearing loss was certainly easier to live with than one of fateful death. She had to take the shot... *Now...* She squeezed. Nothing happened. *Nothing happened?* The safety was on. She flipped the small catch on the side of the Walther. *Nice, Ingrid. So much for all that training.*

A *metallic* jingle came from above Tom's head while crouched low to the floor, searching. He looked up... The keys hung from the... *Goddamn ignition! Why hadn't he checked there*—he cranked the engine on and slammed the Range Rover in reverse.

Ingrid, having just aligned Camorra's forehead once more in her sights, fired—the Range Rover lunged backwards. The inevitable and sudden physics thrust her toward the front. While the bullet missed by several inches, launching straight through the glassless hatch and striking the brick wall of the adjacent building, fragmenting the lump of lead wildly out in numerous directions.

Mike ducked just in time as the broadsword Camorra had pressed to his throat came flying at him out of Camorra's hand. Holding himself as low as possible in his seat, Mike peered up at the blade now severed through his door's window, suspended oddly so within the glass. Having lost hold of her gun, Ingrid watched as if in slow motion as it sailed toward the front, landing with a hard plop between Tom's legs.

He winced, grabbed the gun and fired blindly back at Camorra, who was harshly jolted against the rear of the backseats. Nearly being shot by Tom, Howie threw himself down. He hugged his body to the seat, thoroughly covering his head with his hands, wishing he'd stayed on that old rusty ship of his in the sweet ocean air.

Continuing to blindly fire through the back of the Range Rover, Tom removed his other hand from the steering wheel as he raced just as blindly so in reverse. With his now free hand, and no hand upon the heel, he hit the reddish-colored button along the console. The rear hatch released, swinging up, fully open—the back of the Range Rover slammed into the front of the Mini Cooper parked there.

A truly surprised Camorra found himself quite suddenly sailing out the back the of the Range Rover into open air, only to be immediately caught with a blistering crunch by the Mini Cooper's windshield. Howie and Mike ventured their heads over the backseat, seeing Camorra sprawled quite dramatically upon the now concave windshield of the Mini Cooper. Tom threw the Range Rover into drive, tearing away from the small parking lot into the alley and onto the first street. Ingrid broke into laughter.

"What are you laughing at?" demanded Howie. "We just almost died at the hands of that deranged landshark."

She turned in her seat, facing him. "Just thinking of the look on those poor people's faces when he had to have burst through the door into their little church the same way we did moments before."

Wonderfully infectious, one by one, her laughter spread to the rest of them.

~~ ~~

In the parking lot, Camorra pulled himself from the windshield. Covered in cuts, bleeding, he peeled away a particularly long shard of glass lodged in his side. The blood whispered from his body as it flowed forth. At a frequency much too low to hear, he heard it though.

Wiping the blood generously oozing from his forehead, a burning pain seized up his arm. The female's shot had actually connected, having ricocheted off the brick wall behind him. Examining the wound, the bullet, or more correctly, fragment of which had passed cleanly through the place high along his left bicep. Without another second wasted upon it, he started to jog down the alley in the direction of Carters Supermarket, building speed as he went.

Contact

"You look... shot," Domenico said, stepping off the lift and joining Camorra inside the tent.

At the foldout table strewn with the contents of a first-aid kit, a shirtless Camorra stitched up the wound on his bicep. "Nothing for concern," he said. "Fragment exited on contact." He scrawled a series of numbers on a piece of paper, then slid it across to Domenico. "The number plate to the Range Rover Discovery they're in."

Domenico memorized the plate number. "A photo of them would go a long way." Camorra began disinfecting the largest of the gashes on his chest. He nodded to the paper in Domenico's hand. Domenico flipped it over, revealing Camorra's rather skillful sketches of the woman and her three male counterparts.

"Female is L' Entita, as we know, at least in some form," Camorra said. "The rest are not." From his pocket, he removed the printed photo of the Praesidio Autem Veritas. "They dropped this. Someone had to have leaked it to them. I assume the list of possibilities is short."

Domenico folded the pieces of paper together into a perfect square. "I know your sentiments for law enforcement, Camorra, although now's the time to bring in local authorities. You're going to play nice?"

"Nice enough."

Domenico slipped the folded paper into his pocket. "Points of egress for the entire island are already covered." Placing both hands on the table, he leaned in. "Any premonitions of the Camorra?"

"They will abandon the Range Rover at first chance." Setting aside the container of disinfectant, Camorra stood and wrapped gauze around his muscular torso. "They'll head for an out-of-the-way hotel. A shower and food and some rest will be high on their list of needs right about now. Somewhere on the edge of town."

~ ~ ~ ~

A few miles outside of Tarxien, the Range Rover pulled to a stop along a lone dirt road.

"Now what?" asked Tom, turning off the ignition.

"We walk," Ingrid said.

Howie looked out the window, seeing only trees. "To...?"

Ingrid removed the compass piece from the glove box. No longer hot, she returned it to her pocket. "There is a motel half a mile away, down the other side of this hill here."

"What's your name?" asked Howie. "Girl with a gun?"

"What?"

"Your name," he said. "Even members of the L' Entita have names. If I'm going to be taking orders from someone, I want to know their name."

"Ingrid," she said, opening the passenger door.

"Okay, Ingrid," he said.

They got out. And she led them into the tall grass and pale green trees with flaky bark most tan.

~ ~ ~ ~

At the Roman Curia, within her office of hardwoods and shadow, Lucia Vaccaro rolled the brandy glass back and forth in her palm. The reddish-tinged brandy softly swished up to the brim, nearly escaping its crystal cage. Slowly, she swallowed, releasing the bittersweet liquid to slip down her throat.

If the drink helped dull the ringing in her ears, it was negligible. In fact, that ringing seemed all the greater now, more immediate. Realizing her phone was the cause, and not one of the intense headaches which routinely plagued her, she glanced at the baroque clock on her desk before answering. This specific ringtone disrupting her solitude mimicked that of an antique phone. Rather cleverly and appropriately so, she'd exclusively designated it, the outdated sound it was, to a single contact.

Into her cellphone she asked, "Domenico?" Her eyes closed, hearing the news. The ringing in her ears was now replaced by a resounding silence of the absoluteness of what she'd just been told. "Yes. I heard you. Thank you for making contact. I'll arrange for Oliver's body to be returned here. And Domenico, I'll look forward to the field report, *personally* completed by you explaining the incident in unequivocal detail."

Setting the phone on her desk, she spun it upon the glossy walnut surface. It came to a stop, pointing at her glass, half empty, half unfinished. Her hand, trembling ever softly, took the glass and lifted it from the beautiful and cold desk. She sat in silence, letting the shadows wash over her.

~~ ~~

With a stack of pizza boxes wedged between his side and arm, and a full duffel bag over his shoulder, Daniel stood outside the humble motel. He lowered his fist from the dingy yellow door and looked to the flickering sign displaying the motel's name, 'Sapphire Inn'. He turned back to the aged and yellow paint, most certainly not sapphire or any semblance of blue for that matter, which poorly clung to the walls of the old motel, blistered and peeling.

Inside the motel room, Ingrid, wrapped in a bathrobe, looked through the peephole. "It's only my contact."

A flood of relief flowed through Howie, Tom, and Mike, each in matching bathrobes. She pulled open the door. To the complete surprise of the three men, Daniel entered the room, seeing *he* was Ingrid's contact.

Daniel took in the scene, with the four of them wearing identical robes, hair matted and wet, with all the furniture not bolted to the floor pushed flush to the walls of the small room. It was a strange sight. But not as strange as this room's particular occupants being together in the same place.

Ingrid grabbed the pizzas and duffel bag from him, setting them on the bed. About to introduce Daniel to them, she saw the look upon everyone's faces.

"So," Daniel said, "this is awkward."

Howie approached him. "Quite."

"Look, Howie, I didn't get a chance to tell you," said Daniel.

"Right." Howie turned to Tom, who, along with Mike, had already started on the pizza. "I don't know, Tom, what do you think? Think our old pal Daniel sold out to Ingrid before or after he met with us in his hotel room?"

Tom shrugged, taking a big bite of pizza.

"Before or after, Daniel," Howie pressed. "Come on..."

"Before," Ingrid said, trying to position herself in the space between the two men that was rapidly headed to a place most uncomfortable.

"Let him talk," Howie said. "Clearly, he has no problem talking to whoever about whatever, whenever. And Ingrid, if you want to talk, then, yeah, we'll have a nice talk once Daniel and I are done. About who *exactly* you are."

"Fine," she said. She unzipped the duffel bag on the bed and removed a set of sweats from it and disappeared into the bathroom.

"Howie, I know how this looks to you, but trust me, it's much more complicated," Daniel said.

"Trust you," said Howie, stepping closer.

Mike and Tom settled into the two easy chairs along the

wall, watching and stuffing themselves with pizza.

"Why not fight it out in the parking lot!" Ingrid yelled from the other side of the bathroom door. "Good luck with that though, Howie, Daniel's only former SAS!"

"Please," Howie said, "I think Daniel, who *was* my friend and professional associate, would've mentioned that to me at some point in the seven years we've known each other."

"Well...," said Daniel.

"Really? That's just great," Howie said. "Wait—did you know my father was at the site too?" Daniel's silence spoke the answer.

"As far as I'm concerned," said Mike, "I didn't know anyone else was going to the site."

"As far as you're concerned, this isn't your concern, Mike," Howie said.

Ingrid returned from the bathroom dressed in the sweats. Her sweatshirt displayed the large red and white shield forming the centerpiece of Malta's coat of arms. Its bold lettering proudly stated, 'Virtute et Constantia'.

"Still at it," she said. "Good. Because it's not like we all don't have more important things to be focusing on right now." She took a prepaid cellphone from the duffel bag and tore it out of its packaging. "Don't let your manly feelings get hurt over this, Howie, but whatever loyalties Daniel had to you were moot, when it came to me."

"Thanks for pointing that one out," said Howie.

She programmed the prepaid phone while she tried to explain. "I've been searching for the L' Entita all my life, and Daniel and I have had a very long and very specific agreement, given his unique access to all things ancient and unknown. That he'd alert me to anything even remotely connected to the L' Entita." She finished activating the phone. "And a massive hole in the ground branded with the Praesidio Autem Veritas more than qualified."

Howie ignored her. "You should have told me, Daniel."

"I screwed up," said Daniel. "And if I were you, yeah, I'd

feel the same way." He dumped out the duffel bag, then held up a set of sweats and prepaid cellphone. "I come bearing gifts."

"The Trojan Horse was a gift," Howie said, glancing in Ingrid's direction. "You know, the story, Troy, which burned because men betrayed each other over a woman."

Tom and Mike smiled quietly at each other, and moved on to the second box of pizza.

"Subtle," Ingrid said, glaring.

"I can be more to the point," Howie said.

Ingrid got in his face. "How about this point, if we don't immediately start working together, none of us are going to survive!"

"That is a good point," Tom said, through a mouthful of pizza.

"Right," Howie said, unable to deny her words. He accepted the pair of sweats and cellphone from Daniel. "Will be good to get out of these matching robes and..." He held up the sweatshirt that was exactly the same as the one Ingrid was wearing. "Into these matching sweatsuits."

Mike took a pair from the bed. "These look like they're straight from the tourist shop."

"That's because they are straight from the tourist shop," said Daniel.

~ ~ ~ ~

The sun, swollen and orange, hung low in the sky as Camorra, contrasted vividly in front of it, elegantly flowed through the moves of the Unsu. He'd long mastered all the katas of the martial art of Shotokan, though this was the most difficult. It was a small pleasure in knowing he was the only one alive who could perform the Unsu to completion without flaw, and do it while keeping his eyes closed. And he did so now, barefoot, upon the broken pavement in front of Carters Supermarket.

In the background, Domenico topped off the Ducati's gas

tank. Setting aside the container of gas, he checked the text he'd just received. He studied Daniel's photo displayed on screen, then sent the information to Camorra's phone. "Their contact is former SAS."

Camorra finished the Unsu, drawing his palms together. He held his eyes closed, feeling his mind, body, and being align. From several feet away, Domenico threw the Ducati's keys at him. Camorra's hand snatched them out of the air. Now he opened his eyes, welcoming the reality of things all around him. He straddled the Ducati, bringing its powerful engine growling to life.

Domenico offered the helmet. "Visor's wired for GPS."

"Helmet's too constricting."

"Alive, Camorra."

Camorra tore off on the Ducati, the brilliance of the Maltese ocean and sun at his back.

The Sun Book

*I*ngrid might as well have been alone. Lost in a world all her own at the desk against the motel room's far wall, she translated the inscription crisply illuminated around the base of the compass piece.

On the opposite side of the room, Howie, Tom, Mike, and Daniel sat next to the bed, having designated it as their table. Surrounding them, empty pizza boxes and bottles and aluminum cans and wrappers from every assortment of vending machine food laid arbitrarily strewn in some frenzied aftermath of fervent hunger.

"There's more," Daniel said. "The Santa Alleanza has brought out of retirement their best assassin. I can't strain enough the danger you're—we're all in."

"Think we had the pleasure of his company earlier," said Howie.

"He's... He's like not even human," Tom said. "Like... some prehistoric beast which stalked early man. Still haunting the lost memories of our former selves."

Daniel raised an eyebrow.

"Forgive, Tom," said Howie, "he can be quite eloquent, when he's forgetting to put his foot in his mouth."

"Camorra. That's what he's called," said Daniel.

Tom sat up, hearing the name resound in his ears. "That's not the name of any *one* man. That's the name of an extinct secret society..."

"Yes," said Mike, "membership's steep. Have to be from one of the originating bloodlines of the Sicilian Cosa Nostra is all."

"True," Daniel said. "And nearly extinct. You see, he's the last of his kind."

"I know how that is," Ingrid said, returning with her tablet in hand.

"All done?" Daniel asked.

"With the translation," she said. "We need to start solving it now."

Daniel rose from his chair. "Well, I'll leave you all in Ingrid's very capable hands."

Confused, she followed him to the door. "Where are you going?" Her voice wavered, betraying her.

He took her hand. "I'd try to convince you." He turned to them. "All of you, to come with me, but I'd be wasting everyone's time with that plea."

"Daniel, I, I can't solve this and seek out the answers I need while in hiding," she said. "Now with the actual compass piece, I've never been closer..."

He smiled, his eyes saying what neither of them knew how in words. "You've been closer to me." He placed a kiss on her cheek. For him, her skin somehow possessed the best qualities of both cold and warmth. "After all, there are *special forces* at work, are there not." He released her hand and turned back to the rest of them. "I'll do what I can to draw Camorra away. Since I am all your point of contact linking you to the site, that puts me first in line for who they'll come after."

Howie held out his hand.

Daniel shook it. "The four of you, you have a decent chance of actually solving this mystery."

"Who dares wins," said Howie.

"Do me a favor, keep the SAS membership thing contained to this room. It's not something us SAS blokes look to advertise."

"Secret's safe with me," said Howie.

Daniel left. Ingrid ran after him out the door. In front of the decaying old motel illogically named the Sapphire Inn, she grabbed him, not wanting to let it happen, for him to leave, and do the thing most sensible... *Most logical.*

"Goodbyes are only a matter of distance," he said. He placed the toe of his boot ever gently upon her bare foot.

She hugged him, knowing sometimes a soft embrace was better than a kiss. Then, pulling her foot out from beneath his, she let him go. Returning to the room, she quietly closed the door and scooped up her tablet from the coffee table at the end of the bed. And heading to the TV attached to the wall, she took notice of the mini fridge their underneath. She opened it.

"Honestly, just between you guys," Tom said, "actually, I do feel a bit special. You know, with this assassin being brought out of retirement, and now being on his shit-to-hit list."

Howie nearly choked on the last of the can of Coke in his hand. "Yeah. A real honor." He stared blankly at the wall. "Camorra. Camorra. Camorra... Secret society within the society of the mafia... You couldn't make this stuff up. No, sir, really, you couldn't."

Taking note of Ingrid's obvious solemnness, everyone stopped talking. In silence, she handed out the miniature bottles of wine she'd removed from the little fridge. No one knew if the discount alcohol would be for a moment of celebration anticipated within their near future, or to dull an inevitably pending doom. What was certain, they all knew the bottles were going to be depleted in their entirety, and done so with a great passion.

This was true, except for Tom. "Thanks. But I don't drink."

Strongly resisting the impulse to inquire, she immediately chastised herself for having the thought, and largely just because he was Irish. She silently reminded herself that everyone had their own secret wars within themselves, which stretched out in battles across their life's journey. And that included herself.

She linked her tablet to the TV mounted on the wall, then took a seat amongst them. She set the tablet onto the small coffee table, and drawing in a deep breath, pressed the power button upon the TV's remote. The TV screen lit up. Displayed before them was simultaneously what they'd all been waiting for, yet were clueless to what it was. And in collective solitude, they each read the inscription to themselves.

The site you plainly seek lays within the Sun Book's sacred eight.
Faces precession for the age awaits the great.
To sun rayed land caked in wheat with bull drawn out by ram's watered hate.

Tom blew the air from his mouth in a most defeated manner, letting his lips vibrate as all hope whistled out. "Another riddle. You do understand this, Ingrid? Yes?"

"No."

Tom rubbed his temples as if attempting to spark something within his mind. "Just beautiful."

Howie slid the tablet closer to himself, hoping if he read the words upon the smaller screen, somehow the greater intimacy of it all would inspire some deep human truth. It didn't. He didn't know what he'd been expecting... *Certainly not more enigmatic poetry. Not when his life was on the line. Not when everybody's life was...* His desire for adventure had quickly withered, dissolving to a desperate—frantic need to simply understand.

The feeling spread to each of them. Reality wasn't just sinking in; it was a vacuum sucking them straight into the unknown. For Howie and Tom, this was no longer a hunt for sunken gold. For Mike, it wasn't an archeological dig or scholarly exercise. And above all, for Ingrid, this was not just about her discovering who she was through her past. This was her life... *All of their lives.*

Somehow these three—no, four men, with Daniel's life too, all had become entangled. They all were in jeopardy. It was her doing, at least for Daniel being involved. *Yes, ultimately, it was.* More than any of the others, she was most responsible for this situation. But who was *she?* She'd spent her life clinging to the places unnoticed by others. Certainly, out of all of them, she was the furthest from a leader.

"Who are we kidding," Tom said.

His thick Irish accent jarred her from her thoughts.

"Ingrid's right," he continued, "we're just grave robbers. In the end, that's all we really are."

"And scholars," Mike said.

Tom traded the mini bottle of wine Ingrid had given him for a Coke. "Grave robbers and scholars." He downed the can of Coke.

"Yeah," said Howie, "truthfully, we only managed to solve that last riddle because we *had* to." He emptied his mini bottle of wine.

She watched these three men, supposedly worldly travelers, all seeming to give up before even attempting to try. "So, what's changed? Guys?"

"Nothing," answered Howie.

"Exactly," she said. "What better motivation. Right..."

Mike held up his bottle. "Right. Here's to the adventure." He took an exceptionally modest sip before snarling up his lips from the bitterness of the cheap wine. Quickly, he set the bottle aside as far away as he could possibly reach.

"Why make it so complicated?" Howie asked. "On the L' Entita's part, I mean?"

"Always wanting it easy, kid," Mike said. His tone was somehow even more disapproving than his words. "Life doesn't always provide an 'X' to mark the spot."

Howie's eyes narrowed at his father. "Yes, thank you for that. Believe it or not, Mike, I've actually noticed life's not always simple."

He chucked the pizza crust sitting on the arm of his chair

into the rubbish bin. It struck the bottom of the bin with a resounding thud.

Thoroughly homing in on Mike, he said, "How difficult others can make life is about the only thing you did teach me, Mike. First hand." He stood, grabbing another piece of pizza from one of the boxes on the bed, then pointed the slice at Mike with all the menace as if it were a deathly sharp blade. "And yes, I wish it were an 'X' to mark the spot instead of this... convoluted headache. Because—because you know, considering it's just our very lives dependent upon it. That's all."

In final rebuke, the cheese in its entirety slid off the front of his pizza he had aimed at Mike, splattering onto the floor at Mike's feet. And for good measure, it brought with it all the pepperoni. Howie took a large tearing bite of the now just sauce and dough pizza, then threw the rest into the bin. He dropped back into his chair, crossing his arms.

Ingrid handed him a fresh Coke. "Because... and back to your question, Howie, the inscription was intended for the L' Entita's eyes only." She offered him a napkin.

Mike intercepted the napkin, swiping it away. He used it to wipe up the mess of cheese and pepperoni at his feet. "Always cleaning up after you, kid," he said, throwing the crumpled napkin into the rubbish bin.

"Boys, please," she said, directing their focus to the inscription, "we have two huge advantages over our adversaries. We have the only key to the remaining chambers, being the compass piece. And we have the only one who can translate the L' Entita's language, being, well, me." Her next words came to her from a place undiscovered within herself. "Now we can and we will do this. Anything is possible, if broken down into smaller steps. We only need to find a beginning. Howie, line one, if you will." She felt quite satisfied hearing her own words. *Ingrid, maybe there is a leader within you after all. All you needed was a beginning.*

Howie set aside his Coke and tried his best to let the

sounds of each artfully chosen word within the inscription expel from his mind the anxiety in knowing Camorra grew ever closer. "The site you plainly seek within the Sun Book's sacred eight." The capitalized letters for 'Sun' and 'Book' were taunting, pleading his brain to know something, something he should know. *But what? Capitalized letters begged an actual name...* "A title?"

Ingrid didn't want to tell him his guess was as good as hers, but she had to tell him... them, something. "Whatever this Sun Book is, it's the key to our solving this puzzle and locating the lost library of Alexandria. And saving our own bodies in the process."

"Then," Howie said, "having this book is a bit of a prerequisite."

"More like knowing what it is first," said Tom. He leaned against his chair and popped his back in a most disturbing tone. "Jesus Christ, this is like knowing you have to pass a college exam or you're going to flunk the class, but you know there's no way in hell you can pull it all off. Not in time anyway."

The second he said the words, they'd begun to echo around within her mind. And there, the words stuck. *Jesus Christ. Jesus Christ. Jesus...* like a devilishly catchy chorus, refusing to leave her brain. *But why*—she froze. "Plainly... In plain view... Tom, you just might have something!"

"With flunking school?" he asked.

She scanned the room. "No!" *One had to be here.* "Jesus." She was borderline certain it was here. *But where?* They'd only rearranged virtually the entire room with making space to solve the damn thing. *Jesus...* Her eyes darted in every direction.

Entirely lost at this point, they watched her run to the small dresser next to the bed.

"Anything worth sharing with the rest of us?" asked Howie.

"Tom's a goddamn genius," she said.

Tom frowned at the notion. "I am?" A grin blossomed

across his face. "I am." Judging by the less than convinced looks being given by Howie and Mike, Tom's grin quickly transitioned back to uncertainty. "Why?"

Searching all the drawers, Ingrid turned to the much larger dresser pushed against the wall at the far end of the room. She beelined to it and yanked out the first drawer. *No luck.* She yanked out the second drawer, and the third. Still, she found nothing. Having exhausted that possibility, she sat atop the desk next to the dresser. Her eyes searched around the cluttered motel room, pleading for something... *Nothing.*

What was that tapping? She realized her fingertips had been quite feverously bouncing up and down on the surface of the desk. Her fingers froze. *Of course!* The spot where'd she'd first started from with translating the damn thing...

Driven by that place between caution and curiosity, Howie made his way to the desk as Ingrid tore away its single drawer, expelling the contents across the floor. Dropping to the withered and stained carpet, she fished through the stationery, pens, and tourist brochures. Finding it, still on her hands and knees, she thrust up the Bible into the air.

"For the record, I'm still confused," said Tom.

Howie helped her to her feet. Returning to the others, she dropped the Bible with a satisfied plop onto the coffee table in front of them all.

"Anyone else confused still?" she asked.

Howie and Mike raised their hands.

"Okay," she said. "Anyone here know Greek?"

Howie and Mike again both raised their hands.

"Then you'll know that in Greek, 'Holy' is derived directly from 'Helios', which means 'Sun'. And 'Bible' comes from the Greek word 'Biblos', which means 'Book'," she said. "'Holy Bible' literally translates to..."

"Sun Book," Mike said, finishing her realization while wondering how he'd missed something so obvious... *The world had missed it too...*

The Inscription

*T*he same obviousness hit Howie in the face. Staying sincere to the time and place when written, the original context for the Holy Bible's title translated perfectly to Sun Book. *Perfectly.*

"How'd I ever miss that?" he asked.

Ingrid couldn't help but smile, seeing the same look upon both the father and son seated before her. It was clear now, despite these two men's perpetual butting of heads, their minds worked, well, as similar as that of father and son.

"No, really," Mike said, "I at least should have, at some point, saw that."

"Don't beat yourselves up too badly," she said. "I'm sure the majority of the rest of the human race can ask the same question, if ever they were allowed a pause in their hectic lives to give it a moment's thought. Often, the obvious can prove the most elusive."

The Bible stared back at them in a whole new light. It was the light of the sun. Its letters, stamped into its mass-produced faux leather and thin cardboard cover, were not quite silver, not quite gray. And for a generous moment, they each considered the ramifications of what she'd just said.

Mike tried to clear his mind to be able to speak the words, the idea of it all. "The L' Entita, a society, as ancient and mysterious as they come, hunted by the Church for the knowing of a secret which contained the power to negate the

Vatican itself, hid that very secret within the Church's own religious text, where it's managed to remain to this day, undiscovered."

For Howie, the generous moment was over. He scoffed at the idea. "Yeah, Ingrid, as much as I hate agreeing with Mike, you're telling me, out of all possible places the L' Entita could've chosen to hide it, whatever *that* is, which their very lives depended upon, they chose..." He grabbed the Bible and shook it at her. "The one place the Catholic Church would be guaranteed to look more than any other down through the ages?"

"Well, of course it sounds crazy," she said, "when you put it like that."

"Why does everyone keep telling me that?" He offered her the Bible. "In what way does it sound sane?"

She grabbed it away. "It's the perfect hiding place."

"Not to take sides," said Mike, "but I agree with Ingrid. I mean, we can't argue against the inscription."

"Yeah, okay," Howie said. "It makes for an intriguing venture, but *why*? Why would they take that kind of risk—it's crazy."

Having been sitting quietly, Tom raised his hand. "I think I speak for Howie as well on this. We've been doing this treasure hunting gig a long time, and the Bible being used to hold a secret treasure map is, well, downright perfectly brilliant in its own right. But goddamn, it is brazen, even by the L' Entita's standards."

"Ingrid, you do know what we mean...?" Howie asked.

Ingrid cracked open a can of Coke. "Sure. I know. I'm saying, consider from their viewpoint. They needed not just hide this secret, but *preserve* it. And I guess your choice of words, Tom, will do. Their treasure map, it needed to be hidden somewhere that was both encased, yet concealed within another document or text. And one that would weather the course of history."

Tom glanced at Howie, then shrugged. "It would make for

a bloody good middle finger to the Church, as it were."

"The Bible," said Mike, "at the time, it would've been their best bet."

Howie sighed, letting the logic eclipse over his doubts. "Okay. When you put it like that."

Mike leaned over to Ingrid and whispered, "And that's as good a conceding you're going to get from those two."

"Wait," Howie said, "why Greek? I mean, for the translation with the—"

Anticipating where he was going and their need to make progress, she cut him off. "As opposed to Aramaic for the Bible, yeah, well, simply because all original biblical writings are in Greek, not Aramaic. And I know what you're thinking, shouldn't Aramaic be the original language the Bible had been written in. Yes, you're right, it very well *should* be."

"What she's getting at," Mike said, "if the Bible had actually been composed in the time and place the Church alleges it to have been written, its original text would be Aramaic. Not Greek, like it is." He sensed the urgency rapidly building within in her. "Though, we'll get to that in good time."

Ingrid drew in a long drink from her Coke, letting the carbonation thoroughly bite the insides of her mouth before swallowing. "Moving on. Howie, grace us with line two. Unless, anyone has an inkling what 'sacred eight' means at the end of the first line... No? Okay, Howie, continue."

"Uh, right, faces precession for the age awaits the great," he said.

Mike raised his hand. "Anyone else notice a pattern in the word choices? *Astrologically...*"

Hearing him say it harbored some relief for her. If he, a well-learned man of the world, saw it and thought it too, it must be so. And it meant she hadn't let their situation's direness push her across the line yet, to be grasping at straws, to be creating answers instead of facing elusive and difficult facts. She felt a calm begin to melt within her now. For he saw what she did, a hidden message woven into this passage left and lost by her ancestors so long ago.

"Ingrid?" Mike asked.

Once more, she broke from her thoughts. "Sorry," she said. "Yes, well, the Bible is bursting with astrological symbolism after all." Her peripheral vision couldn't help but take in the lost looks of Tom and Howie. She used her tablet's stylus to underline the words standing out to Mike and her. Collectively, they turned to the TV screen.

The site you plainly seek lays within the Sun Book's sacred eight.
Faces precession for the age awaits the great.
To sun rayed land caked in wheat with bull drawn out by ram's watered hate.

"See," Mike said, "with 'Sun Book', being the original context for the Holy Bible's title, it just seemed a nod to the Bible's astrological significance, as well its roots."

"Which is the lens you were looking at the rest of the passage in," said Ingrid.

"Exactly," Mike said.

Howie cleared his throat. "Uh, astrological roots?"

"More reading, kid, less pirating," Mike answered.

"If I didn't have Captain Hook for a father," said Howie. The loud crunch of Ingrid's empty Coke can in her fist abruptly ended the beginning of their feud.

"First word in question, precession," she said. "As in precession of the equinoxes... Mike, please, and briefly."

He grabbed the last two Cokes from the mini fridge, and offering her one, said, "Trade you for your tablet." Using the tablet's stylus, he brought up a blank page on the TV screen. He drew a large circle. Then, equally spaced out around the circle's perimeter, he wrote the names for each of the signs of the Zodiac.

"So," he said, "the precession of the equinoxes, it is the cycle where the Zodiac's twelve constellations seem to visually, as well in order, one by one, rotate around the earth."

"Earth, being in the middle of all this?" asked Tom.

"Yes," Mike answered, a little annoyed. At the center of the large circle, he quickly made a smaller circle and labeled it, 'Earth'. "With the completion of this cycle, wherein all twelve constellations have appeared to rotate around the earth, it's called the Great Year. Hence, just as the inscription says, precession, age, great."

"That's it?" Howie asked.

"Just, that it takes a long time for this cycle to complete," Mike added.

"Really long time," said Ingrid. "Try somewhere around twenty-six hundred years."

"Is that number relevant to the riddle?" Tom asked.

"As far as could be," she said, "anything and everything is relevant." She took the tablet from Mike. And on the TV screen, she projected his diagram directly alongside the inscription. With the stylus, she underlined all the words now likely referencing astrology.

The site you plainly seek lays within the Sun Book's sacred eight.

Faces precession for the age awaits the great.

To sun rayed land caked in wheat with bull drawn out by ram's watered hate.

"Everyone gets that 'bull' could equal Taurus and 'ram' could mean 'Aries'?" she asked. Accepting their collective nod, she continued. "As it happens, 'bull' is the one word I'm not a hundred percent on. I mean, the translation is tricky. It could as easily be cow, or even calf."

Mike stood, stretching. "Wouldn't exactly fit the astrological theme then. Let's call it good with 'bull'. One thing's certain though, there's no shortage of bulls and rams in the trusty old Sun Book," he said, patting the Bible's faux leather cover.

"That's the problem," Howie said. "Where to begin."

"To sun rayed land caked in wheat... 'land' sounds suspiciously like a place for us to take flight to and get away from Malta," said Tom. "What countries are wheat-heavy?"

"Who knows," said Howie. "When this riddle was written,

the climate was significantly different."

"Boys," Ingrid said, "let us stick to the astrology symbolism for right now."

Having forgotten about the can wedged between the side of the easy chair and his leg, Tom gulped the entirely warm and flat Coke. He immediately grabbed the rubbish bin and spit it out. The splatter of the sticky liquid on the bottom of the bin seemed as blood.

"Those two animals are sacrificial," he said.

"Good, Tom," Mike said, sincerely impressed. "If there's a passage in the Bible that has both a ram and bull in it, then it'd also most likely be in the context of sacrifice." He reached for the Bible, but it was already in Ingrid's hands.

Using the index to cross-reference 'bull' and 'ram', she flipped to the place. "Exodus thirty-four. Howie, if you will."

He took the open Bible, not being able to recall the last time he even touched one. That didn't mean he wasn't familiar with the stories, because he was. Ingrained in him as a child, or, more like seared into his mind with a branding iron forged from nothing less than pure traumatic terror, these tales remained forever there. And like with all his traumas, he had his father to thank for that.

"What's the matter, Howie, you look like someone walked over your corpse," Tom said.

"I just... Reading from this thing isn't much my thing," he answered. "I'll just paraphrase the highlights."

"Begin at the beginning of the passage then," Ingrid said, smiling warmly, yet urgently.

"Right," he said. "Let's see, Exodus thirty-four... So we've got Moses on Mount Sinai getting the Ten Commandments... The Hebrews are tired of waiting around, so they build a gold bull. Hey, okay, we've got our bull. Now, let's see... Moses returns, catching them worshiping the bull. Moses, he orders the Hebrews to murder each other for their punishment. Then, god inflicts a plague upon the Hebrews on top of it." Howie looked up. "I don't know, this, this is *exactly* why I can't read this stuff."

"Oh, here we go," said Mike.

"God loves his people so much, right," Howie said, "but has no compassion whatsoever for the fact he's made them wander around, well, literally BF Egypt for what, four decades. And anytime his people don't adorn him in worship, god becomes homicidal." He sighed, not even realizing his Sunday School PTSD had brought him now to be wrenching his hands tighter and tighter around the Bible. "Love?"

Mike looked like he was about to say something in rebuke to Howie, but Ingrid shook her head at him.

"Preaching to the congregation, Howie," said Ingrid. "So, please, continue."

"Choir...," Mike said. "Never mind."

"Okay, okay, sorry," Howie said. "Uh, Moses announces his arrival with the Shofar." He scanned down the page. "That's it, that's the rest of the passage. So where's the ram in this soap opera?"

"Shofar is a ram's horn," said Mike.

Unable to contain himself, Tom stood, actually knowing something they didn't seem to, or at least being the first to recall the relevant information from his brain. "Also, Moses himself is the symbol for 'ram'." Taking the tablet, he held it up, and clicking on the final line in the passage with the stylus, quickly underlined, 'drawn' and 'watered'.

To sun rayed land caked in wheat with bull drawn out by ram's watered hate.

"In Hebrew," Tom said, "the literal translation for 'Moses' means to draw out of water."

"And how the hell do you know that?" Howie asked, while not sure why he was feeling so annoyed by Tom's uncharacteristic insightfulness. *Why was he so angry?* He needed sleep. They all did. Especially his holier-than-*everyone*-else father, who was yawning in the easy chair there beside him. *God.* Even when Mike was sleepy, he still looked smug.

"Irish Catholic dad. Jewish mom," said Tom.

"And I thought I had complications of identity," said Ingrid, trying to lighten the mood.

"Also," Mike said, pointing to 'sun' in the passage, "Moses means 'son' or 'sun'. Per, the origin of both derive back to the same root, *sun*, as in the big ball of gas."

"That's true, in Egyptian," said Ingrid, "that Moses means sun."

"Egyptian...," said Howie. "*Egypt*—where god forced the Jews to wander around for forty years."

"The same Egypt where Mount Sinai is," said Mike.

"Seems we may have a sun rayed land to go to after all, Howie said.

"Can't afford to screw this up," Tom said. "Go to the wrong country, hell—wrong continent, we'd never be able to catch back up with the Vatican. So how do we know for *sure*?"

"Well, the L' Entita used both the Hebrew and Egyptian translations for Moses within the inscription for a reason. Not just to be cute," Mike said. "Right?"

"For once—twice, got to agree with Mike," said Howie. "It's too coincidental to be coincidence."

"And where do we go when we get there?" Tom asked.

Howie went for the mini fridge. He surely wasn't sure if he wanted to fly somewhere as hectic and sprawling as Cairo without first knowing where in Egypt they even needed to go. "What you're really asking, should we stick around trying to decipher the rest of the inscription. Or, try to get out of Malta now while—if we still can."

"Yes," Tom said, "that's what it's come down to." He leaned back all the way in his chair. "Look, okay, say we risk flying into Cairo. There's a good chance somewhere between here and there, at least one of us sets off a red flag on the Santa Alleanza's radar, or any of the countless agencies at their disposal. Just saying, it's easier to solve this thing while not in the middle of a hot pursuit."

"Let's vote then," Ingrid said. "Everyone wanting to stay,

raise your hand." Tom's hand shot up.

"And everyone for leaving now." Ingrid raised her hand as she said it. Mike joined her vote. She went to Howie, still at the mini fridge. He watched through the window at the ocean at the bottom of the gentle hills and beyond to the noonday sun.

"You didn't vote," she said, placing a hand on his shoulder.

He pulled a bottled water from the fridge and took a long gulp. "Fine." He raised his hand. "Let's go to Egypt." He tossed Tom a bottled water. "Sorry, buddy, but you *were* the one who wanted to get out of here ASAP. Let's hope we're able to solve the rest on the flight."

Tom broke the seal upon the container of orange Tic Tacs in his hand. And pouring half the container into his mouth, said, "Let's hope..."

Expected and Unexpected Guests

*T*he Ducati came to a halt, joining the police vehicles parked in a most disorganized way near the abandoned Range Rover. Camorra stepped off the Ducati. He couldn't stand police. Their method, or lack of, for parking was the least of which. He approached the closest of the police cars. Hearing a branch snap behind him, he spun.

"Been expecting you," the detective standing there said. "Nothing was recovered from the Range Rover." Light danced across the little crucifix pinned to the detective's lapel.

Without a word, Camorra nodded and turned. Slipping the phone from his pocket, he found the screen cracked, though still usable. On screen, he displayed the Sapphire Inn, the closest motel to the Range Rover's location. Returning the phone to his pocket, he brought the Ducati to life.

~~ ~~

Howie led Tom, Ingrid, and Mike up the steps of the Cessna Citation XL. Entering the cabin, something was wrong, terribly so. The door to the cockpit was wide open. The captain and copilot were nowhere to be found.

"You're a hard man to track down, Howard."

The voice came from behind them. The blend of baritone and wheezy softness was unmistakable. Howie and Tom knew beyond any doubt the owner of that voice was Rino Teresi.

He was there, somewhere, obscured from view by the curtain drawn across the narrow aisle at their backs. They also knew they should have expected this moment at some point. But with everything going on, the consideration of this particular danger had evaded them.

They turned to run. Ingrid and Mike did the same with no need to understand the situation to understand the situation. There was a certifiably unmovable wall of a man with a gun at the bottom of the steps. Rino's younger brother, Richie Teresi, stood there. Tom knew better than to even contemplate going for his Colt .45 under his jacket.

"Ah, don't leave now," Richie said. "You might miss your flight."

There was no debating with him, not when the entirety of his immensity, all three-hundred and twenty-pounds and six-foot, six-inches, well-toned, was one-hundred percent dedicated to keeping them on the plane. Likewise, his well-aimed gun, now trained on them, was just a formality. With Richie starting to lumber up the steps, they returned to the cabin.

Hunched over like some overgrown version of Quasimodo, Richie entered the Cessna. The cabin's five feet and seven inches of head room only magnified the menace of his stature. Forced to face their fate, Howie took hold the soft fabric of the curtain across the aisle. With the same reluctant swiftness of peeling away a bandage upon an inflamed wound, he drew back the curtain.

~~ ~~

At the Sapphire Inn, painted in its most dismal yellow, gun aimed, Camorra quickly pulled open the door to the room.

Daniel was seated in the easy chair there at the center of the room, hands entirely relaxed on the armrests. "I've been waiting for you."

Camorra paused for a moment in the doorway, lingering within that space between, neither outside nor inside. "I keep hearing that. It disturbs me, because..." Having let his eyes adjust to the interior lighting, he entered. "It's starting to make me feel like I'm predictable..."

He remained standing, just inside, leaving several feet between himself and Daniel seated there before him. Quite deliberately, he left the door open to his back. The sun streaming in caused Daniel to squint head-on into the light.

"But you, Daniel, here, that's something I myself didn't anticipate." He lowered his gun, keeping it at his ready. "Custodibus quia quod inimicus oms non telum. Quia ille potes necat cum eius animo solum."

"Watch for the enemy who holds not a weapon, for he can kill with his mind alone."

"How pleasant. So, Daniel, you're not only a former member of the most elite special forces on the planet, you're classically educated."

"Qui audet adipiscitur."

"Indeed. I'd ask you where they are. But a man as keen as you wouldn't have placed himself into such a position with actually knowing. This brings us to why then you are here. But we know there's only one reason for that... To delay my pursuit."

"Where does that put you and me?"

"A warrior as rare as yourself, Daniel, I would no sooner choose to end your life than I would choose to destroy a Stradivarius violin." Camorra moved in a little closer. "Unnecessarily."

"The unnecessarily part sounds like a qualifier, Camorra."

"You wouldn't be here if you didn't truly care... at least for..." Camorra watched the subtlest of body language from Daniel. He took in everything, reading past the composure, despite Daniel's exceptional control over his faculties. "Yes, one of them..."

Daniel's pulse upon his throat quickened ever slightly.

"Yes, you more than care for the female. Don't you..."

"They are my friends. And they're in danger."

"What happens to them is not for us to decide. That is for them."

"What're you getting at, Camorra?"

"I will preserve their lives if they choose to give me what they have found, as well walk away. You doubt my words?"

"All things considered..."

Camorra removed the magazine from his gun, placing both on the bed near the door. Daniel stood, ready. Camorra closed the space between them.

"Daniel, don't mistake my aptitude for the combat of man for a wasteful pleasure of it. Leave preserved. In turn, involve yourself no more. Or you'll be no more. Again, what happens next is their choice, and theirs alone."

"Since when is the Santa Alleanza content with loose ends?"

"I'm the one doing the tailoring. So, leave them to me."

"If I don't?"

"Consider the feelings—needs of this woman you love. Are relics of history of more value than that? No. Go back home, Daniel. It's Australia, isn't it. Go, and stay off the grid, like you're so apt at doing. Your friends will thank you later, for staying alive." He stepped aside, gesturing to the open door behind him. "Sometimes, staying alive is the best any of us can do."

Not liking the choice, but he knew this... Camorra was correct. It wasn't the right choice. There wasn't a right choice. It wasn't even the least worst decision to be made. What it was, was necessary. And it was what he had—must do now. He left.

Camorra closed the door, severing the flow of the sun into the room. He turned off the lights and lowered his body to the now vacant chair. The shadows of the dark room washed over him, feeding his solitude.

Past Dues

*W*ithin the Cessna Citation XL's most comfortable cabin, the four of them stood most uncomfortably. Before them sat Rino, barely contained in the plush leather seat.

"What'd you think, Howard, you'd get to write the Pied Piper an IOU," he said. "Richie, what do call that little thing he plays?"

"Flute," said Richie.

"Sorry, I didn't bring my flute," Rino said.

"I brought my gun though," Richie said. "And I can sure make her whistle."

"I believe you," said Howie, truly believing Richie could.

"Now, we're going to have ourselves a little business meeting, so bags on the floor," said Rino. They dropped their bags.

Rino turned to Tom. "Now, Tommy boy, Richie forget to ask?"

Tom knew what was coming next. Carefully, he removed his Colt and gave it to Richie. "What's with the suits?"

Rino stroked the thick Oxford-style tie hanging from his vast neck. "Like it, Tommy boy?"

"We got our MBAs now," said Richie.

"That right?" asked Howie.

"Summa cum laude," Rino said. "From the school of hard

knocks."

"With honors too," said Richie, grinning proudly.

Rino groaned at his brother. "That's what I just said, Richie."

"Yeah, yeah," Richie said, admiring Tom's gun. "Think you're Jesse James don't you."

Tom hesitated on whether to correct him. The hesitation was brief. "James had a Schofield. William Bonney—Billy the Kid, as it were, was known to carry a Colt."

Richie gripped the gun. "And the snotty brat got himself killed dead, now didn't he."

"Now Richie," Rino said, "don't interrupt someone when they're teaching you something. You might actually learn something. And Tommy boy, enough. Now, everybody take a seat. Here, Howard, I saved you a place right next to me. I suggest everyone sit now." At Rino's not-so-suggested suggestion, they promptly seated themselves. Richie, being last in the aisle, struggled to situate his too large of body into the too small of chair.

"Now," Rino said, "this is how this business meeting is going to go. I'm the CEO, and little Richie there across from me, well, he's my business partner. VP."

"Vice president," said Richie.

Rino frowned at him. "Yes. And all of you are the associates. That means try really hard to be quiet during this meeting unless I need some business information from one of you... Being my associates. Now, Howard, don't be rude, introduce everyone."

Howie nodded to Rino. "Everyone, this is Mr. Teresi, the senior."

"Howard, please, it's just Rino, everyone." Rino dabbed with a silk handkerchief at the sweat building along the edges of his deeply graying hairline.

Howie felt his own sweat building. "I stand corrected. It's Rino."

"Really, Howard?" Rino looked sincerely hurt. "Rino,

Howard's *chief* business associate. You haven't forgotten that now, Howard?"

Sliding off his jacket, Howie answered, "Etched in stone, how could I." It wasn't just stuffy inside the Cessna's cabin. It was on the verge of suffocating, with the sun beating down on this aluminum coffin that contained them. For Howie, the heat seemed to be drawing in the walls, shrinking the entire cabin.

With his handkerchief, Rino kept his forehead sweat at bay. "It certainly is etched in stone, Howard." He used the handkerchief to point to Mike. "Now, who are you?"

Mike stared Rino in the eye. "Mike."

Rino cocked his head, awaiting more.

"My father," Howie offered.

"Ah... *Dad.* Richie, you see the resemblance?"

Richie looked to Mike, then Howard. "Can't say I do."

Rino dabbed at his face with the corner of the handkerchief. "Me either. Speaking of family, for those who don't know, Richie here's my kid brother."

"We see the resemblance," said Tom.

Ignoring Tom, Rino turned to Ingrid. "Now... Who is this exotic creature?" He held out his massive hand. She leaned forward, taking it. His palm held hers with a delicateness that should have been impossible for a man of his size.

"Ingrid," she said.

"Deeply, sweetly delicious. Yes. Yes, I see it now. Beautiful eyes for a beautiful name." He released her hand, just as he placed a fat foot upon Howie's shoe, applying pressure. "Since you remember me, your business associate, Howard, then clearly you remember our business meeting we had. In case it's escaped you, the meeting where you borrowed a hundred and thirteen million. Let me say that figure again." He pressed down hard on Howie's foot. "A hundred and thirteen million dollars. Now, please, Howard. Tell me you remember."

"Yes," Howie gasped, fighting back the crushing agony.

"Okay, had to check." Rino removed his foot. "Because my return on investment is past due." He slid his bulging fingers down his tie. "Where's all my little golden eggs, Howard?"

Howie tried to rub his foot back to life. "Rino—" Rino suddenly slammed his great palm against his massive thigh, derailing any train of thought Howie may hoped to have.

"How's the prospecting been for you, boys?" Rino asked, nearly shouting the question.

Getting the go-ahead-and-tell-him-nod from Howie, Tom went ahead and told him. "Mother lode's still at the bottom of the ocean."

Rino conceded to the sweat bleeding below his hairline. He draped his handkerchief across his forehead, tilting his head back. "Sorry to hear that, Tommy boy. So, why don't you explain, Tommy boy—no, Howard, you explain, being my golden goose business associate."

The blood finally returned to Howie's foot. He decided to keep it simple and tell the truth. He hoped, quite deeply, for some kind of sympathy. Even if that sympathy were in the form of something unexpected and strange that only a man like Rino could offer. "Thing is, Rino, we're dealing with a situation with the Vatican."

"I know." He nodded to Richie. "That's exactly what we heard too. Right, Richie?"

"That's what we heard," Richie said.

Rino loosened his tie. "Got to say, Howard, when the Camorra sets his mind... Well, we got to say, he's thorough. And if you don't mind me saying, he's the kind of business associate us Teresi brothers should've conglomerated with to begin with."

"Employed," corrected Richie.

Rino gave him a dismissive wave. "Richie, don't be correcting people. It's just rude."

"You know Camorra?" Tom asked.

Rino smiled at Tommy boy's word choice. "No one *knows*

the Camorra. But I can say, during my time, and a time it's been, yes, I can say I have... Crossed paths with the Camorra on three occasions." He removed the handkerchief, exposing his glistening forehead beneath, and sliced away the broad streams of sweat along the edges of his nose. "Now, Howard, I'll say this, the Camorra, well, one crossing of paths was enough to make an impression. I'll also tell you, Howard, if I can find you, then the Camorra certainly can. And certainly will."

"How did you find us?" Howie asked.

Richie snapped his fingers at him. "Don't interrupt the CEO."

"Richie, I'll handle my own meeting, if you don't mind. Now, where was I before I was interrupted... Ah, yes, Howard, don't interrupt." Popping open the top button on his shirt, Rino pivoted his great neck back and forth. The sweat around his collar acted as a kind of lubricant in doing so. "There's just not many pilots in the position to get away with not filing a flight plan when it comes to intercontinental travel. And you see, I know them all." He frowned, for the first time seriously pondering the ramifications of Howard's predicament. "Richie, frankly, I'm surprised the Camorra hasn't cooked our golden goose yet."

Richie grinned at Howie. "When he says goose, Howard, he means you."

"I got that," said Howie.

Rino clenched his handkerchief viciously in his giant fist, splattering sweat to the floor. "The golden goose, Howard, you see, is only valuable if it produces its golden eggs."

Howie attempted to look confident, though knew that was the last thing he needed to try to salvage at this point. "I got that as well."

Rino's grip, as fierce as it was upon the handkerchief, somehow tightened even more. "Then stop nesting on all the damn gold and pull it the goddamn up!"

He noticed Mike's glare clearly aimed at Howie. "Ah,

looks like dad's got something to say. What say you, dad?"

Mike, no longer able to contain his anger, said what he had to say. "Howie, you can't just give that gold to him. No offense, Mr. Teresi. The HMS *Sussex* is too historically important."

"Dad's a bit self-righteous isn't he."

Howie glared back at Mike. "And then some. Look, Rino, how you expect me to be a sitting... duck."

"Goose," said Richie.

"Golden goose," Rino said.

"Target," said Howie. "To sit there in the middle of the ocean and pull up the gold, when the Vatican has, likely at this very moment, satellites positioned there, just waiting for me?"

"Outsource, Howard," said Rino. "Business 101."

Having someone else pull up the gold hadn't even crossed Howie's mind. It was an impossible prospect. Who could he trust with five-hundred million in gold, unsupervised no less, who also possessed the ability to actually do the job? It was more than an absurd idea.

"And who exactly, Rino?" Howie asked, "would you trust to handle five-hundred million in gold? Just asking, because one-hundred and thirteen million of that gold is *yours*."

"You two treasure hunters tell me," said Rino.

"Jager White," Tom said. The utterly improbable idea had popped into his mind as fast as he'd just blurted it out. Everyone turned to him....

Diamond Among the Rough

*T*he Ducati sat outside the Sapphire Inn. Inside the motel room, Camorra stood motionless, taking in every detail.

"Has housekeeping been in here?" he asked, his shadow casting over the empty rubbish bin.

The employee uniform was too big for the slender frame of the teenage-looking boy beside him. His Sapphire Inn name badge, cocked a bit sideways on the baggy shirt, stated his uncommon name, 'Krispin'. Out of proportion with one another, his features weren't as awkward as his general presence and demeanor, but it was close.

Krispin answered as quickly as he could, for he could tell this man, with his father-like demeanor, demanding yet thoughtful, was someone of mysterious importance. "No, housekeeping doesn't arrive until—"

"Comb the room." Camorra unclipped the boy's name badge. Straightening it for him, he reclipped it. "Only you, Krispin, can find what's out of place within this room. The clues... Only you."

Yes, Krispin thought, *that was true.* Upon Camorra exiting the motel room, Krispin wasn't left just with a desire to accomplish what this man asked, he held a true need to do so...

~~ ~~

Camorra dropped softly into the dumpster behind the

Sapphire Inn. Without disturbing a single item piled before him, his eyes scanned the contents. To anyone else, this jumble of trash would've appeared a random mix, one thing without connection to the next.

There were patterns though, unwritten signatures, and thus, ownership which endured, still linking the discarder of such things to these things. And these four which he now hunted, who knew they were hunted, had been calculated enough to remove their trash during such an urgent departure... He spotted it now, obvious only to him.

Each the same, there were three of them. He carefully fished out the trio of pizza boxes. They were perfectly closed, purposely so. If they'd been tossed into the dumpster, open, like one would do with an empty pizza box, then he wouldn't have seen the specialness, the footprint for that which he pursued.

He brought the boxes to the grassy knoll which bordered the small parking lot. Sitting on the grass, he opened them to find the trash hidden within. And after carefully spreading out each item, he found the one most vital, that broken twig leading the way to his prey.

Uncrumpling the sheet of notepad paper, his mind photographed the handwritten words, the sentences, the *inscription* of a time long passed. On the paper, the three lines were not written one under the next, but corner to corner, forming a triangle.

His eyes closed. In the blackness, he summoned, in perfect detail, the image of the altar within the chamber. He focused in on the empty place amongst the surface of the altar, that pyramid-shaped space. In his mind, looking directly down upon it, he set the inscription written in the shape of a triangle into this vacant opening. It fit, locking in flawlessly, as some great pyramidal jewel.

His eyes opened. The sunlight broke through the leaf-filled branches overhead, reflecting sharply off something specific. Where the light met the object was strikingly bright, shining back fiercely.

Locating the thing, he found its surface was of simple and clear plastic. And to anyone else, that's all it would have been. His fingers plucked the Tic Tac container from the other discarded items laid out there.

With its contents drained, it remained only as a hollow shell. Holding the container to his nose, the small hinged cap on top was open, and he sniffed inside. There was a tangy smell, half artificial, half natural. Silently, he read the single word which made this container of Tic Tics unique from others, 'Orange'.

Returning to the motel room, immediately he saw Krispin had not disappointed. The room from top to bottom was in place as if never occupied, or having only been by ghosts.

Eagerly and proudly, Krispin said, "The Bible. That's the one thing missing."

"Greatness is within you," said Camorra, brushing back the boy's long bangs. He removed from his pocket a Ziploc bag. Carefully, he withdrew a single diamond from the others contained inside. Pinched between his thumb and index finger, he held it out, baptizing the gem within the splintering sunlight creeping through the room's curtains.

"This diamond's grade is FL. Its color classification is D. In other words, it's perfect. Pen and paper, young Krispin."

Krispin seized the stationery and pen sitting neatly on the desk.

Camorra wrote swiftly. Handing the boy back the paper, he told him, "Take this to this jeweler. I've written the address down for you. Ask for that amount I've also written. He will give it. Do not doubt, Krispin, for he will know who has given you this diamond, and he will honor the request."

Looking around, but not seeing anything worthy of the task, he removed the empty Tic Tac container from his pocket and slipped the diamond inside. Clicking the hinged cap securely down, he gave the boy the container. "Go. Shed your shackles. And be."

Plots Quicken

Seated inside the Cessna, Howie gave Tom the look of utter death. "I wouldn't trust Jager with the *Sussex's* gold if my life depended on it."

"Your life—*our* lives do depend on it," Tom said.

"Jager White's the same shmuck who stole your wife?" Rino asked. "Pretty thing she was."

Keeping his eyes locked on Tom, Howie nodded. "The same Jager White who's owner of Great White Recovery, my direct business competitor. Who, for the past twelve years, stole four of my biggest finds during that time."

Rino shook his head at Tom. "And I thought Howard here had been dabbling on the daft side of business as of late. But no, you Tommy boy, really are a—what would we call him, Richie?"

"Obtuse."

"Naw," Rino said. "Let's go all out. Let's go with blockhead."

Richie snickered. "*Now* that's a real-life Greek tragedy..." The snicker had quickly transitioned to rolling laughter. "If it wasn't such a comedy," he managed between gasps.

"Glad your big-little brother is amused," Howie said.

Rino used his handkerchief to sponge along that perpetually sweat-covered forehead of his. "Richie, let the man some sympathy." Noticing the minibar a matter of inches from his reach, Rino's sausage-like fingers clawed at its sliding glass door. The door relinquished and slid open. "Howard's in a sad state indeed, sad indeed." Making his selection, and somehow, using those same plump fingers, he managed to twist the cap off the little bottle of Jameson. "Now, Tommy boy, you know, asking your business partner, Howard, to trust a weasel, the likes of Jager White, is the same as asking myself and my kid bother Richie to trust that same weasel too. Being, we all here are business associates. Oh, not dad over there though. And not Ingrid, beside me here..." He smiled almost charmingly in her direction. "A kiss of exotic elegance itself." He held the smile a touch past everyone's comfort level. "So, Tommy boy, why ask us to trust someone like Jager White?" He thrust the Jameson into Tom's hands. "Picked it for you, being a cut of the Irish cloth and all."

Without partaking, Tom slipped the bottle to Howie.

"That's just insulting," Rino said.

"Don't drink," answered Tom. "Rino, you don't need to trust Jager White. You've got the next best thing. Blackmail."

"*Ah.* Trust, blackmail. Semantics," said Rino. "Go on."

Howie, for the first time, realized Tom's angle. Wiping the bottle, he took a generous drink of the Jameson. "It's a long story."

"So, make it short," Richie said.

"Yes, you two can do that, can't you," said Rino.

"You'll appreciate this story, Rino. It's *golden*," Tom said.

Howie took another gulp of Jameson, and sighing at Tom's crass pun, gave the bottle to Richie's large and reaching hand. "Tom, stop with your puns, and just tell the man already."

Rino pulled another bottle from the minibar. "Puns, long, short, somebody better fill me in."

"*Goldfinger,*" Tom said.

Fumbling with the bottle, Rino got it opened. "James Bond?"

"The same," Tom said. "The original DB5 in the film. It was stolen from a hangar in Miami... Aston Martin. It's the car—"

"I know the James Bond car," Rino said. He turned to Richie. "The car. You know the car?"

"Yeah," Richie said, finishing the Jameson and setting aside the spent bottle. "The car."

"Anyway," Tom said, "the grandson of the oil sheik who had the car stolen, he owed Jager quite a bit of money. Not saying as much as Howie owes you, but it was a lot. So, long and short, Jager got the car in exchange."

Rino handed his bottle off to Mike. "And how you two know about it?"

"Well," Tom said, "it's embarrassing actually."

Rino dug through the minibar, examining each and every bottle. "We're past that. This is a business meeting, Tommy boy. Embarrassment's guaranteed." He stared Howie directly in the eyes. "For some of us here."

"Yeah, Tommy boy," said Richie, "we're past that."

Finding an off-brand of vodka he thought he'd like, Rino tried it. "Richie, please. You're the VP. I'm the CEO. Now, shush, and Tommy boy, continue."

Deciding it best to wrap up this story, Howie took over. "Getting to the point, here for you Rino—"

"That better not be a pun," Rino said.

"No, sir," said Howie. "Three years ago, Tom and I found the Cestos Diamond."

"How's that?" Richie asked, "everyone knows Jager's outfit found the Cestos."

Howie shook his head. "No—see, this is what I'm talking about. Jager stole it from us."

The drinking had begun to change Rino's tanned complexion to an increasingly red one. He tugged at his tie, further unraveling its Windsor knot. "Stolen diamonds, stolen cars. James Bond. How's this get me my gold?"

Howie took the bottle of vodka, sipping it. "Naturally, we, being Tom and myself, went to recover the diamond Jager stole."

"That didn't belong to you two to begin with," Mike said.

Rino and Howie simultaneously turned to him and yelled, "Shut up!"

Howie continued with a mouthful of vodka. "On this recovery mission we *found* our way inside the storage facility Jager uses for his... less than legitimate dealings."

"Let me guess," Rino said, "no diamond, but there was a certain Aston Martin."

"Hold on," Richie said, "this facility happen to be in London? In the borough of Lambeth?"

Howie slowly nodded.

"Bausc Street," Richie further probed.

"Yeah...," said Tom.

"How you know that?" Howie asked.

Rino took back the vodka, and emptying the bottle, said, "Boys, we've been in this world of *business* all our lives. It's our business to know. And betting you two blockheads, one-hundred and thirteen million in gold, you don't even know who actually owns that building you two broke into. Do you?"

"Jager doesn't own it?" asked Howie.

"No, Jager don't own it," Richie said. "He *rents* a space there."

"Storage units for criminals," Tom said, beaming.

Exasperated now, Rino's breathing intensified as he rubbed his face, glowing red, into his handkerchief. "Richie, I'm gettin' the feeling our two business partners here are more liability than profitability." He wadded the handkerchief and threw it at Howie. "Mishka Maslak. That's who owns the building you two blockheads broke into."

"Who the hell's Mishka Maslak?" asked Tom.

Howie released something between a sigh and moan, seeing now what remained of his life was merely a tangled mess of leftovers destined for destitution. "Ukrainian mobster."

Rino grimaced at the crudeness of the term. "A businessman. Renowned as myself." He tilted his palm back and forth vertically so in the air. "More or less."

Howie and Tom shared a look of dread.

"This is good for us, boys," Rino said.

"It is?" asked Howie.

"Yes, yes," said Rino. "He's a businessman. Richie and I are businessmen. We'll get this movie car..." He grinned a great grin. "Then, you'll get your share of the gold, and Richie and I get our one-hundred thirteen million."

"Two-hundred million," Richie said.

About to, by default, chastise his kid brother for interrupting, Rino considered the shrewd business sense in what Richie actually just said. "I stand corrected. Our return on investment of two-hundred million." He placed a truly large palm upon Howie's leg. "Now Howard, having put your poor old business partners, being me and Richie, through so many hardships with all of this..." Rino gave him a look of sincerity as sincerely as he could, and not that it was, but it was an attempt. And an attempt of sincerity from Rino Teresi was as good as the real thing. "That's fair, Howard, yeah?"

Knowing fully well this wasn't a debatable point, Howie nodded. Then Tom nodded. And for moral support, but even greater, for the sake of getting out of there alive, Mike and Ingrid nodded, making their business agreement truly unanimous.

"What shall we call it, Richie, this bonus donated by our associates here?" Rino asked.

"Asshole tax," Richie said.

"Yes..." Having forgotten he'd thrown his handkerchief at Howie, he briefly looked for it. Then he used his tie to dab at the base of his neck, catching the sweat that'd collected within the many rolls there. "Asshole tax, with outstanding penalties. To be paid in full. That includes a relatively small service fee to be paid to Mr. Jager White. You want to remain a gentleman after all, Howard. Now, that's the extent of what your CEO here can offer. In the meantime, don't get killed before we get this gold pulled up. Now, Howard, give me a hand."

After a notable amount of effort, Howie succeeded in helping Rino to his feet.

"Get Tommy boy back his piece," Rino said.

Richie handed over the Colt to Tom.

Tom gave Richie a smile in return. "Don't let the door get you stuck on the way out."

Richie stuck a finger in Tom's face, about to tell him something less than terribly clever, though more than moderately intimidating.

Before the words would manifest, Rino cut him short. "Let's go, Richie. Oh—Howard, here, do keep in touch." He handed him a cellphone. "Direct line to the CEO."

Rino and Richie made their way down the steps to the tarmac to the limousine, awaiting. From the top of the steps, Howie watched as his missing pilot and copilot exited the limo, and started for the Cessna. A single droplet of rain struck his face. He looked up to the graying clouds which had begun to thicken overhead.

Ingrid joined Howie atop the Cessna's steps. "Thought you said they're from Sicily?"

"Don't let them hear you ask that," Howie said. "Born, yes. Grew up, no. New York... They were forged into the men they are today deep from the furnace of Hell's Kitchen."

Inside the limousine, Rino turned to Richie. "Arrange an audience with the Camorra..."

~ ~ ~ ~

Camorra entered the immense pyramidal chamber. It was a conscious effort to adjust his mind to the ways in which physics behaved differently here. Along the diamond-like skin of the chamber, his reflection and shadow seemed to have random deviations of their own. These things couldn't be calculated, and he hadn't the time. Quickly, he joined Domenico at the altar, dead center of the chamber.

Domenico spoke to the handful of men he'd positioned as

sentries there. "Leave us."

Alone now, he turned to Camorra. "Where's this Daniel, the contact of theirs?"

"We reached an understanding."

"Letting him go wasn't the agreement, Camorra."

"I made a judgment call."

"This allegiance to that warrior's code of yours, is it going to be a thing? A problem?"

"I'll find them."

"Without the girl, we cannot locate the next chamber." Domenico gripped the glassy roots protruding up from the altar, as though drawing its secrets deep into his being. "Not the thing they took from here, Camorra, but she... She's their key. She's the only way to obtain what's at the end of all this. And I will obtain it. One way. Or the other."

The Investors

"*W*elcome to Zurich, Miss Vaccaro, I am Mr. Zahren," said one of the two men in the expansive meeting room as Lucia entered.

The second man stepped forward. "I am Mr. Sarasin."

Either man could have been born in his suit for how exact their bodies fit within them. Their suits fit not as a suit, but as a skin upon another skin might if such a thing occurred in the world as she knew it.

"Your journey was acceptable?" Mr. Sarasin asked.

"Yes, thank you."

They remained quiet, as not to interrupt her assessment of the room. For, in doing so, they levied their own assessment on her. The space looked suspiciously like a boardroom any large corporation might have. And why shouldn't this be any different. A conglomerate bank as this was most certainly, by any metric, a corporation. Just, this particular bank had darker secrets... *Much* darker.

Her eyes drew to the table, the room's centerpiece. Elongated and wood, its vast and calm curvature, led the all-white table to end in a horseshoe of gentlest form. It was more rare, expensive, and elegant than any the Roman Curia, or the Holy See possessed.

She could tell much of a person alone from their choice of furniture, and particularly so with tables. She had hers, the black walnut that it was. Domenico had his, the minimalist cutting-edge smart table. These men, they had theirs.

Like this table, Mr. Zehren and Mr. Sarasin, she could see, were a tailored breed. They existed from a place where they were the centerpiece, where all things were built, then sculpted to fit around them. Good, bad, or something else, they were unique and wholly so.

"Please, if you will," Mr. Sarasin said.

She took a seat in the chair he indicated. The table was void of anything except a long glass cylinder. It contained what appeared to be water, some exotic kind, as much as water could be.

Quite ceremonially, Mr. Zehren broke the seal upon its metal lid. And requiring some effort, lifted, and tilted the nearly three feet in length glass cylinder. He poured it into the only thing of particularly aesthetic plainness encompassed by the room, one of the ordinary in size drinking glasses now beside the cylinder of water.

Where had those glasses come from, she wondered. *They hadn't been there a moment ago. Had they?*

He set the glass squarely in front of her on the cold white table. "Water."

Smoothly as could be, he poured two more glasses. Then, they sat themselves directly on either side of her. They took an equally measured sip at precisely the same time and returned their glasses perfectly so in front of themselves. Together, they turned to her.

"You're wondering what is special about this water," Mr. Zehren said. "Wonderment awaits. But, back to the water. It comes from the heart of the McMurdo Dry Valleys in Antarctica. Believed somewhere around one million years, it's by far the oldest known to humans on earth."

"To *any* species," Mr. Sarasin added.

"We've gone through much effort to bring it here. The offering of this most-purity consummated to our lips now," said Mr. Zehren.

Having seen them drink it, Lucia joined them this time, as

they each raised their glasses and swallowed the million-year-old, or older, water. It tasted in her mouth now like... Water.

"Back to wonderment. You're wondering why you're here," said Mr. Zehren. He shared a most mirrored smile with Mr. Sarasin, unlike any she'd witnessed before; it was vexed, with an earnest undertone of hypnotic pleasure.

"Think of us as the ones who represent the investors, Miss Vaccaro," said Mr. Zehren.

"Of the Holy See, of the Vatican, of the Church, of all," Mr. Sarasin said.

"The ones who keep the coffers full when the collection plates aren't so much," said Mr. Zehren. "Such as with the present state of affairs." He consumed the rest of the water from his glass. "Miss Vaccaro, there's growing concern among our constituents that, well, you see, the *traditional* mechanisms of the Holy See may not be up to the task at hand."

"The Church has always placed its faith in the capabilities of the Santa Alleanza," she said.

The two men at her sides exchanged glances, before Mr. Zehren continued, "Yes, the Santa Alleanza... Well, to be direct, Miss Vaccaro, we are in a position to know that after you'd held your initial meeting with their Sovereign Padrino, Mr. Favignana, you'd no sooner stepped off that grand elevator of theirs, and returned to daylight, than Mr. Favignana immediately retracted, well, effectively, all his investments from the Vatican Bank."

Guarding her surprise as well concern for these men's apparent omnipresent knowledge of such things, such things there was no logical explanation for in how they knew, she did her best not to reveal anything with her response. "Mr. Favignana—Domenico, I found him to be a man to indulge caution."

"Indeed, as do we," said Mr. Sarasin. "Which is why we've made... investments of our own. Outside the traditional mechanisms of the Holy See."

"Investments in the best interests of, well, the interests of the Church... at large. And you, Miss... Lucia, if I may say," Mr. Zehren said, "in light of these things, are one of our investments."

"Potentially," Mr. Sarasin said.

Positioned on either side of her, they simultaneously rolled their chairs closer, very close, consuming her space, until there was none left, as if the space itself couldn't be left to chance. It seemed to her whatever these men's next words were to be, would hold an importance that couldn't afford the risk of even that small space. For those few inches, anything could happen in that distance, when one considered all that had already happened. At her flanks, as close as the protruding parts of their high-end office chairs would permit, the arm rests of theirs came to press against her own.

Mr. Zehren watched her eyes. He looked past his own reflection within them, to a place deeper, inside of her. This was her opportunity. If she were to be their investment, then they would be hers. She would now do what she had to. She opened her soul to him, this Mr. Zehren, embracing this violation, his audit of her being.

When he spoke next, his voice was on a plane between a whisper and the sea, besieged, as if still recovering from a summer's gale. "Moving forward, Lucia, this is what we had in mind..."

Closing In

*U*sing an electric wine opener, Howie opened a bottle of red, and began filling glasses of crystal. Leaving Tom's empty, he passed the glasses to each of them seated comfortably in the Cessna's cabin.

"I've been thinking," Mike said, nodding to the inscription on the wall monitor. "We really do hold an advantage over the Vatican, with Ingrid here." He drank his wine, rich, blood-like.

"Our own Rosetta Stone," said Tom, overfilling his wineglass with Sprite.

"I'm flattered, I think," Ingrid said. "So, from our first time around, we know when the L' Entita authored this inscription, they did so by incorporating the conventional languages of the day. Let's consider, through that lens, each word in terms of Hebrew, Egyptian, and Greek, in how each of those could have been used to construct, as well, conceal context."

"Like with anything written in a different period of time," Mike said, "the only sincere way to flesh, as well, flush out the actual intended meaning, is through the text, subtext, and context of the writing. With, the time and place when it was written, taking precedent."

Each, in their own way, turned their focus to the monitor, to the cryptic meanings discovered, and those yet to be, layered within the inscription.

The site you plainly seek lays within the <u>Sun Book's</u> sacred eight.

Faces precession for the age awaits the great.
To sun rayed land caked in wheat with bull drawn out by ram's
watered hate.

As Howie silently read each word one to the next, his fingers found the compass piece upon the table. And pulling the object into his palms so that he could fidget with it, he did so with nothing more than a mind most absent.

Mike churned within his brain the phrase, 'land caked in wheat'. *Why 'caked'? Why that word out of so many others?* The movement of Howie's hands rotating the compass piece around and around, side to side, ever faster, had grown more and more distracting.

Not able to help it, he glanced at the compass piece, ready to yell at Howie to stop shifting it around so obsessively. "Freeze!" He'd yelled pretty much what he'd intended, but his reason for doing so had very much changed in that moment.

And there, in Howie's palm, the compass piece sat at the angle providing a profile view, appearing as the hand-held pyramid that it was.

"Subtle in their directness, aren't they," Mike said.

"Yes," said Ingrid, "so obvious, it's elusive."

Howie and Tom didn't need to ask what they were talking about, as they knew Mike, being the customary know-it-all that they knew him to be, would, without any doubt, lay it out for them all.

Mike gently removed the compass piece from Howie's grasp. "The thing about Greek, is it's Greek, in all its Greekness." Keeping his fingers held upright and curved a bit, he rested the compass piece upon them, perching it so. This gave each of them a clear profile view of its pyramid shape.

"Kid, in Greek, where does 'pyramid' originate?" he asked.

"Uh...," Howie mumbled, trying to retrieve from his brain something so obscure. But not about to give his father the satisfaction of entirely owning the moment, he forced himself to find the answer at the edges of his memory. "Comes from... 'pyramis'."

Mike nodded, feeling a small surge of pride in Howie, even if the feeling was involuntary, coming from a place amidst that most eternal internal tug of war between fathers and sons, to fight, yet to please. And he let a pleased smile slip out that both men pretended didn't just happen.

"And so," he said, "knowing our Greek, we know 'pyramis' means, literally, 'wheaten cake'."

Not seeing the likeness, Tom said, off-the-cuff, "Since pyramids look so much like piles of wheat? I mean, I don't mean that incredulously. Just, you know."

Ingrid sipped her wine and set the glass aside. "That's exactly why, Tom. How the Egyptian pyramids first got their name. People literally thought their shape was similar in appearance to piled stacks of wheat."

"Stacks of wheat, being a common thing for them to see... Remember, Tom, keeping in the context of time and place," said Howie.

"Now, *which* pyramid?" Mike asked.

Ingrid scrawled on the screen of her tablet with the stylus, adding the sum of their progress so far, transmitting to the wall monitor.

(Bible's)
The site you plainly seek lays within the ~~Sun Book's~~ sacred eight.
(Precession/Equinoxes/Great Age)
Faces precession for the age awaits the great.
(Egypt)   (Pyramid)   (Taurus) (Aeries/Moses)
To ~~sun-rayed land caked in wheat~~ with bull drawn out by ram's watered hate.

With it all visually before him, Tom saw it now, the hidden, as well multiple context... He grabbed the stylus and quickly wrote...

Faces precession for the age awaits the great (Great Pyramid)

Howie raised his hand. "When was the term 'Great Pyramid' coined?"

"Actually, that's its original title," Mike said. "Everything after that was, well, after that." He just noticed that Tom, and no doubt having done so accidentally, had removed the period off the end of the line. "Tom, the tablet."

Tom handed it over.

"Inscription's looking a bit muddled in our efforts to de-muddle it. Now, setting the astrology aside..." Mike dropped the punctuation off the ends for the other lines in the inscription, further unraveling its layered secrets, while noting another reference he believed was to the Great Pyramid. He placed the tablet onto the table, and with a satisfied gulp of wine, signaled his completion.

The site you plainly seek lays within the Sun Book's sacred eight (Eight Faces)
Faces precession for the age awaits the great (Great Pyramid)
To sun rayed land caked in wheat with bull drawn out by ram's watered hate

"Ingrid?" he asked, "when you translated..." He held up the compass piece, rotating it, pausing as he turned it from one side to the next. "You did so looking at the inscription as three separate lines?"

"Yes," she said, "because—"

"Because each line within the inscription was contained to a separate side of this pyramidal compass piece here," he said.

"Well, yes, obviously," she said.

"As it was intended," he said. "For one layer of context. And, with removing the punctuation, allows us to connect the ending word in each line to the first word in the following line, forming another layer of meaning. And thus, context."

"Such as 'eight faces'," said Tom, refilling his crystal wineglass with Sprite.

"Eight faces of what?" Howie asked, having quite rapidly become lost.

"As in eight *sides*," Ingrid said. "The Great Pyramid is the only pyramid on the Giza Plateau that's eight sided."

"Look," Howie said, his frustration transitioning to

defensiveness, "I've been to Egypt several times. And most of those times, I ended up, with my own eyes, seeing the Great Pyramid. And it's like all the others..." He held up four fingers.

"Howie, she's right," said Tom.

At this point, Howie had no choice but look to Mike for support. Mike raised his palms vertically next to each other so both his pinkies were flush side by side. Then he tilted his hands slightly inward to create a concave effect.

"Four sides, creased at their midpoints, equals eight total sides," said Tom.

"Yeah—okay, okay, I get it," Howie said, turning to Ingrid. "You're right. I was wrong."

"Happens to the best of us," she said, throwing him a smile. "As Mike had pointed out before, the L' Entita were less than subtle in their obviousness."

"Well," said Mike, "I said directness, but yes, they certainly knew how to make a puzzle within a puzzle."

"And then some," Howie said, opening a new bottle of wine. He rubbed his eyes. "Multiple meanings per word, multiple contexts within multiple languages, all of which can fit together in multiple ways." He overfilled the glass, forgetting he'd been pouring. "Shit."

Spilling, a heart-sized patch of red bled across his sweatshirt, ominously, as if fatally shot. The cotton ate the crimson liquid, spreading it to the size of a dinner plate. Seeing this, Ingrid felt a shiver fall over her, thick and shadowy...

"This isn't a riddle nor poem," Howie said. "This is a Rubik's Cube strapped to a headache." Paying more attention now, he refilled their glasses, and set the depleted bottle alongside the pyramidal compass piece on the table.

"To the Great Pyramid," said Mike, toasting.

In silence, while sipping their wine and Sprite, they watched the mysterious little pyramid. Their reflections cast lightly upon its glossy skin. Shifting in hues, it was surrounded by a thousand questions held by each of them.

"Now what?" asked Tom.

"Now we drink and we sleep," Ingrid said, glass in hand, tilting her seat back. "We have quite the journey in stow."

Collateral Advantage

*T*he saltwater splashed against the hull of the state-of-the-art salvage ship, marked, 'Great White Recovery'. Jager White, the picturesque playboy, stepped from the ship's bridge and onto the deck. His bright white tailored linen suit displayed an impeccably proportioned muscular frame beneath. He was a true male specimen, toxicity and all. Unlike Howie's hardened physique, from years in the field engaged in raw physical exertion, these were the kind of muscles sculpted through an impassioned affair with the gym and vanity.

Closing his eyes, he let the breeze of the ocean embrace his bronzed face, then slide through his highlighted, perfect and sleek hair. He was younger, better looking, and more successful than his greatest competitor, Howie Lyon, in their world of globetrotting and connoisseur all-things-exotic. And he knew well he outmatched his rival on each of these fronts. *Why then did he feel anxiety?* He turned to the plank there, bridging his ship with that rust bucket of Howie's.

Crossing the plank, he held out his hand, greeting the two large, square-jawed men on the other side. Their lack of response and acceptance of his hand made clear they were void of any sense of humor, or personality for that matter.

"You two are new," Jager said, his English accent very much Cheshire in origin, offering yet another layer of sophistication to his presence.

"Arms up," one of the men said.

"Huh?" asked Jager.

The other man demonstrated. "Make like a bird. Come on."

"Seriously now, mate," Jager said.

"Yes, seriously," the other said. Jager raised his arms, and one of them patted him down while his counterpart supervised. Satisfied, they led him for the stern of the ship. Coming to a stop in front of a cargo container suspended by one of the cranes bolted to the deck, Rino and Richie stepped into view.

"Who are you guys?" Jager asked, increasingly confused by the situation.

"Howard and Tommy boy send their regrets for not being able to attend today's business meeting," Rino said. "Mr. Teresi, and Mr. Teresi are who we are."

"But being a business meeting, know us as Richie and Rino," said Richie. "Respectively."

"*Rhino*?" Jager asked. "Like the animal?"

"No... Not like the animal." Rino looked to Richie in disbelief. "Richie, can you believe this guy?"

"Can't say I do," Richie answered. "Look, R-I-N-O."

"Think he's got it now?" asked Rino. "You got it now, Jager?" He didn't give him a chance to respond. "Inquisitive character isn't he, Richie."

Richie nodded, answering, "For a business associate, yes, I got to say."

"Business associate—"

Rino cut Jager off, as his deep gravelly though wheezy voice spoke into the radio he gripped. "Yoshie, commence the business meeting." The James Bond theme started to play over the ship's intercom system. The crane suspending the cargo container came to life. It lifted Jager's ill-gained and ever treasured *Goldfinger* Aston Martin out the open top of the cargo container. There, held by chains linked to the eye bolts upon each corner of the metal platform underneath the car, it hung, swinging in front of them all.

Jager felt as though he had to go to the toilet, cry, and vomit, whilst not sure in which particular order.

Rino spoke into the radio. "Yoshie, give our guest some shade."

Boxed in by Rino and Richie and the two square-jawed men lacking of personality, Jager could only stand where he was while the crane shifted the car directly above him. It swung precariously back and forth over his head, with just its chains keeping it from crushing him. He didn't want to die in this suit, now, realizing what a mess it would make. It was a stupid thing to wear. *Not in white linen...*

"Lower, don't you think, Richie?" asked Rino.

"I think so," Richie said.

Rino raised his radio. "Yoshie, more shade for our associate." With a jolt, the crane dropped the car several feet, sending Jager crouching to his knees. He stared straight up at the Aston Martin now six feet directly over his head.

"Want Yoshie to set her down?" asked Rino.

Eyes glued to the platform above that held the car, Jager frantically shook his head.

Rino shrugged. "Suit yourself. Yoshie, no, he doesn't want you to set the car down." The radio crackled indiscernibly.

"Yes," said Rino, "*don't* set it down. Yes, yes, somewhere out of the way." Jager covered his head with his hands and arms as the car hovered above him for a moment longer. The crane's long boom quite suddenly swung well over the side of the ship. Jager ran to the railing in horror as the car looked to be consumed by the abyss below.

"Jager," said Rino, "now, being, me and my kid brother Richie are business partners of Howard, and we've just made you an associate with us, that makes you associates with Howard. Get it? Good. Richie, what do you call that?"

"Liquidation," said Richie.

Rino frowned. "No—no the other one. The other way?"

"Merger," Richie said.

Rino nodded. "Merger, Jager. So, as partners with... Richie, what's the name?"

Richie dug out a particularly mangled business card from his pocket. "It's... 'Lyon Recovery and Discovery... Recovery and discovery done with a roar. *Roarrrr'*."

"Just the name will do, Richie," said Rino. "Now our business partners, being Howard and Tommy boy, need this gold down there brought up. And you, being our associate, you're going to do that service. And no funny stuff when you do. So, be a gentleman and all, Jager."

"Yeah," said Richie, "a proper gentleman." The sudden increase in wind caused the platform holding the Aston Martin to swing rather violently over the water. Richie snapped his fingers, drawing Jager's focus off the car.

"Don't be rude, pay attention, Jager," said Rino. "Now, for services rendered, you'll receive a payment of one million dollars, to be paid from the gold recovered. Plus, you know, whatever your overhead expenses come out to be." He glanced at the car hanging high over the water. "Hey, Richie, get it? Overhead."

"Yeah, Rino, I get it."

Jager's gaze had drifted back to the Aston Martin. "And the car?"

"Richie, what do you think?" Rino asked.

"Collateral," said Richie.

"Collateral," said Rino. "Do understand, us Teresi brothers know that involving another man's automobile is less than gentlemen-like. But you also got to know, Jager, this isn't your typical business-type situation. Neither do you exactly have a title for this here automobile."

"Yeah, Jager, so be understanding," Richie said.

"He understands," said Rino. "Now, in conclusion of our business meeting here today, as any respectable business associates will do, which us Teresi brothers are doing for you, Jager, we're giving you a choice."

Inside the crane, Yoshie, having dozed off, accidentally

bumped the control lever, dropping its boom—the car dramatically plunged straight for the ocean. Everyone watched, not wanting it to happen, but unable to turn away... Yoshie pulled back the lever just as the platform holding the car made contact with the water.

Horrified, Jager clamped his eyes shut. The sound of the saltwater rushing up around the tires and rims clawed at his eardrums. He needed to pee, but first he had to vomit. He promptly and thoroughly did so, and onto his twelve-thousand-dollar ostrich skin boots. Slowly opening his eyes, he watched as the crane raised the Aston Martin out of the water.

"How about that. It almost went for the big sleep," Rino said. He patted Jager forcibly on the back. "Don't worry, my associate, we'll get that salt all sprayed off for you. Good as new."

"Won't be no corrosion or nothin'," Richie added. He slapped Jager on the back in the same place as his brother had just done, and with a little more added force for good measure.

"What's the choice then," Jager managed.

"Being businessmen of fair and ethical practice that we are," said Rino, "we're not going to force this associate situation on you."

"It's a mutually benefitting suggestion strongly encouraged," Richie said. "*Strongly* encouraged."

"We'd prefer not to have to make a certain auto recovery insurance company one of our associates instead," said Rino. "Richie, what'd we call a pretty boy like this in the penal correctional institution?"

"We'd call him a pretty boy," Richie said.

"Just something to keep in mind, my new associate," said Rino. He put a massive arm around Jager and pulled him close. "Go get that gold." He nodded to the Aston Martin over the water. "Otherwise, that's won't be the only thing needing salvaging."

"Being that car," Richie added.

Rino sighed a great wheezy sigh. "He gets it, Richie. Now, Jager, what's it going to be. Twenty-thousand leagues for old *Goldfinger* here? Or, gold?"

The situation had sunken in good and hard for Jager. He watched the Aston Martin suspended over the ocean. With every sway it did in the wind, his heart beat a little harder. Yoshie, inside the crane, seemed more than eager to release the irreplaceable car to the water.

"The gold's only a league and a half deep," Jager said, correcting Rino. "A league is about three and a half miles. It's really meant as a distance measurement for travel, and not one for depth, mate." He had no idea why he'd just said it.

Rino turned to Richie, then back to Jager. A grin broke out across his broad face. "That's the spirit." His saucer-sized hand swatted Jager once more across the back. "Now, we understand you have a yacht not too far away."

"Yes," said Jager.

"You wouldn't mind having it brought here, so your new CEO and VP can have somewhere to supervise comfortably from while you get that gold?"

"Mi yate es tu yate," Jager said.

"That Spanish?" asked Richie.

"*Yes.* Richie, that's Spanish," said Rino, shaking his head.

Merging Chaos

"*N*o matter how many times I've been to Cairo, the traffic, for lack of a better term, is itself a culture shock," Howie said.

He pulled himself from the compact car that had to be nearly three decades old, but looked twice that. All identifying features were long worn or broken off of it. He rubbed his back. Whatever it was, was far too small. The others followed him out from the car, onto the curb.

"The only thing maybe more jarring than the traffic situation," Ingrid said, "is the two economic extremes."

Across the street along the Nile was a sprawling luxury resort. On their side of the street were lot after lot of collapsed buildings and heaps of trash, stray animals, and starvation brimming every corner. They took in the grim spectacle. Truly, it was a dry ocean of sprawling urban decay.

Right before them, a truck nearly plowed over a kid on a motorbike, which was neither motorcycle nor scooter, though a depraved collage of both. Veering away within the briefest moment before impact, the bike and truck managed to swerve head-on into traffic, erupting a gloriously diverse climax of horns and brake lights all sounds and colors. The truck and bike spun, and performing something far from merging, erratically cut back into the original chaos they'd deviated from.

"*Maybe* more jarring," Ingrid said, reconsidering her prior statement.

Tom checked the text he'd just received on his phone. "Good timing. He's actually up."

"Now that's a miracle. Nuri's never up during daylight," said Howie. "Oh, Tom, use the..." He made quotation marks with his fingers. "*Expense account* to settle with him for the equipment."

Tom grinned, slipping on a pair of sunglasses from one of the many vendor displays lining the walkway. "Was counting on it." He paid the vendor. "Come on, Mike, time to meet a real character."

Mike chased after him down the crowded walkway. "Can't wait."

"Turn your ringer on!" Howie shouted.

Mike held up his cellphone before being swallowed by the crowd, vanishing from sight along with Tom.

"Should've asked if you wanted to go with them," Howie said to Ingrid.

"No, this is good. Just need to acclimate to the energy here."

"Yeah, it's a lot. That bench over there looks just fine while we wait."

Set back several feet from the walkway, he took one side on the empty bench.

"Nuri?" asked Ingrid, joining him.

Howie opened a bag of chips. "Tom and I's contact. From our past adventures in Egypt. And I guess, really, throughout the dark continent, as well Middle East, at large."

She looked at him, a little shocked.

"Did I say something wrong?" he asked.

"You kind of did, Howie. You're not supposed to say 'dark continent' in today's world." She leaned close and whispered, "Could be taken the wrong way."

"Oh, right. But—"

"Yes, I'm aware of its origins being one of geography, with the sun-blocking canopies of jungles and such, but *context*, as we know, gets lost to time."

"Okay. You're right. I apologize."

"So, Howie," she said with a smile, "now this Nuri's going to help you on yet another journey?" Hungrily, she took the handful of chips he offered her.

"That's the plan."

"You're a true globetrotter, Mr. Howard Lyon."

"You make it sound so prestigious."

"To me, it is."

He held up the vibrating phone given to him by Rino. "Business calls." Taking the call, he left the bench and wandered into the wasteland of empty lots behind them.

On the bench, and alone for the first time since she'd entered the site in Malta, she had a piece of solitude for herself and her thoughts. And for herself, it'd been a surprise just how well she'd been doing with being part of a team, as she now found herself to be. Yes, that's what she'd call it, she guessed, a team.

There was a naturalness to it she hadn't expected. Maybe it was because she didn't have much choice. Or, it could have been, simply, the logical thing to do.

But could she take the credit. Could it all, or at least, mostly, be thanks to Daniel? If she hadn't such a deep, preexisting connection to him, would she be doing so well with the others? Certainly not, but she did manifest that bond with Daniel without first having such a link to anyone else. But then again, that link between the two of them, she owed largely to him. Her mind raced with these thoughts, and more. What had she actually done that afforded her credit for anything?

This was self-doubt once more, wasn't it, and at its finest, no less. She mustn't let it cloud her judgment now. It'd done so in Malta, inside the tunnel, when the L' Entita members had come face to face with her.

She'd doubted then, talking herself out of simply making verbal contact with that one, the woman with the piercing blue eyes. *Famke.* That was—*was* their leader, their matriarch.

Despite Famke and her having the same eyes, that deeply cool shade of blue most pale, Famke's had somehow been fiercer, more intense than her own. That, she felt certain of.

It was an odd thing too, to be certain of something about a stranger, but not of herself... Of her own value. If she didn't have faith in her own being, then how could she expect others to? The others... She turned and watched Howie.

Out of earshot, he stood there, framed by the remnants of a little white fence, more zoned out than listening to Rino's lecture on the phone now. The strewn rubble behind the fence could have been the remains of anything. And the trash discarded by those passing by from all walks of life lined the front of the fence like flowers, or other colorful plants, or something more welcoming than the trash it simply was. For him, he saw the beauty in this place, even if it was just things in exile, forgotten to time itself.

In another life, he could have had a white fence of his own. *Though, what an absurd thought.* Paint nearly gone, with the pickets aligned so orderly, one after the other, reminded him all too well of the bars upon his cell in Casablanca.

Not far, and on the bench, she waited, wondering what he was talking to that gangster, Rino, about. Her mind quickly drifted to other things... The man had been married to a model. How reliable could he be? *Really?* She shouldn't, couldn't judge too harshly.

Why am I thinking of him and not of... of Daniel? Well, maybe because Daniel hadn't made any contact with her. *At all.* Was he...

"Ingrid?"

She looked up at Howie, alongside the bench, and for how long, she had no idea.

"You weren't there for a bit," he said, taking a seat. "I mean, you were, but weren't."

Pulling her hand out from under her chin, leaned upon it as she'd been, tried to compose herself. "You were on the phone awhile."

"Oh that, our self-proclaimed business partner, Rino... He just needed me to give someone a call. That's all."

"Jager White?"

The way in which his nod lasted no longer than needed to answer her, it was clear Jager White wasn't a topic he wished to discuss upon this bench with her now, or with anyone.

"About before," she said, "it's a thing of mine, zoning out sometimes." Her stomach began to rumble, and ignoring the hunger, she spoke over it. "My grandfather always told me, if my mind was an ocean, I'd have thoroughly drowned myself long ago."

"What was he like?" he asked, realizing he knew virtually nothing about her, at least of her past.

"Both father and grandfather, really. The first one to make the world make sense to me. I guess."

"Was he one of them, like an actual, practicing L' Entita, you know, like the ones in Tarxien?" His perpetual curiosity made him ask it before thinking better of the timing of doing so. And he hated himself for just now considering the impact it must have had on her, seeing the L' Entita murdered, so coldly entombed by that madman.

He also knew he had to work his way up to the question that he must ask. And this question just now had been a stepping stone. "Now that we're in this together, I wanted you to know I'm not just some glory seeker or trophy collector, or whatever."

"Stop—what do you call it... sidestepping, Howie. Is this your way of asking why I got into this to begin with?" she asked.

"Yes."

"And what do you think?"

"A need to know who you are, via finding out where you came from," he said.

"Well, that's one way of describing it..." His probing had brought it all flooding back to the front of her mind. The implosion of the tunnel, the loss, the regret, all hit her.

Her heart... it felt as a lone buoy. And it'd just been avalanched by a tsunami. She shielded her emotions from him, or did her best. "Yeah—I've been holding back the grief. Not hiding that." *You are though, Ingrid.* "So, don't try to pull that psychological stuff into it either. It's not denial. As if that's even a choice." She edged closer to him on the bench. "Setting the grief aside was just the responsible thing to do. Don't you think?"

"Yeah," he said, both sincerely agreeing with her, as well, wanting to comfort her through doing so.

"I'm not saying there's ever an ideal time... To deal with grief. But we're in a unique way right now, the four of us... You know."

He needed a way to continue down this path with her without further encroaching upon her dignity. He needed answers. Maybe if he waited, then she'd simply open the door herself. "I know. I also know, Ingrid, that holding back grief, sure—yeah, it's doable, to a point, right. Like, I guess, a dam with a crack at its core holding back a mountain of water. Then..." He smacked his fist into the palm of his other hand. "Matter of time." He shrugged. "Yeah?"

"Yeah." Pushing closer to him on the bench, and without realizing it, she told him everything. It flowed from her with the involuntary ease of water. She did so, not because she felt a closeness with him in their mutual situation. But she did so simply because he was there, and he was actually listening.

"It's my regret," she confessed. "Not having said anything, even a word to them, there, in the tunnel when they stepped off the lift. They were *right there*, Howie." She pushed back her hair from the edges of her face. "Such a simple thing... To speak. Why didn't I? I, I'm simply left with no excuse for not having done so."

He resisted the impulse to do the thing he thought other people would do in this moment. Which, was to offer his own contrived excuse for her not having done so. But he didn't, and he couldn't. She was unique, and even he could not bear such a crime as to cheapen uniqueness in its purest form. And she, here, upon the bench next to him, was as much a wonder to the world as she was to him.

"The really, really screwed up part, Howie, is that it isn't the remorse—the regret that's hardest. It's the shame, the internal knowing that my very regret is undefendable, because it's egocentric—it overpowers my empathy for their loss. See, Howie..." The dam within her broke. The words poured out even if she didn't want them to. "I'm more consumed about myself feeling cheated, in not taking the opportunity of telling them who I was, than by their actual death." She turned to him, facing him head-on. "What's wrong with me? I mean, goddamn, because something's got to be."

"Maybe it's the same thing. Their death and your regret. Loss. Seeking out that common thread," he said, closing his mouth rather promptly. He didn't know what else to say to that. Because... *What was there to say to that?* He opened his mouth, slower this time, and let out whatever would come out. "I, I think grief, death, its very nature is about the living, and not actually about the dead. So, in that, it *is* egocentric. And so, you're right, Ingrid, it's a very selfish thing."

His cold honesty sparked some warmth within her. "Yeah," she said. "Come on, let's find some food."

Departing the simple bench set back from the rush of the crowd, they merged into the mass of people along the walkway, doing so with a grace entirely lacking from the chaos.

Hedging the Fund

*A*ll was still in the dark room. There was a neon sign in the dust-layered window. It was a World War Two bomber. The light outlining its wings alternated, tilting up and down, steadily blinking on and off, on and off, simulating the motion of flight for this flightless aircraft.

Barely so, a cluttered desk, many boxes stacked, and the simple wood door near the window were all that was visible. The doorknob turned, not in an immediate way, but in the delayed way in which one does when testing if it's locked. Slowly, it opened.

Swinging inward, the door entered the darkness. The one who'd opened it remained outside. He let his pupils expand, drawing in light, adjusting to his present environment. Only then did he step through. The fluorescent tubes overhead came abruptly to life, revealing Camorra standing there in the doorway. He squinted in the light, now too bright for his dilated pupils. His instincts to let his eyes acclimate to the dark lighting had betrayed him...

"Don't you knock, Mr. Camorra," said Rino, now visible behind the desk within this office turned storage area. "Or, is it the Camorra?"

"Camorra." Richie stood behind Rino, with his broad body pressed back against the rows of boxes crammed into the tight space.

Camorra closed the door. "Mr. Teresi. And Mr. Teresi."

"Formalities out of the way then, know us as Richie and Rino," said Rino. He gestured to the foldout chair stuffed into the corner near the door.

"This stop at the airport was on my list." Camorra drew his finger across the chair, checking for dust. He sat.

"Yeah, we know it was on your way," Rino said. "Bringing us to our business at hand. Now, Camorra, two of the men you're pursuing owe me and my brother money."

"You could say," said Richie, "they're our business partners."

"I wasn't aware," answered Camorra.

"We know," Rino said. "You do know the Teresi family, like with all of the old families of Sicily, holds a long and most *generous* relationship with the Church."

"Aren't you guys from New York?" Rino and Richie both frowned.

"Back to what my brother was saying," said Richie. "In that way, at times, the Church's business is our business, and vice versa." He rested his back against the boxes behind him.

"Camorra," Rino said, "the blood in your veins, as in mine and my brother's flows from the old country. You and me and my kid brother here, we are watchmen, guardians. From the clans of warriors, the original hand of the shadow, of the dark. Our ancestors were the protectors of the Sicilian villages, safeguarding those villagers, who could not protect themselves from outsiders. From those who wished harm and exploit."

Camorra glanced at the clock on the wall. It was broken. "How much?"

"A hundred and thirteen million," Rino said.

"Dollars, U.S.," Richie added.

"You do understand I'm independent of the Holy See?" asked Camorra.

"That we know," Rino said.

"What I can, and I will do for you, Rino, and for you,

Richie, is inform those appropriate to your situation. I cannot make promises." He stood and quickly located a pen and paper atop the cluttered desk. "I trust, being the shrewd businessmen you are, you two have proper documentation of this debt?"

"You can bet your soul on it," said Rino, taking the phone number Camorra offered.

"Believe it or not, your situation is not the first of its kind," said Camorra. "With such a conflict of interest it poses for the Holy See, so there is a contingency, a fund, for such circumstances, provided by investors outside the Church's walls, thus, outside any such possible conflicts for the Church, or its mechanisms. Mr. Teresi, and Mr. Teresi, the two men at the other end of that number are the ones you need. That aside, given my own position with the Holy See, I have to ask. Are you going to tell me where they flew to?"

Having been expecting the question, Rino smiled. "Now, Camorra, being a man of good sportsmanship as you are, you can appreciate the principle of a respectable head start."

"And what of their identities?"

"Got to understand, it's business," said Rino. "Nondisclosure. You know."

Camorra started for the door, then stopped. "Will that be all?"

"For now," said Rino. "Thank you for your time, Camorra." Camorra left as swiftly as he could.

"Pleasant fellow. Don't you think, Richie."

"Pleasant enough."

"Time for some landscaping, little brother," said Rino.

"Landscaping?"

"Yes, Richie... Hedging our bets." Rino read aloud the two names neatly written beside the phone number. "Mr. Zahren. Mr. Sarasin. What kind of names are those, Richie?"

"Couldn't say, Rino."

Rino placed the call....

Eyes Within the Sky

*R*ain, light and misty, caressed the fractured pavement. The tent no longer was in front of Carters Supermarket. An actual building now covered the chasm. Topped off with razor wire, a new fifteen-foot-high chain-link fence framed the perimeter of the parking lot.

Camorra joined Domenico at the double front doors of this brand-new building. "What'd you have the Vatican do, buy the lot?"

"The entire city block actually," Domenico answered.

"At some point, there will be a problem, Domenico, that can't be solved with money. Then we'll see whether the Holy See weathers that storm."

"Until that day," said Domenico, unlocking the front doors.

"What am I doing here, Domenico?"

"It was time to bring in a think tank. Just, these guys are..."

"Different," Camorra suggested.

"They don't get out much."

Domenico led inside, into a medium-sized lab filled with monitors and servers. Two men were in the lab. One of them got up from the monitor in front of him.

"I'm Isaak, your resident liaison," he said, offering his hand.

Domenico shook it briefly, while Camorra did not.

Isaak nodded to the other man, typing away. "That one there with the bad posture is Laurence. Company's best technician."

Laurence waved momentarily, while continuing to type one-handed.

Isaak held out a form. "NDS."

Domenico signed it. "Should go without saying."

"Right, right," Isaak said. "Company policy will be company policy."

Camorra had found a secluded corner in the lab, at a desk.

Domenico went to him. "We're starting, unless you've got something more important."

"Yes," Camorra answered, fully focused on the copy of the inscription he'd recovered from the motel's dumpster. "Did you get what I'd asked?"

"In the draw there," Domenico said.

Camorra removed the Bible from the desk drawer. Feeling Domenico's questioning eyes burning into him, he held up the piece of paper.

Taking it, Domenico studied the words. "This is...?"

"Presumably, what is written upon the item they removed from the chamber." Camorra took back the paper.

"Text me a copy."

"I already did."

Domenico returned to where Isaak and Lawrence sat along the cluster of monitors. "Satellite coverage of the airport at the time their aircraft departed?"

"Yes and no," said Isaak. "The two satellites that were in that alignment window were what you'd call high orbit."

"That, combined with the weather conditions, as they are," said Laurence.

The rain beat steadily upon the metal roofing.

"Where's that leave us?" asked Domenico.

On the central monitor, Isaak brought up what appeared to be a satellite view of Malta. "Leaves us with something better."

He rolled his chair out of the way, allowing Domenico to position himself closer to the monitor.

"The resolution on this satellite feed is far better than anything I've seen," Domenico said.

"Oh no, no this isn't from any satellite." Isaak further enhanced the nearly perfect picture. "This is an HASD."

"High-Altitude Sentient Drone," said Laurence.

Hitting a key on his keyboard, a schematic of the HASD blossomed into view on the secondary monitor. The drone, a winged robot of a thing on the screen, looked otherworldly to Domenico, from a time beyond his own.

"You're making me feel old," Domenico said. For the first time in his life, he truly did feel the possibility of being outdated, ready for decommission. Just another obsolete Cold War-era spy satellite to be dumped somewhere and forgotten... *Stop it. You're not dead, Domenico. Not yet.*

"Say hello to the future," Isaak said. "These little guys can selectively choose their own orbit, high, medium, or low, fully nondependent from the orbit of the earth. Autonomous Algorithmic Mapping... Cross Data Analysis with Real-time Scenario Predictability Augmentation, for both macro and micro events. From *anywhere* on the planet's surface."

He took a long drink from his oversized coffee mug, not that he needed further caffeinating. At the center of the mug was a large all-seeing eye staring back at them. Emptying the mug, he set it aside.

"Hell, these things can determine with hair-raising accuracy the winner of a chess game being played in a park in Chicago just as easily the outcome of a battle in some oil-ripe desert before the firing of the first rocket," he said.

On the central monitor, he progressively zoomed in on the shot of Malta until the Malta International Airport enveloped the screen.

"Or, if you prefer," said Laurence, "a more humanitarian light. These things can calculate the play out of an epidemic or pandemic. On a global-scale even. The applications for natural disaster early warning systems are infinite. Tsunami. Hurricane. Global warming. Take your pick. And if something breaks... Or more like, when these HASDs anticipate the need, they automatically return to earth for updates and servicing—"

"Laurence, man," Isaak said, "can't you see he's on a schedule."

"Right. Sorry. I'm—we're just enthusiastic about this new system we've got here."

Domenico looked to the ceiling. "How many of these..."

"HASDs," Isaak said.

"Yes—how many you have up there?" Domenico asked.

"A lot," said Isaak. "Of course, not all ours, given quite a variety of players have these capabilities now. But... just us, the Chinese, and the Americans, are the only ones who have, well, what we like to call a Sky Key."

"What he means," said Lawrence, "is our drones can tap into any other drones in the air, or to *any* modern satellites. A true universal Bluetooth amongst interorbital entities."

"Not always consensually, of course," Isaak said. "Essentially, going through your neighbor's space mail, as well, trash."

Camorra, loudly tearing a page from the Bible from across the lab, momentarily disrupted their attention. Upon the central monitor, Isaak closed in on the image of the Cessna Citation XL parked at the outer edges of the Malta International Airport.

"No, sir, Mr. Favignana," said Isaak, "with these drones, there's none of that expensive in-space maintenance, overhaul, or complete replacement hassle."

He adjusted the image resolution, enhancing its truly incredible detail. "Technology's exponential evolution has all but rendered the end for satellites. Automated and disposable mobile cameras circling the globe, wholly invisible to radar, that can map an entire city within a couple minutes or read the screen on a cellphone that's a hundred feet underground, through Subterranean Resonance Imaging. A thing of real beauty these are. Oh, here we are, sir." He rolled his chair out of the way again to give a better view for Domenico.

Domenico rested his thumb alongside the timestamp displayed on screen. "How was this aircraft determined to be theirs?"

"Essentially, we worked backwards," said Laurence. "Taking all craft within that time window, we removed each that'd logged flight plans.

"This was the only one without a flight plan?" Domenico asked.

"Exactly," said Isaak. "Interesting, that tail number. Laurence."

Laurence displayed on his monitor the Cessna's tail number. "It's a duplicate number for one of the other jets that took off during this given window of time at the airport. One of the more sophisticated tactics of drug runners and smugglers, and the lot. Well, you get the idea."

"Now that we know how they slipped through," Domenico said, "we can obtain a general heading for their course. Bring up the max range for that model of Cessna."

"Already on it, sir," Laurence said. "Precisely... 1,981-mile range." He displayed the Cessna's potential flight radius on the secondary monitor in front of them.

"Ran an AWDC–Algorithmic Weight Distance Calculation," said Laurence. "You know, based upon the weight displacement of the plane's tires in the images here, to determine if it was fully fueled at time of takeoff."

"That's a lot of area," Domenico said, studying the vast radius on the monitor. "What do we have post take off?"

Isaak feverously typed on his keyboard. "What I'm doing is overlaying the standardized flight paths utilized globally between Malta International and all possible intercontinental destinations on the drone's feed here."

A multitude of superimposed lines radiated out from the Cessna's position on the tarmac. The flight paths arced across the screen in every direction.

"Still a big area to cover, sir, I know," said Lawrence. "So... let's trace forward here in time."

He fast-forwarded through the drone's feed on screen until the Cessna lifted off. Slowing the frame-rate back to normal speed, they watched as the plane rose into the clouds. About to reveal its flight direction, the feed went completely black.

"As you can see, drone's course deviates there from the target," said Isaak. "It'll take some time to determine which satellites and or drones, if any, happened to record the target at later points during its flight path."

"Good thing being," said Laurence, "the HASDs, unlike satellites, which offer separate feeds, these little guys can operate in tandem, as a network, in the truest sense. I'll calculate a log of all active HASDs at present within the possible target radius. Then interlink their feeds."

"These drones have recognition software?" Camorra asked.

Laurence jumped in his seat. No one had noticed Camorra standing there behind them. Not looking at the monitor, Camorra's eyes were on the inscription page in his hand.

"Jesus," said Isaak. "You're like a ghost, man. A ghost-man."

"He does that," Domenico said. "Recognition?"

"Yeah, yeah, live link," Isaak said.

"First, network the drones into a single feed. It'll be faster to locate the Cessna when using the recognition software," Camorra said.

"Clever," said Isaak. "I should've thought of that."

Laurence hammered on his keyboard. "Executing a heuristic search with Dual Tasking Parameter Algorithm... Yeah—yeah the recognition software will cross-reference its scope of field with the aircraft's make, as well tail number. Which, shouldn't take..."

The monitors in front of them rapidly populated with numerous aerial feeds from hundreds of separate drones.

Camorra's finger lunged at one of the feeds on the central monitor. "There," he announced, half a second before the software itself calculated the match.

"That's impossible," said Isaak. "How'd he do that faster than the computer?"

"Where was their plane going?" Domenico asked.

Isaak enlarged the drone footage on the monitor. A pixilated view of the Cessna materialized. He tapped a button and the pixilation faded away. A superimposed likeness of the Cessna tracked the jet on screen as it shifted in and out of visibility amongst the clouds.

"Here," said Laurence, adjusting the controls in front of him. On the monitor, he removed the clouds, then brought into focus the Cessna flying high above the ocean. "Synthetic-aperture radar... What we're seeing is a hybrid rendering comprised by radar, using sound waves to map everything on the screen. Then, converting it to this imagery here."

"Quite useful for circumventing weather conditions. Or whatever visual obstruction, what may you," Isaak said. "Which, satellites are nearly useless when it comes to cloud coverage blocking the..."

The footage again went black on the monitor.

Laurence rubbed the edges of his forehead. "And... back to black, with the target leaving field of coverage."

"Run a trajectory alignment," Isaak told him.

"Right," Laurence said, swiftly entering the commands on the keyboard. "And... Here we go."

A satellite feed came up on the main monitor. They watched the grainy image of the Cessna continuing on over the vast blue of the water far beneath. Abruptly, this feed too faded to blackness.

Still entirely absorbed within the inscription before him, Camorra, without removing his eyes from the paper, reached for the pen clipped to Laurence's shirt pocket. Laurence cautiously eyed him as he did so. Taking the pen, Camorra quickly wrote upon the paper with the inscription.

Laurence frantically punched the buttons on his keyboard. Conceding defeat, he looked up at Domenico. "System's not locating any further points of intersection offering convergence with the target."

"Meaning...?" asked Domenico.

"Meaning, the Alamo Measure," Isaak said, focusing on the keyboard in front of him. "Final ace up the sleeve."

"Or shit's creek," said Laurence. "Depending."

"Depending...," Isaak said. "So, what we can do is model a Statistical Hypothesis Destination... Or, in this case, *destinations*. Contingent on the model and based on flight path at the time, distance traveled, speed—from as many data fields as possible, then it simply, or not so much so, arrives at its—"

"Best guess," Domenico said.

Isaak nodded. "Yeah."

Excluding Camorra, still working on the inscription, they watched the central monitor with locked gazes in ever-mounting anticipation. The system churned, crunching through a myriad of information. Its numerous high-powered processors collectively rushed for the answer...

Camorra dropped the pen and paper on the table. Domenico glanced at it. Written above the inscription in all-caps was, 'CAIRO'. A moment later, the monitor finished its hypothesized projection for the Cessna's destination... The display's map zoomed in on Cairo.

Isaak looked to the paper in Domenico's grip. "How's he do that? *Really*, man."

Domenico answered the radio clipped to his belt. "What is it? What—now? Yes. Tell him I'll be right there." Returning the radio to his belt, he abruptly left the lab with no explanation.

"Go back to the footage of the Cessna at the airport in Malta," Camorra said, taking Domenico's now empty chair.

"Before they enter the plane?" asked Isaak.

Camorra retrieved the paper with the inscription.

"Precisely." He smoothly folded the paper, slipping it inside his jacket pocket.

"Back-tracing now," Isaak said, bringing up the footage of the Cessna parked on the tarmac.

He played the feed at normal speed, with Howie and the group arriving, then heading for the Cessna.

Camorra hit the pause button. "Why is the resolution diminished?"

"Well, because this coverage of their arrival time is from a different feed than when they're inside the aircraft," said Isaak.

"It's satellite coverage," Laurence offered. "Not drone."

"I'll take over from here," Camorra said.

"Absolutely," said Isaak. He rolled his chair alongside Lawrence at the secondary monitor.

"I'll try to back-trace them from here. See where they entered Malta from," Laurence said, energetically.

Camorra zoomed in on the faces of his prey in the frozen frame, mid-walk, to the parked Cessna. Isaak and Lawrence glanced at each other as Camorra typed at incredible speed across the keyboard. He brought up the system's recognition software on the monitor and zoomed in on Howie's image. With a gentle, almost elegant tap of the 'enter' button, he began the system's cross-database search for Howie's face.

"Remap its parameters," he told them. "Put INTERPOL's database at the bottom and all mainstream social media at the top. Ninety-seven and a half-percent probability social media will bring a return before any law enforcement records do."

Laurence quickly made the adjustments on the secondary monitor.

"How long will it take to ID them?" asked Camorra.

Isaak leaned over, studying the grainy image. "Honestly, longer than normal. Given the poor resolution quality we're working with, hour... Two hours, tops."

Camorra typed out a phone number on the screen, then pushed away from the table and rose to his feet. "Send the results to that number when you get them." With not another word, he left as abruptly as Domenico had.

"Those Santa Alleanza guys are a bit curt," Laurence said.

"Yeah, well, so is a day in the life through a spy's eyes. Come on, back to work with you," Isaak told him.

Quid Pro Quo

"*M*r. Lazare, don't you think if I wasn't spending my time here meeting with you then I could be focused on fixing this issue," Domenico said, facing off with the thin man in an understated, though exceptionally expensive suit.

They stood toe to toe along the inside of the perimeter fence of Carters Supermarket, now the property of the Holy See.

"You are not an island, Mr. Favignana. Like it or not, the Santa Alleanza's operating budget comes from the Holy See's investors."

"I'm well aware of our Swiss counterparts."

"Then, you were aware they'd send me to audit the situation after your deputy director's untimely passing."

"I'd hoped they'd have the sense to wait until an appropriate time."

"As it may, here we are."

"And as it may, what is it I can actually do for you, Mr. Lazare?"

"Field reports regarding this present assignment of yours. Daily, directly to me."

Domenico scoffed at this. "*That* is entirely out of the question."

"To the point, Mr. Favignana, the ammunition recovered from your late deputy directory's body came from your own gun."

"Whatever are you implying, Mr. Lazare?"

"Only what your report on the incident states. Which wasn't much. There'd been an internal... discrepancy, was your choice of words. It's the opinion of our Swiss investors, there could be a matter of integrity."

"They think the Santa Alleanza's been compromised in its abilities to keep a secret?"

"My job, Mr. Favignana, is strictly to seek out potential fractures. To stop them from spreading. This is in all our interests. To avoid... things before they start to metastasize. Quid pro quo, Mr. Favignana. Help me help you."

"Good for you. Now let me explain things in a way you'll be able to digest. This isn't a matter of bean counting. An audit to my—to the Santa Alleanza, is by its very nature a great big malignant *thing* that poses a risk to this mission's integrity infinitely more than any brief internal hiccup it may or may not have experienced as of recent. For example, Mr. Lazare, me providing you will field reports now places information that would otherwise be shielded out into the realm of whoever wants to see it can. But if you had any concept as to what I'm talking about you'd know the very nature of the service I provide the Holy See can *only* be obtained through absolute anonymity and surreptitiousness. Thus, Mr. Lazare, the nature of *intelligence.*"

"You're not going to cooperate are you, Mr. Favignana."

"Not if I can help it." Domenico turned and headed back toward the building.

"Mr. Favignana?"

"Quid pro quo," Domenico said, not looking back.

~ ~ ~ ~

Inside the building, and away from that insufferable bean counter, Domenico placed his call.

~ ~ ~ ~

Within her office, Lucia accepted the call, half expecting, half not-so-much expecting it. "Domenico—yes—I gave our Swiss friends a copy of the incident report. Why—because they *required* me to. He told him *what?* No—you *didn't* warn me at the beginning, Domenico—you said skeletons in the closest. *Not* an entire goddamn graveyard under the bed! That's the bed you've made. Sleep in it."

She abruptly ended the call. Dropping her phone with a mild thud, her fingers slid across her desk to the photo there in its expensive crystal frame. It was a glossy black and white of Oliver, sharing an intimate embrace with her. Their lips were locked as one.

You threw him to the wolves, without so much a warning, Domenico... "Quid pro quo, Domenico. Quid pro quo." She drained the rest of her drink and smiled darkly, spinning the remains of the ice within her glass around and around...

Men of Their Craft

*C*amorra stepped off the private plane onto the steps, with Cairo International Airport sprawled out before him. On his cellphone's screen was the single text, 'Here'. He hit send, transmitting the lone word to Domenico, in Tarxien, Malta, 1,058 and one-third miles away, precisely.

Parked not far from the plane was a man leaned quite comfortably against the hood of a Nissan sedan. He wasn't remarkable in appearance and had a face that could blend in most anywhere. Like the car, his suit was tidy and economical.

As Camorra approached, he offered him his hand. Camorra shook it.

"Good to know you, Camorra, I'm Omar Taleb. I'll be your contact with Egypt's General Intelligence Service."

"The Mukhabarat."

"You've heard of our humble agency then."

"The GIS has been known to give Mossad a run for their money every now and again," Camorra said. He needed this man's cooperation, and a compliment upfront was favorable. Besides, he could afford to, as it'd been wholly sincere.

"Yes, well, thank you, Camorra. Our strategy is the reverse of the CIA. Instead of playing incompetent, we like to advertise our strengths."

"Mr. Talab, the list."

"Oh, quite right," said Omar, pulling the sealed envelope

from inside his suit jacket. "It's short." He presented Camorra with the envelope and car keys. "A Nissan Sunny, in silver, as requested. Most common car in Cairo."

Camorra got in, and with razor-precision, opened the envelope. "Short list." A lone name stared back at him. "That's his residence or business?"

"Both."

"Intel's thin."

"It is. Works with his hands. Stays out of the daylight. One of those creatures of the night. Adverse reactions to sunlight and so forth. You know the *kind*. Well, nothing else on him aside from that, I'm afraid." Omar presented a business card. "Call. For anything at all."

Camorra closed the door. Tapping his finger on the card, a thought occurred to him. He lowered his window. "There is one thing."

"Yes?"

"Project Crystal Ball. The one the GIS says doesn't exist, that they don't use to backdoor their way into any app and nearly any database connected to the internet. That one."

"Yes. It doesn't exist."

"That's great to hear. Because it'd be just the thing to use to access the Rideshare Services Records Archive of INTERPOL's that they say doesn't exist either."

"Since it doesn't exist, I wouldn't be cross-referencing Nuri Matar's address with recent rideshare activity, would I?"

"That's exactly what you wouldn't be doing. Say, records for the past twenty-four hours." Camorra raised his window and sped off toward the security gate leading out of the airport.

~ ~ ~ ~

In the large and more than moderately messy workshop, Howie, Ingrid, Tom, and Mike admired Nuri's craftsmanship. Their four custom designed oxygen tanks sat aligned neatly on the concrete floor.

"You got these finished fast," Howie said.

Nuri, a bit past middle-age, looked as one might think one would look with being a craftsman who'd made his living on the backstreets of Cairo. All his life, he'd crafted things others could not for people who valued deeply their personal privacy, as well, their needs for such things. He accepted the roll of cash from Tom.

"Wasn't from scratch, my friend," he said. "Had this design laying around from a prior customer." Not counting it, he stuffed the money into his pocket. "You're going under the plateau? Under the pyramids?"

"What makes you say that?" asked Howie, exchanging glances with the others.

"Oh," he said, forcing a coyness, "the design for these was for someone who needed such a tank for going underneath the Great Pyramid a few years back." He had their attention. "Just saying, Howie, because this guy's the only one alive who's actually seen where it is you seem to be going."

"This information's only of value," said Howie, "if this someone's in Cairo right now."

"Value, as in finder's fee?" Nuri, less than subtly, asked.

Howie nudged Tom, and Tom produced another roll of cash. Nuri started to dig through the paperwork and various pieces of strangely shaped metal, both strewn and stacked across his many worktables. Toppling over a particularly tall stack of books, he dug a dictionary-thick hardcover out. He plopped the book into Howie's hands.

"*Kemet and Beyond: The Correct History of Egypt... Volume One,*" Howie said, reading the title. He flipped the book over, scanning its rather dusty dustcover. "Qeshaun Yousef, PhD, EdD, STD. Distinguished Professor... Modern Sciences and Arts University, Cairo." He handed the book to Ingrid.

"The Cairo part's still up to date," said Nuri. "Not the professor part. Even with being tenured, the university pushed him out after he published this exact book. Suffice to say, what the book had to say, less than diplomatically challenged academia's established version of the historical record."

"No volume two, I take," said Howie.

Nuri returned to digging through the heap on his desk. "Afraid not."

"STD?" asked Tom.

"*Sacrae Theologiae Doctoratus,*" answered Mike. "Doctorate in Sacred Theology."

"Will he want to go along you think, down there?" asked Howie. "I mean, if my team here is okay with that?" He turned to them, not seeing any objections.

Nuri tore a page from one of the many address books piled on the metal table before him. "Hard to say." He gave the page to Howie. "On account of his hand."

"Hand?" Tom asked.

"Lost some fingers when he went underneath the pyramid," Nuri said.

The way in which he said it gave Tom a true chill. "Like from a rock—being crushed or something?"

Nuri shook his head. "Spiders." He lost himself in a blank gaze for a moment. "That's the legend anyway."

"A guide with actual experience down there," said Ingrid, "obviously, is to our benefit. Just..."

"If you're concerned about his pontifical degree in theology," Nuri said, "Qeshaun holds no loyalty to religion. Of any kind. I assure you."

"And I vouch for Nuri's judgment here," Howie said.

"I second that," said Tom.

"Okay," Ingrid said.

"Can we just go back for a minute to this spider issue," said Mike.

"Mike hates spiders," Howie said.

"Almost as much as you hate confined spaces," said Tom.

"Sounds like you've got all the wrong bases covered in that case," Nuri said. He finished packing their equipment into a large tote. And hefting it up, handed it off to Tom. "Good luck with your tour down there."

"Thanks," Tom said.

Opening the old refrigerator against the far wall, Nuri revealed a small arsenal. "I always practice safe business. Considering the kind of people after you."

"Is that a Glock 41?" Ingrid asked.

Nuri removed the gun from the fridge, passing it over. "Indeed."

She slid out its loaded magazine.

"On the house," he said. He pulled two more loaded magazines for it from the fridge and set them into Ingrid's hand. "That address I gave you, Howie, it'll lead you to the shop Qeshaun now runs." He looked at the clock on the wall. "If you hurry, you can still just catch him before he locks up."

"What kind of shop?" asked Howie.

"Near the pyramids," answered Nuri. "From time to time, he's been known to do what you might call unofficial tours... If he were to find the service fee well enough."

"Unofficial is just our kind of holiday," Ingrid said.

Nuri turned on his heels, and holding up his finger, tried to decide which of the three desks along the wall entirely covered in junk it was. Yanking open the drawer from the middle desk, one item at a time, he expelled the most random objects imaginable, until he'd located what it was he wanted.

He handed Howie a wooden, triangular-shaped token. "Give this to Queshaun, so he knows you're officially unofficial. As well, I'll let him know you're headed his way. He's... what you could call cautious. If you know what I mean."

"We all know how that is," said Howie.

"That I do. That I do," Nuri said, revealing the gleaming .44 beneath his shirt.

Choosing One's Battles

*T*he Nissan stopped behind the industrial building and Camorra got out. He quickly scaled the power pole on the corner of the lot. Reaching the right height, he leapt off. His fingers caught the window ledge of the building there. Crouched, he calculated the distance to the roof's edge above him. He launched his body upwards with the power and ease reserved for a tiger, not a man.

Inside his workshop, Nuri watched the monitor before him. Its blinking red light announced the triggering of one of his many motion detectors. This was the backstreets of Cairo, and he had no shortage of complicated clientele. Switching channels on the monitor, he displayed the building's numerous camera feeds.

Surely enough, there was a man on his roof. Using the PTZ control, he zoomed in. He hadn't survived this city and this business, being naïve enough to believe in coincidence. His most recent clientele were being pursued by the darkest parts of the Vatican, and here was this man now... He zoomed closer. Yes, this intruder held a gun. And judging from the skillful footwork as he crept so silently, this was surely a professional.

Nuri's eyes shifted to the .44 tucked into his own into waistband. His fingers danced lightly along the cold metal of the big gun.

"Nuri, Nuri, Nuri... when presented with a true Spartan,

bravery, it does *not* pay," he said, imposing the words onto himself more than simply speaking so. "Come, old man, time to survive another day." Pulling his hand away from the .44, he set a cardboard box over the monitor, concealing it.

With both palms pressed against the edge of his central workstation table, he slid it away, revealing the hole beneath. Climbing down the ladder, his hand took hold of the cable hanging at the bottom. With a swift tug on the cable, the table rolled back, covering his tracks.

Camorra dropped from the now open skylight into the loft above the workshop. As if sound waves paused only for him, he landed not just silently, but void of existence itself. Even the air, unmoving, seemed not to acknowledge his presence. Gun aimed, he scanned for life. There was none. He descended the stairs to the workshop.

Things were far too disorganized. In terms of time, the cost-benefit of searching this place wasn't favorable. Removing his phone, he saw the address Omar had just texted him. His mind photographed it.

Heading for the front door, he knew whatever this craftsman had built for his prey, it'd be something they would've needed to get off the street and to their hotel room as quickly as possible. It was more than ninety percent probable the Uber they'd taken from this workshop to the address Omar gave him was their hotel. Or, had checked out recently from. Either way, their scent was fresh in the air...

Grave Robbers and Scholars

*T*he Uber pulled out of the alley. Merging left, it went down the main street of Aswan Giza. The four of them watched from their respective windows, up at the fog-kissed outline of the Great Pyramid. It sat perched in twilight's ever darkening sky.

The five-minute drive to their destination felt like an eternity, as if each of them had some invisible and unbearable pile of bricks shackled to their very beings. The Uber made the sharp right onto Al Haram. Their anxious silence was broken by the squeal of the brakes as they came to a stop dead center within the deserted traffic circle.

With anxiety both pushing them forward and pulling them back for the journey ahead, they removed their equipment from the trunk of the Uber. Howie, without thought nor notice, took the lead, as they headed across the street. A police car passed in the oncoming lane. Unnoticed as ghosts must be, their group of four continued to the other side.

There, where both a curb and sidewalk should have been but were not, sections of metal fence in every form and kind, collaged together, separated the road with the walkway of dirt and broken concrete. The four of them found their way through a gap in the fence. They continued onward, over and around the various barriers amassed from decades of perpetual construction. It was self-evident these repairs were never completed nor done at a rate ever quite matching the speed of decay now surrounding them.

Ingrid had experienced poverty up close and personal in

Haiti, but nothing before like this, not on this scale. "There's no middle ground in Cairo, is there."

The sprawling luxury resort of the Marriott Mena House directly across, on the opposite side of the street, fortified behind its beautifully marbled-wall, with its extensive, manicured lawn and palms manifesting a modern utopia, all the more contrasted things.

Tom pointed up at the towering pyramids atop the legendary Giza Plateau ahead of them. "Not much changes."

They found themselves in that swath between two worlds, somehow the product of a single species, so divergent, it might have well of been from separate universes. To their left, the hopelessness of urban destitution, inevitable only to absolute decline. To their right, urbane luxury.

"Don't judge too quickly. Egypt's a complex place," said Mike. "Being both part of Africa and the Middle East is no small balancing act."

The police guarding the Marriot's front gate took notice of them from across the street.

Howie quickened his pace, leading them. "Come on."

"Which one is it?" Ingrid asked. "They look the same."

"You mean, condemned," said Tom.

Howie double checked the map on his phone. He stopped at the next building, a little shop. "This brick one..." Three police officers stood a few feet past it.

"The one right next to the police station," Tom said. "Literally."

"Yeah, well, it's got to be somewhere," said Howie. Reaching through the gap in the metal gate covering the front of the shop, he knocked twice. Quite immediately, the door behind the gate cracked open. After a second, it drew inward, opening further.

Soft lighting escaped through the doorway to reveal the thin man standing there. His face was a patchwork of sunken folds of skin, more so than just wrinkles. The light and shadow falling across his eyes and lips made these lines appear even

203

more pronounced.

"Qeshaun, here," he said. "Welcome, travelers. Nuri phoned ahead, said you'd be on your way." He held up his left hand. It was missing two fingers. "I've shown you mine. Now show me yours."

Tom nudged Howie, and Howie dug the wooden token from his pocket and slipped it through the gate. Only after examining both sides of the worn-down coin did this thin man, Queshaun, venture out into the gap of a few inches between the shop's doorway and the gate. It was much too narrow a space for a person of ordinary weight to fit. But he did.

He peered out at the street in both directions before unlocking the metal gate. Howie pulled up the gate and Qeshaun led them into the little shop, more of crumbling than of brick. He snapped the door closed and locked it in ritualistic fashion, securing it with each of the locks spanning the door top to bottom.

"I'd much prefer not to know your names," he said. "Know mine though, and know Queshaun here's to stick a watermelon in your bellies." Tom frowned.

Mike leaned over to him. "Set at ease. Essentially."

"Oh," Tom said, not feeling at all at ease.

Queshaun led them behind the counter of the cluttered souvenir shop to the small yet neatly kept living area at the back. "Please, sit."

They set down their bags containing their equipment, then settled on the old couch along the wall. Each of the walls was covered in maps of Egypt. The ceiling was covered in star charts. The plywood floor was covered in more maps, hand-drawn, of nowhere in particularly recognizable. Nonetheless, these held a level of commitment and detail that demanded their own authenticity. But what stole their attention wasn't any of these things.

Atop the wooden table in front of the couch was a cat, very much mummified. The four of them looked at the cat, sitting there as any living cat may have sat. They glanced at each other and tried to do the impossible, not to look at the creature again for their duration.

Queshaun settled into the rocking chair across from them. "So. You desire a tour from Queshaun." He saw how diligently with their eyes they were avoiding his room's centerpiece. "Don't mind her. She's quite quiet. For a cat."

"She's... lovely," Tom said. "What's her name?"

Appearing somewhat taken aback, Queshaun said, "Cat." Mike rubbed his elbow into Tom's side, a silent plea to keep his mouth shut.

Howie smiled as politely as he could muster. "We need to access the room beyond the Subterranean Chamber."

"Oh, *that* realm. Not much to see. Simply put, just a big room with a strange carving along one of its walls.

"What kind of carving?" Ingrid asked.

"What Americans call a figure eight, remembering right." He began moving the wooden rocking chair back and forth, back and forth. He built a pace and rhythm that gave him an essence as though he'd always been, perpetually so, rocking within this old chair of his. "Hmm... that's about it really."

Ingrid held up the hardcover book Nuri had given her. "Yes, we've seen the photos in your book. What we're looking for is beyond that."

"That's quite impossible, my dear."

Mike leaned forward, but not too far, as to keep a safe range between his face and the cat on the table. "With respect, Dr.—"

"Please, titles are too pretentious for an old man like me," Queshaun said.

"Queshaun," Mike said, continuing, "I've lost all insight of what's possible at this point. And as a fellow academic, that *is* difficult for me to say."

"No doubt you're—all of you are apt in what you do. But, simply, there's a very large and very heavy stone wedged into the passage leading... beyond," said Queshaun. "Such things are quite stubborn to move, even for beautiful young women, and strong, exploratory men."

Ingrid set his book, open to a specific page, upon the table. Queshaun's eyes drifted to the sketch on the page he'd drawn years ago. It was incomplete, with the right side of the page entirely blank. Thanks to that very large and stubborn stone blocking the way, it was impossible to complete the sketch, to map out what was there, beyond. This was a fact he knew. Just as that great stone, it was unmovable, thoroughly blocking any ambitions to finish his life's quest, his mapping beneath the pyramid.

Though, he attentively watched as this lovely woman then placed a paper napkin near his book. The impossible had just become the possible. With his fingertips trembling, he aligned the napkin flush beside his own sketch, drawn from what felt many lifetimes ago. Hand-drawn on the napkin was the other half of his incomplete sketch. It was the unseen section, thus, the impossible-to-know-section of what did lay beyond that stone.

"Where did you get this, young lady?"

"From my mind," she said. "I mean, I just knew what was beyond the blocked passageway. I drew it all out after looking through your book here."

"I see," he said, very much not seeing any logic to what she'd just told him, but knowing she was, without any doubt, genuine.

She leaned over, resting her finger on the place along her drawing. "There, there's a secondary passageway. Concealed."

With an energized conviction, he rose from his rocking chair. "Let's go."

"It's the middle of the night...," said Howie.

"And what do you think, young man, *Queshaun's Unofficial Tours* take place aside troves of tourists? I wouldn't trade my house for an onion peel. No, I certainly would not! Come now, let's know ourselves an adventure!"

He slipped on his jacket and kicked off his sandals, switching them for his old boots near the back door. "Most certainly not, Queshaun goes when he goes." With his foot, he prodded at Howie's pack on the floor. "You've your goodies from Nuri's, so put a move on, will you kids, and let an old man to one last adventure. But do pay him first."

"Yeah, Howie," Tom said, "you heard the man. Visiting hours are for tourists." They took their packs in hand and waited beside Queshaun.

"*Yeah.* You heard him," Howie said. "Pay him, Tom."

Queshaun grinned, not for the money, but for the sensation of really feeling alive again. "And do keep in mind this old man has three ex-wives and thirteen children."

He could have been telling the truth or he could have been embellishing. Either way, none of them would've been surprised. Tom removed a stack of ten thousand dollars U.S. from his pack and gave it to Queshaun.

"You do understand," said Howie, "you're going to have to use that money to leave Cairo. The people following us, they're—"

"Dangerous," Queshaun said. "Yes, of course, Nuri explained. So, don't fuss, Queshaun's not swimming in honey here. I've waited a long time to leave these streets. So, this old man will have somewhere to go out to, into the countryside..." He stopped himself short of revealing anything more, and placed a call on one of the many and outdated cellphones scattered around the room. "Usif? Yes, I have tourists. *Very* well-paying tourists. Yes. See you soon."

They silently smiled, watching this eccentric and wonder man as he commenced to digging through the great clutter atop his refrigerator. Finding an oxygen tank identical to their own and flashlight, he shoved these into a backpack. Then, almost forgetting, he hid the money in an empty butter tub within the refrigerator.

"Doesn't anyone just keep food in their fridge anymore?" Tom asked, trailing behind, out the back door.

Rat and Mouse

*H*ere, within Cairo, this city of secrets, the very crown of Africa, agleam in shadow, the line between what should and what was, was nonexistent. Life shouldn't have been so difficult, but nonetheless was for those born into it, under death's silhouette. Only a few were spared this fate, and only by random chance if their surname was of the right pedigree or economic viability. This unspoken law which governed the desert and its people during the times of the pharaohs was no less true today...

The silver Nissan began to pull into the alleyway. Two police officers awaited, posted guard next to their military-style jeep. And maybe it was an actual military jeep. For what was and who was the military and that of the police was hard, very hard, to discern.

Camorra lowered the driver side window of the Nissan when the police approached with their AKM rifles. He recognized the gun, knowing it to be a little cheaper variation than the standard model AK.

"H10 Pyramids View?" he asked.

"To the left," one of them answered.

Camorra drove slowly down the alleyway, bordered by echoes of dreams long lost for a better tomorrow, stray dogs and stray people, and trash. All of these, discarded, mere remnants, now without purpose. Putridness, decay, and peeled paint framed the buildings as he moved deeper into it all. Sawed-off water jugs lead the way. Each brimmed with cigarette butts, like communal offering plates that only ever collected these burned down and burned-out stubs.

To his right was something less than a restaurant, though more than a convenience store. Next to its dent-canvassed door, the sign in the window, 'Mouse's Den', was as fitting a name as any he'd seen. Maybe his prey were inside now... It held no customers.

A little further down, on the left, he brought the Nissan to a stop. Set back several feet was the hotel known as the H10 Pyramids View. Like the poor state of the Mouse's Den, this place wasn't what it was in the traditional sense. It was something less than a hotel, though it provided the same functions, just barely.

The building was a mismatched ensemble of smaller structures strewn together over time, each in various states of being. Somewhere within laid the hotel. The entire left face of the five-story building was open without a wall. Not that it was missing, because there it was, piled into forever-broken, smaller versions of itself in front.

Camorra entered the hallway strewn with dirt and litter, and worse. Doors, every few feet, which could have led anywhere into anything, lined the hallway. It ended in a board propped against a doorless doorway. To his right was what may have been, by best guess, an elevator shaft, never having had an elevator. Next to this, a staircase, winding and disjointed.

Atop the stairs, he found the plaque on the wall, etched, 'H10 Pyramids View'. The hallway opened into a lobby which was nothing more than a cubby. Here was only a single wicker chair, wooden table with an antique radio upon it, old traveling trunk, and desk. It was something out of *Indiana Jones*, though was impossible to tell if it'd been deliberate or simply was. Behind the desk stood not quite a man, though slightly more than a boy.

Camorra held up a photo of his prey. The boy's eyes reflected recognition. Something else in his eyes too... It wasn't loyalty, but something less personal. Himself, many lifetimes ago, having been a boy of no means, knew the remedy.

Taking in the boy's name from his make-shift name badge, he said, "Ramzi, I'm looking for these four." He set a stack of cash upon the desk, calculating just the right distance between its placement and Ramzi. It was more than a year's wages for the boy. Whatever Ramzi's next decision, it would absolve, and thus justify, his own response to it.

"Know, Ramzi, the way of the world of man. There is no line separating good from bad. There is only belief. Money purchases loyalty effectively as it does betrayal. And in doing so, Ramzi, it frees oneself from the burden of man's falsely perceived morality."

He didn't expect the words, not in their entirety anyway to fully make sense, but speaking them would cause more than an impression upon the boy's subconscious. He waited, and once the boy's fingertips touched the cash, saw the desired decision had been reached. This was a decision that preserved a taste of innocence for them both. Otherwise, he would have brought upon Ramzi a deep unpleasantness, boy or not.

Crestfallen, Ramzi said, "I've been a rat, before... These four paid me not to tell."

"I recognize that, Ramzi. Take solace that integrity is a thing of luxury, and for yourself, this place, this thing you call life, misfortune robbed you of that luxury long ago." Ever gently, he reached across and rested a calm hand on the boy's shoulder. "Are they in their room?"

Shaking his head, Ramzi said, "No, they left half an hour ago." He gripped the money, now in his hand, keeping it close. The touch of it made it tangible, real.

"Where did they go, young Ramzi?"

"There's only one reason why people stay here," said Ramzi, turning to the small window behind him. For the first time, through it, Camorra took notice of the Great Pyramid there outlined in the night sky. It was literally across the street. He removed the small bag of diamonds from his pocket, and selecting one of moderate size, placed it on the coarse wooden desk. He peeled a piece of paper from the pad there and quickly wrote.

"Take it to this address, to this man, and he'll provide the amount I've written." Plucking the diamond from the desk, Ramzi stuffed it with the paper deeply into his front shirt pocket.

"Go now, Ramzi, and shed your shackles. And be." With a pivot, Camorra spun, departing the hotel. In the alleyway, he looked up at the Great Pyramid consuming the sky. "*Pyramids View...* You're only human, Camorra," he said, slipping into the Nissan.

The Plateau

Queshaun, leading the others, exited the rear of the shop, and stepped into the small concrete courtyard.

It contained only a broken-down truck on one side and half an engine block on the other. Not even weeds ventured through the fragmented concrete.

"Wow, all this is yours," Tom said.

"Don't exaggerate my status now," said Queshaun, falsely indignant. "It is ruins, yes, but I live amongst the shadows of the pharaohs." He patted Tom on the back with his three-fingered hand. "And sometimes, the shadows are a good place to be, my redheaded friend. Come, the shadows of kings await." He led for the metal gate at the far end of the courtyard.

This gate brought them to the vast lot behind the line of crumbling shops. They faced a graveyard of abandoned buses, taxis, and tuk-tuks, used up, broken beyond repair, forever cast away. On a path visible only to him, Queshaun took them through the dust-drenched labyrinth of vehicles and carcasses thereof.

Sitting very much in a ravine, the lot tapered up the hill. This hillside transitioned into the immense Giza Plateau. The space between the abandoned vehicles drew tighter and tighter as they grew closer to the heart of this rusted and dusty maze. Distant lights from the impoverished suburb known as Giza offered them little illumination. They climbed over the hood of a gutted police truck, and through a doorless 'fifty-five Chevy.

Voices from the police drifted to them. To their right, up past the embankment strewn with rubble, tattered clothes and trash, the police stood guard along Al Haram. This was the final checkpoint before the street curved leftwards and led steeply up, ending at the summit of Giza's renowned plateau.

Disrupting their gaze across the embankment toward the police checkpoint, Queshaun said, "Don't worry about them." He pointed to the pack of stray dogs bedded down alongside the bus at the center of the lot. "Worry about them." He headed straight for the bus and dogs.

"Didn't you just tell us to avoid the dogs," said Howie, chasing after him.

"Yes," Queshaun said. "It'd be to squeeze a lemon over yourself."

Tom turned to Mike, once more lost in translation.

"Bitter pill to swallow," Mike offered.

Reaching the bus, the dogs laid nested, within lunging distance. As quietly as possible, Queshaun opened the rusty door of the bus just wide enough to pass through. They crept up the old steps. Behind the others, Howie placed his boot onto the first step. It cried out with a sharp creak. He turned, checking the dogs. Surely, the largest of the pack opened one very big and very yellow eye.

This fanged creature snarled the others awake. With a viciousness and agility no dog should possess, he launched his lean yet muscular mass straight at Howie. Frozen, Howie stared at the dog's fangs speeding through the open air— Queshaun thrust the bus's glass door closed at the last possible moment. Slamming snout-first, the dog spider-webbed the glass, ricocheting off with the slightest whimper. He glanced to the rest of his pack, then walked it off as best he could, attempting to salvage his alpha dignity.

By memory, Queshaun located the hidden place along the bus's floor. Howie and Tom slid away the thin metal slab, revealing the hole beneath. Ingrid removed the night vison goggles from the backpack she'd been carrying and handed out a set to each of them.

Turning the night vision on, they descended the ladder inside the hole. Fifteen feet down, they dropped into the narrow passage. At four feet wide and just tall enough not to scrape their heads on the ceiling of dirt, Queshaun led at an impressive pace.

Howie couldn't tell if it was the surges of panic in his mind or if the passage was actually growing smaller as he coursed along. One thing was certain, it was becoming rapidly steeper as they climbed up and under the surface of the plateau for its summit.

The ladder awaiting at the end of the passage came into view. With having a three-fingered hand, Queshaun climbed the ladder surprisingly well. He rapped three quick raps on the trapdoor overhead. A lock released, then the trapdoor opened.

An arm reached down and helped Queshaun out. They followed up the ladder. Unbeknown to the four of them, they entered the headquarters of the Giza Plateau Security Task Force. With the room's lights blinding them, they quickly switched off their night vision.

"This is Usif, my unofficial assistant for my unofficial tours," said Queshaun.

In full guard's uniform, Usif stepped forward. "Captain Usif Riad at your service. Unofficially, of course. You can put fans on your hearts, all, as certainly Queshaun can spin yarn from a donkey's leg." Tom glanced at Mike and Mike shrugged.

Queshaun held up the night vision goggles. "Don't mind if I gift these away?"

"Please," Howie said.

Queshaun gave the goggles to Usif. "A tip, my friend, for helping on such short notice."

Usif opened the door behind him to the closet filled with

guard uniforms. "Should be a size for everyone. Please hurry." They swiftly pulled on the security uniforms over their clothes. Usif led them into a hallway, then through the service door, bringing them outside.

They couldn't help but take a moment of respect and admiration. The three main pyramids upon the plateau stood aligned in all their deserving majesty.

"You know they're big, I mean, you know, from pictures and everything," said Ingrid. "But seeing them in person... Nothing rightfully prepares you for the sheer scale."

Looking up at the trio of colossal stone monuments, or whatever they were or had been, the certainty their presence conveyed was unlike anything else. They seemed to have always been there in that place, even before the ground they rested upon had ever existed. Drawing away his eyes, Tom handed out the body cams he'd brought.

"How these things work?" asked Queshaun.

"Just hit that red button at the top of it... Great, you're recording now," Tom said. In preparation to create their testament for what truly laid beneath the Great Pyramid, they each did the same.

"We must hurry now," Usif said, "and stay right behind me. And, please, don't say anything to anyone when we get there."

In a line, they followed across the uneven ground made from what was dirt more than sand, with rocks of all sizes. Tom crunched loudly on his Tic Tacs as he chewed them by the mouthful. Howie glanced at him, annoyed, and Tom gulped down what remained. Mindlessly, as he often was with small things, he discarded the empty container, tossing it to the unique blend of dirt and sand and rock at his feet.

Seeing now they were heading for the northernmost pyramid, Ingrid stopped. "We're needing to go to the Great Pyramid," she said.

"And I am taking you," said Usif, midstride.

Howie nodded to the one they were on route for. "That *is*

the Great Pyramid."

Having to trust them as they all continued on, she followed, trudging through the sandy dirt. She gazed up at the central pyramid as they passed by. *That one had to be the Great Pyramid... Didn't it?* It was much more beautiful, she thought, than its two counterparts. It was even in considerably better condition.

Queshaun joined alongside her. "You doubt because you know the Great Pyramid to be the biggest of the three."

"Exactly," she said, gesturing up at the center one. "It's *visually* taller."

"So does the sun rotate around the earth."

"That's different," she said, more defensively than she'd liked.

He smiled. "Is the eye not smaller than the brain? Look again. Not at the top, as everyone does. Though at its base."

She took in the new vantage point, attempting to see what he meant... *It was so.* The center pyramid appeared taller because the ground beneath it was in fact slightly elevated.

"See, it is true, my dear. One of *many* illusions cast by our native pyramids."

They reached the bend there to the left, finding themselves at the front of the Great Pyramid. So close, they closed the last few yards. Usif shined his flashlight. About twenty feet up the pyramid, someone flashed back.

Like giant, uneven steps, they climbed the large stones until reaching the two guards. Neither guard bothered to give them a glance. They were much too occupied with the soccer game on their portable TV.

"A tip for my assistant, please," Queshaun whispered to Howie. He held up four fingers on his good hand. Howie nodded to Tom, who passed four hundred dollars to Usif. Who, in turn, passed a fifty-dollar bill to each of the guards. Who, in turn, slipped the money into their pockets, whilst not breaking eye contact with the soccer game. One of the guards handed Usif a ring of oversized keys.

The entrance was to the guards' backs, just a few feet away. Entirely dark and strangely inviting, it beckoned them to enter.

"Savor your last breath of fresh air for a while," said Usif, leading them.

Having never been inside, for Ingrid, the passageway was narrower than she'd envisioned for such a large structure. It offered only enough width for them to pass through single file. As well, it was much more winding than she'd thought it would be. *This was going to be a whole lot less comfortable.*

As they moved toward the center of the pyramid, the height and breadth shifted every few feet, with blocks jutting out here and there in an entirely random way. After, for perhaps three minutes of this, the passageway came to a pronounced fork. One way led steeply up, the other steeply down.

Usif stopped with a halt out in front. He searched along the guard's ring of keys. "This is as far as I go." He removed a key from the heavy ring. "Up is the Ascending Passage, leading to the Grand Gallery. Which is where, I dare say, less interesting tourists seek." He placed the key in Queshaun's hand. "And then, there's the Descending Passage in front of us. Because, my special visitors... Who needs giftshops when there are venomous snakes and spiders. And air not fit for the dead." He stepped aside, revealing the locked gate blocking the passage leading down. A dust-laden and greatly outdated video camera overlooked the gate.

"Don't worry, that hasn't worked in years," Queshaun said. He pushed the key into the oversized and thoroughly rusted padlock binding the thick chain coiled around the gate. With a bit of effort, he turned the key. Mike and Tom slid the chain free, then pulled the gate open, releasing a harsh and hissing creak.

Usif checked his watch. "You've got until dawn. Queshaun knows the drill, so be back here by then. Unless you want to become permanent residents." He removed another key from the ring. "You'll be needing this." Queshaun took the key.

"Enjoy your tour, brave ones," Usif ominously said, before heading for the exit.

The Great Pyramid

*T*he police truck stopped along the traffic circle. The Great pyramid towered in the background. Camorra exited from the passenger door. There was something in the air, in the way the soft breeze caressed the edges of the sand at his feet. He was close. He'd have his prey before the darkness fell to the rising run.

A man stepped from the driver side. He had the rank of colonel upon his ambiguous uniform. There was no name badge, for he was simply known as the Colonel.

He drew deeply upon a Cleopatra brand cigarette. "See, perfectly quiet. I feel your concerns for our great landmarks, well-intended, have been overly enthusiastic, perhaps."

"No," Camorra said, crouched low, his palm tracing over the dirt. His eyes scanned, seeking to separate his prey's footprints from the many crisscrossing the dark ground in every direction. He drifted away from the truck, following the footprints he'd chosen.

The Colonel's eyes, conditioned for an attention to detail, noticed something now. It wasn't that it didn't belong. It just didn't belong at this time.

"See that beige Renault parked across the way," he said. "That's Captain Riad's, of the Giza Plateau Security Task Force. Captain Riad only works dayshifts."

With Camorra's next step, his boot crunched on something. He fished the Tic Tac container from the dirt... The *orange* flavored Tic Tac container. His eyes surveyed the group of tracks near the container. They led for the Great Pyramid.

"You have equipment in the truck?" he asked.

"Yeah, sure. A TRK. Terrorist Response Kit."

"Bring it." Camorra went at full sprint toward the pyramid. The Colonel took a final draw on his cigarette before removing the oversized briefcase from the truck. He gave chase after Camorra.

For the first time in hours, the two guards camped out in front of the pyramid's entrance broke eye contact with their TV. Two men climbed the pyramid in their direction. The man in front they didn't know. But the other they knew well.

Whatever the reason that'd caused the Colonel to be here, it couldn't be good. Though it must involve that unusually large group Captain Riad had taken into the pyramid. At this point they were in trouble, and nothing could change that. They did what they could in that case. They returned their focus to the soccer game playing on their little TV. With the two men's arrival, the guards rose to attention.

"Did Captain Riad go inside?" demanded the Colonel.

"Yes, with a group," one of the guards said. "Only a few minutes ago, sir." Applause erupted on the TV, with the game's winning point. The guard scrambled for the remote.

Camorra took the case from the Colonel. "Wait here." And yanking the flashlight free from the guard's duty belt, he entered the pyramid.

Around the next bend, Usif saw the flashlight beam. He'd been waiting there just within the passageway. He spun and ran. Camorra accelerated after him. Usif reached the unlocked gate leading down. As quickly as he could, he slammed the gate closed and wrapped the chain through it. With the thump of Camorra's boots on the stone floor ever louder, Usif's fingers fumbled with the padlock's rusty hasp. The lock slipped, swallowed deep into the darkness behind the gate.

A flashlight beam fell upon him, illuminating his back. Methodical breathing joined this most unwelcomed light. Usif turned....

Way Down

S eeing Camorra there, Usif ran, taking the Ascending Passage up for the Grand Gallery. Ignoring him, Camorra tore the thick chain from the gate and kicked it open.

~ ~   ~ ~

Queshaun used the key to unlock the steel door blocking their way at the end of the Descending Passage. Collectively, Howie, Tom, and Mike pushed on the heavy door. With a creaking of hinges, it slowly surrendered. They entered.

"Welcome to the Subterranean Chamber," Queshaun said.

He shined his flashlight directly upwards. There was a massive shaft leading straight through the stone ceiling.

"Where's that go?" asked Tom.

"It comes out up about mid-center of the Ascending Passage," answered Queshaun. "But a stone is jammed into the top of that shaft."

"Like the stone blocking the passage beneath Subterranean Chamber," Ingrid said.

"*Exactly* like that one," said Queshaun. "Seems someone, or ones, sabotaged these access points long ago."

Spreading out, they realized the Subterranean Chamber was quite large. Ingrid studied her map of the passageways and chambers long-forgotten beneath the Great Pyramid.

"We're exactly dead center, under the pyramid," said Queshaun, pinpointing their location on Ingrid's map.

"When will we need the oxygen tanks?" she asked.

"You'll know," Howie answered.

Mike wandered to the other end of the chamber, sweeping his flashlight. He found the marking Queshaun had described, carved more than four feet deep into the bedrock wall. It was in the shape of a large... sideways figure eight, or since it was sideways, he realized, an infinity symbol... A very, very large one. It had to have been thirty—no forty feet across, and the width was at least three feet.

"What'd you make of that?" asked Tom, joining him.

"Not the slightest. But see that there," Mike said, pointing to the stains all along the wall and ceiling, twenty feet up. "How the rock is worn smooth wherever there's discoloration."

"That's from water, right?" asked Tom.

"Yeah, and a lot of it. This room, at some point, was filled." Mike lowered his flashlight. "Maybe our guide has a theory."

"This way!" Queshaun shouted.

"Guess that'll have to wait," Tom said. They caught up with the rest of the group at what appeared to be an ancient well shaft. Howie shined his flashlight inside. A metal ladder bolted to the rock led down.

"Well, a well." he said. "More darkness."

"I'd be concerned if it wasn't dark down there," Queshaun said.

"And that's the furthest any living person ever reached?" Mike asked.

"Me, being that person," said Queshaun. "It's what I like to call the Spiders' Lair."

Together, their eyes drifted to Queshaun's three-fingered hand. He took a spray bottle from his pack and gleefully saturated himself with the terrible smelling liquid.

He offered the bottle to Tom. "Spider repellant."

Tom took a whiff. "Smells like camel's piss." He squirted

some on his uniform. Passing the bottle, they all reluctantly did the same.

Howie climbed onto the pale stones around the well shaft. "As I like to say, let's just get this part over with."

Qeshaun seized his wrist. "When you see them..." His eyes grew large. "Kill them."

Pulling away, Howie ignited two flares, and dropped them into the shaft. It took several seconds for the flares to find the bottom. They appeared as little embers far below. Clipping his flashlight to his belt, he lowered himself down the ladder.

In the darkness, it was hard to tell how far he'd descended, but it had to have been thirty feet. Before the soles of his boots even reached the ground, he could hear the... scurrying. He shined his flashlight onto the source of this most disturbing sound. The floor appeared to be moving. But it was them.... Consuming over the floor of stone, only inches from his boots, they moved as a collective, as though a single organism....

Fear the Dark

*E*asily three to four or more times the size of any tarantula, with a leg span nearly as long as his own arm, the spiders Queshaun spoke of were surely there. And they were aplenty. Void of all color except for the cluster of protruding midnight-dark eyes at the center of their massive spider heads, they were white as bone bleached clean and dry. As much as he disliked taking life, of any kind, he disliked the prospect of being eaten alive less so.

He removed the lighter fluid and lighter from his pocket. The spiders were more concerned about their potential next meal than about whatever this fluid was. For they'd begun to use their very long legs to pull themselves onto the ladder, where their prey now stood.

Kicking away the massive spider legs reaching at him, he climbed a few rungs. Igniting a flare, he tossed it as best he could into the center of the horde. With a burst of flame, the flare breathed furious heat across the spiders. They dispersed with a sizzling scurry to the edges of the chamber.

Dropping to the stone floor, he found the original two flares. They shouldn't have burned out so quickly, but were. They looked as though melted by something hotter even than the flame they produced. Using the beam of his flashlight, he briefly surveyed the chamber. It was noticeably larger than the one overhead. He signaled with his flashlight to the others, and they quickly climbed down.

The remaining spiders crowded into a mass at the far edge of the chamber. They did something new, at least to all of them, excluding Queshaun. The spiders' bodies, in their entirety, began to glow with a milky translucence. Even the dead ones glowed in this way.

Focusing on her map, Ingrid tried to ignore this, and find their position. "I don't know which direction we're facing—Queshaun, where's the blocked passage?" He shined his flashlight at the wall twenty feet away. The light revealed a giant and rounded stone jammed nearly a foot deep into the very much square-shaped passageway along the wall.

"Talk about a round peg in a square hole," Tom said.

Ingrid checked her map, then turned to the opposite wall.... The *same* wall where all the spiders had tightly collected into a glowing mass. She ventured forward. Her four male colleagues hesitantly followed.

"You didn't mention they glowed," said Howie, punting a smoldering eight-legged corpse.

"Didn't want to scare you off," Queshaun said.

"Yeah, well, glowing spiders tend to be a dealbreaker," Howie said.

"For *most*," said Tom. "Smells like citrus, musky, and that odor lizards get on their skin."

"As usual, thank you, Tom," Howie said.

"What I'd like to know," said Mike, "is what do these things eat to get so big?"

"You mean, besides the souls of the dead," Tom said.

"Okay, boys, let's not discuss odors or eating for our duration," said Ingrid. She stopped a little over ten feet from the spiders. "Howie." Going no closer than absolutely necessary, Howie sprayed the last of his lighter fluid on the spiders. They started to circle him, with their big black eyes just staring blankly up. Those eyes, they reflected nothing back except their own darkness. Igniting a flare, he chucked it—the closest spider projectile vomited a web of something clear and liquidly, drenching the flare. As the flare sailed through the air, it melted into an oozing, web-covered blob. The spiders scurried back, leaving an empty space where the blob came to land with a splattering plop.

"You didn't mention they spit acid," Howie said, readying a flare with each hand.

Queshaun shrugged. "Didn't want to scare you." Howie threw both flares simultaneously, striking the spider horde center mass. The spiders burst into flame. Blistering and popping, they fled from the wall. As eight-legged balls of fire, they leaped, springing themselves several inches high with their massive legs. The ones that didn't burn to death in the process landed quite charred into the shadows near the base of the ladder, along the opposite side of the chamber.

At the wall, Ingrid booted away the dead ones. She crouched, searching the floor for whatever it was she hoped to find there.

"Anything we can do, my dear?" Queshaun asked.

She removed the compass piece from her pocket. "Watch for spiders." Sliding the compass piece across the neatly fitted and smooth stones which formed the floor, she didn't know what else to try. This pyramidal key had been their guiding light thus far, so why shouldn't it continue to be. As she searched on her knees, the others kept a close eye on the remaining spiders clustered near the ladder.

Tom threw a flare at one of the spiders creeping for them. "At the end of all this, should take one of these back. I mean, a dead one. Being a new species, you'd get to name it."

"At the end of all this, if an old man like me survives such a place as this..." Queshaun's eyes seemed a little penitent. "We know not, not really at all, what lays beyond these walls." Queshaun's honesty cut into Tom's upbeat sense of the world in a way which he didn't know quite how to respond.

"Got something!" Ingrid proclaimed. The compass piece was aglow in a most perfect shade of emerald. She wasn't about to tell them their chances of survival were dependent on a choppy blend of guesswork and hope. It wasn't even a matter of dignity. Just... she didn't want to further their own doubts. And she needed them to believe she held the answers. Because if they believed, then she could too. That, deep inside, she did hold the answers.

The others joined her. She held her palm atop the glowing compass piece. A magnetism coursed through it into her. This tingling and tugging traveled up her fingers, through her wrist. It seeped into her bones as easily as water to a sponge. This wonderful, prickling energy felt as invigorated branches growing and climbing, filling her.

"Just stay back, where you are," she said, not knowing what else to say, not knowing what the next step was to be. No one knew, so silently, they watched.

For the first time, she noticed the temperature of the floor where her knees were touching was much colder than the spot where her hand was alongside the compass piece. Then she saw why. This section of floor, about a four-foot by four-foot area, wasn't stone at all. The color, yes, and precisely so, was the same as the rest. But this single section was... With her free hand, she clenched a fist, and knocked upon it... *Metal.*

The resulting echo proclaimed the empty space beneath and beyond. Hot now, the metal was no longer solid, appearing evermore as frosty mercury, defrosting. Caused by nothing more than her own bodyweight, the compass piece sank, not far, perhaps a quarter inch. But it was enough, locking itself into place. Trying the only thing she knew, she gripped tightly, turning the compass piece. A distinct click of metal from somewhere below them released. By reflex, she jumped off the section of floor as it began to rise.

Behind them, as they all watched this, the spiders knew their prey were unguarded. More, many more spiders revealed themselves, having remained hidden within the crevasses all around, shrouded in darkness. Collectively, and exceedingly swiftly, both creeping and scurrying, they charged, going for their kill.

Oblivious to this attack, before the five of them, the floor panel rose exactly five inches. At one end, somehow attached by an unseen hinge, the four-foot-square section rotated out and away, revealing the hole beneath which led straight down. They venture forward, their flashlights collectively aimed into this entirely vertical passage in the floor—the largest of the spiders struck Mike, toppling him. They faced this ambush of horror as the rest of the sprawling field of spiders attacked.

With a scraping scoop and flick of its legs, the giant spider rolled Mike onto his back. Perched over his face, it hovered, tense, ready to spring, to release its final act... its finale of death. It pressed down a little further, leaving a narrow inch indeed between him and his prey. While the others fought for their lives against the swarm of starved spiders all around, Mike stared up at his pending death, frozen in equal measures of shock and terror.

The spider, overhead, gazed down as if savoring the moment, with its cluster of black eyes, in its prehistorically arachnid way. Its translucent ivory-like fangs slid out, fully revealing themselves. He could see the translucence of the fangs darken as they quickly filled with the acid naturally generated within this perfect and terrible predator.

Its fangs were no longer translucent, but bone white as the rest of its overgrown body. And this hideousness incarnate was now ready to inject its liquid fire into Mike's outstretched and exposed neck. His carotid artery pulsated, as though hypnotized with a dreadful longing for the fangs of the spider....

Forbidden Kiss

*M*ike's eyes involuntarily clenched shut. In self-imposed blindness, he waited for the terrible end—the sound of the gunshot yanked his eyelids open. Fragments of spider splattered. Acid spurted from its decapitated corpse as it came toppling down right for him.

Howie yanked him out of the way. The spider hit the floor, spewing a fierier pool of bubbling death. Gripping Tom's single action Colt, Howie fired the remaining five rounds into the swarm of spiders rushing Mike and him. He threw the empty gun to Tom and pulled Mike to his feet. Tom swiftly reloaded, firing into the seemingly endless spider horde.

Ingrid dug through her pack for the bolt gun. Finding it, she turned to shoot, but tripped. The gun fell into the hole in the floor. Queshaun dumped out his pack, and grabbing his own bolt gun, fired, anchoring a bolt near the hole. With Tom and Mike battling the spiders, Howie locked a carabiner through the eye of the bolt. Ingrid immediately secured the rappelling line. Howie ignited a flare, throwing it in the hole.

As an entangled mass of legs and hate, the spiders made their final charge. No time for thought with who went first, Queshaun scrambled down the rappelling line. Then Tom, Mike, and Howie, while Ingrid ended up last.

"Hope they don't decide to use their acid on the line," Tom said.

"Why would you even think of something like that!" Howie shouted, climbing down.

"Uh, guys," Ingrid said.

Howie froze. "The compass piece."

She went back up the line. "Howie, follow me."

Queshaun handed up his now nearly empty pack to Tom. "It's water proof, flame proof. And hopefully, spider proof." Tom passed it off to Mike, who passed it to Howie.

The spiders covered the hole. Their grotesque legs dangled down, feeling, probing for anything they could devour. Ingrid stopped climbing, barely out of the spiders' reach. With one hand gripping the line, Howie pulled his knife from its sheath. He sliced an opening through both the top and bottom of Queshaun's pack. Losing the knife, it sailed down, sweeping past Tom's ear, past Mike, then nearly hit Queshaun as it continued.

"Head's up," Howie said, very much after the fact.

Tom glared up at him. "Thanks for the warning."

Taking the pack, Ingrid slid her arm through it like a warrior's bracer. "Hold my butt."

He'd heard clearly, but lost as to why she'd said it. "What?"

"Just do it!" she yelled. He held her. She released the rappelling line. Her weight pressed down into him, and he did his best to prop her up. Igniting her last flare, she thrust up through the mass of spiders with both hands. With her arm enveloped by Queshaun's pack, her hand protruded out the top. She gripped the flare, fighting off the spiders. Her other hand found the compass piece still locked upon the elevated floor panel. Her fingers couldn't quite reach....

She pushed up further. The spiders moved in, seeing their prey's head was now in view. Her hand took hold, and unlocking the compass piece, dropped it to Howie. Barely catching it, he stuffed it inside his pocket. The spiders' legs and mouths rabidly tore at the pack thinly shielding her arm. She slashed back with the flare. Thoroughly, they spewed their webs of acid. One of the cleverer spiders pinned her arm against the floor with its legs. The others converged on the pack, soaking it. Her arm became exposed as the material melted away. The spiders' midnight eyes stared upon their prey as it hopelessly struggled. Their retractable fangs rapidly extended, swelling with acid, glistening down, so close to her bare flesh....

Slipping, Howie lost his footing against the wall he'd propped himself against—his grip on the line broke free. Falling several inches before regaining hold, he'd left Ingrid dangling, with her arm pinned by the spiders—the sudden jolt tore her arm from the spiders' clutches, sending a searing pain through her shoulder. She shared a second of wholly unpleasant eye contact with the closest spider as gravity sucked her away. The spider spewed, hissing, sending forth a sizzling stream. A dime-sized blob of acid struck her forearm with a stabbing burst.

As she fell through the empty and dark air, she screamed in horrific pain from the spider's kiss. She sailed past Howie. He reached out, missing. The acid cut through her uniform. It burned away the cells of her flesh with the graceful ease of melting ice. She plummeted past Mike, then Tom. They failed to stop her fall most terminal. The acid made its way to the meat, cutting a hole deeply into her muscle at the center of her arm. As it devoured her flesh at a speed matching her fall, her scream stopped. For the pain now was too great to continue even in proclaiming it. She closed her eyes, accepting the hateful embrace of stone awaiting her....

Someone caught her. Her eyes opened. Submerged in darkness, barely, she could make out the deeply weathered lines which consumed Queshaun's kind and creased face. He pulled her with a strength even he didn't know he possessed, bringing her back to the rappelling line. She took hold of the line with both hands and did the best she could to block out the burning pain, which truly was the most excruciating of her life.

Leading them, she climbed down the remaining twenty feet to the stone floor below. Sweeping the area with her flashlight, and with no spiders in sight, only then did she examine the burn. All she could tell was it was deep and hurt tremendously so. She tore a piece from her uniform and wrapped the wound. Moving close to her, Howie cringed, catching a glimpse before she finished dressing it.

"I'm...," he started to say.

"No," she said. "Don't be sorry. I wouldn't have an arm otherwise." His hand on hers, her eyes drawing him in, they stepped close....

Off the Map

*I*nsensitively, Tom pushed between them. "We're here."

"Let's figure out where here is," she said, removing the map from her pocket. Before they could, collectively and suddenly, they had the onset of intense headaches.

"Now?" she asked.

"Now," said Howie.

As quickly as they could, they strapped on their compact oxygen tanks. Qeshaun handed out the digital watches that monitored their tanks' oxygen levels, and they secured them to their wrists.

Howie read the timer ticking down on his watch's display. "Everyone's got three hours."

"Let's just hope that's plenty more than we need," Mike said.

"Going to have to be," said Ingrid, returning her focus to the map. "According to this... We're in the final chamber."

"Then it, what we're looking for," Tom said, "whatever it is they locked away down here, should be here..."

"Who's *they?*" asked Queshaun.

"The L' Entita," Ingrid answered.

Queshaun didn't believe his ears, but after what'd he'd experienced with these strangers so far, he hadn't much choice. "You didn't tell me this was about *them.* The L'

Entita."

"Didn't want to scare you off," Howie said, patting him on the back.

He headed for the closest wall. There was something there upon the surface. The others joined him.

"Water stains," Howie said.

"Tom and I saw the same thing back in the Subterranean Chamber," said Mike.

Queshaun ran his hand over the water wear that covered the wall. The walls, floor, even the ceiling, were smooth, worn perfectly so by vast amounts of water, he knew must have at some point, coursed through this great space.

"This whole place was submerged. With each of the chambers, one to the next, that we've seen," he said.

"It'd take a river, or a lake, for that much volume," Mike said, left with more questions than answers.

"Kind of like the Nile," Tom offered, following along the wall toward the far end of the chamber.

"No," Ingrid said. "Whatever the source, it had to have come from underneath and up. Not the other way around."

"She's right," said Queshaun. "Look at the direction of flow upon these markings. They travel up from the floor to the ceiling. All the way to the chamber we just came from, and further."

Ingrid left them and went to the other side of the chamber. "It's breathtaking..."

The entire wall, twenty feet high by at least fifty feet long, painted with pristine detail, showed both the Giza Plateau and surrounding Nile Valley in their prime.

"I've never seen something in all my years as well preserved, not even close," Queshaun said, approaching tears.

The immense mural depicted the pyramids upon the plateau encased in brilliant white granite. This was, of course, how they each knew the pyramids to have originally been. What they didn't know of was the vast moat revealed there, brimmed with water surrounding the Great Pyramid.

The ruined path which remained today, running between the Sphinx and the Great Pyramid, was, according to the mural before them, no pathway for foot traffic. It was an aqueduct which channeled water from the pyramid and down the steep hill there to the Sphinx. And there was not one, but two sphinxes, with moats of their own.

"My god," Queshaun said, "look at how close the river was, not just to the top of the plateau, but to the pyramids themselves."

"Modern estimates are off literally by miles," said Mike.

"Off by miles, like virtually everything they believe about the entire region," Queshaun said. "Our—what do you call them, body cams, they're getting this?"

"Yep," said Tom, "every last bit."

Ingrid, having wandered off further down along the wall, noticed something out of place. Within the sprawling mural, the rising sun with its crown of thorn-like sunrays blossoming up, there was another image, lightly painted around the sun. She shined her flashlight directly on it. *Yes...* There was what appeared to be the outline of a book which neatly framed the sun.

Even on her tiptoes, she could not reach the place there several inches or more above her head. "Hey!" They quickly went to her.

"I need to get up there," she told them.

"To the sun?" asked Howie.

"To the sun," she said.

He saw now the soft outline of the book encasing the rising sun overhead. "Sun Book. Subtle. But I can't reach that. That's nearly seven feet high."

"That block over there," Tom said, going for the rather perfectly shaped stone block on the floor not far behind them. It was about twice the thickness and size of a standard cinder block. Howie followed him, wearily anticipating its weight. Requiring much less effort than he thought, he lifted one end while Tom took the other.

"What kind of rock is this?" he asked, pleasantly surprised.

"I know, right," Tom said. As they tilted the stone while carrying it, a wave of dust, which sparkled, slid off. Even in the uneven lighting from the group's crisscrossing flashlight beams, whatever the stone was, glistened with brilliant crystals. Ingrid directed them to the exact place to set the stone. She stepped up onto it. As if specifically tailored to her precise height, the stone aligned her perfectly with the rising sun.

"Huh," said Tom. "Almost like that stone was meant for that spot." Ingrid wiped away the layer of dust that'd remained on the painting of the sun for untold millennia. At it its center awaited a thinly grooved outline of an exact square.

"Compass piece," she said.

Howie removed the little pyramidal device from his pocket and handed it up. She locked it in by its square base. With a twist of her wrist, the compass piece turned. Below her, the painting of the Great Pyramid slid back, recessing into the wall eight, maybe ten inches. She unlocked and removed the compass piece, then jumped down. They entered this slender passageway along the mural. Their flashlight beams revealed only more darkness within.

Queshaun smiled, taking in this chamber. "Well, my dear, appears your map's incomplete."

"Wait, where is Ingrid?" Howie asked, his flashlight beam not finding her amongst them. Veins of light, which looked strangely like an immense circulatory system, began to flicker on all across the walls. These glowing veins were a gentle radiance of teal, bathing them all. The illuminated walls stretched for as far as they could see, revealing how truly massive the chamber was.

Within the new light, they saw Ingrid. She was near the hidden doorway they'd entered from. She'd placed the compass piece into the slot there on the wall, that she'd noticed, but they'd failed to. They realized now she'd been the one to activate this lush and gentle teal illuminating the chamber. She took a moment, falling under the spell of this place. It was beautiful, entirely so, all of it....

Gun raised, with oxygen tank and mask on, Camorra entered through the passageway, shrouded in silence. Without a word, he stood there, behind this woman, this modern version of the L' Entita. His fingers, snarling, talon-like, reached out....

Captive Survivors

*I*n a fleeting series of surreal motions, Camorra grabbed Ingrid, placing her into a neck lock while pinning her arms behind her. With his other hand, he took the compass piece from the wall and simply left. Adding to their horror, from the moment Camorra had taken the compass piece, the chamber door had begun to close. They ran as fast as they could. Reaching the door, its thick stone seamlessly locked flush into the wall, sealing them inside.

It couldn't have gotten any worse. Then it did. The serene blue lighting that branched across the walls faded. It wasn't just the death of the light, with that gentlest teal illuminating their way, that was gone. It was the extinguishing of their hope. They were nothing more than prisoners in the dark, captives to this tomb.

Hauling her over his shoulder, back the way he'd come from, Camorra mused at how perfect it'd been. And, yes, it'd been entirely uncalculated with both her and the compass positioned so opportunely near the doorway.

He set her down in front of the rappelling line hanging from the hole overhead. "Climb."

"And the spiders?"

"I killed them," he said dispassionately.

To be void of such emotion could only be from the sum of a life lived in solitude. This she understood all too well.

And she did not doubt him, not for one moment, knowing he'd killed each and every one.

She climbed. As she did, a realization arose, and one she hated. He and her held more similarities than she did with all the others now locked within that chamber combined. What she hated was this had forced an involuntary connection, a rapport with him. And that was infuriating. He was all the things she despised. He was... *Like* her. He was the last of his kind. She was the last of hers. He was a survivor. And upon reaching the top of the hole, she thought... *That's exactly what I'll do now. Survive.*

Something brought her to pause there along the edge of the hole in the floor. Even through her oxygen mask, the smell in the chamber where the spiders had been, but no longer were, was thick. It was an extremely bitter odor lingering with the pungency of melted rubber. The spent and strewn thermite grenade canisters told the spiders' terrible end. For she knew of thermite. Her grandfather had used it to clear their small strip of farmland in Haiti of boulders and stumps. Like those hard to eradicate things, the spiders had largely been vaporized by a heat only comparable to hell. Their remains, which still remained, were twisted knots of char.

Having climbed free of the hole, Camorra stopped her. Something was happening. She could feel it. Her heartbeat increased. A couple of paces behind her, he slid the tactical knife from its sheath clipped to his thigh. Hand gripping the knife, he crept, advancing on her.

Converged Divergence

*C*amorra leaned down next to where she stood, severing the rappelling line from the bolt anchored there. The line fell into the hole, landing in a coiled heap on the floor of the chamber far below.

Returning his knife to its sheath, he ordered, "Go to the ladder near the wall and climb." Keeping a single stride behind, he followed her toward the ladder that led up through the well shaft.

Unknown to anyone, concealed in the dark, Captain Usif Riad waited a few feet away. He clung to the bottom rungs of the ladder, hidden there within the shaft. Wearing the night vision goggles Queshaun had given him, the surrounding blackness appeared green. With the approach of their footsteps, he decided on the best course of action. Using one hand, he carefully removed his secondary gun, the .38 Special holstered upon his ankle.

Reaching the bottom of the shaft, Camorra again brought her to a halt. He shined his flashlight up into the thirty-foot-tall opening. There was only emptiness. He removed his knife, slicing the straps on her pack. It fell from her shoulder to the floor. He frisked her, finding nothing of consequence.

"Climb."

Not questioning his order, she climbed the ladder as quickly as possible. Reaching the top, a revolver was placed into her hand. By who, she couldn't see, but the coldness of the gun was most welcomed. She pulled herself up out of the shaft. Usif, there, gave her a nod, sliding off the safety on his service pistol. She fought the urge to lock back the hammer upon the .38. Camorra would surely hear it, giving away their much-needed element of surprise. And that they required, if they were to have any chance at all. Taking position on opposite sides, they aimed down into the well shaft.

Camorra's hands appeared first as he ascended from the darkness. There weren't many times during his life he'd known surprise or been outwitted. Though the female and that corrupt captain of the guard presently aiming guns at him from their strategically superior positions, had done just that.

Within a nanosecond, Camorra calculated all possible outcomes contingent upon his actions. Both targets were a little over four feet away. They had him perfectly situated in a crossfire. At this close of range, it was a certainty that at least one of them would deliver a devastating injury. He could neither release the ladder, as it was a three-story fall to the stone floor below. Worse, he had both hands gripping the rung before him while his gun was still holstered at his side. Those were the facts. And that was okay. He'd simply wait and let them be the ones to shift the odds to his favor.

Ingrid held the .38 tightly, having expected a violent response from Camorra. She'd been prepared to actually kill him. But he hadn't responded... at all. She wished she could have simply shot him right then and there, though she knew she couldn't without just cause. He revealed nothing except his impervious stoicism. Now she recognized this man's, the pure predator that he was, most dangerous quality. It was his unpredictability.

"Climb," she ordered.

Calmly, deliberately, Camorra climbed out of the well shaft. Now fully inside the Subterranean Chamber, standing on flat ground, he recalculated his options. Preserving a safe distance, they held their guns leveled on him. Circling around, Usif positioned himself at Camorra's back, and Ingrid stepped to his flank.

"You're left-handed like me," she said. "So, left hand on your head." Camorra did so. She began to embrace the empowerment the gun afforded. It felt good, in a less than good way.

"With your right hand," she said, "remove the compass piece from your pocket. Very, very slowly." As he did, she tracked every second of every motion. She adjusted her hold on the gun's handle, letting its contour settle in a most natural way amongst her palm, skin, and pulse. Her eyes looked past his actions, and beyond the surface upon which those actions spoke.

She watched the muscles along his throat, neck, and every place his skin was exposed. Despite his left palm, unmoving and flat upon his head, it could tell her much. Being his dominant hand, it'd be the first to reveal through involuntary movements any attempt for escape. This was where she'd hold her focus.

Having Usif to assist in this situation did little to alleviate her anxiety. And she felt as that old blind man from one of her grandfather's stories. It seeped into her mind now. The old blind man, fishing upon the sea, had caught a great shark. It was monstrous in size. But it sensed the man was blind. Concealing its strength, the shark allowed the old man to believe he'd reeled in a plain and simple fish. Once the shark was within striking distance, it devoured the old blind man in one merciless gulp... *The end,* as her grandfather always proclaimed so cheerfully upon conclusion of one of his colorful stories.

Continuing to track Camorra's movements as he ever-slowly removed the compass piece, she wondered what exactly her grandfather had meant for the moral of such a grim tale. She'd only been a child when he'd told her. But again, the blood-soaked stories of Biblical wrath Howie had been subjected to as a child in Sunday school were no less traumatizing. Though, being blind, at least the old man had an excuse for his folly. She had none.

Her finger tightened on the trigger. She didn't want to wait to give him the opportunity he needed to kill her. She had a purpose much too important. It was kill or be killed. That was the justification she needed. *He needed to die. Just do it. Do it now.* She could deal with living with it afterwards. Being alive with regrets was far better than being dead with none...

She exhaled. Her finger released some pressure on the trigger. She could do it she knew now, with shooting him dead. But that wasn't her. It'd forever alter her energy, her vibration of being. Now she *really* hated him. It wasn't for his unyielding pursuit to stop her from her life's goal. It was because he'd brought her to challenge her own character. And she'd nearly done so, and in the process, would have made herself even more akin to him.

"Slowly," she said, "slowly lean down and slide it to me."

And just when she'd believed Camorra's next action to be of compliance, and thus of predictability, it was not. He simply shifted the position of where his right hand was. He brought his hand from along where'd he just removed the compass piece out of his pocket, to now a few short inches over the mouth of the shaft. There, he held the compass piece hostage by nothing more than his palm and the threat of gravity. But it wasn't a threat. A man as he, of action, wasted no time with such hollow things. He'd let gravity have its moment. His fingers released the compass piece....

The three of them watched the effortlessness of the physics of it all. The beautiful little object was there, and then it wasn't. What happened next was that everything happened at once....

Usif's finger squeezed the trigger on his gun. Camorra's right hand, open at his left side and perfectly level with his waist, needed only a flick of his wrist. He sent his knife sailing out from its sheath. The blade sank into the side of Usif's neck. In the same moment, the crack of the bullet exiting Usif's gun reverberated off the walls.

Ingrid fired, deliberately aiming for Camorra's left

shoulder. She jumped over the pale stones which encompassed the well shaft, dropping into it. The bullet from the .38 hit high, though still found the flesh it demanded, and barely. It skimmed, lustfully raking, searing away a path of Camorra's skin.

Everything disappeared from Ingrid's view as she sank deeper through the shaft. Falling, desperately trying to wrap her fingers around one of the metal rungs of the ladder, guilt hit her. She'd just abandoned Usif, the very one who'd provided her this escape. The guilt grew outmatched, with a conflicting relief of no longer being forced to face Camorra.

Her fingers grabbed hold of a rung twenty feet down. The snap of her body, torn between gravity clawing her downward, and the will of her arm muscles refusing to release the ladder rung above her, the burn wound on her forearm erupted to life. As best she could, she lowered herself one rung to the next for the remaining ten feet until reaching the floor below.

A series of gunshots resounded throughout the Subterranean Chamber. Their echoes spiraled down the well shaft, flooding her ears with the possibilities of what'd just happened. The utter silence that followed was no less ambiguous.

In the dark, she found her pack on the floor from where Camorra had cut it off of her. She scooped up the pack. Removing her flashlight from it, she searched for the compass piece. It was half sunken into an entirely charred corpse of one of the spiders. Holding her breath, she fished it out, both grateful and disgusted the corpse had served to break the fall. She secured this pyramidal key of mystery into her pocket and ran. As she ran, she pulled the coil of rappelling line from her pack. She'd need it just up ahead, remembering Camorra had severed the line from the bolt there. She pushed her weary legs harder. Her fellow searchers of truth... Her *friends* needed her.

Archetype

*T*he anticipation surged within them both dread and hope as the hidden doorway slid back, opening. Tom steadied his Colt within his hands, leveled at whatever was to enter. Howie, boots placed firmly on the ground beneath him, took a stand. Mike, alongside his estranged son, knew what they all must know, that only the compass piece could open this door. And Queshaun, who'd lived a life's course nearly all by his own terms, realized he truly held no regrets having taken this final journey. There was only one question now. Was it the assassin who hunted them, or the woman with a veiled past, who'd guided them here....

Entering, Ingrid tilted her flashlight toward her face, revealing it was indeed her. Tom lowered his gun. She fit the compass piece to wall, awaking the veins of soft teal to illuminate the chamber.

"No time to explain," she said, removing the compass piece from the wall, returning it to her pocket. "Whatever we've come for, now is the moment." Seeing past the relief in their eyes, she noticed something else. "You found something..."

"We didn't have much else to do," Howie answered. "You're going to love it." He took her hand by nothing more than on impulse. "This way."

He led them all toward something beautiful... Something full of unanswered questions. The veined lighting along the walls became less and less visible as the walls themselves on either side of them drew further and further away. Until, finally, the width of the space was so great the walls couldn't be seen. After a stretch of crossing the expansive chamber, the beams of their flashlights illuminated what they'd found in her absence. She didn't recognize at first what she was looking at, other than it was stones, and a lot of them stacked row after row upon each other.

"Watch this," said Howie.

Collectively, they shined their flashlights up at the structure. It was a pyramid. The thin organic and amber-colored film growing upon it, covering it completely, began to glow.

Fully aglow, she could see the scale of the pyramid. It looked as though it could be a hundred feet long, and by that much tall. She didn't need to know the exact dimensions to know whatever they were, were perfect.

Her eyes arched up, following to the top. She realized the height of this chamber's ceiling was much, much higher here than from where they'd first entered. It was so high she could not see where the darkness above ended and the ceiling began.

What it must have required to build such a thing as this so far beneath the earth was something only her ancestors, the L' Entita, could have achieved. Before even having a chance to fully take in its beauty and brilliance, Queshaun ended their moment of pause, and began to climb the pyramid's face. They each climbed the stone blocks, leading higher and higher for the summit.

Reaching the capstone there at the furthest point, she saw this pyramid for what it was. It wasn't decorative or some kind of extravagant mock model. The pyramid had only one face, the one they'd just climbed. What was before them was a catwalk leading straight out from the capstone and onto a great platform, which was designed as a kind of observation deck.

She stepped to the edge of this deck, fashioned not of

stone but of metal, witnessing that which sprawled out two stories below them. "And I thought the mural was impressive. It—this must be two-hundred-foot-square."

"At least," said Mike.

The model there of the Giza Plateau and the Nile Valley, in its prime, was meticulous in detail and realism. Like the pyramid they stood upon, the entire model possessed an ever-thin layer of that strange organic substance, aglow in the warmest shade of amber. It gave the whole area a truly golden radiance.

The alarm for Ingrid's O2 monitor went off, declaring the last of her oxygen was about to be consumed. Having forgot about the ticking clock upon her wrist, she glanced at it. She was out of time. Mike's, then Queshaun's O2 alarms went off. Tom's began to beep.

Howie eyed the moss aglow upon every surface. Forced to take a gamble, he removed his oxygen mask, then carefully slid off Ingrid's. "There's air flow in here. Enough anyway."

They all removed their masks.

Ingrid drew her hand across the metal railing at the edge of the catwalk, collecting some of the glowing moss. "This stuff, whatever it is, we have to thank."

"We have your ancestors to thank," Mike said. "For having the ingenuity to use a plant which could provide both air and light."

"You're one of them?" Queshaun asked.

She'd never truly considered herself an actual member of the L' Entita. *But why not?* She *was* now somehow walking the same path they did so long ago... "Yeah. I guess I am." She led them single file down the narrow stairway, toward the ancient model.

"What're we looking for?" Howie asked, as they made their way to the bottom of the stairs, and into the series of catwalks which branched out several feet above the sprawling model.

"We'll know it when we see it," she answered.

They each followed a separate path. She ventured along one of the slender catwalks toward the Giza Plateau upon the model. She stopped directly over the Great Pyramid.

Dramatically oversized in scale, it towered over the rest of the model at around seventeen feet high and maybe, she thought, by twenty-five or twenty-seven feet across. She knew it had to be as good a place as any to search for her answers. The hidden doorway into this chamber was located within the mural's depiction of the Great Pyramid. So, there was a kind of logic to it, in hoping this model too held a similar pattern.

She only wished she knew—really knew for certain if she was actually thinking like an L' Entita, or simply pretending to... *Be one!* She sighed. *Ingrid, your self-doubt.* There it was once again. Was she, just as this pyramid model, nothing more than an archetype of the L' Entita, once great, now all but an extinct relic...

There wasn't time for this. Self-doubt was a selfish act. She must lead the others, and could not expect them to follow if she didn't even trust her own ability to navigate. While the others moved aimlessly along the catwalks further and further from her, and while in the wondering of it all, her eyes wandered across the mock model below her. A realization set in.

Her mind flashed back to the terrible moment inside the Tarxien cavern, with the death of the L' Entita. She'd yet to allow herself the luxury of shedding tears for them. The fact remained, just as she remained alive, she was the last of what remained of them.

Regardless, incomplete, not full in scale, or whatever else, she was the only version which existed. She was the only one who held the blueprint to whatever grand design the L' Entita had intended. That's what mattered now. Lost to her thoughts, she hadn't noticed Howie beside her, overlooking the Great Pyramid.

"It's the only one that you can see inside of," he said.

"Huh?"

"The pyramid... It's a cutaway." He pointed down at it. "See from this angle."

Sure enough, when she joined him, leaning her head over, tilted as he had his, it was true. Designed as a cross-section model, they could see each chamber and passageway contained within.

Taking her hand, he led her. "Watch your step, there's steps," he said. They followed down to where the steps came out at ground level into a broad and open space encircled by the model.

"You located something?" Queshaun asked, shouting down from the catwalk.

"Think so," Howie answered. "Ingrid found it."

He glanced at her and grinned, silently speaking to her he knew she hadn't the answers to everything they needed answers to. The tenderness within his eyes said this was okay. And his touch, from his fingertips to the top of her hand... Well, she wasn't sure. But it was kind, or perhaps something more...

A Pyramid Within a Pyramid Within

Queshaun joined them, interrupting what may or may not have been the beginnings of a moment. "What's this all made from?" he asked. "Not stone nor wood."

"The same unknown metal the compass piece is," Howie answered.

"Maybe it's unknown because they used it all building this place," Queshaun said. His curiosity trailed off, refocusing on the model. "Ah, yes, just as with the painting, the Grand Causeway of the Plateau there bridging between the pyramid and the sphinxes is not a causeway at all, but an aqueduct. Look at how reinforced it is. That was for water weight, not foot traffic, my friend. How has history missed that detail, I surely don't know. I missed it too."

Their eyes followed from the dry and dusty moat encircling the Great Pyramid, to where water would've channeled down along the aqueduct to the twin sphinxes below, with their own moats. There were other aqueducts as well, bigger ones which fed and led off from the moat surrounding the Great Pyramid. Though, these, if they held water, would have led it up to the very top of the plateau. There, the model depicted vast swaths of croplands. These fertile fields blanketed the entire area that should've been forsaken wasteland long claimed by the Sahara Desert.

"How were they generating enough pressure to overcome

gravity, and send the water up the plateau... To create all that farmland there in the model?" asked Howie. "Christ, they had an entire irrigation system rigged up. For miles... beyond."

"Add it to the list of history's unsolved mysteries," Ingrid said.

"For once, just once, I'd like to get some of those answers," Queshaun, giving way to his frustration, said.

"Hang around long enough, boys," said Ingrid, "and you just might."

Mike and Tom joined on the observation platform overlooking the Great Pyramid.

"Well, that's not to scale," said Mike, pointing to the pyramid.

"We noticed," Howie said. "Where were you two?"

"We know now what this room—or I should say, we know what this cave is," Tom answered.

"It's a naturally occurring space?" Ingrid asked.

"Yeah, it's pretty clear to see, over there a ways, where the model ends," Mike said.

"Then we're in the L' Entita's actual chamber," said Ingrid.

"Seems so," said Tom. "By the way, what this entire place, if you care to know, is an engineering station."

"Engineering station?" asked Howie. "You mean for when they built the pyramid itself?"

"No," said Mike. "An engineering station as to *why* they built the pyramid."

"Do tell, young man," Queshaun said, his curiosity welling up as to what they had to say of his native pyramid.

"It's not a tomb," said Tom.

"I could've told you that!" shouted Queshaun. "I *did*, as a matter-of-fact, in my book... That got me fired." He grabbed Tom by the collar, desperately craving the answer he'd hunted through ruins and books all his life for. "Tell me—what is it?"

"It's a machine," Mike said, offering nothing more.

"For *what*?" Queshaun asked, begging now. "What does it *do*?"

Tom shrugged. "Well, we don't know." He broke away from the old man, needing an answer he didn't have, nor was his to give.

"But it was made—designed to do *something*," Mike said.

"I came here for a lost library, and now you're telling me this," said Howie. "The Great Pyramid is some kind of machine. And that's *the* big secret of the L' Entita's?"

"There is a library," Ingrid said, with a sudden effort to comfort him. "At least, there was."

"Kid, all we can do is search and see what we find," Mike said.

"Well...," Tom, somewhat sheepishly, said, "we did find some books over there beyond the model."

Howie wanted to embrace Tom, hearing the news, as well strangle him for only now telling him.

Queshaun meekly placed his hand on Howie's arm. "Don't cut the corn before the harvest." He gave him a light squeeze. "So, one thing at a time, yes?"

Seeing the aged-wisdom within Queshaun's eyes, Howie knew he was right. He set aside his need for the moment to see what secret volumes of lost knowledge the chamber may contain.

He turned to Ingrid. "Should've asked before, but didn't want to bring it up."

"You're asking if Camorra's coming back for us," she said.

"Yes."

She gave the only answer she knew to be true. "I don't know. I mean, he could still be alive."

Howie noticed something particularly odd about the model. The amber glow of the moss covering the surfaces all around reflected differently off the Great Pyramid than on the rest of the model.

Realizing the same, Ingrid said, "The pyramid's the only part of the model not crafted of metal."

Mike leaned as far as he could over the railing. His fingers made contact with the dusty surface of the Great Pyramid below. "Stone, it's made of stone." Leaned over as he was, he saw something more... He ran his hand across the pyramid's dust-laden moat, uncovering the water stains beneath.

Helping hold Mike, now thoroughly hanging over the side of the railing, Howie removed a bottle of water from his pack and passed it down to him. Mike poured the water into the pyramid's moat, and Howie pulled him back up. Instead of doing what seemed intuitive, with running downhill through the aqueduct leading for the sphinxes, the water flowed through the front entrance of the pyramid. Its deliberately sloping passageway guided the water ever-deeper inside.

They watched, transfixed, upon the model as the water made the same journey they'd taken only hours earlier. Reaching the branch in the passageway, gravity led this little river steeply down toward the Subterranean Chamber. Building speed, it coursed through the well shaft within the floor of the chamber, then flooded into the room that'd held the spiders.

And that was as far as the water paralleled their own course. Unlike in reality, on the model, the large stone jamming the passageway along the wall was absent. The water shot through, funneling into the tunnel there.

It followed down along the right side of the pyramid, to where it channeled beneath the pyramid itself. As they tracked its course, the water flowed under the model's engineering station and continued to surge through the subterranean tunnel, straight for the other side of the pyramid. There, this massive 'U'-shaped tunnel upon which the pyramid nested, curved sharply upwards, arching the water along the pyramid's left side, and back toward ground level.

Though, before the water could return to ground level, it swiftly diverted into a much wider tunnel positioned there directly to the left of the pyramid. Obstructed, the water didn't flow through this tunnel, and instead quickly pooled up. As the dust dissolved, melting away, something beneath the water revealed.

Howie leapt, swinging over the side of the railing, dropping rather loudly onto the pyramid model. His fingers found the protruding object, a plug. No bigger than a silver dollar, it wouldn't budge. Using his flashlight, he knocked the plug loose.

At first, the water drained, just as they expected. Then, with the quietist and slightest of dribbles, water flowed upwards through where the plug had been. After a few seconds, a lot of water, much more than what the bottle had contained, rose up, flooding back through the passage in the opposite direction from which it'd just come.

"Missed your calling, Howie. Should've been a reverse engineer," Tom told him.

"Just have to settle for rewriting history, I suppose," said Howie.

The water, on reverse course, quickly backtracked along the 'U'-shaped tunnel, through the room with the spiders, up through the well shaft, returning to the Subterranean Chamber. Tom and Mike had forgotten about that strange infinity-shaped design carved deeply into the wall of the chamber until now, seeing it within the model. As the water level drew flush with the infinity carving, a distinct and profound resonance began.

Teasingly gentle at first, it rapidly grew. It bled out from the place upon the model in increasingly throaty bursts. The platform on which they stood started to sing in the same raucous tone, harshly coaxing their bodies into this forced harmony.

"What's happening?" asked Tom.

"Bet my beard it's going to be like jasmine," Queshaun said.

Tom stared blankly at him.

"Right, English...," Queshaun said, his voice vibrating with the resonance. "What's happening is happening perfectly. So, don't let it eat your face."

Letting out a sigh, Tom decided to simply embrace the

limbo he was inevitably finding himself in with the language gap. Returning his focus with the others, the water filled the Subterranean Chamber on the model. Though, instead of flowing up through the Descending Passage, it began to circulate over and over again within the infinity carving.

The water perpetuated this looped-course faster and faster, as though it'd be stuck doing so for eternity. As the water continued to flow into the chamber, though without flowing out, the pressure rapidly built. The faster the water circulated around and around the infinity symbol, the louder the resonance grew, becoming a roar.

"It's creating a compression of some sort," Howie said, guessing, not entirely certain. "Wouldn't you say, Mike?"

"That'd be my assessment," answered Mike. "To what end..." He shrugged.

Suddenly, upon having reached just the right amount of pressure, a vacuum formed, surging water straight up the shaft in the chamber's ceiling. As it accelerated its circulation around the infinity carving on the wall, the amount of water flooding the chamber dramatically increased, radiating out a frighteningly awesome resonance. And whatever was happening, was speeding toward climax.... The water shot out the top of the shaft, and into the much wider Ascending Passage above it.

Queshaun pointed to the place of intersection where the shaft met the Ascending Passage. "That's where the stone is presently jammed I'd told you about."

"Clearly, someone *really* didn't want the actual pyramid to be in operational order," said Howie.

Continued to be forced up the Ascending Passage, the water filled the space. It pushed higher and higher, entering into the largest of the passageways within the pyramid, the Grand Gallery. The Grand Gallery channeled the water ever steeper, for the top of the pyramid.

"It's going to enter what they've erroneously named the King's Chamber," said Queshaun.

"Then why they call it that?" asked Tom. "A pharaoh, nor body of any kind, was ever found in the pyramid. Yes, as it were?"

"Bet my beard, young man," Queshaun said, "nor any evidence there was ever a body or bodies. Or any indication the pyramid's intent *ever* was to be a grave." He frowned. "Hate to beat the same camel, but I wrote a book. And yet, if you question these things, my friends, these things they tell you with zero evidence, then these same individuals who dare don't deal in facts, they call *you* the crazy ones."

Fearing he was heading for a soapbox, he slowly exhaled, and subduing his frustrations, watched the water flow through the model. There was a certain satisfaction seeing it all physically so. *Nothing* was more tangible than the truth. No matter how much the rest of the world denied it, it still didn't change what was true. Before his eyes, the water surged into the extremely modest and crudely crafted space above the Grand Gallery, known as the King's Chamber.

At the very same moment, a shift in pressure allowed water from below within the Subterranean Chamber to travel up the Descending Passage. Reaching the end, it shot straight out the front entrance of the Great Pyramid, filling the moat there. While back inside the pyramid, the water swiftly consumed the King's Chamber.

Going the only place it could, the water raced upwards into the chamber's tapered ceiling. Clearly within the immense cut-away model, they could see the six stones positioned there along the ceiling. Each stone, equally spaced out from the next, sat horizontally so, one atop the other. Above the sixth stone was a shaft leading straight up through the exact center of the pyramid.

The water slowed, taking time to seep in around the spaces between one stone to the next. Upon the water's contact with the first stone, the humming resonance, still intensely pulsating, though they'd grown used to, abruptly shifted to something stronger, a deep and steady thumping. First their bodies, then everything within the cave, harmonized to it.

"Hey, Mike," asked Howie, "you know how big these actual stones are?"

"Ceiling's three-stories tall. Stones are seven, eight feet, I think," Mike said.

The water steadily rose to the second stone.

"Each stone is precisely six-foot-square, with six feet between them," said Ingrid.

They glanced at her.

"Let me guess," said Howie.

"No," she said, "not from my grandfather. I have... I have no idea how I know that. Things I don't even know, they're just... there. Crazy it sounds, I know..."

As the water eclipsed the fourth stone, their bodies grew numb by the terrific intensity buzzing and thumping through them.

"You can bet your heart and eyes, she's right on those dimensions," Queshaun said. "As well, in the ancient Egyptian system of measurement, the shaft there in the ceiling above the sixth stone is precisely six-hundred and sixty-six micro cubits in diameter."

"Six, six, six," Tom said.

"The most sacred number of the ancients," said Queshaun. "Signifying knowledge, understanding, wisdom, and enlightenment. Control over one's fate through a disciplined mind."

"The perfect inverse of its opposite," Ingrid said. "Seven, seven, seven, another sacred number of the ancients. Prosperity through luck. A life willed by chance."

"*That* you got from your grandfather," Howie said.

Surpassing the fifth stone, the pulsing deepened, completely subduing their senses, and triggering a truly mind-altering sensation. Reality felt less real. Their thoughts, abstract and freely shifting, were more certain than anything they could see.

Colors and shades faded, leaving everything a deeply paled

version of itself. They couldn't speak, unable to find their voice or be heard over the awesomeness of the sound. The stone model of the Great Pyramid seemed, or perhaps did change in appearance.

Its precision-crafted lines no longer appeared straight. They looked more and more as waves, drifting, shifting, bending, rippling out and away. Perception of depth and scale began to fluctuate.

In one moment, the model felt as though it was nearly large enough to be the actual pyramid. In the next, the cave surrounding the space they were in was several times bigger, or that they were considerably smaller. The incessant thumping, deeply screaming freely through their flesh and bone, through the stone, through the earth alike, grew. Anymore, and they were dead certain the atomic bonds holding their very bodies together would explode.

Then, the water swallowed up and over the sixth and final stone—

More than a Headstone

*A*s if a switch flipped, the rapturous vibration ceased. In its place, a numbness filled them. The calmest of hums birthed from the heart of the pyramid. Harmonics entirely soothing melted away the borders between themselves and what was around. All within the cave came to match perfectly in frequency of existence.... A hypnotic rapture most intimate.

Collectively, their eyes closed. All things hummed with this unified timbre, as though a single heartbeat. For the briefest of moments, all was still as silence washed over them, over the model, over the cave. Drifting out further, this tangible peace wafted into the earth itself.

Suddenly, upon the model, the water shot upward through the riffled walls of the shaft, spiraling as it surged for escape. Climaxing, it erupted out the top of the pyramid's capstone. On contact with the open air, the water transformed to mist.

As one, their eyes opened. A sublime euphoria constricted, tightening around them. It drew through their pores, inside their mouths and throats. Saturating their lungs, it brought them to be utterly re-energized, vitalized far beyond any long and deep sleep.

The pyramid's moat coursed with water, flowing down through the aqueduct to the twin sphinxes, filling their own moats. There were other aqueducts, larger, which branched off from the pyramid's moat. These led up the model's plateau, and continued far beyond the pyramid itself. Atop the plateau, at the furthest edges of the model, was an intricate irrigation system. It generously fed the patchwork of lush farmland there. The mist blooming out from the capstone had taken a life of its own on, blanketing across the entire model.

"Uh, guys, why is the mist glowing," Tom said, backing away. In an intensifying white, it did glow.

"What the hell were they doing here?" asked Howie.

Queshaun gripped his shoulder. "Oh my." His grin was broader than any they'd ever seen a grin could be. "Oh my..." Mike joined in the revelation. With a grin of his own, he turned to Queshaun slowly, knowingly.

"What they were doing, young man," Queshaun said, "I'll tell you what they were doing."

"*Not* a tomb to satisfy the whim of a lone dead guy, I take," Tom said, facetiously.

Queshaun shook his head. "No. Not a tomb for a guy who went through all that trouble, yet somehow forgot to place a single hieroglyph anywhere at all upon or within the Great Pyramid indicating it was for him. Or documenting it anywhere for that matter. No, my friends, once and for all, all this trouble and critically vital resources were not spent on a simple grave." He slashed his hand through the illuminated mist that'd now brightened the entire cave several times over. He held his grin, knowing he'd been right... *All this time.* "They were cloud seeding, my friends."

"Cloud what?" Ingrid asked.

"Cloud seeding," said Mike. "Essentially, they were pumping moisture into the air, creating, as well controlling rainfall... to manufacture ideal growing conditions for crops."

"After all, the Great Pyramid *is* a machine...," Howie said.

"Is it so hard to really believe," Queshaun said. "The greatest empire of the day, using their precious resources to build something as valuable as food production, as opposed to throwing it all away on the vanities of one man. One man, who had his children's futures at stake. His entire legacy... Dynasty at stake... Would he really have thrown that all away too? Come now, it's only logical, with the expansion of their empire, and of globalization, their food output would also demand and parallel that *same* level of expansion."

"Does make more sense," Tom said, "designing something so precision-engineered and complex to be, well, more than a headstone."

"They simply, or not so simply," said Mike, "combined fluid dynamics and acoustics to meet their agricultural needs."

"A ram pump in other words," Queshaun offered.

"Precisely," Mike said. "*That's* what the Great Pyramid actually is."

"Can one of you two PhDs," asked Howie, "kindly illustrate to us grave robbers, whatever a ram pump is?"

As they'd been speaking, the water pressure within the model had been steadily growing, bringing the output of mist atop the pyramid to its optimal and maximized levels. With it, the accompanying resonance had also been increasingly into something of what a few hundred trombones would have sounded like clustered together inside this cave.

Mike progressively elevated his voice while he tried to explain as simply as he could. "Avoiding getting too technical with the jargon, before there were electric pumps for pumping large volumes of water, more advanced cultures used ram pumps. In how they were using that here, well, sound, in the form of intensive vibration was utilized to break and separate the hydrogen from the rest of the water. And to achieve the sheer volume they were managing, they combined immense pressurization with this vibrational resonance. And *that*...," he said, pointing to the plume of glowing mist escaping through the pyramid's capstone, "is what we're all seeing. The hydrogen. And Tom, to answer your question, that electric illumination you're seeing within, is just that, the resulting electrical charge from the separation of the hydrogen. Really, a rather beautiful byproduct of it all."

Noticing the emotion welling up within Queshaun's eyes, Mike turned to him. As a fellow academic in pursuit of the truth, he understood what Queshaun must have been feeling at that moment. Not to the magnitude of what was now seizing the insides of this weathered and beaten down, though, entirely resilient old man, but... *Yes*, he understood clearly.

He leaned in close, resting his arm along Queshaun's shoulders. "It's something. Isn't it." The two men shared in the awe of seeing this incredible and forgotten machine, even if it were only a model of the real thing, working, providing life to the living, to all around it, as intended.

"Yes," Queshaun answered. "Always, they'd refute my assertions that their entirely unfounded claims, lacking absolutely zero evidence, were less than accurate. They did this with one simple question." He looked to them all. "They'd ask, 'then what is the pyramid if not a tomb?' My lack of an answer, my lack of proof was all the proof they needed to discount me."

"You've got your answer now," Mike said, feeling Queshaun's body release heavy sobs, which flowed from him in a series of deep trembling waves. He held the old man as the glowing mist flowed all around them. The mist was thick, wrapping itself along their bodies. It was as a blanket woven just for them... To cocoon lost souls in need.

Queshaun leaned his head over the edge of the catwalk, weeping as silently as he could. He clenched his eyes. With what dignity he could maintain, concealing himself there, he allowed fully the tears to flow down his deeply creased face. The salty water escaped from his weathered skin, leaping off, guided downwards by the invisible hand of gravity. The swelled droplets landed, bleeding out onto the dust-laden base of the pyramid model below.

Howie, entirely focused on Mike, had never seen his father so emotionally apt toward another human being. It did trigger a pause of jealousy, or something. Whatever the feeling, it was brief. He pushed it away, knowing the embrace did the two men some good. It did them all some good... Despite their discoveries so far, they still remained in the bowels of the earth. There was no certainty their skin would ever taste daylight again.

An unraveling of thoughts occurred to Tom. And as these things manifested themselves, he held not the slightest for how or why. "Not to disrupt the moment, guys... The water pumping up through the model must be coming from somewhere..."

"That could lead to a way out," Ingrid said.

Queshaun wiped his tear-streaked face, and drew his head up, away from the railing of the catwalk. He moved back alongside Ingrid. His eyes smiled wetly at her.

"It really is lovely," she said. "The pyramid." She felt the deep thump of the machine flow up through her feet, legs, and inside her. "When it beats... A heart for all the world."

"A song for something as exotic and mystifying as yourself," he said, pulling a smile from her, this woman, mysterious and enchanting.

"Uh, everyone," Mike said. They crowded in around at the railing directly overlooking the pyramid. Where Queshaun's tears had pooled up along the model, it'd partially, and revealingly so, washed away the dust. There was a perfectly carved square-shaped groove. Mike leaned over, using his index finger to clear out the rest of the dust.

Stepping back, Ingrid took his place. She extended her long and slender arm to the groove, locking the compass piece in by its base. It turned, clicking as it went, completing one rotation. Refusing to go any further, she released it.

Feeling the same deep fear they all felt, dread seeped into her that some piece of the mechanism had over time deteriorated or had broken or something somewhere had gone amiss, indefinitely ending their journey before they could reach the end, to seize the great truth awaiting them there...

A weathered hand set on hers. She looked up at Queshaun. He removed his hand, turning his wrist in the air counter-clockwise. She tried the simple motion upon the compass piece. It pivoted around counter-clockwise one complete rotation, then released itself into her hand.

The model of the Great Pyramid descended straight into the stone floor beneath it. Coming to a graceful stop, only its capstone was visible above the floor. This pyramidal stone of perhaps three inches in height began to glow. Not terribly bright, though it looked as daylight.

"Your hand," Tom said. Her eyes drifted to the compass piece cupped within her palm. The enigmatic inscription around its base was also aglow.

Quickly and gently, the section of catwalk they stood upon began to lower. They rode it down to where it stopped, level with the model. There was a soft metallic click, then the railing of the catwalk folded up and away to the side, presenting them with an opening through which to enter. They stepped out, going to the place where the capstone protruded from the floor.

With the compass piece still held in her hand, she could feel a fierce and tantalizing magnetism drawing to it from the capstone. Letting it lead her, she advanced. They watched with a dreamlike daze threading itself through each of them. A few inches from the capstone, her fingers receded, her palm opening, exposing the compass piece. These unseen forces of magnetism took hold of the compass piece. Entirely seen, it appeared to float through the open air between her and the capstone. The flat and square base of the compass piece came to rest impossibly balanced, perched atop the tip of the capstone.

"Huh," Tom said, pleasantly baffled.

The pyramid model continued its descent into the floor, taking with it the compass piece. Slender slabs of stone slid out from somewhere unseen within the now open hole before them, forming a spiral staircase deep into the darkness. The pulsing of water coursed up from the opening. It beckoned them in unspoken words, *Come Forth.* Bringing her flashlight to life, Ingrid glanced at the others, then started down this simple though elegant staircase....

The Egyptian Chamber

*T*he staircase brought them into another naturally occurring space. By no means small, though it was more modest than any of the rooms they'd explored before.

Pain from the spider's acid burn still surged deep in her arm. This agonized kiss of the arachnid's she'd embrace, for she wouldn't make the same mistake. Unpleasantly reminded, she retrieved the compass piece off its perch atop the capstone barely protruding from the floor.

"This is cozy," Howie said, sweeping the shadows with his flashlight.

This chamber seemed round, perfectly so. It must have been forty feet in diameter. The ceiling, coarse and uneven and of buttery-colored rock, was about seven and a half feet tall. The floor, damp and smooth, was of the same buttery yellow.

Their flashlights were activating the luminescent, amber-hued moss covering the walls. They did so deliberately, holding their beams close, charging the moss. No longer needing their flashlights, they continued deeper inside.

Carved from the rock, spanning floor to ceiling, shelves all along the walls encircled them. Howie knew what these shelves once held. This had been, at one time, the place for the L' Entita's most cherished library. Now barren, maybe it was true. Maybe the volumes of hidden knowledge had succumbed to the tides of eternity.

"At least there's air down here," said Tom, running his hand across the copiously thick moss.

"There!" Ingrid shouted.

The beam of her flashlight led them to the place. On the highest level for the shelves, along the ceiling, eight volumes, neatly in a line, were all that remained of the library.

"Infinity," said Howie.

He pointed to the sideways figure eight carved into the base of the shelf, directly below those eight volumes of books.

"Sacred," Queshaun said. "In ancient Egyptian... 'Sacred' and 'infinity' held the same meaning, as their contexts in how you know them, began as one. To be infinite, was to be sacred. To be sacred, was to be infinite."

"Ingrid?" Howie asked, "what's the first line of the inscription again?"

"The site you plainly seek lays within the Sun Book's sacred eight," she recited from memory.

"*Sacred eight,*" Howie said, realizing the newfound meaning. He jumped up, reaching for the eight volumes awaiting him on the shelf... His fingers fell short... by several inches.

"Who's lightest?" Tom asked.

Queshaun raised his three-fingered hand.

"Second lightest?" Howie asked.

Ingrid shed her pack, stepping forward. Howie boosted her onto his shoulders. As if it were preordained, in some impossible way, for her and him to be here together, they formed the perfect height. She pushed away the ridiculous thought. *There was no way. Not even the L'Entita could have foreseen such a thing so far in the past so deeply into the future.*

"Ingrid... You're getting heavy," Howie said.

Mike joined in helping hold her. She shifted from her thoughts to the task at hand. The impulse drove her to do it. She shouldn't have, but did. Both eager to move forward as quickly as she could, as well compelled by the fear of Camorra coming for them, she grabbed as many volumes as her hands would hold.

Ancient and frail, their bindings broke, showering Howie in loose pages and torn covers. With horror, they watched as these sacred texts floated, thoroughly muddling, swirling all around. Then, in final reprimand to their hopes, the remaining volumes slipped, no longer having their counterparts as support, fell, throwing themselves to the stone floor in a most devastating manner.

"I'm sorry," she started to say, but then, she wasn't, not at all.

For what stared her in the face absolved her of any guilt. Something remained before her there, no longer concealed behind those volumes, now fallen. And what it was seemed, at least in that instant, if not of greater importance, was certainly more relevant.

Spitting on her fingers, she wiped away the layer of dust. She aimed her flashlight. Glittering in the light was a sun, carved from crystal in all its blazing glory.

A few inches in diameter, held there, nearly flush, it protruded slightly, inlaid into the wall at the back of the bookshelf. More compelling than the sun's beauty was what was at its center. There, a triangular-shaped keyhole begged to be penetrated.

Slipping the compass piece from her pocket, she guided the tip inside. It fit seamlessly. She turned it. With a click, the compass piece locked in. It began to rotate on its own. Though she knew this magic must have been by some unseen mechanism.

The sun encircling the compass piece started to rotate in the opposing direction. It did so in a ticking fashion, as though counting down. Having completed exactly one-half turn, both the sun and the compass piece simultaneously came to a stop.

As she returned the compass piece safely to her pocket, a hum began from the crystal sun. A perfectly shaped triangular beam shot out from the keyhole. Of rich and vibrant indigo, it ended at an unremarkable place on the floor near Tom's feet.

Tracing his hands along the stone, Tom found the grooved outline there awaiting the compass piece. Queshaun handed him a knife much too large and menacing for a man of his age to possess. With the sharp tip, Tom picked away the grime caked within the groove.

"Throw me the compass piece!" he yelled.

"Why not let her down now!" Howie yelled back.

"No, he's right. I have a feeling we'll still need this sun," Ingrid said, keeping her head tilted away from the beam as it surged out from the sun's center.

"I have a feeling too," Howie said. "It's called gravity."

She glanced down at him, and mouthed, 'Patience'. Then, as best as she could, with her feet bridging between his and Mike's shoulders, threw the compass piece. It fell short of Tom's outstretched hand... Queshaun grabbed it out of the air and passed it to him. Tom locked the base of the compass piece into the groove. And he waited for it to do its thing...

"All in the wrist!" Ingrid yelled.

"Right," he said, twisting the compass piece clockwise.

A skull-sized section of floor directly beneath began to elevate. Tom scrambled to his feet. Queshaun joined him in backing away. With the compass piece still locked on top, it came to stop at waist-level, forming a pillar of stone.

Three more shafts of stone started to rise from the floor, equally spaced, with this first pillar positioned at their center. Square in shape, and maybe a touch larger, these three in their own right seemed to be more of a column than pillar. As they extended up, they did so slanted inwards at an angle destined to meet. Their ends came together, arching to a point. And the pillar crowned with the compass piece stood directly beneath this point.

If one knew the dimensions of the three columns, then they'd know their design was flawless. Each was six inches in width. Six feet of space existed between them. And their point of intersection, directly above the center pillar, was six feet high. Truly, it was perfect.

"What the hell is it?" asked Tom.

Howie took it in as best he could with his head turned awkwardly back, while still holding up Ingrid. "A triangle..."

"Thanks for that informative observation," said Tom, moving to the pillar at the center.

Queshaun followed. The beam of indigo now ended upon the floor directly at the base of the center pillar. A gentle buzz emitted from the compass piece atop the pillar. Queshaun and Tom felt its vibration flow around them, through them. It built into a hum, the exact same hum generated by the crystal sun.

"Feels like we're inside a tuning fork," Tom said.

"I'd say... We are," Queshaun answered, steading himself with a hand against Tom's shoulder.

The hum filled, saturating intensely within this place containing the three columns centered around the pillar. Cocooned within this space, the vibration accelerated, circling around and around. Somehow, for Tom and Queshaun, time felt different, not faster nor slower inside this field, but distinctly... *Different... Altered.*

Neither Queshaun nor Tom had anything to compare this effect to. At best, either man could say he sensed a severance and separateness from the fabric of time and space, freed from that dimensional plane where their bodies were contained. The invisible cyclone of sound pressed them toward the floor.

The stone floor felt soft. This softness flicked in and out. Between moments, the stone beneath them appeared visually nonexistent.

Tom gripped Queshaun's hand. The whirl of the hum, circling, circling, circling, merged the lines which separated. They could neither see nor feel where the other began or ended. Even the columns and the pillar seemed to bleed away. Everything that had been separate was as one, as the space between things was no more.

Utter blackness took hold for them. Still, they could hear the rush of the air, the trembling of it, blending with the churning of their hearts—everything came back. It was as it'd been, with just a gentle hum pulsing forth from the pillar. Or perhaps, it was coming from the compass piece upon it. They collapsed to their knees. Releasing hands, they searched for their bearings as their hearts returned to a steadier pace.

"Where in the hell did you guys go!" shouted Howie.

"Go? We've been here the entire time!" Tom shouted back.

Without a chance to continue their discrepancy in perspective, the compass piece, in its entirety, began to radiate in richly fierce indigo.

"Well... That's new," Tom said.

Still bridging the shoulders of Howie and Mike, Ingrid was nearly nose to nose with the 'sacred' symbol carved into the base of the stone shelf. Her body was tired, her mind drained. Why hadn't her ancestors made this less difficult? They'd had the power to do so, make this journey less... less of a journey.

What the hell do you want from me? She demanded an answer from them from beyond their graves. Or, who knew, perhaps graves were beneath them. Or, even, perhaps, it—her demand now was one aimed at herself... In some loop of infinity coming full circle.

She couldn't tell anymore where the place where her ancestors ended and where she began. Her life was not her own, but an assimilation. She felt that to be true. To what end, she was at her wit's end.

As if her demand had been answered through light rather than sound, the 'sacred' symbol became aglow in the same bright indigo. In that moment, Mike, holding up half her weight, tilted his head in order to pop his neck, releasing the accumulating pressure. Staring up toward Ingrid, he could see the vividly glowing Egyptian symbol for 'sacred'. With his head titled so, this infinity symbol looked as a figure eight.

He spoke aloud to himself. "Faces eight... Ingrid, see if that thing will turn." He and Howie strained under the weight of continuing to hold her, as she grabbed the symbol where it protruded ever slightly from the wall. She twisted. With some effort, it rotated. Coming to a stop, straight up and down, the symbol now appeared as a figure eight.

The beam streaming out from the sun caught the top of the figure eight. She wiped away the dust from the eye of the 'eight', revealing the lens contained within. Immediately, the beam intensified, shifting in course, shooting across the room. It struck the compass piece atop the central pillar.

"Now?" asked Howie, teeth gritted and arms shaking.

"Now," she said.

Mike and Howie lowered her. The three of them joined Tom and Queshaun in front of the compass piece. Through tired yet eager eyes, they squinted at its brilliance. Then, it happened....

Precession

*W*ithout understanding it and without a word, they watched, hypnotized. The illumination from the compass piece began to bloom, deeper, stronger, steadily intensifying. Then in what could only be perceived as some kind of prismed effect, slivered beams of indigo shot out from the four faces of the compass piece.

There were four distinct beams of the vibrant indigo... At first... In the next second, thousands of them radiated forth. Exponentially multiplying, they became what had to have been millions. In the following moment, there was nothing less than an infinite array of beams shooting out in every direction.

Most curiously was that the beams, which should have intersected with the five of them standing there, did not. The burning slivers of indigo refused contact, leaving a thin layer of space encapsulating them. The beams bent in curved ways which beams of light should not be capable of.

Disjointedly, these beams continued on their course. Fully illuminating the chamber, the ends of each of the beams birthed feelers. Probing like electric tentacles, they pulsated, searching along the chamber's surfaces of cold, damp rock within the subtle glow of the amber moss.

"What is it doing?" Howie asked, knowing no one possibly had any inclination, but rather as his own response, in awe of the spectacle playing out.

He reached toward the beams over his head. They shifted their course, sensing, evading, or perhaps, protecting him.

"Don't, kid," said Mike, genuinely concerned for his son's safety.

"Or I'll break it," Howie said. "Doubtful."

The multitude of beams began to merge. They melted together, resulting in four broad shafts of light. Moving upwards for the ceiling, these became perfectly vertical, while remained separate.

Directly over their heads, the ends of the beams converged, interlocking into a brilliantly steepled point of light. As the beams each flowed from one of the four facets of the compass piece, the pillar holding the compass piece began to recede into the floor. Like electric Velcro, the interlocked point of the beams along the ceiling slowly and somewhat violently started to tear free from one another, releasing a broken blend of convulsed hisses and uneven flickers.

Howie took Ingrid's hand and moved away, toward the edges of the rock walls. The others did the same. And silence washed over everything, absolving their fears. Even the steady hum of the beams dissolved, absorbing to a dead quiet.

The pillar disappeared into the stone floor, bringing the compass piece flush to ground level. Elegantly, the steepled ends of the beams of light completed their separation, gently blooming. Downwards they glided like floating silk, each reaching out for one of the surrounding columns of stone.

None of them, having noticed exactly when it'd happened, saw that upon each of the four columns there was a brilliant shard of crystal now protruding up, roughly six inches in length. In chorus, the four beams made contact with the crystals, becoming swallowed into these long glittering shards. In a most alluring manner, their deep indigo transitioned to a soft yellow.

Glowing before them now was an inverted pyramid fashioned from these four beams of light, linked from the capstone upon the floor up to the four columns positioned squarely around it. Then, in sequence, a beam of yellow released, one crystal shard to the next, to form a perfectly square base for this brilliant pyramid of light. They drew near as their thoroughly overwhelmed curiosity masqueraded for bravery. Out of impulse, Ingrid extended her hand and touched one of the beams. Though she could not feel it, her hand would not pass through. The light was solid, as if congealed illumination.

"I can't believe you just did that," said Howie.

"You sound like your father," she responded, keeping her hand pressed to it.

The soft yellow transformed at once to gleaming gold. The gold seeped into the large and open area at the pyramid's center. It spread out in veins. As an interlinking network of light, it pulsed as it sketched, carving three-dimensionally in gold, not gleamingly so, but opaque, upon the blank triangular-shaped space.

What it drew was obvious. It was the inside of the Great Pyramid, with each chamber and passageway. It came to a completion, having transformed the negative space into an exact cutaway of the Great Pyramid. Ingrid's fingers wrapped around the closest edge of this pyramid etched in light. Again, compelled by an urge, she pulled downwards.

With having given it more than enough force to spin and do so quickly, it defied her and it defied the laws of physics in how she knew. The pyramid did rotate. Though, sluggishly, stopping between one pivot to the next in a strangely segmented way. It wasn't so much in slow motion as much as it paused between frames as it traveled through the fabric of space and time. Perhaps gravity was to blame. Whatever the cause, it was strange, but such had become normal by this point.

In rotating, the beams of hardened light twisted and broke off from where they connected to each of the four facets of the compass piece upon the floor. They severed not rapidly all at once, as glass would. Though, did so as a lake's frozen surface, with many simultaneous fractures coursing steadily, patiently, and methodically across its smoothness, spreading piece by piece through disconnected shards. Until, finally, enough pieces had collectively broken, that the whole seamless plane gave way as some sort of shattered mirror tearing free to birth a million uneven versions of itself.

Like so much here within this place forgotten, they could only observe from their limited perspective, and had to accept they held not the understanding. They knew what should be taking a second or two was now closer to a minute or two. Their own motions and gestures while they watched it happen were significantly faster, at normal speed, than the pyramid.

This lag between themselves and that of the pyramid summoned conflicted sensations within their bodies. There was a kind of collective motion sickness building. Their brains had drifted, becoming out of sync with what they were seeing and feeling from what should be happening. They knew now their expectations, all their expectations, were relative.

Thankfully, the nausea, laced with a bit of dizziness, faded to a dull headache for them all. This was a relief owed to their own consciousness, as their awareness was expanding. Their brains recalibrated, as they were transcending what they knew to be possible. There was no going back, for they'd witnessed this light, long hidden from humans... To *others*.

Having completed exactly half a rotation, the pyramid came to a gradual stop. Now right-side up, and broken free of its source from the compass piece, the pyramid of coagulated light stood before them in midair. It didn't float, because it didn't move nor did it hover, but was entirely stationary, just weight-free, held by nothing. At least, nothing they could see.

"Seriously," Tom said, "they're just showing off at this point." He glanced at Ingrid. "Or, you are..."

"H*ow* exactly is this light continuing to exist?" Howie asked.

Ingrid withdrew her hand from the pyramid of light. "By this point, you should really recognize, Howie, there are a lot of answers I don't have."

Imprinted in Mike's mind, the rotating movement of the pyramid continued to play out. He closed his eyes. The image solidified clearly upon the black canvas before him now. Seeing a familiar shape, he locked it in place. It was so familiar in fact that it brought a sense of déjà vu. "Wait—take it back to where it was on its side."

Ingrid reached for the pyramid. She pulled her hand back before making contact. Told by a voice from within herself or from somewhere or... *something* else, she knew touch wasn't necessary. She thought it to be. The pyramid shifted in reverse, quickly. Abruptly, it stopped. They had an exact view of the pyramid positioned upon its side. The reason Mike had wanted it so stared them all in the face.

"Huh," said Howie. "How about that. If you turn the Great Pyramid sideways, with a cutaway view of it, the entire layout of its interconnecting passageways and chambers create a shape nearly *identical* to that of an infinity symbol."

"How can anyone honestly still believe the story that uneducated laborers built the Great Pyramid?" asked Queshaun.

"How in christ holy hell has everyone missed that! Christ— we're not special," said Tom, nearly shouting, "We're... grave robbers and scholars, right—old gold and broken manuscripts are our thing. Not... this. This is..." He sighed deeply, unsatisfied, brimmed in the belief his question here and now... His cry of why, it would never be answered.

Wanting it so, she silently asked. The pyramid rotated on its own, half a turn, upwards.

She smiled most knowingly. "And..." The pyramid came to a stop right-side up...

"Now," she said, "those very same interlinked chambers and passageways making the infinity symbol appear as a figure eight." She turned to them. "Don't you see? The Great Pyramid *is* the inscription's 'sacred eight'."

"So it is, my dear," Queshaun said, deeply so, somehow

completed now in his life's pursuit. "To be fair, a reason why this discovery hasn't been realized before, Tom, all of you— you've got to remember some of these chambers and passageways here are unknown to the general public. The authorities that be, who have their established farce of history at stake, have kept these shut off to the people. What we're seeing here is a *complete* picture. And that, my friends, is a rare thing. Completeness. Maybe the rarest of things."

"To be fair," Tom said. "Fair enough."

"And for the record, my lady, are you moving that with your mind?" asked Queshaun.

She shook her head, figuring it out inside her own brain before trying to answer. "For the record... No. I think... more of a communication between it and myself." She turned to him, confident her honesty would quench his scholarly nature. "A request that was granted, you could say."

A rich beam of indigo shot straight up into the air from the compass piece. Positioned on the floor, the beam penetrated the base of the pyramid directly above it. Upon contact, the pyramid's core became an empty, blank space once more. Rapidly, the beam drew, sketching in glowing indigo, filling in the space.

Completed before them now was the Praesidio Autem Veritas, encapsulated within the pyramid. A much more concentrated beam, laser-thin, shot out from the all-seeing eye at the center of the Praesidio Autem Veritas. As if on an invisible axis, the pyramid began to slowly revolve clockwise. Then, while the floor remained unmoving, the walls of the circular chamber started to turn, doing so counter-clockwise.

Ingrid spoke the words as they entered her mind. "Sacred eight faces precession..."

"Precession," Mike said, smiling. "A slow orbital rotation." They watched the pyramid slowly rotate. Abruptly, the beam shooting out from the all-seeing eye came into alignment with the symbol of the figure eight on the wall. All movement ceased. As the eye's beam now penetrated the crystal within the figure eight, the entire bookshelf they'd believed was carved from the rock, slid back, disappearing into the wall.

"That's original," Tom said.

"Had to originate from somewhere," Howie said, leading them all for the open passageway. Reaching the dark opening, he shined his flashlight, peering his head inside... Less than an inch from his face was a spider. As perfectly disturbing as those they'd encountered before, though this one was significantly larger, and particularly hungrier. The spider lunged—

The Queen

*I*ngrid's boot connected heartily with the spider's head, launching the eight-legged horror backwards several feet. It landed upon the entangled mass of spiders awaiting deeper inside. With a subtle crackle and pop they all distinctly heard, the spider pulled itself to its feet, and flexed its back sharply upwards. It drew open its mouth, sliding its retractable fangs out, fully exposing them for all to see. Small spheres of glistening acid dribbled from the fangs' hollow tips.

"And we've got spiders," Tom announced.

"Well observed," said Howie, taking the bottle of spider repellant Queshaun offered.

Tom stepped forward. "Plug your ears."

He fired his Colt. The head of the still snarling spider exploded, showering globs of acid searingly onto the surrounding spiders.

"Nice, they're not immune to their own poison," Tom said.

He unloaded on the rest, then stepped back out of the way. Howie sprayed the repellant at the swarm advancing for them. As the great mass of spiders' bone-like legs scurried across the floor, the stone trembled with the sound. It was something between a clickity-clack and claws dragging along old sheet metal. Emptying the spray bottle, it was obvious the repellant hadn't phased the spiders.

"It must be stale," Queshaun meagerly offered in his own defense.

"Must be," said Howie.

Strangely and fully aglow now, the spiders seemed to almost march as they closed in. The ones spearheading this tide of terror raised up the front of their torsos, making their bodies look even larger than they already were. These terrible creatures moved as a collective, as a single organism.

They retreated from the spiders to the center of the chamber. Swiftly spreading out, the spiders encircled their prey, who were now trapped. Doing the one thing they could, the five of them positioned themselves back-to-back, facing their fate.

Tom inventoried his remaining bullets, revealing he had not nearly enough. "You know when people reach that point with confronting death, and in the utter thralls of sheer desperation, start to beg in an ever-deepening loop of depravity.... Not like this, not like this... *Not like this.*"

The spiders, enveloping the floor of the chamber, drew closer, with their clickity-clack and clawing of their legs upon the stone. They did so until there was less than a foot of space separating them from their prey, there huddled, pressed to each other at the centermost place within the chamber.

"What are they waiting for?" asked Howie, both grateful and in dread of the delay.

"Their queen to eat us alive," Tom said, off the cuff, without considering the inconsiderateness of his words.

The others glared at him. With a twist, Queshaun popped open the hinged top of his oxygen tank. A soft hiss flowed from the broken seal.

"Your tank's full?" asked Howie.

"Yours is too," answered Queshaun. "All of yours are. Oh, didn't I tell you—the tanks automatically refill in oxygen-rich environments. Tom, your bullets."

Tom gave him his remaining bullets. Queshaun dropped them inside the tank and locked the top back in place. What could only be the spider's queen, entered, passing through the shadow-filled doorway into the chamber. Everyone turned to Tom.

He raised his hands in defense. "Hey, how was I to know they actually have a queen."

Considerably larger and somehow managing to surpass with her hideousness, she faced them, with ivory-like fangs extending. Her mass of pitch-black eyes reflected only darkness. The spiders parted like a sea, receding back. And the queen strutted clickety-clack, clawing down the open pathway straight for her feast, long-awaited.

"As I like to say in these precious moments, whatever you're doing, Queshaun," Howie said, "do it faster."

As fast as he could, Queshaun released a hose from its place on the tank. Igniting a flair, he jammed the inflamed end into the hole where the hose had been. "This is for my fingers, you bastards." He chucked the tank.

The five of them collectively dropped to their bellies, their hands and arms shielding their heads. Before the tank could land, the flare's flame raptured with the oxygen within the tank, directly so over the queen. They dared not look up, for the reverberance of ricocheting bullets filled the air. The tank blossomed gloriously into an inflamed ball, spewing forth shrapnel most generously....

Ascending

*P*ressed to the floor of stone, they watched the disturbing spectacle amidst the aftermath. The remaining spiders not killed by the blast began ravenously devouring the pieces, once their queen, now splattered across the chamber.

"Reverse black widow-ism," said Tom.

Having seen their window for escape, Howie pulled both himself and Ingrid up. "Let's get out of here before these cannibals finish their first course."

They ran across the spider-strewn chamber, kicking and leaping as needed. At the furthest end of the chamber, they found the staircase there, or what once had been. It provided no guardrails and disappeared high into the darkness above.

Mike took a handful of the crumbling wood. "Oak..." The broken splinters spilled through his fingers to the floor. "I think."

"They must have transported it here," Queshaun said. "Like so many other things."

Howie headed up the precariously steep and thoroughly rotted staircase. "Don't care where it came from, just as long it'll hold our weight."

Carefully, they climbed the steps which squished underfoot, feeling more like mushy sod than wood. With each step, they anticipated it to give way, and hoped someone around them would grab and save them. Reaching the end, the staircase proved a rare and welcomed uneventful venture.

Passing through the large open doorway of stone awaiting them, they entered the chamber there. At their feet, they found what remained of the chamber's twin metal doors. Deep and broad dents covered them.

Clearly, some climatic conflict had led these great doors to be torn from their mighty hinges. Ingrid crouched down, running her hand across the cool, dusty metal. The coldness upon her skin offered no answers, other than the doors had been crafted from the metal of the L' Entita.

Howie pulled a bottled water from his pack, and taking a long swallow, offered it to her. After having a drink herself, she poured the rest onto the door. The thick dust melted away, revealing the large inlaid Praesidio Autem Veritas.

She led. The realm which laid before them was vast. On the smooth walls carved from the bedrock, there were metal hooks. Upon these hooks hung torches. Tom ignited a flare and held it to the torch there in front of him. To no avail, it wouldn't light.

"Like there'd still be oil left in those," said Howie. "It's not like a movie."

Mike removed the small container of lighter fluid from his pack and squirted some onto the crumpled fabric wrapped on the head of the torch. By the torchlight, Ingrid held up the compass piece. Cupped in her hand like a crystal ball for all to see, she gazed with hope and a will unyielding.

In answer, it began to glow of rich indigo. Brightly pulsing so along one of its four faces, it led them in the direction of their answers... To something great, something long lost to their species.

Lighting torches along what seemed an endless wall, they passed immense stacks of unused building materials and tools, organized, still awaiting use, as if all abruptly abandoned. Paintings covered the walls. Vividly, they depicted moments of emotion, capturing everyday life along the Nile Valley.

Chariots lined against the wall, intact, virtually perfect. And then they found the skeletons, dust covered, still in grimaced poses spread out all along the stone floor. How ever they'd met their ends, it hadn't been kind. Whatever had happened had been swift, and left no one spared. There was row after row of scaffolding, and most impressive, an enormous lift, once used to bridge between here and the chambers above.

Reaching the end, they came out onto a towering platform that offered an array of ancient controls, levers and shafts and gears running hundreds of feet in length, disappearing into the walls and ceiling so high above. The scale of this place matched the Great Pyramid itself. This station overlooked an immense and open bay-like doorway. The room beyond was of stone, but what it offered couldn't be seen.

Leading her male colleagues, Ingrid silently read over the labels along the control station. Some were written in the L' Entita's lost language, while others were in ancient Egyptian. Absentmindedly, Tom leaned against the panel closest to him, his hand pressed atop a rather large lever....

"The fact that there's ancient Egyptian here alongside the L' Entita's language does beg some interesting questions for history. To say the least...," said Mike.

Howie moved Tom's hand gently off and away from the lever, knowing not what would happen if its position were to be changed, but knowing it'd quite likely be less than ideal.

Mike turned to Ingrid, wanting answers. "Thought the L' Entita were engineers of religion. And only so." He gestured around them. "This is a product of the L' Entita much more than of the pharaohs."

She addressed all of them as she spoke. "There's a lot— most I don't know. But I'd not assume too much a distinction between the pharaohs and the L' Entita of the time..." As she spoke, the answer they needed in that moment gave itself away, doing so in the form of one of the control labels. And it wasn't by any measure the best idea, but it was the only possible out she saw for any of them.

"Yes...?" Tom asked, feeling her gaze wholly upon him.

"The lever near your knees, give it a tug downwards," she told him. "It controls that big lift we passed, that, if still working, can take us up."

Eagerly, he did. Defiantly, the lever stopped about halfway down. With Howie's help, they moved the lever to its lowest possible position.

"Now the one right next to it, pull it down too," she said, directing their efforts for escape.

It wouldn't budge despite Tom and Howie fully exerting themselves. Mike joined in. Finally, the lever broke free. It slowly pulled down, but froze, refusing to go any further. Howie raised his foot, sending the others retreating back. He slammed his boot upon the lever, glaring back at him—the thick, yet wooden lever snapped in half. Howie found himself tumbling forward, falling into the control panel before him. With a splintering crunch, every lever protruding from the panel broke off.

Mike pulled him up. "Nice. Very nice."

Frantic, Queshaun grabbed Ingrid, pointing to two of the levers Howie had broken, but not before having shifted their position upon his fall.

She read the labels written in ancient Egyptian. "Ram... Water—we've got to go!"

Before they could ask why, she sprinted for the now rapidly closing bay doors thirty feet out in front of them. In no way able to keep up with her pace, they fell behind as she passed through the two giant doors....

The Chariot Up

*T*hrough the now sliver of doorway they slipped, with the thud of the heavy doors sealing closed behind them. They nearly ran head-on into the metal guardrail there. Ingrid grabbed Howie, sparing him this fate. He peered over. On the other side of the rail, the floor dropped twenty, maybe twenty-five feet, straight down.

This cubed-shaped room appeared to have once held, as well directed, vast volumes of water. Large slots in the ceiling, sixty feet high, seemed to have functioned as a kind of reverse drain for the water to travel up through. The wall at their left side, was just that, a solid wall. The wall to their right, ended in a massive metal grate, also meant to feed the flow of water. While big, not even Queshaun could've fit through the gaps in the grate.

None of these impossible routes were what Ingrid had in mind. Looking past the guardrail, and directly across from them, she saw the enormous and perfectly round tunnel. She estimated it to have been forty feet wide. Where it led was deep and dark.

"Down there?" Howie asked, anticipating the path of most resistance.

She nodded. "We must hurry." Howie yanked the rappelling line from his pack, securing it to the guardrail, and lowered himself. The others followed as quickly as they could. They ran across the waterway there of stone to the other side.

Twenty feet above them, the tunnel awaited. Along the base of the wall was a debris pile of rock, sand, and wood. At the center, a chariot was tilted vertically on end. Of rotted wood and brittle metal, this chariot appeared it'd implode at any moment, bringing the knotted pile with.

With as much care as frantic-induced-speed would allow, Howie led their climb of the chariot. Reaching the top, and pushing himself as fast as his courage would tolerate, he lunged for the ledge nearly four feet overhead. His fingers caught, and he pulled himself up. For the others still clinging to the chariot, there was a great vibration coursing through.

"Unless that rumble is from the ghost of a racing Arabian, we *really* need to get out of here," Mike said. The chariot teetered. Howie grabbed Ingrid's arm, reeling her onto the ledge. Th vibration trembled everything. Howie reached for Queshaun—the chariot snapped in two, tumbling down, unraveling the knot of debris. Collapsing, it spewed in a wave across the floor. A single wheel, all that remained of the chariot, bounced out and away. Queshaun dangled from Howie's grip. Ingrid hung dangerously over the side, barely holding Mike. Tom swayed by fingertips wrenched upon Mike's boot. Swiftly, Howie pulled everyone up.

"Let's never do that again," Qeshaun said. The roar of water flooded their ears, sounding as a thousand or more chariots racing for them.

Ingrid drew in a lung full of stale air. "Run."

"You want us to run *toward* the oncoming tidal wave," Tom said. Flipping her flashlight on, Ingrid sprinted into the tunnel. The slap of her boot heels against the stone, first blending with the water's roar, then were swallowed by the thunder of this pending tidal wave....

Ram's Watered Hate

*T*heir flashlight beams swung widely out in front of them, slicing the dark insides of the tunnel as they ran toward their own doom. Water flowed harshly past them now, of a few inches deep, tearing at their ankles. Rapidly deepening, it struck, ramming at their legs and knees with an icy resistance. The sheer and absolute coldness didn't feel as water, but as things which pierced, incessant stabbing chills, injecting frozen shards to their cores.

"I don't want to be the first to die of hypothermia in Egypt," Tom said, fighting against the rushing river.

With the water eclipsing their shoulders, Howie grabbed Ingrid's hand. They each interlocked their hold to each other, pushing forward.

"There—there it is," Ingrid said, aiming her flashlight, illuminating the rungs of the metal ladder along the right side of the tunnel fifteen feet away.

As one, they trudged through the hateful water assaulting their bodies, tearing free their packs and equipment, wholly ensnarling them with a frigid frenzy, devouring all energy. The water surged over their heads. Howie's eyelids snapped shut, feeling his eyes would certainly freeze otherwise. Lungs burning for air amidst the icy water washing over him, unable to see, his fingers took desperate hold of one of the metal rungs.

Pulling himself up, and forcing his eyes open, he refused

to release the ladder as the ever-deepening water thrashed his body. Ingrid caught one of his flaying legs, and climbing up it, got herself onto the ladder. As the water continued to rush higher and higher, faster and faster, they fished out the others.

They forced their frozen and thoroughly numb fingers to grip the rungs as they climbed. The dark waters, chilling all the way through them, brimmed over the mouths, noses, and eyes, over their heads. Fueled by fear alone, they pushed themselves, managing a fragmented gasp of dingy air here and there.

Howie broke free from the water's grasp, finding the final rung. The metal door, half-hanging from one hinge, stared down at him. He aimed his flashlight, badly flickering now, into the partly open doorway. The beam died, succumbing to the darkness.

"Anyone still have a flashlight?" he asked. "That works?"

Mike handed his to Queshaun, passing it up the line to Howie. Flashlight aimed, he peered inside the doorway. Seeing nothing which possessed eight legs, he entered. Shivering, the others followed.

The air, it actually felt as though it contained some life, not stagnant and tainted with old death, as the air of the tunnel. Single file, they made their way through the narrow passageway as it brushed along their arms and shoulders. For the first time, Howie felt neither panic nor anxiety for such a tight space.

"Stop," Ingrid said, as they reached the rather sharp leftward bend in the passageway.

Other than being where the pathway turned as it did, it appeared as the rest of the walls, as blank dusty stone. And she would have believed it to be. Though, the compass piece, now burning within her pocket said otherwise. With a badly trembling hand, as they all continued to shiver, she pulled out the compass piece. Its face, closest the wall, glowed in a soft emerald.

This was it. She knew this slab of rock to be the entrance to the final chamber, here in Egypt. *Just... how does it open?*

They all wondered this, staring, shaking, too cold, too exhausted to think or talk. Queshaun collapsed to the floor. Fearing he'd died right then and there, Ingrid reached for him. But then, he steadied himself, holding her hand so, he began to wipe away the dust caked in the groove, that only he'd noticed there at the base of the wall.

Smiling with relief for him and for all of them, she handed over the compass piece. Sliding it tip-first into the little triangular groove, he locked it in. The seamless section of wall slid out, sighingly so, shedding away its dust.

Ingrid unlocked the compass piece, returning it to her pocket. Slipping through, they entered the blackness. Though, it was only dark for a few paces, passing the gentle jog there, and finding the place beyond.

It wasn't a chamber, not really. It was a room, and the smallest of any they'd entered thus far, by far. The walls, ceiling, and floor gleamed in the same bright white granite that once encased the pyramids. Even the thin layer of dust upon the room's surfaces could not dull the granite's polished gleam.

Where to go was obvious. The only thing occupying the space was whatever laid upon the large table at the center of the room. Whatever was there, was covered by a vast leather hide.

"What do you think's under it?" asked Howie.

Ingrid shrugged, expecting anything, knowing nothing.

Tom reached for the long hide of leather. "King Tut."

Queshaun, thoroughly missing Tom's sarcasm, answered, "He's already been—" Tom yanked away the exceptionally large leather hide....

What Truth Lied Beneath

On the table, carved from nothing less than untold and painstaking amounts of time, entirely fashioned from a mosaic of bone, laid a topographical map of the world. Perfect in every way, at a sweeping twenty by twenty feet, forming an exact square, it was a marvel unto itself. They spread out, encircling the table.

"Bit macabre," Tom said, touching his fingertips to the peaks of the Himalayas, jutting up ten inches from the surface.

Both agreeing and disagreeing with his assessment, Ingrid said, "Yes... It's beautiful."

"Your people didn't do anything small, did they," Queshaun said.

"Not when it mattered." Ingrid's eyes scanned the map for a triangular or square groove. Finding none, she searched the edges of the table, for something, anything. She set the compass piece on the map. "If anyone has any ideas, by all means..."

Howie located the Giza Plateau. It felt natural to begin there and work backwards. "I like how they included these little landmarks throughout the different regions of the day." His index finger rested on the tip of the two-inch-tall Great Pyramid.

"Maybe more than a nice detail," Mike said. "Could be a way to gauge when the map was built. What do you have there anyway?"

"Don't know," said Howie, running his fingers across the small and empty slots all along the Giza Plateau and beyond.

"Locations for Egyptian obelisks," Ingrid said. "Or, at least where they'd they started out being."

Howie took the compass piece, and going to the place on the map, carefully positioned it within Vatican City, alongside Saint Peter's Basilica. "You mean, before they were all hauled to Rome."

"All except for this one," said Tom, pointing to the inch-tall obelisk sitting in front of the Great Pyramid.

Removing the little obelisk in question from its slot on the map, Howie pointed it at him. "And what obelisk, Tom, do you recall seeing upon the Giza Plateau?"

"Right," Tom said.

"All the obelisks were moved," said Queshaun. "Especially that one."

"Then why was it the *only* one that was still in its slot here on the map?" Tom asked, grabbing the obelisk away from Howie.

"If there's a discrepancy, "Ingrid said, "it's intentional."

Not really sure why, as was the case for many of his actions, for impulse wasn't governed to reason, Tom went to the Great Pyramid on the map. It... *glowed.* He took hold of the little pyramid and yanked up.

It tore free from its place. He opened his palm, revealing the two-inch pyramid. Though, it was no longer aglow. And... it wasn't of bone, not like the rest of the model. It was... *Yes,* of that strange and unknown metal.

"You broke it!" Howie shouted. "Why would you do that?"

Tom stared at the little pyramid. "It was glowing. I just... Just had to take it. Didn't you see it glowing?"

"No, Tom, it's not glowing," Howie said.

"You two," Mike said, shaking his head.

Ingrid glared at Tom. She took both the little pyramid and obelisk from him.

"Tell me, Queshaun," said Mike, "why especially that one?"

"What?" asked Queshaun.

"You said especially *that* one..." Mike reached for the obelisk, and Ingrid gave it to him, who, in turn, handed it to Queshaun.

"Because..." Queshaun brought the obelisk alongside the compass piece there, sitting in Vatican City. "That's the *one* that's been in Saint Peter's Square since thirty-seven A.D., brought there for the construction of Caligula's circus, where the Vatican, the headquarters for Christianity, now so clearly rests.

Mike shook his head. "The one in Saint Peter's Square, the Romans took from Heliopolis. Now a suburb of... Cairo." He pointed to the place on the map. "See, there? About twenty miles northwest of the Great Pyramid."

"If you'd read my book, young-timer," Queshaun said, "then you'd know there was a preexisting temple where the Great Pyramid now sits. And when that temple was constructed, that's also when that *particular* obelisk was built there in front of the pyramid. *Later*, it was moved to Heliopolis."

Howie suppressed his grin, never having seen Mike get so called out, and corrected.

"Well," Ingrid said, "seems you're both right. And according to my grandfather, when an obelisk was initially positioned at an institution's doorstep, be it the temples of Egypt, the Vatican, the U.S. Capital building, et cetera, wherever, it symbolized a passing of the torch between the old to new, regarding the powers that be. And as we know, this torch itself is the symbol for the secret knowledge, held and controlled by those very same powers that be."

"This knowledge, being, the long-established devices for social control?" asked Mike. "Just want to be on the same page here..."

"Yes," she answered. "And in my ancestors' case, devices

that had been perfected to an exact science."

"With religion being the apex of which," said Howie.

"Well, yes," she said. "Don't you see, the sense of it all couldn't be more perfect... When the transfer of power happened between the old, Egypt, to the new, Rome, so did the symbol of that power."

"Egypt's obelisks," Tom said.

She nodded. "Those beacons to the sun. The torches of knowledge. To be placed at the heart of Rome, upon Rome's founding of their new means for universalizing, and thus controlling their empire..."

"Rome's most powerful creation, Christianity," Howie said.

"Precisely," she said. "While using the old, Egypt's own religion as the template, to conceive the new."

"Yes," Queshaun said, "anyone with a mind of their own and ability to read can know as much, if they're *sincere* in desiring such. But, my dear, to stay on track with where we are here and now, did your grandfather tell you of the origins of the obelisk?"

"Think I know where you're going with this," she answered. "Obelisks, all were positioned ever carefully to be illuminated by the first light of day, as well the last of it, with the rising and setting of the sun. As so, originally, they were meant as a symbolic gesture of respect to the sun... The giver of life unto the world, as my grandfather would say."

Queshaun smiled. "Couldn't have said it better myself, my dear, if the sages had whispered in my ear. I'd just add, that 'obelisk', within its original context in Arabic, means 'messiah'." Gracefully gripping the small obelisk of bone, he tapped it atop the dome of Saint Peter's. "And 'messiah', the root for which, of course, means anointed or enlightened one."

"Or, in ancient Egyptian...," said Mike. "Bearer of the torch."

"Leading us back to the Vatican," Howie said, "back to

your ancestors, Ingrid, the L' Entita."

"Or," Tom said, "in contemporary translation, the infamously famous Society of the Morning Star."

Ingrid turned to him, quite surprised by his knowledge of such things... *Secret* things. "Yes, well, that's no longer a title spoken. Not amongst the living."

"No telling what will come out of Tom's mind or mouth," said Howie, grinning at his long-haired Irish friend and business partner. He slipped the obelisk from Queshaun's fingers and set it into the empty slot within Saint Peter's Square on the map. "Full circle."

"Okay...," said Tom, speaking to be what they all wondered and needed to know. "What now?"

Seeing the little phallus-shaped shaft tilted slightly to one side within its slot, Ingrid adjusted it. Aligning straight, it clicked into place. She quickly retrieved the compass piece as the entire map began to tilt completely up on end. It rotated around, bringing its reverse side to lie flat before them. This map, no longer a twenty-foot-square depiction of the world, had become one solely of Vatican City.

"A Vatican City of the fourth century, or so," said Mike, glancing at Queshaun for confirmation.

"By the layout of Saint Peter's, yes," Queshaun said.

Beautifully detailed, Saint Peter's Basilica then rose up from the rest of Vatican City. After having done so three feet straight into the air, it stopped. Revealed beneath, at eye level, was a continuation of the map itself. Though this one charted the labyrinth of chambers and passageways that filled that truly dark realm below Vatican City.

The complex was vast, a city of its own, hidden. All the while, the world of daylight above had continued to evolve. Tom double-checked his body cam, ensuring it was still recording. Starting atop at the floor level of Saint Peter's, their eyes traced down to the enigmatic Vatican Grottoes concealed beneath.

They followed deeper, to that grim and shadowy place

known as the Vatican Necropolis. And lower still, through this subterranean maze, their eyes led to the much older, preexisting necropolis underneath. Far into the earth, and perfectly centered beneath that great eye of Christianity, Saint Peter's Basilica, laid the realm which beckoned them.

There, the L' Entita's most elusive and sacred of all their lost chambers awaited. Consecrating this truth, the chamber began to glow with an emerald most inviting. By this new illumination, they saw it at the chamber's center, the unmistakable Praesidio Autem Veritas.

Starting slowly, the symbol beat, pulsating a soothing hum. Magnifying, it shed out onto them a lush indigo. The light from this darkness deeply within, spread, bathing over the subterranean world under Vatican City.

"Jesus...," Howie said.

"Christ," Tom said, completing the perhaps overused response. Nonetheless, it was the... *perfect* response.

"Holds to the L' Entita's bravado," said Mike. "I mean, with being located beneath the Vatican itself."

Ingrid's fingers tapped upon the glowing chamber within the model. Not knowing why, at least why right now, she started to feel a kinship to her past, to those authors of great beauty, of great horror, and more. "Maybe we'll all get to finally find out how, and *why* exactly, the L' Entita, who were commissioned by Rome to create Christianity, ended up quite *literally*, demonized. And hunted down through the millennia, by that very church...," she said, not so much for them, but for herself. For her... *blood.*

"That is the billion-dollar question," Mike said.

Queshaun turned to them all in their moment of fear and awe. "How do I say this, my friends... I am both happy and sad to not be going with you, to complete this journey of yours. This quest..."

Howie removed his cellphone from his pocket, and used its camera to trace the route they'd need to take, starting at the Vatican's front doors.

"Hey...," Mike said.

They followed his gaze to the doorway of entirely normal size now open within the far wall. Howie cut in front of them, heading for the doorway. Ingrid pushed past him, taking the lead.

"Let's go," she said. As she did so, the small pyramid fell from her hand.

Howie caught it, then coolly as he could, offered it to her. Ignoring his attempt at charm, her eyes instead locked upon that little triangular object in his hand. No longer appearing as pale-bone-white, it glowed golden.

"Told you," said Tom.

Taking it, she rotated it around in her fingers. The underside was hollow. She pulled the compass piece from her pocket.

It was aglow in the same golden hue. Having forgotten all about those odd little grooves on the end of the compass piece, she ran her finger along them now. They watched as each of her hands slowly brought the two objects together.

How ever long they'd been separate, could not be known. But they each knew it had been something near an eternity. With a whispering click, the small pyramid fit over the tip, becoming a capstone for the compass piece, locking perfectly into place....

Lion's Den

*T*he passageway on the other side led them steeply up for fifty feet until it dead ended in a large pile of rubble. There were fragmented walls and a sunken ceiling. Piles of broken stone and large rocks laid in heaps. Everything was uneven, partially submerged in sand and dirt.

Howie wiped away the sweat beaded along his filth-streaked forehead. "Can't see it, but I can feel that heat. The sun's got to be just on the other side of whatever all this is."

Leading, he sucked in his sides, then pushed past the narrow gap between two massive blocks of stone. They followed him to the other side of wherever they were. He could feel the faintest of airflow dance lightly across his sweaty face.

Before him was a dust-laden wall. It was of the strangest looking material. He dug his fingers into it. The crumbling and clumpy powder of it was easy to recognize.

"We've hit a wall." He turned to them. "Drywall."

Grabbing fist-sized rocks, they smashed a hole. Breaking through, they found clothes hanging in front of them.

"Seems you've discovered a closet," said Mike, sliding aside the clothes.

Not sunlight, but light nonetheless seeped in around the seams of the sliding closet door. Howie slowly opened the door. A soccer game played on a TV in front of empty foldout chairs. The small space, with its table, microwave, and fridge, appeared to be some kind of break room.

They ventured out. Written across the wall, amongst the various sports posters there, was something in Arabic. Quite large, painted in red, it looked dripping, bloodlike.

"What's it say?" Howie asked.

Queshaun recognized the phrase. He should, as he'd been here in this very room before. "Lion's Den." He knew with a resounding certainty they must leave right now. "This is the police station," he said, grabbing a handful of jackets from the closet.

"How do you know that?" asked Tom.

Queshaun pulled on a jacket. The embroidered police badge and lion's head on the front stared them all in the face. "My brother worked here."

"Your brother's a cop?" asked Mike.

"Was," Queshaun answered, offering them the jackets.

Sliding them on, they followed Queshaun to the doorway. He peered out, making sure the hallway was clear. They moved as quickly as they could down the all-white brick hallway, passing the series of closed doors on either side, toward the exit sign beckoning their escape at the end. Unrealized in their urgency, their boots, entirely still wet and thoroughly caked with dirt and sand, left a swath of muddy footprints on the bright white tile floor.

"Where's Ingrid?" Howie asked.

Still in the break room, she stepped out, holding a can of Coke. One of the doors between her and them opened, and two police officers entered the hallway. They moved toward her. Heart racing, she tilted her head down, briskly passing.

She joined them, from where they'd watched in suspense at the other end of the hallway. Handing the half drank Coke to Howie, he took a long gulp. The coldness of the metal and condensation wetting his hand felt good, though not that it justified her recklessness just now.

She'll be the death of you, Howie. And what a death it could be... He passed the can to the others. Finishing the cool Coke, Tom started for the door marked with the 'exit' sign.

Queshaun grabbed his arm. "No, my friend, there's an alarm." He crouched to his knees. "This way."

He led, turning the next corner, entering another hallway. Tom peeked up into the window spanning the wall. Queshaun pressed his finger to his lips.

Through the window, they all now saw why he'd had them crouch. Half a dozen police officers at work stations in less than organized rows occupied the large space. All the way across on the other side of the room, they could see the glass double doors with the sunlight streaming in. Their freedom was in sight, though the relatively short distance, it was far indeed.

"Let's just go for it," Howie said, rising to his feet.

Taking the lead, he headed through the swinging door with a roaring lion's head painted upon it, and entered the inner most lair of the Lion's Den. Single file, they headed straight down the center aisle of the long room.

"Look," Tom whispered. Their wanted posters stared back at them, tacked to the bulletin board upon the wall amidst the sea of seedy faces on display. They continued at ever-increasing pace, and wouldn't stop until they reached the double doors. The last officer they had to pass suddenly stood from behind his desk. Causally, he glanced, nodded, then went for the water cooler along the wall.

Thrusting open the glass double doors, departing the Lion's Den, that familiar voice they'd all learned to loathe, entered their ears. There, within the lobby, Camorra stood. Shrouding himself in as much seclusion as he could conjure while on his cellphone, with his back to them, to anyone who might pass through, he faced the blank white brick wall before him.

The slosh of their still wet boots floated out into the lobby, mingling in the air with Camorra's hushed voice, blending together in the glass encased space. Eyes wide, jaws clenched, hearts in their throats and elsewhere—everywhere except for their chests, they moved at a conflicted pace, governed by both urgency and stealth. Slogging past him mere feet away, they pushed through the final set of doors... Daylight was truly, and justly so, blinding.

Camorra stopped mid-sentence in his phone call, hearing a noise which didn't belong. There'd been the distinct sound of feet... *Wet* feet. The double front doors swung back, returning to their closed position. The lobby was empty. He was alone. But he hadn't been. His eyes scanned. *There.* There were the wet muddy boot prints across the center of the lobby floor, leading out and away from the police station.

Abruptly ending the call, he exited the lobby into the glaring light of day. The boot prints disappeared at the bottom of the steps, already sucked up by the dry air. The sun, fully perched in the sky, stood as the lone and silent witness to whoever had slipped so closely past him.

Before him, atop the Giza Plateau, was the congested chaos of tourists, vendors, and everything in between, desperate to see and desperate to sell. Upon the steps, the last of the wet boot prints were erased by the heat of the day. And he knew they were gone without a trace, with their trail having grown cold by the sun's hellish breath.

Following the prints back through the police station, he found himself at the closet door of the break room. Pulling it open, he entered to the crunch of freshly broken drywall underfoot. Mockingly, the hole in the wall there glared back at him. He raced along the tight debris-lined pathway that came out into the steep passageway down.

Swiftly descending the passageway, he found the room with the meticulously designed model of Vatican City awaiting him. With a blink of his eyes, his mind photographed the same route the eyes of his prey not long so ago had gazed on. It'd lead him to that most hidden and secret chamber of the L' Entita beneath the Vatican...

* * **

In the break room, Camorra closed the door and turned off the TV, and lowered himself to the metal foldout chair there. He reconnected his call he'd been forced to end with Domenico. "I apologize for the disruption. You've returned to your office?"

In cloaked solitude, behind his desk at the Santa Alleanza, Domenico had indeed returned to the *nearly* impenetrable confines of his office. "Yes. You have news."

"They've escaped the pyramid."

Domenico let the words settle, but more importantly, he let their implication simmer, reaching a point of percolation within his mind. He'd hoped this whole thing would have taken care of itself nice and neat, as he so preferred things to be. Though no, the tombs of Africa had failed to entomb those who he sought, along with what they sought. And since he couldn't be sure of what precisely was being sought, just that it would prove most devastating to the Church, as well its divinity, or perceived divinity, his rules of engagement on the matter now must be... *Elevated.*

"Domenico?" Camorra asked at the other end of the line. He'd heavily awaited Domenico's response for the duration of this entirely uncomfortable pause. And he needed one, of some kind.

Domenico rose from behind the desk. His eyes fell upon his family coat of arms on the wall. Legacies all around were at stake.

There was only one answer to give. It'd be done with the utmost clarity. For clarity was the currency by which perfect calculations were obtained. And thus, results. And he needed—required Camorra's calculations to obtain precise results now more than ever.

Camorra had been in the past, and would be in the present, the *only* one to obtain such results. He was the perfect predator, a lion amongst... sheep, bears, tigers... Whatever the scenario may be, it did not matter.

Domenico held tightly the phone. "The girl cannot continue on her present course. Or, *any* course."

Camorra had deliberately waited to inform Domenico he

was aware of the female and her group's next destination, and what an impeccably unlikely one it was. He first needed to gauge Domenico's response to the news. In this unforgiving business, no lie, no matter how perfectly crafted, could ever compare to the effectiveness of allowing the other person to make an assumption in place of such a lie. Assumptions were infinitely more powerful, as they were a product of the subject's own inception. And Domenico was no average subject.

"Camorra?"

This delayed response had also been deliberate, perfectly calculated. It'd mirrored Domenico's own delay in response. Now things were equalized. "I understand." He breathed deeply. "The task will be managed accordingly." He ended the call.

He did understand. He understood that from this point moving forward, with or without his own participation, Domenico would continue wholly toward the means for which he'd just so clearly stated. Sitting there on the metal foldout chair, he stared into the blank TV in front of him. His reflection stared back at him from this dark, square void.

He could not deny the deviation he faced. Domenico must be forsaken in order to preserve his own oath to the Order of the Camorra. His next action would be an irreconcilable one. It would be a reckoning for everyone. Not the least of which, for his own self.

Camels, Horses, and Betrayal

*M*any miles away and free of the chaotic congestion of Cairo, the five of them traveled upon the backs of camels in single file fashion. Queshaun spearheaded their beast of burden endeavor through the countryside. Down the dusty road he took them, weaving around one final bend in their pastoral expedition.

The road continued on, but he brought his camel to a stop. And they all followed in the same way, drawing their reins sharply taut. At this place, both of dust and swelled with lush green, there was a homemade, though artfully so, gate framed over the drive here. It led into a grove of mango trees, ripe and full, for as far the eye could see.

Queshaun read to himself the words elegantly carved across the sign in Egyptian Arabic.

"What's it say?" asked Tom.

"Mangoes and Hash," Queshaun answered.

Ingrid pulled her camel alongside Howie's, at the place directly under the wooden gateway, and awaited their next entrance into that which was unknown. "It says, 'Don't worry, Be happy'."

Atop his camel, Queshaun bowed to them. "Yes. As I said... Mangoes and Hash."

He led them down the drive lined by the mango trees on either side. A short distance, past the first turn there within the drive, appeared a robust and lively woman on a gleaming midnight Arabian. A plume of dust flowed out behind her. She rode sidesaddle at a speed not fit for even the most daring of youth.

Pulling the beautiful horse to a truly skidded halt, she yelled out, "Queshaun! My silly brother-in-law, what a marvelous day to see your marvelously silly face!"

"Think they know each other," Tom whispered to the rest of them.

Queshaun ran his palm down the Arabian's snout. "Onyx, you're radiant as ever."

The camel beneath him released its bowels quite generously. It followed this with some blend of snarl and hiss, exposing its crooked, oversized and yellowed-teeth.

"And what a less than radiant camel, my silly brother-in-law," the robust woman said.

Queshaun rubbed the camel's long neck. It snapped at him, then spit. Quickly retracting his hand, Queshaun gestured to the woman. "Everyone, this is Fernanda. Fernanda, this is everyone."

She waved to them. "Glad to meet you, everyone. Gumaa won't be back until sometime near dusk." She briefly looked them over. Their more than disheveled state was more than obvious.

"Plenty of time for everyone to get washed up, fed, and watered," she said, spinning her flawless Arabian, Onyx, and leading with a brisk gallop.

Mike readied his camel, looked to the rest of them and smiled. "I don't know about you all, but a mango farm is sounding pretty damn good about now." He dragged the back of his palm across his forehead, mopping away the sweat that'd been so effectively drawn out by the swollen Egyptian sun over their heads. "Queshaun, our guide to life's sweet fruit, lead away!" He almost fell off his camel while saying it.

Queshaun took chase for the Arabian already out of their sight. The glistening and beautiful black horse led into that realm before them, which contained untold amounts of mangoes, swathes of shade, and a promise of peace, even if just temporary.

~ ~ ~ ~

Domenico sat across from Lucia, her desk bridging the awkward threshold. His unannounced visit to her office there in the Roman Curia had her feeling more than off balance. The fact this was her realm afforded her no counterbalance. *What all did he know?* She couldn't know, not fully. She knew, however, quite clearly, she was the one which commanded the arm of the Roman Curia, a thing of widespread power. And it had weathered worse storms than any relic of inconvenience and forgotten history.

Blocking out Domenico's words as he spoke, she repeated within her mind the only thought she could assemble in that moment which dispersed the fear she refused to reveal outwardly... If she had afflictions of self-doubt and insecurities, despite a lifetime proving the exact opposite, then it was at least conceivable he too, the mighty and mysterious Domenico Favignana, Sovereign Padrino for the Santa Alleanza, had afflictions of his own of similar, if not the same, buried deep within his being.

As he finished, having spoken his piece, she gave him a look which could only be interpreted as a woman possessing full confidence. He brought the crystal glass to his lips and drank the water, signifying he was indeed done saying what he needed to say. Continuing to reveal nothing but confidence, she less than confidently thought to herself, *he was simply fishing.*

"Well, Domenico, it makes sense, if one didn't *want* this operation to be a success... with, as you just said, having cut the Santa Alleanza off from vital resources, such as that think tank you use, and from any other outside sources which can aid an endeavor of this caliber." She made sure her words had a chance to solidify in his mind before continuing. "And if indeed, that's the case, what can I do to help, Domenico?"

He finished the glass of water, and let her try to read every gesture he had to offer, every potential reveal latent within the language of his body. His hand returned the crystal glass from where he'd lifted it, back to the small table beside the chair where he sat. That was the place where his and her shadows converged, bleeding darkly together.

From the forceful and unforgiving hand of experience, he knew, as any spy who'd survived for so long must, it only paid to deceive when absolutely necessary. Otherwise, before long, one had woven a less than symmetrical web, a strand at a time, precariously zigzagged one sticky line of lies to the next. He knew too, from this very same experience, every slivered strand of this web had to be proved true, ever after. And that was an *impossible* thing to manage for such a web as this woven thing, needing unweaving in a most desperate way, not in the time he had to work with anyway. *No.* There wasn't a spy alive that talented.

He couldn't know in an absolute sense where these tangled strings would lead. *If* she was part of this movement against him, against the Santa Alleanza, and thus of the interests of the Holy See itself, then she would do all she could to keep that fact concealed. Yes, no doubt she'd give a flawless portrayal, serving her part in the conspiracy and betrayal. She'd play her part perfectly, a tactician as she, as a spy playing a politician. Or was it the other way around...

In any case, she'd provide him as much help as she could, camouflaging her true face... *If* she was part of it all. This ball of lies and spies had begun. Now, she and he were masquerading with their masks most obliging. They were partners, even if they were adversaries.

And provided she do so, he'd readily accept, without hesitation, any assistance she'd provide. In turn, he'd play his part ever convincingly, using the genuineness of his genuine need to amass as much help as he could before all hell came crashing down... Before the collapse of this immense web of deception gave way from the gravity of it all, ensnaring him, her, and whoever else alike with its deathly and sickly stickiness.

Though he'd get his answer to the question that he'd now set in motion. It'd arrive in the calm right before this collapse. *If*, by then, she remained the only source outside the Santa Alleanza to continue providing him help, then he'd know it was deliberately allowed to be so. And she'd be dealt with. *Swiftly* so.

The pause in his response back to her felt as though minutes had passed, but in reality, it was only a few seconds. He smiled, and nodded slightly, insincerely sincere in acceptance of her gesture for a helping hand. "Yes, thank you, Lucia, I can use all the support I can get in this time... Wholly, I fear for all our souls with this darkest hour encroaching upon the light of our Church most holy."

~ ~ ~ ~

Camorra stood in the waist-deep grass, before the fence made from scraps of wire weaved together, looking more as a web than fence, and fed the horse on the other side from his hand the somewhat dry, somewhat green grass. The horse paid no mind to the prop plane as it set down onto the private runway a few yards behind Camorra. The plane continued on and away down the runway, and Camorra turned.

He wiped off the few small pieces of grass remaining on his palm and waited for the older model Mercedes now approaching. Pulling onto the grass, it parked alongside the crudely fashioned fence which bordered this runway located within the eastern edges of Cairo. Rino exited the Mercedes, joining Camorra near the fence.

Camorra handed him a wad of the long grass. Without really looking at one another, the two men fed the lone horse on the other side contained there by the fence. The fence appeared not stable enough to contain anything, much less this horse.

"Alone, today?" asked Camorra.

"Richie had a prior... matter."

The horse ate all the grass in Rino's hand. He pulled more grass, sprouted up there where it reached up to the edges of his thick and broad fingertips.

"Your investment, Mr. Teresi, it has brought forth dividends."

"Good news. But I must ask why the fast return on our venture?"

"In the words of the Santa Alleanza... Things have changed. They have their boundaries. And I, mine."

"And you, Camorra, aren't one to be kept within the fences set forth by others."

The horse's teeth chomped dangerously close to Rino's portly fingers. He yanked away his hand, back to his side of the fence. Removing an unsealed envelope from his jacket pocket, he slipped it to Camorra. "Here."

Camorra took it and opened it, revealing the property deed.

Rino tore free more grass, continuing to feed the horse despite the near encounter with its teeth. Not sure if the horse was greedy or grateful, he cared neither way. "Not the villa you requested, yes, I know. That comes later. You'll find this one of generous value though. Consider it a retainer." Seeing Camorra's hand tighten upon the deed, his lips coiled, smiling coyly, knowing he'd retained *the* Camorra, hooking this prehistoric creature of legend and lore.

Mangoes and Hash

"Camels are the Dutch of the animal kingdom," said Gumaa to them, seated in his backyard around the campfire. The flames repelled the darkness of the late hour. Gumaa looked noticeably similar to Queshaun, their features quite the same, though Gumaa's less weathered, less strained by time.

"Please forgive my brother," Queshaun said, "he truly says what he thinks."

"And I think what I say," said Gumaa. "As the Dutch would say, I don't mean it in a condescending way. I'm just saying it is what it is. Like camels, there's particular things and traits they're good at. Perhaps, the best at. Take the Germans, I wouldn't buy their wine, but trust them to manage the train schedule, I would every time."

"Well, I got to agree with you, Gumaa," Howie said. "Once to the Netherlands was once too many." He gazed out across the grove of mango trees at their backs, and past it, to the Nile in the moonlight. The water seemed to levitate over its course of gentle turns as it floated perpetually into the night. The pop of the embers inflamed at the heart of their modest, though ample fire brought him back to the moment.

"Gumaa, I've walked all seven continents, and I sincerely believe you've chosen one of the most... what's the word I'm looking for?" Howie asked.

"Tranquil," Tom said, for once capturing actually what he

wanted to hear.

"Yes, tranquil," he said, feeling envious in a contented way. "What's your secret to having it figured out?"

Gumaa fed the fire another piece of cypress wood. "Wasn't always this way." He placed his arm around Fernanda, and sliding her slightly closer to himself, smiled at her. "What finally got us on track though, was to understand happiness—it's a task, a duty for oneself, and no one else's responsibility. It needs fuel and care as to not burn out." By the firelight, he took Fernanda's hand and squeezed it warmly, tightly. "Of course, there's those who help us keep that most critical fact of life in mind."

She leaned her head into the nook of his shoulder, and as if one, they watched the flames thoroughly rapture the wood, melting it into ash.

"So simple," Howie said. "And only requires a lifetime of experience to realize."

Ingrid watched Howie watch them, and felt many things, many things indeed. She raised her glass with the wine, dark and red. "To life," she said. "And the seeds we plant while being here." They each held up their glasses, letting the flickering oranges and reds of the fire reflect off the crystal and wine. In satisfied silence, they watched the sparks leap out of the flames, freeing themselves into the lukewarm air, and drift along the night like seeds themselves.

Tom drew deeply on the smoke from the pipe in his hand. Its bowl, brimmed with hashish, looked to him like chunks of chocolate. "To mangoes and hash," he said, offering the pipe to Mike.

Collectively, they spoke the mantra as one. "To mangoes and hash." All except Mike, whom Tom still held the pipe out to.

"What is it?" asked Tom.

Mike took the pipe, and not smoking, passed it on to Howie. "What lays ahead? Where do we go from here?"

Howie pressed the pipe to his lips and pulled in the smoke.

Holding it a moment, he released, blowing it out and away into the gradients of darkness before them. "To the Vatican." He gave the pipe to Ingrid, and she smoked from it, then passed it to their hosts, who smoked it as well.

Mike let their hash smoking play out in almost ritual fashion, to complete itself full circle, before responding. Doing so just felt right, somehow more appropriate... Letting them first grow dulled by the misty gray nirvana breathed out by the pipe instead of just presenting the news he knew they'd take negatively. Having reflected wholly upon it, he decided the best way to say it was just to say what was on his mind, like their resident sage, Gumaa would, in speaking what he really meant...

He cleared his throat. "What I mean, is we know Camorra's alive. And we must assume he followed our path to the map. They'll have the Vatican on complete lockdown. Or worse, they'll have a noose set for us. Either way..." Taking the teapot filled with what his hosts had described as an, 'All natural and groovy stress relief experience,' sitting beside his empty wineglass, he poured himself a steaming cup and sipped, feeling utterly stressed by the prospect of dying in the city of saints.

The pipe returned to Howie. Leaning back upon the lush grass cool to his skin in the night air, he let the smoke generously saturate his lungs. "Stick to the office if you can't handle the field."

Mike set the teacup down, clinking it to the table's surface there with more force than he meant. "Yes, yes, very manly, kid. You know, to know the difference between a man and a kid, is, well, kid, to know what battles are winnable and what's... just plain suicide." With his frustration with Howie rising, he gulped the stress relief tea, emptying the cup. Abundantly burning the insides of his mouth, he was left even more stressed.

"So typical," Howie said, grinning lazily, now flat upon his back amongst the grass. The sea of stars above blanketed all.

"Queshaun? What do you got to say about that?" He tilted his head, looking for an answer from him. But alas, Queshaun was asleep in his chair beside the fire, chin slumped against his shoulder, evidently dreaming of better things.

Mike had anticipated such a response from Howie, but it didn't change a thing. "I'm the bad guy because I'm the rational adult. You know, kid, being responsible is a fact of life. Once you get to my age, which happens faster than you can know, your sureness of youth is long gone, no longer by your side as you dig yourself into your own grave."

Howie held his gaze upon the stars. "Mike. You know what... You belong with the Dutch... In one of their so cheerful museums way high up there in their little tower at the top of the world." He smirked at the vision of it as it entered his entirely relaxed mind. Tom and Ingrid knew to stay safely quiet on the sidelines during these father-son moments.

Though, Gumaa could no longer do so. "Howie, don't you think, if you were your father, you may feel the same way?"

"If I were my father..." Upon the grass, he let the thought wander around within his brain, not sure at all what Mike may or may not feel. "May... be." He sat up, leaning back against his arms, with his palms flat on the ground. "What's your point?"

"Points are too tiresome for men of my age."

"Men of age," Howie groaned. "How about I want to do before I'm too old to do. How about that? Men of age?"

"Sure," Gumaa said. "Just saying, it's possible your father's concern could be more for you than for himself." He finished his wine, perhaps having let the wine speak for him a bit more than what was wise for a man of his age.

Mike stood abruptly, illuminated by the firelight behind him. "Haven't we seen great things already—everyone?" He turned to Ingrid. "Isn't that enough? It is for me."

"My reasons are not yours." She looked to them all. "None of ours are."

"Exactly," Mike said. He went to Gumaa, shaking his

hand. "Goodnight." Then he shook Fernanda's hand. "Goodnight, and thank you both. For the rest you, I wish you the best." He nodded. "Life *is* seeds." He left, entering the house through the door on the back porch, alone.

The meaning within the words Mike had spoken, this variation of the very same words Ingrid had also said, remained long after he'd departed. Adrift in their ears, these words lingered, refusing to settle. *Life is seeds...* Despite its eerie echo within their minds, if it were an epiphany, its significance had yet to germinate true meaning for them. For certain, it would be one of many things awaiting them along their journey ahead.

They came back to the moment. The cypress wood popped, bursting at its center, blooming embers which appeared like seeds aglow. So fiery, though their glow faded as they floated into the night, succumbing to darkness.

All Roads Lead

"*T*hink I slept the entire time on the flight over here," Howie said to Ingrid, encompassed by the lights of the city within the night. He sat across from her at the two-person table. On the other side of the stone wall next to them, the Thames made its winding course along the edge of Rome. The waiter, or cameriere, as Howie knew the Italian context of the word to be, brought them their cappuccinos.

And drinking tenderly the creamy dark liquid, Howie tried to get a good angle of the river, looking down from where they sat, but couldn't. "The water's just situated too far below." He sipped and sighed, returning his focus to her. "Everything here is built directly upon the old, layer after layer of discontinued versions of itself. Raw, earthy, exposed."

"But that's Rome," she said. "Isn't it? I mean, shadows of its past, imprinted one to the next. That's its charm. Magic?"

"Yeah. Suppose you're right about that. To think of it, it's us, humans. It's life. It's... all that perpetual evolution of renditions passing through the dark void..." He could smell the place as he spoke, musing his existential whims to her. There was enchantment all around, flowing deep, one layer to the next. The softness of hazelnuts, dampness of the river and recent rain, and of course, of coffee beans, all filled his senses.

His thoughts came back to Rome. "Once, and still the great essence of the empire of ancient times, but having evolved into I guess... multicultural capital of Italy, here and now. Yeah, that's its charm, Ingrid. It is charming, that I'll give you." He glanced to his watch. "Would you like to go?"

"No. Not tired. Slept the whole way here. Just like you, remember."

"Big day tomorrow. With whatever happens."

"How ever it does, Howie, will be by design. Tell me, Mr. Howard Lyon, why are you doing this?"

"How do you mean?"

"*This*. Our Bible Quest," she said.

He raised an eyebrow. "I like that. Sounds like something. You know?"

"Yeah, it does. So... Why'd you get into this line of work? Running to, or from something?"

"How much of an influence did Mike have on me you mean?"

"I mean, don't bring your father into it. What kept driving you to make it a reality?"

It'd been so long since someone had asked... had wanted to know what drove him. "The thing, that thing, I love about history, no matter how much the powers that be, being whatever powers those may be, attempt to scour away and cover the truth, truth's fingerprints will always remain to be discovered. And by those who simply choose to seek it."

"You choose to seek."

"You as well."

She smiled. And so did he. Across on the other side of the Thames stood Castel Sant'Angelo illuminated in golden yellow. This nighttime lighting of the castle bled into its aged walls also of a yellowish tinge. Their eyes were destined to find it along the skyline. And did so at the same time. There it was, the iconic fortress standing guard to the entrance of Vatican City. This sentry of stone had stood for the centuries long past. It felt as though it was both daring and inviting them to cross the bridge linking Rome to Vatican City.

That city, with its famous monuments of marble openly

displayed to all, yet with history veiled. Howie knew history, and history knew that place known as Città del Vaticano. It was a place equal in measures of eternal bliss and hellfire.

And for the two of them, with their drinks along the waterfront, yes, they could have been just another normal couple on some much needed and overdue holiday. But the realm of the Vatican aglow within their vision held this daydream in the night at bay. They'd just have to make do with what they could, enjoying the little time they had for the little things, such as a quiet evening.

For her, everything she'd done since she'd departed her home in Haiti was new, was foreign. And it helped here and now to speak of things as if they were on some outing of leisure, instead of a journey for answers which brought them both danger. Or, worse.

"I could get used to these private flights of ours," she said.

Setting aside his tiny and empty cup, he smiled. "Globetrotting isn't without its perks." It felt the right time to ask. The small talk had, if anything, largely brought that about. "Something I've wanted to ask you."

"Yes?"

"The name Ingrid, it just doesn't sound very Haitian."

"That's your question? My mother was Haitian. My father, Scottish. He's to blame for my European name. Now, you have another to ask, don't you?"

"I do. Something that's been bothering me ever since the chamber in Malta. If the inscription on the L' Entita's compass piece was written before English existed, then how exactly can you make translations between the two languages so flawlessly... With how it rhymes even?"

Despite her touch of disappointment felt for his question being academic and not of a more personal nature, she couldn't help but feel a smile break over her lips. "Well, Howie, in that case, you can perhaps guess the true origins of the English language. The authors of that native tongue of yours."

The thought hadn't occurred to him, not until she'd just said it, but it made sense. *Perfect* sense. "The L' Entita."

"Since we're on it, and not to burst your bubble, Howie, but as well the authors of your native land, those deliberately chosen lucky-thirteen colonies."

"Wait—what?"

She held back an ever-sly grin. She'd let him dwell upon that for a bit, and it served him right for having such a singular mind so held to history, and not to other things. *The smaller things.* She beckoned for the waiter, and pointed to the gelato on the menu. The waiter nodded, seeing them as nothing more than another couple here, in the now. He returned inside the café.

"You like cold things?" she asked.

"Sometimes." His mind wasn't on dessert. It was on the fact neither of the two questions he'd asked her had been the one most begging on his mind. Both, though, had been a lead-in for what was. As she watched him from across the small table, he sensed she sensed he was holding back. It was time to just ask. "What are your plans, Ingrid, after we've completed this thing?"

And there it was, the question she thought he wanted to, but wouldn't ask. It wasn't just one question, but a Trojan Horse filled with many other questions which all led in a specific direction. She kept a calm within her voice. "Oh, I don't know. I won't go back to Haiti, not to live. I'll travel. For a time, at least. And you, Howie? You'll continue searching for sunken ships and pirate gold, ever to be the Flynn-type bachelor?"

"One does what one is. So, what of Daniel? Is Australia in the cards for you?"

"Who knows, but I'll tell you something. The cards are bullshit, Howie. A spectacle of fifty-two smoke-filled reflections. None of which are of oneself. No, not off running to Australia as a love-struck girl. Well, at some point I'm sure Daniel and me... Our paths, despite star-crossed as they are, will cross once more. That's in the stars, I'm certain. But after this, as I said, yeah, some travel will do me good."

Not that she showed it outwardly, even a touch of the sweet sentiment she held regarding Daniel. Certainly, it was there, just latently so. The memory of Daniel and her and their shared embrace outside the hotel in Malta flashed brightly so in her mind. *Was it more than a memory?*

It was... A moment that'd remain readily within her. "Honestly, eventually, for a time, I believe, Howie... Daniel, he'll always hold a place within me, without out actually needing to be next to me. If that makes sense."

Noticing how close their hands were to one another upon the table, she tapped the top of his palm with her fingertips, severing the closeness. "Howie, why did you end up divorced? I mean, besides work stealing time, and all that?" She'd blindsided him by her question. That, she was good at. He saw she seemed to enjoy doing it as well.

He'd asked her about Daniel, having witnessed it back in Malta... Daniel walking out the door of the hotel room. That had been what it was... A drifting of roads between two people. *But why did he feel so caught off balance by her question?* It was only the natural course of the conversation... He asks something personal, then she does in return, pulling each in closer...

Perhaps, yes, perhaps it was because it was *her* asking and not so much the question itself. "The road which leads to divorce? Not any one thing. Work, of course, not to escape the question with that scapegoat. Best answer I can sincerely give... People, they drift apart, given enough time. You know?"

"No, I really don't." She leaned up off the seat of her chair and peered down over the stone wall at the river far below. "I think people are stationary. And..." She tiptoed her fingers, walking them along the edge of the wall like a precarious young girl might do if tight-roping on a narrow path she was told not to, but did so just for that reason. "I think, everything else, that's what's moving." She lowered back to her seat, meeting his eyes. "Yes. I'm quite sure of it now. That's what's drifting, everything else. And, it's people who just need to reach out. Grab onto something as it moves past... Past themselves in this world adrift."

The waiter brought them their gelato, swiftly moving on to the next table. They started in on the cold, rich and thick treat. And they were, truly, as any couple would seem on a night such as tonight in Rome.

Howie sat there across from her, thinking maybe she really, actually was right. Maybe people didn't drift apart, but what they did or didn't attach themselves to did. That maybe some things, such as love, romance, and the like, those were the things which traveled in opposing directions, and did so at a rate faster than other things.

Maybe that was the never-ending fate of people, such as Ingrid and him... Well, not her and him, but of normal people—of couples, to be entangled by these things adrift. And only to have those things pull diametrically so, until stretched thinly as shadows, breaking free from one another, to be left once more, alone and stationary unto this world.

He ate his gelato, letting the cold bite into him. Finished, he pushed away the empty dish. "You know, Ingrid, you're quite a unique kind of person. Peculiar, but nicely so."

"Thank you."

When she said that simple response, that was the moment, and for no particular reason he could draw distinction for, a 'simple thank you' from years ago spoken from his wife—ex-wife's lips to him, entered his mind. The absoluteness hit him. He realized his wife, Bexley, and he had ended, adrift, alone on their separate ways. The reason was not because of the drifting apart, not because of the rifting of life, but because they stopped trying to hold on to each other while adrift.

Things felt too stationary at this table. He stood. "Music's playing down the way." He held out his hand. "Care to dance?"

"Sure. As long as you lead." Hand in hand, she rose, and they began down the road toward the music.

"And where are you two headed?" Tom called out after them, poking his head from the café's doorway. Then, he heard the music too, coming from the open courtyard not far down the way. "Ah." He joined them on the curb. "Before you go, someone's here to see you..."

Mike stepped from the café. Neither Ingrid nor Howie, so engrossed in each, had even noticed him enter.

Tom nodded at Mike. "Look who decided to show up to risk life and limb on our adventure so reckless in this place of many roads well-traveled and those, not so much so," he said poetically so, wrapped in his Irish accent, while presenting Mike to them as smoothly as he could, in hopes of a productive reunion, or at least productive enough.

"Howie."

"Mike."

Both men nodded curtly. Ingrid squeezed Mike, not his hand, but more intimately and a little higher, above his wrist, thankful he'd changed his mind, glad for his expertise, as well company. Her hand released him, and with her other hand, gripped Howie's. Howie led her down the road into the night.

"You kids don't be too late now!" Tom shouted. "Got a big day come the rise of the sun." He turned to Mike. "Come, let's enjoy our Roman holiday."

They returned inside the café and found a place at the bar. Mike ordered a glass of wine, red, and one he'd not tried before. And, Tom, not that he didn't appreciate the alluring aroma of Mike's wine, ordered an Italian cream soda, butter rum in flavor.

The Italian folk music known as Tarantella drifted out from the courtyard, with its many columns generously wrapped in both grapevines and soft white lights. Terraced wooden beams overhead the dance floor, adorned in light as well, shed down upon the multicultural patrons submerged within its charm. And the adjoined restaurant, in Roman fashion, was busy, too crowded. Most of the people were seated, enjoying their food and drink.

Howie and Ingrid entered the courtyard and joined the few there dancing. Everyone moved to and from and back again, along each other, their simple movements shadowing life. No one danced the same, as there were no rules, not here and not now. The places everyone came from were wrought with rules, requirements, and limitations. Regardless of how many roads each had taken to bring them here, they'd inevitably find themselves back in those same places. But *this* was their time.

Howie led Ingrid to the dance floor, her hand cupped in his. They danced, doing so unlike anyone else. Here, they were anonymous. Here, they were just Ingrid and Howie. They were alone, just the two of them... Just two more people who'd followed one of the many roads into the night... *Just like everyone else*, they thought, if not believing, trying to believe so.

As he danced upon the cobblestone, Howie saw his shadow cast on the wall. There was a brief, though deep foreboding in that shadow before him. He knew his purpose now. Tomorrow, he'd lead. He'd be the hero. And as the hero, not of the screen nor of paper, he'd be most vulnerable to the cost of this role. For what did distinguish a hero from the rest, he thought, if there was neither risk nor *sacrifice*?

The music flowed through him, and he felt it. Music was the freedom of now. Rifting their bodies to and fro it was without rules. It was adrift. All his worries could flow out, taken away by this rhythmic current. His eyes met her eyes. Those eyes of hers, piercing, wise, beyond justification, vivid, they were... *stationary*... Of a time without time.

They were the only thing that was as far as he could see in any direction. And he saw in her eyes that she too recognized what his shadow had foretold. Written without form upon the wall, it said that a hero's beginning was entangled to its own end. That was why he needed to kiss her. It was also why he denied himself and her this action, both simple yet complex.

Sweaty and hearts beating, they ended their rhythmic movements with the culmination of the song. He'd given her the first dance and the last. But now, brimmed with emotion, motionless, while everyone else around them danced, moving in chaotic elegance, they felt it. It felt a dark end....

Grottoes

"*I*t's not literally Saint Peter's tomb," Tom said. Within the towering walls of Saint Peter's Basilica, they moved with the wave of tourists, seeking answers. The answers they sought however, required a deeper truth. They headed along the nave toward the far end, to where the high altar of Saint Peter's was.

"Even by the Vatican's own admittance," Tom said, continuing, "it's just their *tradition* to refer to it as that."

"Thanks, Tom," Howie said, "think we're all aware there wasn't actually any such person, historically speaking."

For the elderly woman in the crowd with her grandson, who overheard these two men's words, it was particularly shocking, because both men wore the traditional long black cassocks designated for priests. She gasped and glared, and gripped her grandson's hand, and pulled him away and out of range of hearing any further blasphemy.

"God, only place I've seen that gets away with charging their tourists money to use the restroom," Tom said.

"Only restroom with gold-plated ceilings I've ever seen," said Howie. "Doesn't come cheap you know."

Mike joined them, in a cassock of his own, now before the massive bronze baldachino, the Baroque canopy-like structure towering eight stories over the altar. "Can't believe I let you two talk me into this."

Tom grinned that grin only he could. "I don't know. What do you think, Howie? I think it's a natural enough look on Mike, a man of the cloth, as it were."

"As it were," Howie said, glancing up at the thick beams of light streaming in from overhead while positioned directly under the dome. Perfectly round, at four-hundred and forty-eight feet high, the dome stared down upon him like a giant eye, watching everyone and everything. "Where is it exactly...," he started to ask, but Ingrid, in a black and white habit, and features nearly too eye-catching for any nun to be allowed to have, had already located the place.

Behind a steady stream of tourists, she led their incognito group of four, entering inside the truly immense and awe-inspired Pier of Saint Andrew. The statue of Saint Andrew itself was stunning, and eerily so. As Saint Andrew, if he'd actually existed, had been dipped in liquid marble and encased skin-deep. The result, a likeness nearly identical to life itself. The pillar it was carved from was colossal, as much as it was beautiful, wrapped in ornate oak leaves and gleaming of veined marble.

As fast as the crowd would allow, they descended the staircase inside the pier, leading them below into the Vatican Grottoes. The fervent tourists hungry to see the mysteries beneath the Vatican spread out through the underground corridors, providing the four of them the perfect cover to blend in. Everyone's footsteps merged together as one upon the Tuscan marble floor. Their hushed voices of awe culminated into a great, undiscernible whisper, which echoed off the virgin white walls of stone.

"This way," Mike said, taking them down the main passage.

The hallway-like space was lined with cubbies with

arched entrances on either side. Roped off, they contained marble sarcophaguses holding deceased popes, and diplomats who'd found favor with the institution which now held their remains of dried-up bones. The four of them stopped at the entrance to the decorative though modest-in-size room branching off from the main passage. A metal plaque on the wall proudly displayed the name of the place, 'Chapel of the Madonna of Bocciata'.

The tall dual gates to the chapel were fully open. Half a dozen onlookers had already congregated inside, taking photos with the room's centerpiece, the fresco of the Madonna della Bocciata, along the chapel's far wall, dyed in what was once rich blood-orange, now somewhat bled out and faded. Howie checked his watch, not wanting to enter too early, though neither too late.

Quickly, while as casually as they could, they peeled off their long and black cloak-like garments, revealing the Vatican workman uniforms beneath. Shedding these grimly dark cloaks of the Church and bone-white collars, they transitioned in mere seconds from clergy to that of the construction team stationed within the Vatican Necropolis directly beneath where they stood. Acting with all the authority afforded one dressed in the workman uniforms, they entered the chapel. They took the stanchions with red ropes suspended between their polished bronze poles that were sitting along the chapel wall.

"Please," Howie said to the tourists inside the chapel, "this area is now closed."

Groaned complaints slipped through the mouths of the disappointed sightseers as they dispersed from the space.

"Ruining vacations the world over," Tom said, helping Howie position the stanchions and ropes across the entrance to the chapel, sealing it off.

"I'm faithful they'll manage," said Howie. He pulled up

the sleeve on his uniform and monitored the minute hand rotating around the face of his watch. "Perfect."

"Now, where it pays to be a stuffy academic who reads copious amounts of history," said Mike, leading to the marble slab along the right side of the chapel.

At first and even second glance, the slab very much appeared to be part of the wall itself. So often overlooked by tourists, carved upon the slab was a marble relief of a knight. A cloak shrouded his face. The sword gripped by both his hands, gloved with chain mail, displayed a symbol that appeared to be three 'sixes' interlinked. These three interlinked sixes formed the eye of the sword's pommel, located at the very end of its handle. Behind the knight was a strange, and borderline otherworldly landscape, identical to the one found on the painting of the Mona Lisa, if one were to take notice of such things.

But even you, Mike, an academic of things lost and forgotten, of things hidden, find such information rare to come by, he thought, taking a moment to locate the place there at the top of the marble relief. The decorative and leafy edge of the veined white marble framing the knight had the lightest indentation upon the center of one of its decorative leaves. In anticipation, he looked to them, then pressed his thumb firmly down, and tried to believe the ancient manuscripts he'd read over a decade earlier were correct, were true...

And... *maybe they weren't. Maybe it was all bullshit.* He couldn't deny the doubt, not now that nothing happened when he pressed upon the spot. This was the right place. It was the *only* place to be pressed upon.

"It's supposed to slide or what?" Howie asked.

"Slide," Mike answered.

With a sharp thud, Ingrid kicked at the narrow piece of marble wedged quite tightly. They all saw it now, nearly concealed within the tiny gap there at the bottom of the marble slab where it met the floor. Howie left Mike and joined Ingrid at the opposite end of the ornate relief, and helped her work to knock the sliver of marble free.

Tom kept watch behind them, at the tourists wandering through the corridor. Some paid them glances, but continued on after seeing the roped off entrance to the cherished little chapel. He deeply hoped the onlookers made the assumption the four of them were simply workers doing whatever it was they were doing.

The toes of Ingrid's and Howie's boots both came down at the same time, finally kicking away the small piece of marble. Mike pressed down upon the intended place on the leaf once more. The slab of marble budged, perhaps four inches. Together, they managed to push it out just wide enough, then passed through quickly.

Necropolis

*W*hen they entered the secret passageway, they found darkness and metal beneath their feet. There were cold walls a few inches from their bodies on both sides of them. It was of rough stone. The moderate dampness of the place brought a collective shiver through their beings. A steady crunch beneath their feet was the result of the walls, having suffered centuries of decay, and shedding lumps of themselves in fist-sized wads of fragmented stone to the metal walkway.

Howie used the flashlight on his phone to guide their way down the sloping passage, leading them two stories below Saint Peter's Basilica. It took no more than a few minutes to reach where it ended, at a barred gate. A padlock, quite dated but not ancient, secured the gate.

Beyond these bars was more darkness. Pungent waves of mildew swept into their nostrils. There was another odor too, not as crass to their senses, but more bitter. It was the scent of old death.

"Personally," Mike said, "I prefer this route for accessing the necropolis, I mean, to the one they make the tour groups use outside the basilica. You know the one, next to that terribly pretentious souvenir shop."

Howie gripped the lock upon the gate and shook it. "I prefer a way not locked."

They searched along the floor for a stone worthy of the

task. Ingrid, finding a particularly large one, handed it to Howie. After a couple of swift strikes, he broke off the hasp on the lock. He pulled open the gate, and they entered into the Vatican Necropolis hidden below the grottoes.

Tom wrinkled his nose to a scent most murky permeating from this underground crypt of the dead. "Why was that passageway even there?"

"Ah," said Mike, "yes, this here was a bit of a backdoor for the Ammantato Invisibile... As to smuggle in their Vatican-sanctioned spoils of war into the secret vaults beneath Saint Peter's... Back, before they started using the vaults deep within the mountains of Switzerland."

"Who?" asked Tom.

Mike thought a moment, seeing no way to word this delicately. "Eh, the group the Church replaced the Templars with after the pope had them all mass murdered," he answered as best he could, as they made their way through the dark, mildew-laced stone corridor.

Seeing Mike's explanation hadn't helped, Ingrid leaned her lips close to Tom. "The Ammantato Invisible were Vatican state sanctioned mercenaries. Infinitely more vicious and violent than the Templars."

"Vatican sponsored pirates... Fantastic," Tom said, grinning.

Ingrid frowned. "Well, that's not really—"

"*Pirates*," Tom said rather loudly, his voice announcing it down the narrow corridor, echoing through the dark.

This brief corridor ended, and before them now was what may have been any dark alley to be found in the center of Rome, where things still remained ancient and lost to time. Certainly, it didn't look as though they were underground. The path beneath their feet was narrow, and an actual street of stone, level and smooth. On both sides of this alley-like path were structures that appeared as buildings of red brick, seamlessly connected one to the next.

These were the mausoleums, as they appeared not as one

would envision them to be, but as actual buildings or as houses, with normal to scale doors, windows, and patios. They reached one, two, and three stories up toward the shadows above. There, the sky-like darkness concealed their ceilings' ends. The open doorway for each mausoleum offered them passage inside. Large lightbulbs strung out along the tops of the mausoleums brought the dramatic contrast between the light and the dark.

"Which one is it?" asked Ingrid.

Howie unfolded his tourist map of the necropolis and drew from his pocket the photo he'd taken from the Vatican model in Egypt. Comparing both, he found the route they needed. "Mausoleum U."

Mike took the map, checking his suspicions. "Yep. That's what they call Lucifer's Tomb."

Their collective stare begged, *Why?*

"You'll see." He handed back the map.

Footsteps approached from somewhere inside the necropolis. They slipped inside the doorway directly to their right and hid in the shadows. Casual voices in Italian joined the pending footsteps. Howie checked his watch. The workers assigned to the necropolis passed by, and continued along the narrow pathway toward the main entrance, leading out into Saint Peter's Square.

"Never late for lunch," Howie said. He led, climbing out of the open mausoleum, quickening their pace upon the pathway, straight for the center of the Vatican Necropolis, to that place known as Lucifer's tomb.

Camorra awaited them in Lucifer's Tomb. Shrouded in silence and darkness, he listened to their footsteps as they unknowingly drew closer. Flat on his back, he laid within the tight space carved into the wall, low to the ground. A little slotted cubby intended for a corpse, but it did quite nicely to conceal the predator from prey. His pupils had expanded, adapting to the dull lighting for quite some time.

The infamous mosaic was across from him there, on the

wall. While waiting, he'd come to relish this piece of art. The vibrant reds and oranges framing Lucifer, the Light Bearer, on his white horse reared up on two legs toward the comet-like sun... Or perhaps it was another star. Whatever it was, was power... The greatest of power, that of knowledge, and the will to both wield and use that power.

Letting them draw in closer, closer, the vibrations of their footsteps deepening, he admired the mosaic of Lucifer and of his brilliance in the illuminated shadow of the sun. Their footsteps were strong now. Intersection was upon them all... They entered the mausoleum. Stopping in front of the mosaic, they eclipsed Camorra's view of the Morning Star.

Ingrid rested her fingertips along the edge of the tiny colored tiles making up the mosaic. "The bringer of light... Of knowledge. Of wisdom."

"Anything they can do to demonize free thought and will," said Tom, somewhat cynically. "Forgive the fitting pun."

"It's true, they're no champion to people's freedoms," Mike admitted, "though still, being fair, modernity's Vatican is the largest provider of charities and humanitarian aid in the world."

At what cost," Howie sharply responded, having had about all he could bear from Mike's posturing as Church apologist.

"This isn't the place, and certainly not the time," Ingrid said.

"Another time, another place," said Howie. "Knock on wood." He rapped his fist upon the center of the mosaic. The solid thud announced clearly their entrance into the hidden chamber would be more difficult to find than that.

He lowered his fist from the wall. "Well, hell, that was my best guess. Anyone?"

"Look for any kind of symbol that could be associated with the L' Entita, something we've seen before or a variation of," Ingrid instructed them. Her self-doubt and fears of inadequacy encroached upon her, for once again, she didn't have the answer for them.

They spread out, searching. The mausoleum was somewhat smaller than the chapel from which they'd passed through, that was somewhere above them now. The paint had faded badly on the walls, and in places was nonexistent. Modest cubbies carved into the walls themselves, spaced throughout, held nothing, or at most, fragments of dust-laden pottery.

There wasn't much to investigate. A semicircular nook of a few feet across was high up on the center wall. Crowned above it, gracefully painted, though worn, a picture of a large peacock. A few other smaller birds, similar, yet different in appearance and colors, which could have of parrots, perched along these archaic walls of the mausoleum.

Camorra intently watched them as they worked. This was the first time he'd observed his prey in their natural way of being, and not distraught with guns pointed and voices and emotions tense. He saw they had nothing particularly special guiding their way. Just... their will and earnest nature for the exploration for answers. For... the *truth*. *That most dangerous thing.*

This simple revelation for what compelled them relieved the conflict. As herein laid the problem, not for himself, but for Domenico, as well the likes of whomever served the interests... *self*-interests of the Holy See. And *that* was the problem, but more so, the danger. He knew, as they must too by this point in their journey, nothing was more dangerous than a truth denied its shining light, shackled in concealment for far too long.

Tom, having exhausted all efforts, and without thought to it, a bit irately stomped his foot upon the floor there where he stood, near the central wall of the mausoleum. It too gave a hard thud, eliminating the chance of the entranceway being below their feet. Glancing at it now, the floor he'd first believed to be of dirt, wasn't. It was just simply layered in a lot of dust and filth.

From his pocket, he removed the one bottle of water

security had allowed him to enter with. Sipping from it first, he poured a generous amount onto the floor. It wasn't nearly enough to wash away the layers of grime which blanketed there, but it was enough to expose the masterfully crafted tile underneath.

Focused within her own search, Ingrid moved to the wall Camorra had hidden himself at the bottom of, inside that carved out alcove intended to cup a corpse. Her knees came directly into his field of vision. Aside from a patch of peeled paint of an indiscernible shade, the wall was utterly blank. She saw the shadowed hole near her feet. He watched her knees as they began to bend. She started to crouch down to examine the place where he was, just a few inches away...

He slid his gun from its holster and held it steadily upon his chest and slowed his breathing to a perfect silence....

Sacrifice at Lucifer's Tomb

*A*t the other end of the mausoleum, Howie took noticed of what Tom had stumbled upon, or more so, had stomped upon. "Dump the rest." Tom emptied the bottle of water on the floor. Revealing the entire mausoleum was built at an unperceivable slant, the water began to flow to a very specific place at the base of the central wall before them. This created a tidy little pool, triangular in shape.

Oblivious to what they'd found, she felt she'd found something as well. As to what, she didn't know. Not allowed to pass through the basilica security with a flashlight, and having failed to charge her phone, she had no light to cast illumination upon this current darkness. She knelt before the alcove. It was barely visible. There was just an outline inside that cubby within the wall, lush with heavy shadow. The light dimmed in that place in an unnatural way.

Needing to know, and at the mercy of whatever spell this was, her hand reached out toward the shadow. Her fingers extended, sinking into the space. Her head, very, very close now, her eyes strained, mesmerized. Yes, there was something there, the contours of a...

Camorra, faceup, flat upon his back, with his free hand, began to reach for Ingrid's outstretched fingers. He watched those tantalized fingers which searched so closely, searching for the truth. A piece of paper couldn't have passed between the tips of their fingers, converging, on the cusp of intersection. He could feel the heat from her body as he prepared for their touch—

"Ingrid," Mike said, suddenly from behind her. Causing her to jump, she turned to him, while awkwardly still crouched.

"They found something," he said.

The light from Mike's phone held at his side cast its soft glow upon floor only a few paces away from the alcove. Camorra's hand trembled there in the open darkness, something it had never done before. His fingers nearly touching hers, as she faced the other way, still holding out her hand directly for his. His heartbeat began to rise. That too was a peculiar sensation. He smiled upon the shadowed outlines of hers and his hands. For, they resembled the Sistine Chapel's iconic centerpiece with God's and Adam's fingers about to touch. *So close...*

Ingrid rose and followed Mike to the others. A few inches directly above where the triangular pool had formed was another mosaic. They hadn't noticed it at first due to the film of dirt covering it. Lowering to her knees, she cupped her palms together, scooping water from the pool. She splashed it upon the mosaic. They worked quickly to wash away the dirt.

"What is it?" Mike asked.

The colors, muddled, nearly gone, but the image remained. Three-foot by three-foot-square, the mosaic displayed a tree. Like a complex and upside-down root system, its branches were spread out, filled with leaves. And with something else...

"Are those...," Howie began to ask, though realizing what hung on the tree was precisely what they appeared to be. Suns, no larger than apples, dangled ripely aglow throughout the tree's branches.

"Forbidden fruit... Bearing *knowledge* to man," said Ingrid.

Tom knocked on the mosaic. The echo confirmed their point of entrance concealed behind this unique and beautiful piece of art.

Grabbing one of the mausoleum's loose bricks strewn along the floor near the wall, Tom headed for the mosaic. "So, let's take a bite."

"Don't even think about it," Mike said, desperately searching the mosaic's edges, looking for a way to remove it intact.

Howie glanced to Ingrid, who nodded for the go-ahead. They wouldn't just eat of the tree of the knowledge of good and evil painted upon the mosaic. They'd shatter it. It'd been created beautifully so, without flaw into the wall. Majestic, it was perfect. And that would be its downfall. It'd be their sacrifice to gain entrance.

"Here," Howie said, taking the brick from Tom's hand. He glanced at Mike, who stood behind them, arms crossed. The others moved back. He repeatedly smashed the brick into the center of the mosaic until it cracked, caved, and shattered, leaving them an opening to pass into. Howie tossed the brick and peered in with the light from his phone. A gust of stale air swept past him into the mausoleum. Gasping on the unpleasant taste, he pulled his head back.

"Want me to lead?" Ingrid offered.

"Most certainly not," he said. "I have chivalry to think of."

"Please," she said, rolling her eyes, "men with their sexism guised as swashbuckling."

He drew in a breath, tried to relax his mind, and climbed inside the small passageway. "You're not replaceable, my lady. Tom and... Mike even, can replace me," he said, the square space amplifying his voice in a deep and ominous way.

"No need to foreshadow your doom," Mike said, entering. Ingrid and Tom followed.

Alone, in shadows all his own, Camorra pulled his body from its resting place, and went straight for the opening. He could still inform Domenico of all he knew. Domenico would have to understand, because, despite his delay, he'd be delivering these four to him. Domenico would be pleased by the end of it too. Bemused even. How could he not be.

All this time, the L' Entita's hidden secret was beneath the Vatican. The Santa Alleanza could not ask for a more convenient location in which to control, cover up, and dispose of any threat to be found there. It would be perfect. *Flawless.* He wouldn't though, not with reporting a thing to Domenico. He'd already made up his mind. This fall from grace with Domenico, and the other, grimmer consequences yet to take fruit would be his sacrifice, and his alone to bear. *All...* would likely burn.

Fall unto the Underworld

*W*ith the flashlight from his cellphone guiding the way, Howie crawled through the passageway that was much too small. He'd assumed the three-foot by three-foot hole that he'd passed through would have opened up into something wider, even by a little. It hadn't. In fact, it felt things were growing tighter. This could've been inside his mind, with the deepening tide of panic drifting in.

He thought about each of the places he could be instead. Even a dig out on the Sahara Desert, baking in the sun, was infinitely better. Or, as he was most accustomed to, the deep sea. The ocean entered his mind because of the water now. Not a lot, but enough to be noticed, it was there between his body and the stone floor. And it was flowing slowly and coldly, very coldly in the direction he crawled. A chill closed in upon him, along with the damp and cramped mildew-coated walls.

An ocean, any one of them, that's where he wished to be. Not that he particularly enjoyed putting his life at the mercy of an air tank while under water. But it was wide open space for as far as the eye could see, and beyond. The less space, the less control he had. And he needed that, control—the cold wet stone beneath him was suddenly no longer beneath him.

His phone was gone and he plummeted through the darkness. *God, impact was really going to hurt at this distance and speed*—his body hit with a tremendous splash into a deep pool of water. The welcomed fact it wasn't rock or stone was short-lived. The shocking awe of just how cruelly cold the water was consumed his entire being with stabbing pain.

Thrashing up, he pulled himself to the surface. In the dark, he grasped wildly for anything. There—there was the wall. Of smooth rock, it denied a hold of any kind. He pressed his palm to it, letting it guide him. Then... the strangest thing he saw...

A small light came flying down through the dark, straight at his face. One thought and one thought alone took hold, as he uncontrollably shivered from the frigid water. *What the hell is that?* He reached for it. Slipping through his fingers, whatever it was, hit the water a few inches out in front of him. He grabbed the object aglow before it could start to sink too deeply.

Realizing he now held Mike's phone in his hand, he shook the water off and aimed the phone's flashlight. The rock walls weren't rock walls at all. They were the walls of mausoleums. And the pool he was in wasn't just a hole with water. Once built upon dry earth, this place was now partially submerged.

He knew where he must be. This was the second necropolis beneath the first. And he must be close to the L' Entita's secret chamber, as this was the lowest level beneath the Vatican.

"Howie?" Mike's voice echoed down to him.

"I'm alive!"

"What do you see?"

Howie let the phone's light trace across the surrounding mausoleums. There were endless tombs and graves. "More dead people!"

"Oh. Why didn't you take the stairs?"

"What stairs?"

"The stairway directly on the other side of the hole you fell into! Didn't you see the stairway?"

"No—I fell!" *What kind of question was that?* Howie glared in the dark. *Leave it to Mike.*

"We're taking the stairs!"

"I'll meet you here!"

"How will we find you?" Mike shouted.

"I'll be the only one holding a cellphone down here!" Howie swam to the edge of the water to where it gradually transitioned to dry ground, or at least to where things weren't submerged.

The first necropolis above may have been impressive, but this place was, by all measures, an entire metropolis for the dead. It was like another Rome beneath both Vatican City and Rome itself, with how far it appeared to sprawl. Mausoleums, great and small, simple and extravagant, and everything in between, were everywhere. It was a maze, a complex, a great city where no one lived, but everyone was here, with their veils of stone. There was nothing he could compare such a place to, not on this scale, nor grandeur.

Not far at all from the water's edge, he leaned against a massive gravestone of marble. He wrung out his clothes and managed to get his shivering under control. Their voices came from somewhere in the darkness.

He held the cellphone above his head, trying to see the top of the gravestone towering over him. Being far too large for any gravestone, it had to be some kind of monument. It was nearly to the same scale as that eight-story tall baldachino inside Saint Peter's Basilica.

How could he have mistaken this... *thing* as a mere grave marker. It was hard to see in the poor lighting, but the marble structure appeared to taper out in a rounded kind of way forty or so feet above his head. There, it formed some sort of bowl. And the section that comprised this bowl appeared to have been another forty feet tall itself.

Seeing their flashlight beams, he waved the light from the cellphone in their direction. No one needed to speak, for this site was a sight not to be spoken of or simply seen, but digested, and thoroughly so, with all of their senses. After the long moment had passed, they turned their focus from the metropolis of mausoleums to the bowled structure Howie leaned against, with his hands tucked up under his armpits, subduing residual shivers.

"That's a hell of a torch," Tom said, illuminating the deep groove brimmed with oil carved along the base of the structure.

Grabbing Tom's flashlight, Howie aimed toward the massive bowl shape. Mistaking the thing for a gravestone was one thing, but... *not* immediately recognizing it as a device to birth light unto this place, that was something else entirely. If he was to lead, then he needed to at least know what the hell he was looking at while doing so. His focus shifted to the flashlight. "Tom, where'd you get a—"

"Flashlight? From one of the worker's tool belts they left after they went to lunch." He removed the cigarette lighter from his pocket. His thumb softly rubbed over the four-leaf clover stamped upon its face before handing it to Ingrid. "Do the honors."

"You don't smoke," she said.

"Lucky charm, from an old archeologist friend. Retired now."

She ignited the lighter. "Let there be light." She lowered the lighter to the vein of oil. The flame kissed the oil, and like a great serpent of fire, it bloomed brightly in rich yellow. The flame raced up the base of the enormous marble torch, disappearing into the vast reserve of oil contained within. It took a few seconds for the flame to travel the eight stories above them to the massive bowl, erupting into something glorious indeed.

Now they could truly see this city of the dead. The light revealed the narrow viaduct of marble running from the midsection of the bowl, and spanning high over their heads out for fifty feet into the distance. This viaduct bridged to the next great torch of equal size.

It too blossomed into flame. After a few seconds, another, and another, and another did the same. Two dozen, maybe more, of these massive torches erupted to life. Until finally, the vastness all around spilled forth light, crackling with fire.

"Have you ever seen a sight even close to this?" asked Howie.

"I've never even imagined such a thing, not as this," Mike answered for them all.

"Where is all the oxygen coming from?" Tom asked.

Ingrid pointed to the immense grove of plants in the distance. Prehistoric and taller than they, this thickly sprawling entangled nest of vegetation was a jungle unto itself.

"As to the rest of the science of the ecosystem, you've got me," she said, shrugging.

"We'll be sure to send down a botanist in the future," said Tom, "at some point... But first, okay, let me just wrap my mind around one thing. Originally, this... and for no lack of a much better word, graveyard, was built here, because, you know, the ancient Roman ordinance said it was illegal to bury the dead within Rome's city limits. Then, the necropolis above us was built on top all this here. *Then*, Nero built his thing, that giant racetrack thing..."

"Nero's Circus," Mike offered. "Or, Caligula's. Whichever."

Tom nodded, having forgotten the rather obvious title. "Then, on top of that, the first Saint Peter's Basilica. And then, the second Saint Peter's Basilica constructed on top of *all* that."

"Don't forget the Vatican Grottoes, that, at some point, they decided to stuff between the present basilica and the *second* Vatican Necropolis," Howie said.

"Moving on," Ingrid said, stepping forward, "whatever we're looking for will take a whole lot longer if we don't split up."

"Haven't you watched any horror movie. *Ever*," said Tom. "Right after the group splits up is when they're each picked off one by one."

"Everyone stays within visual distance of someone else," said Howie. He turned to Ingrid. "Anything else?"

She nodded. "It's a good assumption what we're looking for directly relates in some way to one of these graves."

They spread out in different directions down the streets, lined with what looked to be endless monuments for the dead. As Howie ventured deeper, eyes watched him. These eyes followed, hidden in the dark. Howie continued on along the road of stone and dirt and the occasional stray bone he'd chosen from the many untold roads.

Ingrid and Mike, not long after choosing their own separate roads, came to a place of intersection. Face to face, they were bathed within the firelight of the mighty torches towering above.

"You had the same inkling as I," he said.

"Appears so." Stepping out of the light and close to the place, their eyes drew to the edifice casting its great shadow down on them. While they gazed upon its macabre elegance, the same eyes that'd watched Howie from the darkness now watched them. It drew closer, silently melting the distance between itself and them.

Mike waved in the air, and yelled, "We found something!" He and Ingrid waited for the others, somewhere in the distance, obscured by the mausoleums and elongated shadows.

Having just noticed what was atop, the crowning jewel to this immense mausoleum, Ingrid set her hand along Mike's cheek. She turned his head, leading his eye.

"We found it," she said. Amplifying her voice into a shout the others would be destined to hear, she proclaimed it with all her soul. "We found *it!*"

From the darkness, the eyes watched. It'd wait just a little longer... For the others...

Originem

*S*teepled atop this towering mausoleum, the L' Entita's Praesidio Autem Veritas was illuminated by the flicker of the great torches. The eye at its center gazing down upon them couldn't have been more ominous. Their team of four stood there at the mausoleum's great doors, gazing back. The tapestry of light and shadow from the flames danced across their faces, across their bodies, and most of all, across their souls. The mausoleum appeared to be built into the hillside of rock directly behind it. There was no telling for how far into the earth it went.

"Went looking for the tallest one," said Mike. "Follow the money, right."

"Alexander. Flavian. Herod," Ingrid said, reading the three surnames emblazoned proudly into the elaborate marble crest above the heavy dual doors of the mausoleum.

"*The* three most powerful families in the world at the time," Howie said.

It began to set in what they actually were up against. With not just who pursued them in their present, but the legacy of this power from the past. These weren't just names. They were titans of their time, and no less than master architects of history itself. For the four of them, the odds of at least one or more of them ending in a grave of their own felt quite high.

The compass piece grew uncomfortably hot inside her pocket, and Ingrid removed it. Softly emitting an amber glow, the heat receded. Upon the mausoleum's marble crest, words in Latin revealed themselves, illuminating in a vivid and silky gold, while encircling the three surnames. Then symbols, each distinctly unique, appeared along the crest. Above the crest, another word in Latin appeared, deep and crimson.

"Originem," she said, looking to the single word above the rest.

"Origin," Mike said. "Meaning, in Latin, 'to rise'."

Ingrid named off the symbols. "The anchor, boat, fish, olive branch, and star."

Mike pointed to these. "Each, and in how they're arranged, formed the Flavian family banner. The equivalent of their coat of arms. Also, these were the first symbols of Rome, when it was founded upon Palatine Hill. These symbols of Rome, they go all the back to the very origins of Rome itself... One thousand B.C."

"Well," Howie said, "how about that, the Flavian family banner and crest for Rome of the first century are the exact same as those for the earliest symbols of Christianity."

"Huh. I never made the connection until now...," Mike said. "But you're absolutely right, kid. Every single one of these symbols are the very same, originally used by Christianity." He shook his head. "Sometimes, guys, I'm telling you, I think the most obvious pieces to a puzzle are those left to be discovered until the end. I mean, *these* symbols, along with the carvings of the Flavians' face profiles, were on the Roman coins of the first century. I actually have one in my office at the university..." His annoyance with himself deepened, realizing... "Ironically, right next to my bookshelf packed with books on the origins of the Church." He sighed, not at all feeling clever or wise, but a dusty old man who'd missed far too much in his time.

"Intriguing," Tom said.

"Intriguing indeed," said Mike.

Ingrid quickly stated the Latin phrase aglow upon the marble crest, eager to move on in their journey. "Fili Vir."

"Son of Man," Howie said, translating the Latin.

"The official title of Titus Flavius, the first century Roman emperor," said Mike.

"Isn't that Jesus's thing? That title?" Tom asked.

"So was rising from the dead, being born of a virgin, walking on water, et cetera, et cetera, et cetera," said Mike. "But we well know now, when it comes to this Jewish god-man, nothing is, shall we say, kosher, at least regarding the originality of any of his attributes." Picking up on Ingrid's growing impatience, he turned to her. "Mind if I give a quick detail or two on this phrase? Given it's carved here, glowing brightly so, it just might prove important later."

"Please," Ingrid said.

"Thanks," he answered. "Briefly, you see, 'Son of Man' derives from an older version of itself. Being, 'The *Sun* of Mankind'. Literally, meaning the sun. That gaseous ball within the sky. A common, though, revered phrase shared by many of the ancient pagan cultures, simply expressing their respect for the awesome power of nature."

"And why's it emblazoned across the front of this mausoleum containing the three most powerful families of the first century?" asked Howie.

"Aside from its implication the remains of Titus Flavius could remain inside," said Mike, "I don't know. Though, only one way to find out. And all I can tell you, Titus took this phrase from the Druids, and designated upon himself. In doing so, he made this title known to *all* across the Roman Empire."

Feeling a burning need—longing to enter the mausoleum now, Ingrid slipped the compass piece inside her pocket, then stepped past them for the doors. "Druids?"

"Yeah," Mike said, following. "Titus was the one who wiped them from the face of the earth. Every. Last. One."

"Nice guy," Tom said.

Mike glanced up at the Latin phrase carved above them.

"Yeah... You have *no* idea."

Ingrid placed a single hand on one of the marble doors more than twice as tall as she, and pushed. The door swung inward with an ease which surprised them all. Howie pressed on the other door, opening it too, allowing the light from the great torches to flood inside. Together, side by side, as if one, they entered....

Strategic Alliances

*T*he air was cold here within the mausoleum. Everything was cold, at a temperature not meant for the living. By the torchlight and the lights which they held, they could see that the space inside went far into the rock behind the mausoleum. As well, the gradient of this aisle-like pathway progressively sloped downwards.

A marble bowl of nearly three feet in diameter stood upon a pillar also of marble a few paces just inside. Mike ignited the oil brimming the bowl. Howie did the same to the first torch on the wall. The oil-filled vein along the wall birthed flame to the rest of the torches. In the flickering light, it appeared that every surface within the mausoleum was of marble.

They followed down the center aisle. To their right, were what was about twenty ornate sarcophaguses of marble. To the left had to have been around the same amount. Each, spaced out perfectly in a row, was neatly and orderly so. And each was as much beautiful as it was unique.

The artistry which had transformed these great blocks of marble into truly lifelike likenesses of who they contained had no equal they'd ever seen. Uniformly, all the sarcophaguses showed in the same place the name of the individual held within. These were etched signature-style, as though by that person's own hand before they had died.

"Talk about a strategic alliance," Tom said.

"The trifecta of true power for the first century," said Mike.

"You guys," Ingrid said. "Mike, you'll like this."

They joined her in front of the sarcophagus. 'Titus Flavius Fili Vir' was carved elegantly.

"Nice, Ingrid," Mike said. "The Son of Man himself. And look—these other two either side of him. Vespasian, his father. And Domitian, his younger brother."

Beautifully emblazoned across the tops of their sarcophaguses was their family banner, the same symbols of the early Church.

"The more I learn of history and academia, the more I see it's not without its own flaws," said Mike.

"How do you mean?" Howie asked.

"I mean, the tour office selling tickets to tourists outside the Roman Forum will swear up and down the Flavians are entombed at the Mausoleum of Augustus, despite having no proof it's so. Suppose it sells tickets, though."

Ingrid had moved on. They matched her pace, knowing time was slipping away from them. At a depth that had to have been fifty feet inside by their estimates, they reached the last of the sarcophaguses. This brought them face to face with the rock wall there, marking the end of the mausoleum. Over time, sections of the marble slabs covering the wall had broken off, exposing the coarse rock behind.

"Well, this is romantic," said Howie. With the literal dead end, he found himself arriving at that ever-inevitable question. "What now?"

"Uh, that what now," Mike said, pointing to the soft glow bleeding through Ingrid's pocket.

Armed with hope and with belief in her ancestors' extraordinary foresight, she removed the compass piece aglow vividly indigo. Before she could even raise it or move it or do anything with it, the exposed sections of rock along the wall began to glow, and in the same indigo.

"Starting to feel there's an actual design to all of this," Tom said.

"An *actual* design," said Ingrid, grabbing one of the broken pieces of marble piled up at the base of the wall.

They saw now what she meant. There was some form of an image peeking through on the exposed rock. They each grabbed pieces of broken marble and smashed away at the remaining slabs still clinging to the wall.

With nearly all the marble slabs broken off now, the lushly illuminated Praesidio Autem Veritas stood before them, inlaid in that mysterious metal upon the wall. Ingrid raised the compass piece, moving it toward the symbol. The closer she drew it, the brighter the indigo grew.

"Wait, why's it not inverted?" asked Tom.

None of them had paid it any thought. Not even Ingrid had noticed, who certainly should have. She'd been too caught up in the moment and magic of it all to have really observed this most obvious deviation of her ancestors' sacred symbol.

"Who... knows...," said Howie, sighing.

"Is there a place to lock in the compass piece?" Mike asked, while running his hand across the coarse surface of the rock.

They joined him. Their hands and fingers and eyes and hearts all searched for that familiar groove. But they found nothing resembling it anywhere on or near the place.

"Ingrid?" Howie asked.

"Yeah?"

"How about just placing it against the symbol?"

Why not? She held the compass piece to the Praesidio Autem Veritas, choosing the center of the eye as Howie's proposed point of contact. After a long moment, and one which pushed her to the very edge of complete doubt, the compass piece began to resonate within her hand.

"Anything?" Tom asked, nervously.

"It's vibrating," she answered.

She opened her hand, showing them all the compass piece as it trembled. Its indigo had become a deep emerald. Before their eyes, the glow of the Praesidio Autem Veritas transitioned to the very same emerald.

"Green means go," Mike said.

"Let's hope so," said Ingrid.

The convulsing of her hand brought on by the resonance had become just too much. She released the compass piece... It did not fall though. Instead it remained exactly where she'd held it, against the center of the eye upon the wall. Somehow, by technologies not known, let alone understood to them, the compass piece stayed flush to the pupil of the symbol's eye. Howie pulled Ingrid back a few feet from the wall.

"Huh. That's different," Tom said.

Just as he finished saying it, the compass piece began to slowly turn clockwise, with its base still remaining flush to the eye of the symbol upon the wall. On its first turn, with a great click, and in an oddly lagged way, the symbol itself also started to rotate clockwise. The compass turned again with a click. And a brief moment later, the inlaid symbol followed. With the third turn and click of the compass piece, the symbol, after a short pause, rotated, bringing it to be perfectly inverted.

Compelled, Ingrid reached out. She took hold of the compass piece, then pulled back toward herself. The compass piece, somehow, still holding to the place on the wall, brought with it the section containing the glowing symbol. Upon sliding free from the rest of the wall, the weight of it all immediately pulled her down to her knees. The section of wall fell, hitting the marble floor, shattering.

Howie helped her to her feet. Opening her palm, she revealed the compass piece safely nested within, no longer aglow. Before them, an entrance into the wall of rock awaited, in the symbol's pentagram shape. They started to venture toward its dark borders...

Behind them was a click. This was a different kind of click than the compass piece could produce. It was one they dreaded. They turned. A few paces away, those eyes that had watched them from the shadow-kissed realm of the mausoleums came forth.

Revealing himself, Camorra stood there, gun aimed.

"There's nothing in my power to cause you to trust me."

These words he grimly hissed were unexpected, though they wholeheartedly agreed with the statement. The gun staring them in the face only helped solidify it.

"Conversely, there's no way for me to trust you, not based on your own freewill alone," he said. "This impasse of ours does not change the urgency we're collectively facing. The four of you, I need you to do something."

"Shoot," said Tom.

They turned to him and glared.

"Yeah, poor choice of words," Tom said.

Howie shook his head, returning his focus to Camorra. "Being?"

"I need you to continue on with your course of action. To get this thing that you're searching for."

"The catch?" Howie asked.

"Once you've got it, I need you to give it to me. This is where the trust issue becomes an issue."

"Explain it to us then," Ingrid said.

"Me being here alone, without the full resources of the Holy See beside me should tell you. Given our present location."

"That's a good point," Tom said.

Howie pressed his finger to his lips.

"Right," said Tom, promptly closing his mouth.

"He's been alone every time we've crossed paths," Howie said to the others.

"You can give us that gun," said Mike.

Camorra shook his head. "Again, the trust issue." He stepped forward, bridging the space between himself and Ingrid. "I'm going inside." He reached for the compass piece still resting on her open palm.

She let his fingers make contact with its cool metal surface, then closed her hand, covering over both the compass piece and his fingers.

He cocked his head at her ever slightly. "Excluding her,

the rest of you can follow. Or, not." He wrenched his hand free from hers, taking the compass piece as he did so. Feeling it within his hold, he smiled at them. This wasn't a smile done in a pleasant way, and not in a happy, or even partially content way. It was one which was done in a way that conveyed, with undisputed clarity, he was the one in control.

Then, he, along with his unsavory smile, as well the compass piece, were gone, disappearing into the darkness of the pentagram-shaped opening along the wall. Ingrid immediately entered behind him.

Tom started to follow. He stopped, feeling the matching looks of disapproval from Howie and Mike. "Look, guys, right now, he's in power. Call it a strategic alliance." He pushed past them, immersing himself into the dark space of the pentagram.

The Lies Above as so Beneath

*U*pon entering the passageway, Howie and Mike nearly tumbled over each other, as the ground of smooth stone beneath their feet had suddenly become extremely steep, slanting downwards. It'd only been for the narrow rock walls on either side of them to catch themselves upon that'd saved them from this fall, which could've proved a tremendous distance down. By the light of Mike's cellphone, it was hard to tell just how far the passageway went.

The grade forced even Camorra to a modest pace. And it wasn't long until Howie and Mike had caught up with the others. As the passageway was only wide enough for two at a time, Mike and Howie moved side by side. Ingrid walked alongside Camorra.

"I'd say you've been replaced as team leader," Mike said.

"Yeah, well, don't say it then," Howie told him, more than annoyed by his father's skillful ease to get under his skin.

The passageway came to a gentle bend to the right. Around this slight jog, their path ended. Facing them was a wall of rock, smooth, like that beneath their feet.

Upon the wall was what had to be a door of some kind. It was in the shape of a true triangle, and it pointed straight down. Crafted from the same mysterious metal the compass piece was, it appeared to be a single and solid panel with no seams of any kind.

Its edges protruded out from the rock a good six inches. While, from one point to the next, it was seven or eight feet across. Large, it was by no means the biggest they'd seen thus far. Surprisingly minimalistic, there were no apparent markings to be found upon it. There were, however, characters written in the L' Entita's language carved into the rock itself above this strange triangular door.

"The lies above as so beneath," Ingrid said, giving them her best translation.

"As above so beneath," said Howie.

"Believe that's the gist," she said. "Everyone, if the L' Entita had a motto, this would be it. And they enjoyed their wordplay. Dual meanings. Hidden contexts. All the things we've come to know them for by this point in our journey."

"Both meanings of 'lie', then?" Mike asked.

"Without a doubt," she answered.

Deciding it best to let the one most experienced to do what they do, Camorra handed her back the compass piece. What she, nor none of them knew, was he'd secured a tracking chip to it upon its base. Tiny and nearly invisible, he was quite certain they'd never notice.

She brought the compass piece close to the metal panel. A triangular keyhole began to glow upon the panel. She slid the capstone that was attached to the tip of the compass piece into the keyhole. The others watched, feeling, and increasingly so, just along for the ride or journey, or whatever this was going to become.

The triangular panel began to change in form, confirming their belief it was indeed some kind of door. As it did so, it opened in a way they'd never seen before. Silently, the panel transitioned from an inverted triangle to a pentagram. This metamorphosis wasn't overly slow nor did it occur too fast as to not see precisely in how it was achieved.

Simultaneously, a new point along both the left and right sides slid out at an angle identical to how the points on a pentagram should be. The two existing points on top grew as well, angling out like horns which crowned the pentagram. Upon completing this change, its metal surface suddenly fogged over as though it had an abrupt shift in temperature. This thick and clinging vapor quickly melted away.

The surface of the now five-pointed panel no longer appeared metallic. It was like a mirror. Their five reflections gleamed perfectly back at them. The mirrored surface started to flicker, then rippled softly, as if a gentle breathing was escaping from it.

Ingrid grabbed the compass piece where it'd locked into this mirrored and moving surface. Before she could release it from the panel, a beam of light shot straight out of the base of the compass piece, blinding her head-on. Letting go, she jumped back.

The beam created a three-dimensional projection of another pentagram. It too appeared as though fashioned from mirrored glass. They stepped away, as this projection grew until it matched perfectly in scale the pentagram on the wall. The beam from the compass piece tilted upward, elevating the pentagram within the projection.

It did so until this pentagram of light was far overhead and positioned directly above the pentagram on the rock wall. Upon contact with the rock, the pentagram formed by the projected light no longer was of light. It was as solid as its counterpart. And the beam from the compass piece ceased to be.

"You don't see that every day," Tom said.

Not a second had passed with him speaking, and the top pentagram had begun to rotate itself while still holding to the wall. It stopped once it came to position perfectly pointed upwards. Before the five of them, now were these two identical pentagrams, one atop the other. And mirrored versions of themselves, the top one pointed up, while the bottom one pointed down. Each cast their own vantage point, clearly so reflecting the five of them standing there in front of the rock wall.

Quickly, though not immediately so, the mirror-like surface for the bottom pentagram faded away, as though made from thin ice, evaporating into nothing. Left in its place was a pentagram-shaped door leading straight into the rock wall. The compass piece remained in the place where it'd been. About eye level, it appeared suspended in the open air, unmoving.

Camorra, apparently unphased by any of this, checked his watch, then took a large step forward toward the open doorway—the top pentagram swung free from the wall. As if hinged by its two bottom points, the pentagram tipped straight over and down. It came to a swift, though smooth stop, filling perfectly the empty doorway also shaped as a pentagram in the rock wall below it. The compass no longer appeared as if suspended in the open air. As though the mirrored panel of the pentagram had somehow passed right through it, the compass piece now was flush and secure upon its mirrored surface.

With a sincere shock in his eyes, Camorra leaped back, nearly impaled by the point on the pentagram when it'd swung down. All of them, especially Camorra, couldn't help but feel as this had been a warning of some kind. They'd never seen Camorra reveal anything except deft control. Perhaps he was just a man, after all. Perhaps...

"Well... there's a door, again," Tom said.

Their focus wasn't on the pentagram-shaped door though. It was on what was reflecting back at them in its mirrored surface. The reflections of themselves were inverted, perfectly upside down, while everything else around them in the image was right side up.

"Above, so beneath," said Ingrid, with her voice low, not by volume, though, bewitchment.

From Howie's lips escaped something lost between a sigh and stifled moan drowned in enchantment he'd never known. "You couldn't make this stuff up. You'd have to have seen it for thine own self to know such things exist in the shadows of these places forgotten..." The brief daze evaporated away, and he turned to Ingrid. "So... do we knock, or what?"

How the hell should I know, she thought. The thought was short lived. For, at exactly that second, the compass piece glowed to life, pulsing its lush emerald hue.

"Green, for go," said Tom.

Camorra glanced at him, more than unamused.

"Green for...," Tom started to explain to him, but decided it best to just close his mouth.

Ingrid took hold of the compass piece. But as she did so, it, along with her hand, sank straight through the other side of the mirror-like door. With the ease of water, the reflective material filled in around her wrist, concealing both her hand and compass piece, now sunken behind it.

Unseen, with the compass piece in her grip, she tried to pull her hand back through, but it felt as though it was immersed deeply in mud, congealing. As she fought against its hold, the glassy surface stretched thin, becoming a swirl of elastic and liquid. Ripples spread out across their inverted reflections on the mirrored panel.

Camorra stepped beside her. "Turn it around."

"So the tip is pointed toward the glass?" she asked.

He nodded ever slightly. By her sense of touch alone, she rotated the compass piece in her hand so that its tip now faced her. As she pulled it toward herself, Camorra's cleverness proved true. The tip of the compass piece pierced the mirrored surface. As she drew it through the rest of the way, the compass piece, aglow in emerald, grew hot within her hand. Bearing the heat, she continued to pull until it stopped. The compass piece securely locked once more upon the pentagram's mirrored surface.

She started to rotate the compass piece counter-clockwise. A mechanical kind of clicking released with each pivot. As she turned it, their reflections within the mirrored surface followed the motion, rotating one click at a time. And only their reflections did so, rotating, while nothing else contained in the mirrored surface moved.

Completing one full turn, the compass piece released with the slightest hiss escaping from somewhere behind and unseen. She gripped it tightly in her palm. Stepping back from the mirrored pentagram, she saw that their reflections were now right-side up, as they should be.

Camorra held out his hand. And she set the compass piece into it. He zipped it inside his pocket. She paid him no resistance, due to what was happening in the pentagram's mirrored surface. Each of their individual reflections drew in a sliding and drifting motion toward a separate point within the pentagram. Before them now, they each saw their own reflection staring back, contained in its own point on the pentagram-shaped door.

"Five of us. Five points. Preordained, or something?" asked Howie.

"Or *something*," Mike said.

For no reason known to science, and certainly by no result of where he was positioned, the bottom point of the pentagram was the one which held Howie's reflection. The mirrored surface filling this point faded, melting away into nothing, taking with it his reflection. The point containing his reflection was the only one to fade away. An inverted triangular doorway stood in its place. Eerily, the rest of their reflections each remained.

"Hope that's not an omen of some kind," Tom said, bluntly so, swatting Howie on the back.

Howie frowned, recalling the ominous feeling he'd had the night before while dancing in Rome. "The thought hadn't entered my mind until you said it, Tom..."

By an instinct found only in leaders and those ill-fated enough to be heroes, he took a step for the open doorway. Camorra's hand on his shoulder abruptly stopped him in his tracks. Much more careful this time, Camorra extended his arm, penetrating the space, proving it could be passed into. He entered, obscuring himself into the shadows beyond.

The four of them looked to one another, now bonded by this journey, this quest into the unknown, long past a measure not fully understood. Nonetheless, it was entirely felt, touching them, burning now deep inside each of them. They too entered the doorway, each knowing what the others had decided without words in that moment, committing, if needed, and most likely, required, their very lives to... *At no cost, would Camorra be allowed to take the truth they sought...*

The Italian Chamber

O n the other side of the doorway, Camorra found the L' Entita's chamber. It was real, despite being a place seated only in legend. He turned on his flashlight. It was a naturally occurring space, vast and open.

By all measures, it was a cave. Certainly, it was large, but nonetheless just a cave. The width of which, fifty feet he calculated it at, was still narrow enough to be able to see the rock walls on either side of him.

In contrast, the cave appeared long, and greatly so. A thin film of algae or something moss-like grew in swaths along the cave's walls. It vibrantly glowed in amber upon contact with the beam of his flashlight.

Smooth, though uneven, the walls all along and near the doorway were covered in primitive paintings. There was a large bull depicted being slain. The leader of the group painted there, spilling the bull's blood for sacrifice, was strikingly similar to how any pope he'd ever seen would be dressed during ceremony. He knew well enough his history to know what this cave had once been.

The others were now behind him, standing there just inside the doorway, their shadows casting upon him. He felt certain they'd follow him, driven by their own curiosity. What else could they do except accept. He moved deeper inside the unknown and dark place. So did they.

Howie shined the flashlight he'd taken from Tom onto the

paintings. "Mithraism."

Walking beside him, Mike couldn't help but feel impressed by his son's correct assessment. "Yes. When Rome founded Christianity, they built their headquarters for it, with Saint Peter's Basilica, right literally upon the existing headquarters for Rome's principal religion of the time. Being, as you said, kid, Mithraism."

Tom caught up beside them. "You're saying this is *that* actual cave?"

"Yes," Mike answered. "Isn't that precisely why, Ingrid, your ancestors placed their own headquarters within this ancient place designated for belief? And why they left these paintings intact. To preserve the true origins of the Church?"

Out in front, following closest to Camorra, she turned back at them, but only for the briefest of moments. "I suppose." She returned her focus to Camorra, and quickened her pace, leaving a greater distance between herself and them.

Camorra and Ingrid, leading, and Howie, Tom, and Mike, following, ventured further into the black, somewhat cold, and absolutely silent cave. It wasn't long until the paintings along the cave's walls on either side of them stopped, becoming blank slates of rock. The width of the cave grew narrower, drawing inward toward them, and was now perhaps thirty feet across. Camorra's flashlight revealed the rock wall where the cave appeared to come to a dead end.

"The compass piece," Ingrid said. "The key..."

Camorra gave it to her. She held the compass piece up. At the exact center of the wall, and at a height of about three feet, a square-shaped groove came to glow in electric-green. She locked the base of the compass piece into this keyhole. A few inches away from where it was locked upon the wall, seams began to form. In the same electric-green, they created an outline in the shape and scale of any ordinary door.

Without a sound, this section rock slid rather swiftly straight up, rising into some concealed space within the ceiling. She unlocked the compass piece from the wall, and

Camorra held out his hand. She returned it to him. Passing through the doorway, they saw the immense thickness of it, with easily being ten feet deep.

This passage delivered them into what had to be the actual chamber. Upon being touched by the light they brought, more of the moss or algae-like substance they'd come to know, glowed in amber all along the walls. It awaited them there at the center of the rather modest chamber.

Together, Ingrid and Camorra came to stop at this large and rectangular table. It was longer than any of them were tall, and several feet broad. The table was of stone, smooth and precisely crafted so, so long ago. The top of the table, inlaid into its stone frame, appeared to have been formed from a single shard of crystal. Milky and semi-clear, the color of it wasn't anything visually spectacular. Though, the size of the crystal was extraordinary, filling perfectly the table's sprawling surface. The others joined them there at the table's edge.

Camorra laid his palm flat on the face of the crystal, cool to his touch, then turned to all of them. "Where is the library of the L' Entita?" Just as he'd anticipated, each of their faces revealed their disbelief of him knowing *what* they'd been searching for. Their faces also told him that they, like him, had expected the lost library, saturated with the darkest secrets of history, to be here somewhere in this subterranean hole. Before they could enact their natural response of asking how he knew of the library, he gave Ingrid the triangular shaped object, that little pyramidal key of the L' Entita. "Shall we?" He drew away his hand from where he'd had it upon the table, exposing there the triangle-shaped groove carved into the table's surface.

Ingrid locked in the compass piece to the place. The tabletop of crystal glowed to life. It became clear, like pure and still water. Encapsulated within the crystal's surface and within it deeper, down to it its bottom, pastel colors floated in misty clouds. Bleeding into each other, the colors vanished, and the crystal's surface became white as daylight.

Then, at the very center of the tabletop of crystal, a tiny black dot appeared. Expanding, it grew to the size of a crystal ball. Only, it was the blackest black they'd ever known. Within the several feet deep surface of the crystal, this flat, one-dimensional circle transitioned into a three-dimensional sphere. A thin white line opened across it horizontally, splitting it perfectly in half. The line grew wider. As eyelids would, it opened, to reveal the large black pupil at the center of the sphere.

Three more black dots materialized, positioned around the spherical eye. Then, lines took form, connecting between each of these dots, to create the inverted triangle now framing the eye. Several more black dots came to be upon the bright surface, spaced around the triangle. Lines spread out, linking the dots, creating a pentagram, the final piece to this familiar symbol.

Camorra gazed upon it. Complete now, this symbol, the signature of the L' Entita, the Praesidio Autem Veritas, softly pulsed, illuminated like some high-tech and modern logo... *Exactly* in the same way another table had... A memory flashed before him... Seated at a table, large and smooth, centered within an office, empty, just as this cave appeared to be, a logo pulsed hypnotically. It came from the table's surface, glowing up into his eyes...

There was only one place he'd seen such a thing... The smart table contained within the headquarters of the *Santa Alleanza*. After all, he'd been under their employment for several years, and from not that long ago. As strange as this glaring similarity was, it was not a priority, nor relevant to achieving his directive of the moment. Nor, he knew, none of these individuals within this cave held the answer for this coincidence. But someone, in another place, and close by, certainly did. He'd wait for that answer, only Domenico could provide... *For the time being.*

Not knowing why she did, she just did. Ingrid reached out and tapped the pupil of the eye. With her touch, the black pupil became a fiery ball of oranges and reds, rapturing into a perfect sphere aflame.

Radiating out, the flames consumed the Praesidio Autem Veritas. Skin-deep within the crystal, this fire looked as though sealed beneath a thin sheet of ice. Within seconds, it had filled the entire surface of the table. Freezing, the fire became fractured crystal facets, embers most frozen.

A hair-thin seam of brilliant blue light began to spread horizontally across the center of the table's crystal face. It neatly divided the surface into two equal halves. The seam grew wider, moving out in each direction, until it was no longer a seam but a large opening that had somehow devoured the crystal entirely, leaving it nowhere to be seen.

With the crystal apparently now gone, they ventured closer, up to the table's edge, and peered inside the large space left in the crystal's absence. What they saw, like so many things on their journey, was something unlike anything they'd witnessed, nor ever heard of anyone witnessing....

Nonequilibrium Static Magnetic Influx Wave Oscillator

" *W* hat the hell is it?" asked Tom, and in no way actually expecting an answer.

"Nonequilibrium Static Magnetic Influx Wave Oscillator," Ingrid said, telling not just him, but all of them. She'd forgotten, long ago, about this device. And she, of course, had never actually seen one. But, based upon her memories of how her grandfather had described this mechanism designed by her ancestors, it had to have been such a device.

"The thing Tesla never was able to get working?" Howie asked.

"The thing Tesla had no business in taking liberties with," she said. "This machine existed long before him. As you all can see. And mistakenly, as he'd assumed, it wasn't intended to serve the needs of electricity. It was meant for genetic memory."

"Is there a, you know, shorter name for this?" Tom asked.

"Actually," she said, "in the words of my grandfather... Sphere-thingy." Resting within the cavity of the table was a sphere. It was about the size of a cauldron, with two simple loop-shaped handles on either side. At the very top of it was a perfectly round hole of perhaps four inches across. Like the table, this sphere seemed crafted from a single and immense crystal.

Beside the sphere, laying flat, was a disk. It couldn't have been more than half an inch thick. Noticeably a few inches smaller in diameter than the sphere, this disk appeared to be fashioned from the same kind of crystal. Unlike the sphere's surface, void of all markings, the disk was completely covered in the unknown characters of the L' Entita's cryptic language.

And finally, beside the disk, rested the compass piece, safe and secure. Somehow, it wasn't lost when the transformation of the table's surface occurred. The crystal or the table, or something else altogether, had preserved it.

Perhaps stranger than any of these things, was what was lining the table's cavity. The biotic or biotic-like membrane seemed to breathe or beat like a great heart or other organ of some kind. Rhythmic and steady, it drew in itself, then exhaled, continuously. The sphere and disc sat sunken slightly into this softly moving tissue, held there to it.

Not able nor even wanting to resist, Tom reached inside the cavity of the table and touched the lining. It felt warm. It felt alive. He pressed harder. Its pulse traveled through his own fingering tips, then into his hand, dispersing up and through the tissue of his arm.

"Uh..., Tom," Howie said. "Your hair is standing up."

"Right," said Tom, pulling back.

Camorra nodded to her, and Ingrid leaned over the edge of the table. With both hands, she took hold of the disk. As if nested into this biotic membrane, when she tried to lift the disk, it seemed to resist her efforts with an intense suction.

She pulled harder. Still, it did not release. The lining beat faster, its breathing accelerating. Deciding not to fight it, but not sure as what else to do, she left her hands upon the disk and stopped pulling. As if sensing, with an awareness which recognized it was *her*, the disk released, and she removed it with ease.

They peered down into the table's cavity, watching with repulsed curiosity upon the indentation where the disk had been held there within this pulsating membrane. The disk-shaped outline pooled with a runny, though chunky, kind of mucus. Then, all at once, the membrane drew in on itself, released the disk-shaped outline, and became as the rest of the lining, as if the disk had never been there.

Mike went to grab the sphere. "Things usually have handles for a reason."

"Let me," said Ingrid. He moved aside, and she took hold of the sphere by its handles.

They watched in silence, collectively thinking the same thought. *She wouldn't be strong enough to lift the crystal sphere.* And this was simply due to how much it must have weighed.

Calmly, she rested each hand upon a handle. Then, when she'd decided this thing, whatever it truly was, had an understanding with not so much her, though with some level of her consciousness locked away within her DNA, did she try to raise the sphere. She'd expected it to allow her to do so, as with the disk... It did not.

Mike's words echoed within her head, '*Things usually have handles for a reason*'... *What if they weren't handles at all.* She tried pulling one of the handle-like loops up. Nothing happened. She tried turning it downwards—it clicked, then rotated half a turn. She did the same for the loop on the other side.

This time, when she lifted by the loops, the top half of the sphere came right off. It was shockingly lightweight and required no more effort to lift than an empty box of cardboard. The inside of the sphere half she held was mirrored.

Retrieving his flashlight from Howie, Tom shined it inside the now half sphere within the table. The beam shot sharply off its mirrored lining, momentarily blinding them. Tom sheepishly lowered the flashlight, and Camorra yanked it away from him. Taking the disk, Camorra placed it inside the sphere half within the table.

Ingrid set the top half back onto the bottom half, making the sphere whole again. The compass piece, calmly resting next to the sphere, seemed to call to her. It lightly glowed. The glow disappeared. *Had it actually glowed?* She took hold of it. It wouldn't budge. She turned it clockwise. In three clicking pivots, the compass piece made one complete rotation.

In perfect silence, as slender and smooth as sword blades, four crystal shards rose up from the stone floor, positioned flush along each of the table's four corners. The four crystal shards were milky, and each of a different shade. One was a faded cherry. The next, sandy and tan. The third, a deep emerald with speckles of pale sunburned orange. The fourth and final one, it was black, neither dull nor glossy, just black. The crystal shards pushed up from the floor, until stopping maybe three inches or a little taller than the edges of the table.

"Liked their crystals," Tom said.

Camorra noticed the narrow but deep line carved into the top of the crystal that was black. He went to it. The line began just below the crystal's blade-like tapered point and ran straight down its side for two inches. He traced along it with his finger. And he found where it ended in a small hole, which was slightly wider than that of the carved line.

"Please," Ingrid said to him.

He stepped away, giving her space to do with the crystal whatever it was she intended to do. She placed her finger upon its tapered point. Pressing down, it punctured her skin. After a moment of pressure, her blood ran out her fingertip. The grooved line captured every drop with the efficiency and eagerness as that of an offering plate.

Again, an image seized upon Camorra's memory. He couldn't place why. If only he could recall where. *Where?* The question haunted him. *Why was it begging upon his mind so?* Then... Involuntarily, his eyes closed. He felt himself drifting to a place familiar yet distant...

There, he saw the same room inside the headquarters of

the Santa Alleanza, which contained their smart table. It was of a time from several years before, and his face appeared a little younger, the wear upon his features a little less. Domenico took form within the office space. He placed his finger upon his DNA scanner, letting the needle pierce his skin. Crimson fluid released from his fingertip. A single drop escaped the needle from the scanner. This droplet ran down the arm of Domenico's suit jacket. Its dark red line was narrow and slender... Like the blood groove along a sword blade...

Realizing he was within his own mind, and not inside the Santa Alleanza, he quickly opened his eyes. He would never leave himself vulnerable like that, but he could not stop his eyes from shutting when they did. How long had he been like that, unaware of his present surroundings? It had been long enough to cause them all to now be staring at him.

Not drawing enough blood to continue to fill the groove, Ingrid placed her left palm onto the point of the crystal. Puncturing her skin, the blood flowed, now filling. It reached the hole, becoming captured. With the first droplet entering deep inside the crystal, a tender though distinct resonance began releasing from within. She stepped back.

Each of the other three crystals, positioned along of the edges of the table's corners, released a resonance as well. All were similar in both strength and pitch, though still noticeably different. An aura, matching each of the four crystals' colors, began to float out in misty layers, from and along the entire length of these shards.

The resonance grew perpetually louder and deeper. The colors of the four auras wove together, though did not bleed and muddle. They held their separate hues, and linked to one another, like pieces of vaporous wicker, forming a large and translucent patchwork.

Growing, the crystals' resonance coursed through all, until finally, each distinct pitch blended, harmonizing into a single great trembling. It streamed up through the floor, through the crystals, long and blade-like, and throughout their bodies. This all-consuming harmony flowed along the patchwork-cloud of colors now encircling them, moving across it as waves.

Positioning itself directly over the table, the cloud of color began to twist and form a ball of swirling, fiery hues, aglow. Balling up, it drew down into the open surface of the table. They saw the sphere within was spinning. For how long, none of them knew.

This ball of color sucked along the spinning sphere's silky edges. As it did so, the sphere seemed to drain away the colors themselves as the hues dissipated into a thin and pale mist of no shade at all. The sphere accelerated, faster, faster, until appearing to levitate.

It did so, rising straight up from the table's cavity. Flush with the open surface of the table, it hovered there, twirling around and around ever quicker. With the sphere only a blur now, the table's smooth and crystal surface started to return, manifesting itself.

As ice freezing over, it solidified, sealing the cavity in the table, while leaving the sphere to spin in place upon the table's sleek crystal face. The sphere spun at such a rate its skin appeared transparent. All they could see of it was the mirrored lining contained within.

Dissipating to a gentle hum, the resonance grew a bit tantalizing in its pitch. And a pencil-thin beam of corresponding color emitted out the top of each the crystal shards, drawing into the spinning sphere. The light beams did not bend nor break upon entering the sphere. Physics here, in how they knew, seemed not to govern this technology shrouded in mystery.

Instead, the four beams of four different colors remained unbroken, bouncing, reflecting infinitely so off the sphere's mirrored insides. The beams thrashed within, blurringly, frantic, chaotically. Entangling in form and color, they created a fist-sized orb of pure white light.

Then, a moment of silence and stillness, before this orb shot straight up and out the hole in the top of the sphere. The orb hovered before them all in the open air. Light started to flow through the hole atop the sphere, creating an illuminated field of soft color. Wafting from the sphere as translucent fingers of light, it floatingly absorbed into the bottom of the orb hovering above it.

"Bit like a projector," Tom said. "If, turned directly upwards, as it were."

Ingrid realized she was gripping Howie's hand. *How did that even happen? Had he noticed?* He looked to her hand. He stared at her now as she kept her gaze locked upon the projection in front of them, pretending she hadn't noticed. *Why didn't she simply let go?*

Their focus returned to the projection. The orb expanded outwards in every direction, immersing them within this ball of ever gentle and swirling world of light. It spread, consuming the chamber. Perfectly bright white, everything appeared as fresh snow, and as silent. The white light faded to a near transparent. A three-dimensional landscape took form as though they were standing there within this place. It was a forest raptured with summer. Two humanoid shapes materialized. These figures, now before them, manifested within this beautiful space, brought Ingrid to gasp. For she knew them, and knew them well...

Memories Unknown

*T*he images weren't just a representation of these two individuals. It was a memory, somehow extracted from within. The scene she saw, they all saw, was a personal one. It did not belong to them. It was something that had no right to be taken and displayed and played out for their eyes.

There was a young girl in a sky-blue floral dress and an elderly man in shorts, vest, and leather moccasins. Both she and he had skin deeply tan. They walked side by side, following along a trail used by the many animals that existed in those woods. Songs of birds and streams of midday sunlight seeped through the leafed canopy from above. To the rest of them, those woods could have been anywhere. But they weren't just anywhere, not to her.

"That's my grandfather... And me. When I was a little girl."

"That's not Haiti," Howie said.

She immediately released his hand, having entirely forgotten about their hands still clasped tightly together. *How could he respond like that—that's not's Haiti?* "No, Howie, it's not Haiti—that's not the point." Small wisps of air hissed through her gritted teeth as she spoke. Hearing it, she tried to compose herself. This wasn't the time for anger at him, or at any man.

"This memory of yours," said Mike, "it must have been taken from within your DNA. That's the only explanation, logically speaking."

Realizing he was right, "My... blood," she said. "But why *this* memory?"

Entirely unsure himself, he shrugged. "Maybe it's a marker somehow. You know, to identify, like an establishing shot?"

"Maybe," she said.

Suddenly, the images began to move in reverse. She and her grandfather walked backwards down the mountain trail. The effect increasingly sped up as if in rewind. Then the memory ended, transitioning into another.

The new scene played out forward, as it should. A boy, no more than ten, ran down a strip of beach. The perpetual rhythm of the ocean brushing along the sand sounded as real and immediate as if they actually were there. A light-haired woman dressed in linen chased after him. She caught up to him, lifting him up. He kissed her while placing a sandy hand along her cheek.

Ingrid did not recognize the memory, as it was not hers. But she knew well that brief moment, framed with the boy in the woman's arms, hand to cheek, with kiss shared. It was a photograph she possessed, one of only two she owned of her grandfather. The other one was of when he was in his mid-eighties, shortly before he'd died... "My grandfather. As a boy..."

A man, also in linen, entered the scene. He held up a camera, old and cumbersome, and tried to steady his shot of the mother and child in their embrace. Things began to move backwards once more, from one scene to the next. Faster and farther the images blurred by, with only a glimpse of something recognizable to her eye every few seconds of her grandfather's boyhood.

It was hard to watch her grandfather captured in these moments. She missed him deeply. This all had been draining for her. And it hurt. Her mind hurt too, trying to rationalize what they saw, lacking context. Parts, yes, made sense in how it was possible. But parts definitely didn't make sense to her.

"I... don't know these things. These belong to my grandfather. How—"

Camorra, having been silent for a long time, saw she was the key. She needed to be handled as such, guided and directed to the right place. Only then, within that right place, would the truth be unlocked that their lives now all depended upon. "You know not what your DNA knows." It was the first time, or seemed to be to any of them, that Camorra had participated in their joint effort. They listened, earnestly so, as he continued.

"Your memories are not yours. They don't belong to you. Nor mine to me. They belong to our DNA," he said. Now, he hoped, she would commit her focus in full to their collective goal. He needed this from all of them in order to move forward.

Focused, and with no illusions, Ingrid and Camorra now led their journey. They watched the images shift before their eyes and minds. A church steeple materialized, appearing strangely, though fittingly as a scaled-down obelisk. It drifted away. A birthday cake, small and round, covered in thick chocolate frosting, came to be, then was no more.

Finally, they saw what could only be a womb. Without needing to know, they sensed this tiny fetus contained within, bald, ugly, and curled up, suspended in fluids, bound by umbilical cord, must be her grandfather. That memory too reached its beginning, ending there.

The rewinding of memories increased, steadily accelerating, as it shifted to the memories of her grandfather's father. These images continued to blur by in reverse, rapidly ascending Ingrid's family tree. Each passing frame pulled them a generation closer to the origins of the L' Entita, to where it had all begun. That was where the keyhole locking away the truth awaited them all. No longer seeming as separate lives lived, these passing memories appeared as one single vein of moments racing by.

"Why does it show the memories like this?" Howie asked.

"How do you mean?" she asked.

He pointed to the sphere flowing with imagery. "Like this—not from any particular point of view. If it was your memory, wouldn't it have been through *your* eyes?"

"What if this works like a composite," said Mike. "In that forest, maybe it was memories from both you and your grandpa. After all, your DNA was his too."

She looked for the words to make it make sense. "So... A chain linking one person to the next. So that the sum of their experiences is some kind of... collective pool?"

"Essentially, yeah," he said. "The entire cumulative human experience, from the very first human, spanning all the way to the seven billion of today, all of those memories preserved and stored inside a single strand of our DNA. The answers to our—life's most prevailing and perplexing questions just a pinprick away. Think of it..."

They did, deeply so, and the implications it'd bring crashing down onto modern society and evolution alike if unlocked. As they witnessed these shifting images of lives past, they realized it wasn't just the weight of the Vatican upon their shoulders. It was the impact their decisions would have on humanity's future. The ripple effects... Those would be eternal.

Encompassed within the projection, generations fell past them as easily and plentiful as droplets of rain, bleeding one into the next, flooding their senses. For Ingrid, she felt her mind sinking, drowning into it. Her eyes closed. Trance-like, she moved to the sphere, transparent and spinning, upon the table's crystal surface.

Its mirrored insides, projecting and reflecting. Its beam of lush imagery, fervently flowing out the top of this sphere, drawing up into the orb, afloat. And they, at the center, would be witness to it all.

She placed her left hand upon the edges of the spinning sphere. To her, with eyes closed, it felt as though it was unmoving. To them, all watching her, it very much appeared to be spinning, just as it had been.

In her mind, completely out of her control, the thought arrived. It was a very specific date and a very specific location. Instantly, the blurring images stopped in front of them. Things came into vivid focus, as if the place and the time were truly there, 360 degrees, and no longer just a projection.

"Christ, is that...?" asked Tom.

Howie nodded, slack-jawed. "It's..." The word escaped him.

"Breathtaking," Mike said, finishing his son's intended sentence. "Simply and utterly breathtaking..."

The First Century

*F*irst century Rome, in all its glory, manifested. Ingrid's hand still pressed to the spinning sphere, helmed what they saw. Her eyes stayed shut, but inside her mind, or perhaps from somewhere else, she saw just as clearly as they.

Camorra moved a few paces away from their group, a little further down, along the edge of the table. There, he watched silently, observing everything that was revealed by this device, and by them as well. Characters written in the L' Entita's language had begun to overlay along the top edge of the lush imagery of ancient Rome.

All at once, feelings flooded Ingrid, ones not hers. It was an odd, though not overwhelming, sensation. She realized it was coming from the four of them, brought on by their inability to understand the L' Entita's language. It was their confusion which had entered her. This machine, it could merge the boundaries between things. Human emotions and sensations were not exempt, but readily accepted, consumed, and projected upon whoever could connect, to feel, to experience it. She thought of the language they needed to see it in. And as simply as that, it shifted to English.

Reading what was now displayed there to himself, but not intending to do so, Howie spoke aloud. "The Year Sixty-Seven Common Era."

"There's no Colosseum," Tom said, looking around.

"Right," Mike said. "The Flavian Amphitheater, as it was called, wouldn't be built for about another three years."

"By Vespasian Flavius," Howie added.

"You do read after all, kid," said Mike.

"Wait," Tom said, "if the Flavians built the Colosseum and did all these things and had their own dynasty even, then why am I just now hearing about them?"

"Yeah...," said Mike. "Think we've all got that feeling. Bit like their role in history has been deliberately swept away."

The imagery of the projection moved them deeper into the ancient city. The front gates of the Imperial Palace towered now in the foreground. The sphere drew Ingrid closer to it, her left hand bonding to its glistening surface. She brought her other hand against it too.

From within the place behind her closed eyes, where she envisioned the palace's gates, she felt the stones underneath her feet. A mild breeze, having escaped the sea, and traveled across the coast to arrive here before these grand gates, swirled through her hair. With her hand outstretched, the sensation of the air passed between her fingers. She was there. *Or was it here?*

For the four of them, no one had moved. She still stood where she had been, leaned fully toward the sphere where it continued to spin on the table. But something quite strange, from their perspective happened. Her hands sank into the surface of the sphere as it spun, disappearing, becoming one with the mirrored lining within.

She felt what they felt. It was amazing, as well amusing to her, that each of them felt such similar things despite their many differences. Camorra too, he had entirely human thoughts...

Jesus. She was reading their thoughts now. This wasn't something she wanted. She wouldn't want them, nor anyone to be invading her mind. *Was she choosing this? There was no way to tell. But why? Why was it so? There had—must be a reason, a function of some sort for this connection to the others. Yes, of course, connection. They needed to experience what she was experiencing, and in the same way. In union.* They needed to read *her* thoughts...

Thinking it so, made it so. By her mind, she directed them. And by all measures of their senses, they were now inside ancient Rome. The chamber containing them dissolved, vanishing into nothing more than a vague memory, rapidly unraveling.

It was jarring at first, traveling through time and space, moving so freely, though not of their own will, but of hers. As she guided them, she feared what they may come to think of her, see her as. For they must realize by now, as her awareness increased as to what she was, truly was, so did her power. *What if that power was too much for her?*

Her concentration drifted, and their movement through the city became even more jarring. She tried to bring her mind back to the helm at the sphere. They skipped in both time and space in leaps from street to street, as if the distance between, in one moment was there, then erased in the next.

"My brain and body have the hiccups," Tom managed to gasp.

Even Camorra was thrown off balance. In fact, he felt quite nauseous. Regaining her focus, she brought them to where she saw herself standing. In one blurring leap, they found themselves abruptly before the Imperial Palace's front gates.

"*Now* I feel like barfing," said Tom. He leaned over, gripping his stomach.

The mention of the word escaping Tom's lips was enough. Camorra vomited violently onto the street, in front of all alike, palace guards, and those passing by. The four of them glared at Tom.

"What," he said, his stomach settling.

"Do you think they see us?" asked Mike, trying not to look directly at the palace guards standing sentry just a few feet away, on the other side of the gates.

"We see each other," Howie said, swiping his hand at

Mike. His palm made contact with Mike's stomach. "Solid enough too."

"Hell we are we!" Mike shouted, jumping back. His reaction startled them. For him, Howie's hand had just passed right through his body.

Though, to them, Howie's hand had connected quite harshly. Tom poked at Mike, feeling the contact his finger made.

"See," Mike said. "Right through."

Howie stepped close to Mike. "Really?"

Fist tightening, he did something he'd wanted to do for, well, for the duration of his life. He swung with all his might... His fist met Mike's nose with a wrath the others found quite disturbing. This excluded Camorra, who saw it mildly humorous, but would never expose such an emotion openly.

For Howie, the only thing strange about the moment of contact with Mike was that Mike didn't even flinch, or move, at all. Howie had certainly felt it, and the pain within his own hand increased now from it. And the others, they'd heard the crack and smack of the collision.

Despite having seen and heard it and having himself done it, Howie realized, for Mike, it hadn't happened. Because, for Mike, if it had, the force of his fist would've knocked his father off his feet. That he was certain of. He smiled, though just a touch. The bizarre physics of their situation, actually, were proving quite therapeutic.

"This palace is...," Mike started to say, struggling for the single right word.

"Ostentatious," Ingrid offered.

"Obscene," said Tom. "By the way, who was—is emperor?"

"Nero Claudius Caesar Augustus Germanicus," answered Mike.

"Or, before he changed his name," said Howie, "Lucius Domitus Ahenobarbus."

Mike smiled. "Very good."

"Nero," said Tom. "That's all you got to say."

Howie and Mike nodded at the same time, while simultaneously answering, "Nero."

"The one and only," Ingrid said.

"For those who care to know," Mike said, "as it has some interesting and perhaps non-coincidental parallels to Alexandria, the original place for the library now lost. Like the library, Nero's first palace burned to the ground atop Palatine Hill sixty-four A.D."

Camorra waited quietly. He'd grant this academic a little slack, as he might indirectly mention something of value for a later time on their journey.

Mike continued, and drew his finger away from Palatine Hill in the distance, back to the immense grounds of the palace before them, in the Roman Forum. "He had this colossus of a palace built after the fire. He created it in the likeness of the city of Alexandria, with his innermost sanctum at the center of this palace, designed after the layout of Alexandria's library no less."

Howie raised his hand. "And Nero's chosen name for his palace, the Domus Aurea, meaning 'Golden House'. Which, its original Greek context means, Chamber of the Torch, AKA Bearers of Light, or knowledge."

"He did so because Chamber of the Torch was the original name for the Library of Alexandria," Camorra flatly stated, ending their tangent.

He'd no sooner said it and a horse carrying a Roman officer came rushing down the road near the palace entrance. Camorra stepped into the path of the horse. They watched, thoroughly conflicted about what they wanted to have happen in that moment. Camorra stared the horse dead in the eyes as both it and the officer passed right through him. The others saw the horse in one second about to trample Camorra to death, then in the next second, appear directly on the other side of him, continuing to gallop down the road.

Camorra stepped out of the road and faced Ingrid. "Now

where?"

She turned to the palace. Her eyes closed.

"So, how are we going to get in?" Howie started to ask. Before he could finish, they found themselves within the interior of a large and lavish chamber inside the palace.

Gaining his bearings, Howie steadied himself against a pillar along the wall. "Ingrid, please, please warn us before you do that."

Mike scanned the room adorned with silk tapestries, marble busts, and ornate hardwood furniture. The unprecedented blend of architectural styles which formed the palace was everything and more from what he knew of history. "This is the Emperor's Chamber."

There was the sound of locks releasing from on the other side of the chamber's towering double doors.

"Can't believe I'm going to actually see Nero," Mike said, growing thoroughly giddy.

"Technically, you're seeing a reconstructed composite of memories," said Howie. "Remember."

The doors opened fully, and six guards entered. The Captain of the guard, who was now standing mere inches from where Tom was, drew his gladius sword, a rather simple in appearance and one-handed weapon. Invisible to the guards, Tom was nonetheless deeply uncomfortable with the situation. The captain thrust his sword out, directly on trajectory for Tom's face....

The Three Generals

*C*lenching his eyes shut, Tom dropped to his knees. Sweeping the sword through the air, the captain of the guard led his men down the center of the chamber. Hands ready at the handles of their swords, they spread out, searching. Tom opened his eyes. The others stood there watching him.

He got to his feet. "Hey, a sword is still a sword," he said.

"It's alright, buddy," Howie said, resting a hand on him. "Can't unlearn the stove's hot."

The captain returned to the open doorway and tapped his sword handle to his breastplate. His men lined up in formation behind him, evidently signaling the chamber was indeed secure. Emperor Nero entered. Wearing slightly more decorative armor than the captain of the guard, Nero was nonetheless dressed like an officer in the Roman army. It wasn't how any of them imagined him to be.

Even Mike, who knew the most intimate of historical details, had envisioned him to be dressed in the distinct royal ropes exclusive to the emperor of Rome. Everything he'd read of Nero, it'd indicated the man had been of flash and pretense. He, like them, knew now they'd have to unlearn what they believed of history, starting with these small details, and work up to antiquity's most ill-sweeping presumptions.

Another officer entered the chamber, armor bearing the mark of a general. With a wave of his hand, he dismissed the guards. The five of them watched near the center of the chamber, unable to hear this general as he spoke to Nero, his voice hushed and hurried.

Consumed by curiosity and yearning for truth, they creeped, closing in on the two men. Close now, they listened, invisible, like the phantom spies they were, from their place deep in the future, far away from the here and now. Camorra kept a little further distance back from the others. Always, he maintained his own space, his own realm for being and doing, as the last of the Order of the Camorra should, and only could.

Howie strained his ear, understanding a word or phrase here and there. "Latin."

"Kind of comes with the territory," Mike said.

Ingrid hoped it to be. The low and fast-moving words exchanged between the general and Nero no longer where in Latin, but in English.

"Anyone know who this guy is?" asked Tom. "He really commands a presence."

"Yeah he does," said Mike. "More so even than Nero. Whoever he is, he's important. Vespasian Flavius was the top general of the day, in today's terms of rank. But... this guy isn't Vespasian. He's too young, and the temperament's all wrong."

The general motioned for Nero to follow. And Nero promptly did so, not like an emperor, but as a soldier taking an order. They followed as well, through the open doorway, and down the hallway there painted brightly in white.

"Even bigger on the inside," Ingrid said.

"Well, it does have three hundred rooms," said Mike. Covering the walls were extravagant and gilded marble fountains and reliefs, enormous statues, paintings, and countless precious jewels centered around great inlaid pieces of ivory. Even waterfalls flowed out from the tops of the hallway walls. It'd felt as though they'd walked the length of a football field, but were only halfway down the hallway. They came to a stop at a single door of normal size.

The general unlocked the door, and he led Nero through. They followed, entering the surprisingly small courtyard on the other side. Behind the others, Camorra paused for a second, letting his eyes acclimate to the daylight. A slight breeze flowed. Tall white walls surrounded them squarely on four sides, a true courtyard. The tiled mosaic floor under their feet covered the ground in every direction. Pillars ran the length of the courtyard, stretching high into the sky, up to the towering rooftop of the Imperial Palace. From the shade of one of these courtyard's pillars, another officer stepped out, revealing himself in the sunlight. Emblazoned upon his breastplate, a wolf gripping a spear in his teeth. He too had the mark of general.

Mike immediately recognized the sharp features of this man's profile. "Vespasian Flavius. That symbol upon his breastplate, 'Into the wolf's mouth', as it was known, that's exclusive to the Primus Pilus, the highest military rank one could hold in ancient Rome."

"Making the other general his son...," Ingrid said. "Titus Flavius." Vespasian moved to the open center of the courtyard. And everyone drew in as well.

Nero, clearly frustrated, spoke, drenched in embittered disdain. "Why haven't you dispatched the forces to Jerusalem? Tell me, Vespasian. Is it fear?" Titus stepped forward. Vespasian quickly shook his head, and Titus backed off.

"My men haven't been paid in nearly a year," Vespasian said. A heavy underlining of justified defiance coated his words.

Nero's frustration quickly thickened. He heard well his general's defiance. "*Your* men?" A bee landed along Vespasian's thick and tanned neck. Its stringer nearly penetrated. Vespasian's eye contact remained unwaveringly so with Nero. With reflexes only gained from the battlefield, and a love only a son could hold, Titus flicked the bee away.

He promptly returned to his place, a few paces from alongside his father, as ever the good soldier.

Seeing his words carried no consequence for Nero, entirely missing their mark, Vespasian continued. "Rome cannot afford another military campaign of the undertaking required to do what you demand done. The treasury is dry. Your private reserves, even they are depleted beyond any measure known." He stopped himself short, avoiding mention of Nero's wasteful excess, which had only served to decimate Rome's overall cause.

The five of them watched the intensifying exchange. The sun, directly in the sky, didn't help. It beat down upon all of them, drawing out beads of sweat as large as that bee of the first century had been. The sweat, heavy upon them now, did little to ease the growing temperature as the breeze had stopped.

Tom wiped at his face. "This is awkward." Camorra tilted his head at him, and Tom understood the unspoken meaning, abruptly shutting up.

Nero, wanting to have Vespasian flogged right there for his insolence, but entirely aware of his dependence upon him, being his best tactician, found himself hopelessly conflicted. "How is it you're so intimate with my private finances?" He balled his fist, then pointed at Vespasian.

Titus secretly hoped Nero would lose control and strike out at his father. It'd be all the repercussion he'd require to chop down this weak, decadent man, painfully not fit for emperor. He *needed* to crush this... imposter of an officer who wore the uniform, but had less experience on the field of battle than any infantry man. More than hating him, his fist gripped the handle of his sword sheathed at his side. He burned with an eager sincerity for Nero's blood.

Vespasian sensed the youthful zealous and soldier's will within his son. It was time to speak, to draw upon his experience of age rather than the sword. Clearing his throat, he stepped forward, and when he spoke, his voice was calm, though his words were stern. "As the commanding officer of Rome's army, it's my business to know, and know well, the financial situation which funds her, or in this case, is failing to do so."

Nero glared back at him, dressed as an officer, but was the furthest thing from. Unlike the highly trained officers of Rome, adept both physically and mentally, Nero was beyond frail. He lacked heart and conviction. Worse, he was incompetent. And Vespasian hated this about the man more than all his other shortcomings. Getting Nero to grasp even the simplest of concepts when it came to managing anything was a deeply skin-clawing annoyance. It was a task he dreaded more than any enemy within the frenzied heat of battle.

How could he get him to understand? With the sunlight gleaming off Nero's heavily engraved breastplate bearing zero blemishes, virgin to the field of battle, the answer literally blinded him. *Ah yes.* "Do try to see my position. As general of the army, I lead Rome's soldiers to victories. The spoils of those victories, a percentage of which, as promised to *your* soldiers, have instead gone in whole back to Rome. These men have families. See now, these are my responsibilities as general to the soldiers of Rome. As emperor, which, makes you *general* of all of the Empire of Rome, have all of her battlefields to navigate. Daily, you have an embattled sea of politics under your command." He gracefully brushed away the bee when it returned, intent to land upon his shoulder. "We both only continue to be generals as long as there's money to do so. That money has to come from somewhere."

Nero couldn't help but smile. *Maybe there was a future after all for Vespasian, even as self-absorbed as the man was.* "I understand. I do, Vespasian. So, as the general of Rome, my order is to go to Jerusalem."

"Vespasian's more a politician than Nero ever will be," said Mike, impressed by the general's diplomacy. For them all, pursuers of the past, it was an unprecedented front seat, and exhilarating insight into the very heart of history. It was an experience perhaps more fulfilling in certain ways than even the L' Entita's treasure of knowledge they collectively sought.

Vespasian bowed to Nero. "As you command. My son, Titus here, and I, we will bring this victory you seek over the Jewish rebels, barbaric bastards they are. Alas, effective in their vicious ways. But it will be at the price of Rome's economic ruin."

"Nonsense," Nero answered with a wave of his hand. "Money cannot ruin this." He flailed out both his pale and thin arms to the sky. "You, you should know by now, Vespasian, what Rome is. It's the will of the gods themselves. It cannot fail. We—it is too great. And *I* command it. And you, her army, the greatest the world has ever seen. Now, go, the both of you, and be great. Rome eternal!" He stomped his sandaled foot to the tiled ground and slapped his right palm to his breastplate.

"In the mouth of the wolf," said Nero.

"May the wolf die," said Vespasian, out of tradition rather than respect.

The discourse had gone exactly how Titus had predicted it would. And Titus was right. This was their opportunity to let Nero impale himself. They'd bide their time and wait for the will of the people to shift to their side. The public was as the tide of the sea. A good spectacle could turn their mind in any direction. And nothing was a greater spectacle than war. Then that is when Nero would be brought to the flames... Vespasian paused in his thoughts. For some reason unknown, he was compelled to follow to a point just outside his peripheral vision. Turning his head to the place, his eyes found nothing. He *felt* something though.

For the briefest moment, Camorra thought his eyes had made contact with Vespasian's. Though, he knew it must just have been his own respect and natural will to connect with this rare man, a man who was a true follower of the warrior's code. It was the path least traveled in a world of men among men. He was a man who could move in appearance between wolf, serpent, and sheep. While, Nero was a sheep dressed as a wolf. Camorra released a sigh. For what was the first time in his life, he was starting to feel like he actually was in the right era for himself. Perhaps he'd stay. *What prey he could spill the blood of in such a place as this...*

Titus pivoted upon the beautiful mosaic tile, turning for the door. Vespasian returned his focus to Nero. His eyes wanting to say more, though he denied his mouth the pleasure. He quickly followed his son.

"And Vespasian," Nero said, pointing at him, "leave the bookkeeping to me." Without another word, Titus led his father inside the palace.

At once, the color drained from all things....

Astral Projection

*I*ngrid...!" Howie yelled, seeing everything around him bend and fold, then fade away.

"It did it on its own!" she yelled back, able to hear him, though unable to see him or anything else except for herself.

Like a photograph slowly taking form, their surroundings came into being. They found themselves boxed in by tens of thousands of Roman soldiers marching down Appian Way, Rome's central road. The color guard leading the vast army out of Rome held high the Flavian Family Banner.

Time flowed faster than it should be. The sky shifted from day to night. Cycling so, it was neither blue, gray, nor black, but a gradient of all. Star-filled sky, moon aglow, clouds, and sun coexisting, it was crisp and clear above them as they continued onward.

The dry fields, stone pines, and rolling hills of southern Italy passed by as they traveled away from the western side of the Italian peninsula to the eastern side. The parched landscape ended with the gleaming Mediterranean Sea. Hundreds of single mast ships waited the army along the port there.

"Okay, hold on," she said.

Knowing she'd be immediately seasick upon stepping onto any ship, she closed her eyes, seamlessly folding time and space, skipping this part of their journey. Immediately so, coastline came into view. Glassy water with small silky ripples drifted slowly in and out along the shore of tan stones and sand. Stepping off a ship they held no memory of boarding, they found themselves in port now among sun-beaten buildings.

"Ptolemais," Mike said. "Right below Tyre."

"Syria," Howie said. "Always never wanted to go here."

"Reconstructed composite of memories," said Mike. "Remember."

As they spoke, they were once more flanked and boxed in by Rome's vast army as it marched them along out of the port town, traveling further south through the Roman province of Judaea. In one moment, having been on the ground, now they found themselves viewing the army from an impossible angle. At a bird's-eye view, elevated at what must have been thirty feet, maybe more, they saw five people failing to march in rhythm, while neither dressed as soldiers amongst the uniformed ranks. Their brains began to catch up with what they were seeing... realizing those five who didn't belong were... *themselves.* They were without their bodies.

"Uh... Howie?"

Howie heard clearly the question, but could not see Tom, nor any of them. "I know."

"Just go with it," Mike said, his body absent, while voice was rich with enthusiasm. Free for the first time of the physical confines of his body, it was both scary and empowering. *Was this like astral projection? Science be damned, it must be. If my body's still in the chamber, then how am I looking at myself below me? Stop overthinking it, Michael. And just enjoy the ride.*

Continuing to rise, they could see farther than any human eye should have. The curvature of the earth was there. Above it, like an eternal hallow, was the gentle blue of the atmosphere. As if guided by an invisible tether, they held course with their bodies far below.

The Roman army flowed as a great ribbon of armor, stretching out over the land for miles, keen, intent for death and glory. Superimposed, the word 'Galilee' took form upon the stretch of dusty landscape before them. Galilee, from what they could see, appeared as a cluster of villages. The men of Galilee, gravely outnumbered, embraced their families for the final time, then took position outside the villages.

"Such courage," Mike said. "They see clearly as we the sixty-thousand Romans coming for them. Yet, there they stand, ready."

Before even the first death, everyone knew the outcome. The five of them, the Galileans, and certainly, the Roman army, could feel it with certainty. Spearheading the army, Vespasian and Titus jointly gave the order to their archers.

With the release of their arrows, an immeasurable sum, it formed a cloud of merciless wooden shafts and piercing metal-tips. As the arrows arched down back to earth, they found their mark, sinking in and through the hearts, bodies, and iron wills of the men of Galilee. These men's collective fall spilled forth a great vibration across the battlefield.

No more than a few score of men remained alive. Detached from the horror awaiting them, the Galileans charged. Wielding broken swords, crudely fashioned knives, work tools of every kind, they faced their fate. With a wave of his hand, Vespasian sent his first legion of calvary, a number of men on horseback far more than necessary, to intercept the gallant, though doomed charge. The remaining Galileans, ever brave, fell swiftly.

With the end of the battle, more slaughter than warfare, the five of them arose, sinking deeper into the sky, which held the sun and moon in equal measures. Their invisible tethers unraveled, breaking their connection. It was an odd sensation, tearing from one's own body.

In fear, they shouted. The rich blue glow of the atmosphere swallowed them. Free from the will of gravity, space was closer than the ground so far, far below. Suddenly, they plummeted. The roar of the air tearing past was deafening, muting their screams....

Prisoner

*A*s they tumbled through the open air toward death, they found themselves once more imprisoned within their physical bodies.

"Back inside our bodies at least!" Tom tried to yell over the roar of the rushing air.

Pillars of smoke rose high into the sky, proclaiming victory for the Romans. What little remained of Galilee rapidly burned to the ground, leaving dried up puddles of ashen nothingness. The smoke swirled around them as outstretched fingers unable to stop them.

Reaching terminal velocity, the earth rushed toward them at a 118 miles per hour. Less than ten feet from impact... the air became thick as glass, catching them. It spit them out onto the corpse-strewn battlefield.

Pulling themselves up, they saw Vespasian not far away. He climbed onto his charcoal-gray horse and led the army south. The snap of a dried and dead olive branch brought them to turn their focus away from the departing army.

A man, well dressed for the first century, stepped from the broken stones concealing him. Leather bound his wrists. Legs bent, with his palms leaned against the front of his shins, he gasped for breath.

The man's dark eyes and long beard seemed familiar to Mike. Titus revealed himself now, drawing his sword. In one swift motion, he brought the tip to the man's throat.

For Ingrid, knowing now this man's identity, the lost pieces of history scattered across the ages, spanning millennia, were quickly beginning to align. "That's Josephus."

Of course. Mike knew he should've recognized him. Titus prepared to drive the blade in. Whatever inaudible words Josephus then swiftly spoke, effectively disarmed Titus's wrath.

Titus seemed to measure what'd he'd just been told. He released him and rapped his sword to his breastplate. A group of soldiers immediately joined him. Titus placed Josephus upon a horse, then climbed onto his own. Single file, he led down the road in the direction of his father and their army.

"Who was—is Josephus?" Tom asked.

"Joseph Bar Mathias... If you've got to ask," Mike said, "then you don't need to know at the moment."

"Can you for once not be a condescending," Howie started to say. Without a sound, all became liquidly. Bending and folding like silky paper, as the plane woven of time and space crumpled into itself, drawing them thoroughly into the fabric of existence....

Spilled Blood and Wine

S hapes took form, filling in around them. They found themselves inside a building of brown brick. With their backs to the wall, next to the dual front doors, the structure before them was long, narrow, and hall-like.

An official gathering of lawmakers of some kind filled it. Their voices were hushed whispers flowing with the day's finest gossip. These first century men of Rome sat on either side of the hall upon marble benches that ran the length of the building. Modest and austere, the most decorative part of the interior were the marble reliefs which served as a kind of wall three or three and a half feet tall along the face of the benches. These reliefs were carvings of numerous Roman figures, whom must have been historically significant, though none they recognized.

Camorra calculated the interior's dimensions to be eighty-two feet long by fifty-six feet wide, or somewhere nearly that. He knew where he was now. He'd seen the outside of this building in passing. It'd been a few years though, during a meeting in the Roman Forum, with Domenico no less. The bare and brown exterior of the building imprinted into his memory was even less remarkable than this interior of the same dull brown. Nonetheless, and as he knew through and through, appearances and importance often did not imprison one another.

And Mike, of course, knew where they were simply from

the signature red and green and white tiled floor beneath their feet. "Curia Julia. It's the Curia Julia." Howie and Tom's blank stares reminded him that the others didn't hold a PhD in history, but more significantly, didn't spend their days inhaling the words of ancient manuscripts as freely as one would air. "The Roman Senate building at the time."

The doors directly behind them had begun to open. Before they could turn to see, Nero, with jug of wine greedily held in both hands, entered, bordered by his entourage of six guards. They passed right through them, invisibly so as they were, and headed down the center of the hall. Unseen to all, Howie, then Camorra, led the rest of them, following behind Nero and his men.

Nero took position upon the elevated platform at the other end of the hall and faced the Senate. His men, three on either side, stood calmly and carefully, watching. They hoped by the will of *all* the gods that Nero would manage not to completely spoil another session of the Senate. Alas, even the gods had their limits. Nero, after all, was drinking his wine, and that never ended well for anyone.

Camorra brought the others to stop, now standing directly behind Nero and his men. With this vantage point, they each saw just how oddly shaped Nero's head was, and not just overly large for his body, but actually nonsymmetrical. Nero, attempting to commence session for the Senate, was too drunk to begin to even speak, ending in some slurred mumble no one understood, not even himself. He buried his face into the jug of wine and gulped greatly, with streams of purplish-red running down both sides of his mouth. He released a deep belch before his audience, both amused and not.

The senator closest to Nero stood. He pointed his finger straight at Nero, who was too absorbed by his jug of wine to pay notice. "You make a mockery of Rome." Saliva sprayed out from his mouth as his words rebuked his failed emperor. "You make a mockery of us. You make a—" The jug of wine crashed at the senator's feet, smashing into a plume of sticky wine across the tiled floor.

The senator jumped back. His eyes were afire. A shard from the jug protruded from his calf. Blood trickled from the place, entwining with the wine, then dripping, snaking down his leg.

Nero's lips turned upwards, sneering into a most satisfied smile. "Emperor..." He thought about this, then changed his mind. "Supreme Emperor General," he managed somehow, stringing three words together coherently enough to be understood.

The senator stooped and tore the shard free. "Supreme?" He hurled the shard at Nero. "Supreme ass of a horse!"

The shard safely sailed several inches over Nero's oversized head. This didn't prevent Nero from releasing a scream of terror. The shard continued to sail and right at Tom, then passed through his forehead, clattering to the floor.

Still positioned behind Nero, as best they could make out, it seemed Nero had begun to relieve himself right then and there upon the beautifully tiled floor of the Senate. As he did so, he suddenly drew a knife from its leather and metal sheath strapped to the thigh of his closest guard.

Eyes wide, blank, and glassy, Nero pointed the six-inch blade of the knife. Letting out a bloodcurdling, whooping cry, he lunged for the senator spurting forth blood from his calf. Nero's guards reached out, attempting to stop this spectacle of derangement.

"Can't say I'll ever complain about modern politicians again," Tom said.

A horde of senators converged upon Nero, wrenching away the knife mere inches before it could sink into their fellow lawmaker. The entire Senate was now on their feet, and had begun to encircle Nero, where he was upon his knees pressed to the beautifully tiled floor. He frantically tried to wipe away the wine spilled on his clothes, but it'd set deeply into the fabric. Desperate, he futilely kept wiping at the stain.

His guards unsheathed their swords. They held their blades aimed downwards at the floor, as diplomatically as possible in this impossibly undiplomatic of circumstances. Pressing through the crowd, they made a pathway to Nero, deftly careful not to spill any further blood. For, in doing so, they, along with their emperor, would be torn to pieces.

These no longer were senators, but patriots of Rome, angry as wolves, clawing at the cusp of vengeance. Nero's guards lifted him to his feet. The injured senator, defying the threat of the guards' blades, ventured closer, taunting them to strike.

He pressed his outstretched finger to Nero's wine-soaked chin. Then he drew in his finger, clenching his hand into a tight fist. He leaned his fist into Nero's sticky skin. The senator's voice was shaky and bitter as he spoke. "Fool." His fist pushed harder against Nero's chin. "Your fate is sealed." With his other hand covered in his own blood, he raised it high into the air. "You hear me. Sealed with the blood of Rome's own."

As Nero's guards dragged him steadily backwards along the wall for the doors, he saw the unanimous hatred in the eyes of the entire Senate. The terrifying truth of the senator's words took realization across Nero's face. This hate was for... *him*.

Every senator followed, as a pack surging forward, hungry for Nero. Reaching the dual doors, Nero suddenly attempted to break from his guards' hold. He convulsed, snapped his jaws open and closed at the senators, though did not release any words. He howled wildly at everyone, thrashing his arms and legs as a rapid beast could, and surely would.

Breaking free of his men's hold, he stretched out both arms in front of him. With his long, thin fingers curled, he grinned wildly at the senators just inches away. The senator closest drew a knife.

Another revealed a knife. And another raised a long blade, more sword than knife. These three senators, armed, wielded their weapons, ready to stab, slice, and penetrate any part of this lunatic standing before them. Nero, eyes holding no awareness for his actions or thoughts, with his bony hands bent into little arched talons, his fingers shook with fear and rage as the senators' blades reflected back grimly in those glassed-over eyes of his....

Besieged

*N*ero's guards tore him back, then dragged him out the front doors. The five of them followed. Their surroundings began to morph....

"Here we go again," Howie said, just as everything warped and rippled.

The lighting became as dusk. Sounds of evening birds and insects drifted through the dimly lit space now surrounding them. Wooden floorboards were under their feet and barren walls were before them. Through a large and open widow was the Italian countryside. The sun was quite low, nearly melted away.

At the far end of the room, a small ball of light appeared. It connected itself to a candle that was held in someone's hand. More candles were lit. Nero's face was embraced within the shadow, amongst the trembling candlelight in the breeze. With the sun now gone, twilight slipped through the window.

They ventured closer to this self-exiled emperor. Empty and smashed wine jugs covered the floor. His face, smeared with dirt, pale and unshaven. He crouched down with a candle in his grip. Holding it low to the floor near the corner of the room, they saw now the lone and dead servant. The handle of a knife protruded from his chest.

Many torches appeared from outside. Numerous voices, angry, could be heard. A mob awaited Nero, alone, without guards or hope.

Nero's eyes frantic, stared through the window out at them. He mumbled something and saluted them as the military man he so very much wished to be. Then he went and sat slowly, deliberately, and almost calmly next to his dead servant.

His hand trembled as he drew the knife from its sheath at his thigh. He aligned the blade to his own chest, to the place where he best guessed his heart to be. Ingrid turned her head away, unable to watch. The blade sank sluggishly into Nero's chest. After some gurgled gasps, it was done. In the candlelight, his eyes reflected nothing, besieged with emptiness.

None desired to venture closer to the scene where Nero had just taken his own life. They averted their eyes and wished to be taken from this grim, dark place. Even Camorra, he found no value nor valor within this act compelled by fear, even with what a great deal of courage such an action required... To do such a crass and lonely thing.

"Now we go," Ingrid said.

Without question, they followed where she led, appearing to pass straight through the wall before them....

Depleted

*T*hey entered a great chamber completely of marble. Torches secured along the walls warmly illuminated the cool marble surfaces.

"It was—is real," Mike said. "The Imperial Vault..."

"We're back inside the Imperial Palace?" Howie asked.

"Yes," Ingrid quickly answered.

"So... where's the treasure then?" asked Tom.

"Nero used it to build the palace overhead," Mike said.

The large and beautifully ornate treasury vault was virtually all but depleted of anything of value. Footsteps flowed down the marble staircase leading into the vault. Vespasian entered, wearing the deeply purple robe reserved exclusively for the Emperor of Rome.

He held a single sheet of papyrus. Thoroughly displeased with whatever he saw upon it, his eyes drifted away from the paper-like sheet to the empty treasury. His grip tightened on the papyrus, crushing it into a yellowed ball. He chucked it directly at Tom, who instinctually ducked, but a moment too late. The balled papyrus passed straight through his face, falling to the charcoal-gray stone floor.

"Why does that keep happening?" Tom asked.

"Right place, wrong time," Howie said.

Ingrid nodded at Vespasian's purple robe. "Though not for Vespasian."

"Yeah," Mike answered. "Upon destroying the entire

region of Galilee, Vespasian and Titus received news of Nero's death. Vespasian sent Titus on ahead to sack Jerusalem, while he himself rode straight back to Rome. And with Nero gone, well, there was no one who could challenge Vespasian's claim to the throne, so to speak."

Vespasian slumped against the wall, slid to the floor, and stared vacantly at the depleted treasury vault. His fingers gripped the edges of his purple robe. He turned away from the immense empty space before him and focused on the robe.

Quickly, he pulled himself up with the noise of footsteps coming from the staircase. He placed a look of stoicism on his face just as his son Titus came into view. Titus wore the breastplate his father had, emblazoned with the wolf, signifying he now held the highest rank directly below emperor, that of Primus Pilus.

The five of them followed this father and son, the two most powerful men in all the Roman Empire. They went to the furthest corner of the vault. Not having noticed it before, within the shadows, there was another door.

Removing a key of iron from his pocket, Vespasian unlocked the door. They entered. In the torchlight within this inner vault, numerous large metal chests sat neatly stacked.

Titus led to the closest chest. Vespasian joined him there. As silent witnesses in search of the truth, their group of five watched and listened intently so to these great men of Rome.

Vespasian rested a heavy hand on one of the chests. "How is it, Titus, you bring news of a*nother* Jewish uprising?" Gently, he withdrew his hand. Suddenly, he slammed both his fists onto the chest. "Tell me! How is it these Jewish rebels not only don't fall, they continue to grow stronger?" He shook his head, waiting for an answer. "Be the son I need you to be. If you don't know what that it is, it's called..." He breathed deeply. "Being the son of the Emperor of Rome!"

Just now, releasing his fists still clenched upon the chest, he set a truly weary hand to the breastplate Titus wore, seeking out his son's heart. "I cannot be both in Rome and do your job as general for you. I don't care what you have to do to finish this... Just make it so."

Titus pulled away from his father. "And what am I to do? I destroyed Jerusalem. I destroyed their Temple. 'Not one stone will be left on another', as Josephus said to do. I took their holy texts. And yet, they keep..." He raised both his hands and balled his fingerings into fists of his own. "They keep going... Keep rebelling. Their minds and bodies know no end. I tell you, Vespasian, there is no *reason* for it."

"Then there are more copies of these texts, my son. Simply, you failed to take all from their temple and bring them here, locked away out of their sight. Out of everyone's sight. See, that is what drives them. They must have more copies. There is always a *reason*."

Titus leaned upon the chest. "I did not fail. The Temple was the only place the Jews thought sacred enough to keep their precious texts. Josephus dare not lie of such things."

"Ah, Josephus. You've grown too close to him. He's a traitor to his own. How can you trust a man as that? Has triumph dulled your mind so? It was by *his* deceit to his own which gave you swift victory over Jerusalem."

"You vex my mind you speak of. It's *because* I keep Josephus close that I know if he's deceitful." Thoroughly exhausted from everything, he rested the side of his face against the marble wall near the chest. The coldness of the marble felt good to his skin. "It's what's inside their writings. That's our true enemy. That's what *keeps* them fighting."

"Tell me, Titus, what that is? What's in these chests here that we've so faithfully kept locked away? *What* exactly is in those texts which keeps these people willing to die?"

A new voice, a woman's voice, invaded their secret realm there within the soft crackling light of the torches. "That's the question the two of you should have been asking to begin with." The voice had no face, not yet. Even for the five of them, invisibly watching the emperor father with his general son, they could not see her.

Titus and Vespasian reached for their swords, only to discover their swords were gone. At the darkest part of the vault, the shadows themselves began to separate down their center, revealing....

The Crossing of the Blood

*H*aving in one moment been invisible, like the five of them, and in the next, simply there, the woman appeared. She was tall and fair skinned. The hooded cloak she wore partly obscured her face.

Her cloak, dark, as though crafted from the shadow, contrasted her pale skin even more so than it already was. She moved without sound, as if her feet didn't even touch the stone floor as she walked. She stopped within an arms-length of the two men positioned at the many locked chests.

Raising her cloak just enough to show them both their swords were tucked safely away beneath, she sleekly shed her hood, now fully exposing her Scandinavian features. Her shoulder-length hair was short for the time and place. It was a style neither man had ever seen before on a woman. And the color, her hair was extremely light, blonde, nearly white.

"This is the most secure room in the world," Titus said.

"Says little of rooms," she responded. "Or of security. The most of something is the least of other things. You are the most powerful general in all the world, yet there are a handful of Jews in Alexandria, as we speak, who are on the brink of overthrowing the city there. And you are powerless to stop it."

"How do you know?" Titus started to ask, but found his voice to suddenly fail.

She ran her finger along the metal chest next to him. "Power in itself has its limitations. Rome's rule by force has forged you an empire. But such force, it's not sustainable."

"Who are you?" asked Vespasian. His voice was casual, calm, almost warm. "If you wished us harm, I believe you'd have brought it without first showing yourself. And while capable, you've chosen not to. You've done so for a reason."

She moved closer, not to them, but to the chest. "Ever adroit. Titus, pay your father mind. His diplomacy will take you farther than any army's able to. My name is Ameci. Beyond a name, who I am is not vital. What is, I can answer your question."

"What question?" Vespasian asked.

Ameci placed both hands upon the chest. The metal felt warm to Titus now, uncomfortably so, with his palm still touching it. He pulled away.

She drew her left hand across the chest, hovering it just so over the keyhole. "I can show you what it is that keeps men fighting. That keeps them dying for something that cannot be seen, at least to the senses of man."

Ingrid, feeling, rather than seeing it, was lured toward Ameci. She saw now by the dancing torchlight something familiar in Ameci's eyes. They were unnaturally, intensely blue. They... were the *same* as her own. She crept closer to Ameci, taking a place across from her, just on the other side of the chest. She glanced at the others to see if they were to follow. Though only Camorra did.

"She's L' Entita," he said.

"Yes," Ingrid answered.

When she returned her eyes to Ameci, Ameci seemed to be staring directly at her. The two women's startling blue eyes connected in a place between space and time, a place without borders. In their moment of connection, Ingrid's mind flooded with thoughts not her own, but those belonging to Ameci. There was an unspoken permission with which they flowed to and through her. In that way, she'd been given the right to read... No, *feel* these thoughts.

A single instruction solidified within her mind. *Believe.*

Just believe. A calm confidence wrapped itself around her, soaking in. Her body devoured its comfort. This frequency unseen between Ameci and her harmonized.

The others seemed oblivious to this communication. They held their own focus on Vespasian and Titus and... Ameci. She realized she could no longer hear what was being spoken between the Flavians and Ameci. She could hear only the thoughts of this mysterious women as they resounded as silent echoes throughout her mind.

My friend, breathe, please breathe. Know I am with you through and through. Now, see as I do. These thoughts dissolved away as vapor within her. Another quickly took form. *The Flavians have overestimated the power of the sword. Their success will ultimately disarm them, bringing them their defeat.* Then, as though a switch shut off, Ameci's thoughts flowed no more.

"For the first time in your lives," Ameci said to Titus and Vespasian, "you're cornered by a problem the blades of your swords cannot solve." She began to lift the chest's lid.

Titus moved toward her. "It's locked..." The lock, nor the great weight of the chest's heavy lid, held any consequence for her, for she opened it with an uninterrupted ease. Vespasian joined his son alongside Ameci. The three of them, aligned before the chest, looked inside at the secrets contained within.

Ameci's perfectly shaped fingers hovered for a moment before removing a particular scroll. "With all reverence, Vespasian, and Titus, how can you expect to understand their faith, when you have none yourselves." With a twist of her left index finger and thumb, she untied the bit of leather binding the scroll, letting it unroll.

By the torchlight, she read silently this sacred text of the Hebrews. She held securely, though delicately, the scroll as she started to speak. "The greatest power is not found in truth. But in belief." She parted her cloak, showing them their swords were in fact not beneath. "Why is this? Belief is a thing being true. Even if it is not." They checked their sheaths at their sides. Their swords, as if having never been removed, were there.

"Yes. Were they always there?" Ameci skillfully rolled the scroll back up. "That is the question, when all is done, you'll still be asking." She returned the scroll inside the chest.

"Why?" Vespasian asked.

Ameci removed from within her cloak a piece of paper, not papyrus, but actual paper. "Because belief requires a reason."

She placed the paper flat onto the chest before them. They closed in on this perfectly smooth and bone-white material of far finer quality than any papyrus they'd ever seen.

"A contract," Ameci told them.

Vespasian scanned the artfully written document. "Our blood? You desire our blood?"

Her steely blue eyes told them, father as well son, they'd not receive an answer as to *why.* They could either accept this or reject it.

Vespasian ran his finger along the place in the contract. "And what is this of Josephus?"

"It's simple," she said. "The only way to be able to trust him is to give him something he doesn't have. Something his life will be dependent upon. That which will force his loyalty."

Vespasian turned to Titus. "She wants us to make Josephus part of our bloodline."

Titus immediately scoffed. "A *Jew* with our family birthright."

"Did he not unlock the hidden gate within the wall of Jerusalem, securing your victory for you, Titus?" she asked.

"Yes, at the threat of my blade, for I'd have ended the breath within his body."

"Then grant him this title, and he will surely unlock the gate to Judaism itself, securing *Rome's* victory once and for all over Judaea."

"The Jews have been lions amongst the greatest warriors of the world... for thousands of years," said Titus. "What you speak of is ending such a legacy. To transform them into... sheep. You can't simply change their history."

"Sure you can, Titus Flavius, great General of Rome," she said, with unwavering confidence and belief, as if she could indefinitely see the shadow cast by the future itself. "My dear Flavians, before you rewrite history, first you erase what's been already written."

"Like with the Druids," Titus said.

She shifted her focus solely to him. "Yes. Just like that, with ensuring their history was lost. Forever. Now, do it for the Jews. And, Titus, this is exactly what you're going to do. In every direction heading out of Rome, dispatch a task force. They are to eradicate all documentation even referencing the Jews for all of this century. They are to burn all records. All, of everything. I trust you know how I mean."

"What of Josephus?" asked Vespasian. "What further role can this traitor possibly play?"

As though willing it, her shadow suddenly eclipsed over Vespasian. "What you don't know of Josephus's past will be the very thing to decide his role into your, the Flavian's future, Rome's future. *Our* future."

"Tom?" Mike asked, intently watching from the shadows swirled within the torchlight.

"Yeah...," Tom answered.

"How long do our body cams record for?"

Tom smiled. "Better part of two terabytes. So, don't worry, we'll capture it. All of it." Camorra drifted closer, continuing to separate himself from the rest of them, drawing to the center of this scene which seemed to be destined to determine things, many things echoing far into the future... into his present.

These five, eavesdroppers of the past, had begun to finally taste the truth shrouded behind the curtain of time. Now they craved more, imprisoned by the freedom it beckoned. Their eyes held to Ameci, this cloaked woman, as she immersed the leaders of Rome into her masterful plan that'd direct the fate of an empire, and the will of the world with her hand.

"How, Vespasian," she asked, "is it, you believe, Josephus rose to the position that he did before his capture, as the central architect for the Jewish rebels?"

"By his blood," he answered. "He was born into it."

"Yes," she said. "It was written, locked away in his blood before even his birth. For his father was the chief guardian of the Temple itself. You see, my dear Flavians, your Josephus was groomed from the earliest ages, to know the codes layered within the sacred Hebraic texts."

"What codes?" Titus asked.

"Codes are everything," she answered, by not entirely answering him. "They are the locks which conceal the secrets. You still believe, by this point, Titus, that you happening to personally capture Josephus, lone survivor of that Galilean massacre, was by chance? Hmmm. How easily success causes us to miss the details which brought that very success..."

In her eerie way of walking without seeming to touch the floor, she placed herself exactly at the center of this inner vault, letting the torchlight bathe her in a gentle and golden aura. The two Flavians followed, hooked into her enchantment, needing it as air now. She loosened her cloak around her neck, exposing her pale and smooth flesh there. "Having chosen so or not, the Flavians' fate has bled into the bloodline of Josephus's own. He is the key to the universal empire that will bind all."

Raising her left hand, she performed what the five of them had always known to be the Catholic sign of the cross, and what Vespasian and Titus, of the first century, had never witnessed before. "The *Crossing of the Blood* has happened." Without a word more, she tilted her head away, and looked Ingrid dead in the eyes. The virgin white marble enveloping the vault and them became as melting wax. Things were as a photograph reversing itself, fading.

The Fathers, the Sons, and Gods

*W*ith a dizzying rush, they returned to the small courtyard of the Imperial Palace. A starry sky, more stars than any of them had ever seen, glistened down. Ameci and the Flavians stood before a round table of marble at the courtyard's center. They joined them.

"Tell me," said Ameci, "what caused this conflict with the Jewish rebels to begin with?"

Vespasian and Titus glanced at each other.

"They refused to worship the likenesses of the Roman gods we had placed within their Temples," Vespasian answered.

"You stuck statues inside their most sacred places of worship and they rejected it," she said. "And you were surprised by this? If you do not see the problem, my dear Flavians, then how can you hope to understand the solution? You cannot force a god onto someone who already has one. Hmmm. What do you do then, clever men?"

"You make their god our god," said Titus.

She smiled. "*That*, Great Titus, is the solution. Let us just do so with a little more adroitness than dumping statues of Jupiter inside their temples. Now, I trust you two can appreciate the function of the imperial cult."

"Imperial cult?" Tom asked, turning to the others as they so silently and invisibly gazed upon what was taking place.

"Using religion to dictate politics to the people," said

Howie.

"'God wants me to be president'," Tom said.

"Uh huh," Howie said. "Just the Romans took it a step further. I am a god, thus, by divine right, I'm unchallengeable. Total immunity."

"Right," said Mike, "and perhaps the more critical element to the imperial cult was the divine claim to authority it established for the respective family in power. We're talking dynastic politics. The emperor is a god. So, his son, by default, is also a god..."

"I see," Tom said, nodding. "Securing a single bloodline to power."

Ameci pulled their attention back to her as she swiftly clapped her hands twice. Immediately, Josephus entered the courtyard.

"As we've all seen," she said, "you cannot conquer the Jews militarily. It must be done politically. To do that, you must understand the Jewish system of politics. Josephus, tell them."

"In my culture," he said, "politics and religion are interwoven as threads to a blanket. They are the same."

"See," Ameci said, "it is no different than the Roman system. You Flavians believe war is spectacle. But a war for one's soul, *every day* of their life. Now, that is true spectacle." She held up a silver coin. "This denarius. Two sides. The front, a profile of a man seen by the people as a god. Neither a man nor a god. But a *symbol.* That is religion. That is the side we let the people see." She smiled. "Yes, religion. A system where logic and reason are unnecessary, where one's decision making is exclusive to emotion."

She flipped the coin. Catching it, she showed the reverse side. "While the other side, that is for us to know. To understand. Full of symbols, which only we wield the true meaning of. This is the realm of politics. Where you, Josephus, and you Titus and you Vespasian, the policymakers, will operate free from the people's scrutiny."

"Your ancestor is creeping me out," Howie said.

"I know," answered Ingrid.

Ameci nudged Josephus closer to Vespasian and Titus, pushing him into their circle's center.

"How are we going to do this?" Titus asked.

"Josephus," Ameci said.

"A new religion," Josephus answered. "Binding the Jews to Roman will. In Rome, an emperor rules by divine right. In Judaism, prophets are the key to this divine right."

Ameci rested a hand along Vespasian's wrist, measuring his pulse, feeling the song of his *blood* as she did so. "Now, Titus, being the younger of you, it must be him."

Almost trance-like, Vespasian nodded.

"Titus," said Ameci, "we will anchor you to a Jewish prophet. This will give you, a Roman, divine claim in Judaism. Hence, *political* right over the Jews."

"You crafty snake, Josephus," Mike said under his breath. He turned to his fellow seekers of truth. "Topology... Anyone? No? Okay, so topology was used to establish a foreshadowing from one prophet to the next in Hebraic text."

"Repackaging of old into new," Tom said. "Ireland holds no shortage of such tales."

"Most appropriately, I'd say," suggested Ingrid, "Jesus, he's a direct repackaging of all the thousands of messiah sons of gods before him—Horus, Mithra, and so forth."

"Exactly," Mike answered. "Rome's Jesus is a direct repackaging of Joseph of the Old Testament. One only simply need read Matthew and Genesis side by side. Deeper though, with Hebraic topology, these connections were established covertly, *encoded* into the text, subconsciously indoctrinating the reader. A deliberate pattern is created, repeated over and over again to be absorbed into the reader's mind, *without them even knowing it.*"

"It's precisely how the Romans interlinked their Christianity's New Testament to the Old Testament of the Jews," Howie said.

"Shhh," Camorra said, stepping from his place along the

shadowed wall.

They directed their focus back to the conspirators before them.

"And what *Jewish* prophet am I, the Great Titus, to be anchored," said Titus.

"Your pride will be the end of you, my son," Vespasian said.

Ameci nodded to Josephus.

"We're going to create one," Josephus said. "A new one. A pacifistic one to defang the mighty Lion of Judah."

With a gentle wave of her hand, Ameci drew them in closer together, around her. Though, while they encompassed her, it was her shadow, which was the one who surrounded them. From within her cloak, she removed a slender piece of bone of a few inches long. Both ends of it came to a sharp point.

"A pen," she said, setting the contract on the table. "You know where the ink comes from." She held it out to them. "Freewill. You also know of the great rift which resides between free and will. It's in the form of consequences. If you don't sign, the Jewish rebels will continue their course. Your army, that, while great and powerful, costs millions to maintain. Millions in expenses in order to extinguish a fire which costs the rebels nearly nothing to ignite. Not before long, fires, not just from these rebels, but by others who'll follow their example, will spread across your empire. It is an exceptionally large empire with a great many places ripe for flame. In the time being, as these flames of chaos divide, taxes cannot be collected. Rome will fall."

Titus plucked the pen of bone away. Puncturing his palm with its point, he felt his blood somehow being sucked, drawn up inside this piece of bone. Using his blood, he placed his signature, large and elegant and warmly crimson, forever burned into the beautifully crafted paper. He offered the pen to his father. Vespasian drew his own blood, signing his name below his son's. Josephus then signed. His signature was perfect, revealing he possessed the greatest grace with a pen.

Ameci took the pen and contract, gathering them up, and hid them away under her cloak. She faced Josephus. "From this day forward, you will be known as Josephus Flavius. You, just as your children's children, will be a Flavian. Now, we erase the lion, and in place, place a lamb. Not before long, dear Flavians..." She flipped the silver denarius high into the air, sending the silvery starlight from above rippling off of it. "The Jews will be *rendering unto Caesar what is Caesar's*."

Catching the coin, she opened her hand, revealing this little circle of silver to be gone. She turned, and quite deliberately, let her fingertips brush against Ingrid's arm.

Ingrid *felt* Ameci's touch. Her hand had not passed through her. Was this woman of the past... *More than a memory of blood?*

Ameci nodded ever slightly to Ingrid, promising a great reveal, the *greatest*, awaiting them all, as she led for the doorway....

The Eye

eaching the door, Ameci paused. "Have faith."

"What'd she mean by that?" asked Tom.

Josephus and the Flavians faded away as the five of them followed Ameci through the courtyard's doorway. The palace was no more. Ameci was no more. They stood upon a sliver of a ledge high within the sky. The Roman Empire was spread out several miles below them.

Ingrid hovered one foot over the vast open space. She didn't doubt Ameci's words, only herself. *What the hell is 'faith' even?*

Camorra pushed past, setting both feet into open air. He stood there in the air as though on solid ground.

"That's what she meant by that," said Howie.

"Thanks," Tom said.

Ingrid closed her eyes and freed herself from the safety of the ledge, joining Camorra. Reluctantly, the others did the same. Upon doing so, they saw now the countless bonfires which burned across the empire.

Ameci's words silently screamed within their ears. *All records documenting first century Jews are to be destroyed.* The gift they'd been granted, as witnesses to history, in this sharply unique and original way, was double-edged. And it cut deeply.

Such a horrific loss of culture on this scale was nearly unmeasurable. They could only hope the Library of Alexandria had survived its own flames. That its treasury of knowledge could still be reclaimed.

These tens of thousands of pillars of smoke from the fires cut vertically up the sky, like prison bars solidifying across the earth. The pillars of smoke converged not far below them, intertwining, swirling into a single juggernaut of ashy gray gloom, thick and hateful. A shape began to form within this coagulating knot. Sculpted of smoke and terror, the Praesidio Autem Veritas, vast and dark, now stared up at them.

Blotting out everything else, it devoured over the countryside, rewriting all within its inky gaze. The pupil of the eye, a hundred feet across, expanded, opening into a tunneling vortex churning with teeth, if smoke could manifest such things. Vast tentacle-like shafts of smoke drifted, snaking up. They reached out for them.

Calmly, Camorra accepted these. He relaxed his body, and he let his arms hang loosely, freely at his sides. The tentacles of smoke wrapped around him, drawing him down for the open eye. A hint of a smile tugged at his lips, and they watched and wondered what disturbed things could such a man have seen as to not know terror in this moment. For their own screams, they never had a chance....

The Serpent's Gift

S wallowed by the eye of the Praesidio Autem Veritas, there was nothing of smoke. Nor, did they know the scent of fire. They fell. Though, instead of accelerating, their fall slowed the deeper they traveled through the center of this great vortex. The bottom of the vortex constricted shut, denying them a view of the ground. Only a pinpoint of hellish red light awaited them there.

The walls which contained them coiled like a great serpent. It breathed, bending inwards and outwards, fluctuating, contracting. A luminous vapor, brightly light-green as an exotic snake, hissed as it released, flowing from these coiled walls, thickly misty, filling the open core of the vortex.

They drifted, leaflike, down through its gentle glow. Somewhere they'd crossed an invisible line, involuntarily so, transitioning from a state of terror to one of near tranquility. It did not matter to them now, realizing the vortex was an actual serpent, towering from the heavens down to the earth. That was okay. Strange, yes, but okay, as they held no fear for it.

Ingrid pushed herself for the walls. Brushing her finger across the scaly surface, it drew blood. A tiny single droplet bubbled up from her fingertip. It flowed upward, releasing itself into the lime-green air.

Expanding to the size of an apple, it was lush and crimson, and begged for her touch. It hovered there before her as if dangling from a branch unseen. They brought themselves near, as she took hold of it. In her hand, she saw it to now to be an apple, the most flawless one any of them had ever known.

She raised the apple to her lips. And she swallowed the flesh, red and white and juicy. It tasted as an apple should. Just... *perfect* in every way. She gave the apple to Howie, who took a bite. Passing it around as they floated slowly down through the great vortex of a snake, they each consumed this apple most perfect.

Tossing the core, Mike said, "You know, in Genesis, it doesn't actually specify the kind of fruit they ate from the Tree of Knowledge."

"Yeah," Tom said, "well we wouldn't want to be historically incorrect with the mythological story now would we."

Howie watched as the apple core drifted past him. It seemed to gain speed as it fell. "The point wasn't the kind of fruit. It was the kind of tree. The Tree of *Knowledge*. It was a metaphor for evolving oneself with knowledge. To choose ignorance or enlightenment."

Ingrid took his hand, and they descended together, the others trailing a little behind.

"Until Christianity came along," she said, "muddling up the original context the Jews had written."

"Look!" Mike pointed.

The bottom of the vortex opened, transitioning into the immense head of a snake. Its deeply yellowed eyes dilated, glaring zealously up at them. Its jaws drew wide, fully expanding. A vast, forked tongue snapped out, reaching for them. Midnight dark, it glistened and glowed, and burned. Neither flesh nor fire, a blend of both, it cut through the electric lime mist emitting off the coiled insides of this great snake. The apple core, adrift, softly made contact with the tip of the forked tongue. Immediately, it shriveled, becoming a tangled puff of mold.

"I want to go home." Tom retracted his legs up as tightly as he could from the tongue lashing out at him only inches away.

His foot touched the snake's tongue... He clamped his eyes shut. The tongue, then head, faded away, leaving a great hole straight through the bottom of the vortex. The ground, eighty feet below, danced in flame, raptured with a bonfire bigger than any they'd ever seen.

"Better?" Howie gripped Ingrid's hand tightly, their drifting becoming a plummet.

With the smell of fire entering his nostrils, Tom opened his eyes. "No—not at all." He quickly shut his eyes again.

Camorra torpedoed his body, pinning his arms flat to his sides, and aimed his head straight down. He sailed past them, roaring for the fire below.

"What's wrong with that guy," Howie said.

"A considerable sum," Mike said, catching hold of his son. With his other hand, he gripped Tom's hand.

The four of them raced toward the flames....

A Tale of Two Campaigns

*E*xpelled from the bottom of the vortex, the black sky met them, with the bonfire below. Fifty, then forty, then thirty feet, it licked up at the night with long searing blades of orange and red and yellow, entwined with tips of white. Its feeding grew louder, snapping and spitting giant embers. Tremendous, the fire was several hundred feet across by a hundred or so high. Though there was no heat, not at all. The sweat clinging to their bodies was from fear alone.

"Have faith," Ingrid told them all.

With the towering crimson flames snarling up, nearly upon them, the fire began to part, as though a ruby sea spreading so down its center. And down they drifted, down to the ground.

Flanked by walls of towering flame, they rushed along this inferno's pathway. Before them, in the far distance, awaited the Imperial Palace, its marbled-silhouette beautifully illuminated against the scorched palette of night. They ran, exiting the parted sea of fire.

All around, hundreds of Roman soldiers fed the flames pile after pile of Hebraic text. A cloaked figure was there amongst the soldiers, noticed only to them. Shedding her hood, it was Ameci. Her eyes were fierce and coldly blue in the firelight. She reached out for Ingrid.

Ingrid offered her hand. "Hold on," she told the others.

From all things, the color drained. The distance between

them and the palace folded upon itself. They found themselves in a white marble room and knew it must be within the Imperial Palace.

This place seemed to be Josephus's personal chambers. He was there, before a vast oaken desk, along with Titus and Vespasian. Illuminated by a halo of torchlight, Ameci set a piece of crisp white paper on the desk.

Vespasian took it, and seeing clearly the signatures in blood, looked sharply up at her. "You've entered into contract with the Herods and Alexanders. Without consulting us—"

With a raise of Ameci's hand, Vespasian's voice failed him. "If you believe you can keep Rome's heart beating on your own," she said, "then, dear Flavians, you've already failed."

Titus turned to his father. "She's right. The Alexanders and Herods are the wealthiest and most powerful of all the world."

"Yes," she said. "Now what is certain, what keeps your empire current, is currency. You have none. Your vault is dry. Its lifeblood gone. Endless war drained all, leaving bodies strewn across the land. And simply said, you can't tax the dead."

"Taxes," said Titus.

She nodded. "Life *and* taxes. The Alexanders, they will manage Egypt, taxing all there. The Herods will do the same for Judaea. That is where the wealth is. Ignore the rest of the empire. For now. We will soon wet our throats with new blood as it comes flowing in." She smiled. "We will flood our insides with it. Do not doubt, for you Flavians, your bloodline will be as eternal as the veins of these marbled walls."

Invisibly, Mike turned to the others. "And now, we see how our holy trinity of power came to be."

"All at the behest of my ancestors," Ingrid said.

With another wave of her hand, Ameci glanced at Vespasian and Titus. "Leave us now."

They left.

She suddenly grabbed Josephus's wrist, savoring his pulse as its vibration coursed into her fingertips. "Josephus, I have a task of great importance for you. This will be our... *Testament.*" She pressed the back of his hand to her cheek, pulling herself in very close to him. "This, Josephus, will be the book which you were born to write."

Releasing his hand, she set herself upon the oaken desk. "You were present for Titus's campaign against the Jews, from its inception at Galilee, all the way to Jerusalem's fall."

From her cloak, she removed a scroll. Unrolling it, she placed is squarely before him. "As I've instructed here, step by step, in *exactly* so, you, Josephus, will depict this triumphant campaign of the Great Titus, Son of Man, the warrior."

Pulling a second scroll from beneath her cloak, she unrolled this too, laying it flat on the desk. "In another separate, though entirely parallel campaign, beginning with Galilee, and spanning to Jerusalem, and ending there, you will depict a pacifist prophet. The first of its kind, for all visionaries of your people, of the Lion of Judah, have always been of the fiercest warriors, spillers of their enemy's blood. Listen clearly, Josephus, this second campaign that has never happened nor ever will, make no mistake, it will be mightier than a thousand Romes. It will be sharper than a thousand swords. And all will know its words."

Turning for the door, she paused. Removing an apple, she set it softly so in front of Josephus at the desk, then left. Pen in hand, he began to write as the scrolls before him instructed, and exactly so.

"In the first century," Mike said, "the contextual definition of the word 'gospel', meant successful military campaign. And it's easy to see how that has eventually evolved to mean good news."

Josephus's five silent, invisible witnesses from another time drew in from the shadowy walls, into the light. As he wrote, the ink, a special kind indeed, rose from the page, manifesting shapes, forms, and things unknown. These lines spread out, consuming before them a world written in words, painted in images, and devised for deception. For their unlikely group of five, they melted into it, surrendering their beings to be immersed within this plane now flooding the room of marbled veins....

Fishers of Men

*T*he Sea of Galilee glistened in the blazing sun. Heatwaves peeled off the soil of sand and fragmented rocks, dancing up into the parched air, bending the horizon lined with squat and barren hills. Titus was there beneath a tree along the shoreline. As he spoke, his voice was not close enough to hear, though the earnestness within the twelve men around him was clear. Tens of thousands of Roman soldiers camped along the towns of Galilee.

With Ingrid leading, they joined Titus. Camorra drifted a little further away, always maintaining his own space from the others. His focus led to the Roman armory, agleam, set up outside a large tent not far from Titus and his men.

"Now I tell you, brothers," said Titus, "fear is part of man. It is natural to his heart. Even to ones hardened as your own. Am I without fear? No. I embrace it was a woman, as gold, as the finest wine. It is for you to command."

"Titus's twelve disciples," Howie said.

"That's what he called them?" Tom asked.

"Absolutely," Mike answered. "His closest and most trusted. He kept them within a sword's reach. At all times."

As he spoke the word 'sword', Titus drew the sword at his side. He tapped it upon his breastplate. "Run from it, and I tell you, it will control you. It will destroy you. Control *it*, my brothers..." He pointed his sword at them. "And you'll hold the will of the world in your grasp, by the hilt of your blades." Lowering his sword, he turned toward the sea. "Control your fear, and it will melt away from your hearts easily as your sharpened blades remove the flesh of your enemy."

"I'd say," said Ingrid, "this depiction here of these events is from *The Jewish War.*"

"Say so," said Mike.

"Which is?" asked Tom.

"Josephus's literature," Mike answered, "*The Jewish War,* Josephus's account of Titus's military campaign against the Jews. Per Ameci's—the L' Entita's instruction."

"What we witnessed from before was the actual, historical fall of Galilee," Ingrid added.

"This here, is the Roman propaganda version in other words?" Tom asked.

"Fiction, more like," said Howie. "Literature, as Mike said. But, yes, which was used as political propaganda by the Romans."

Titus thrust his sword high into the air. He let the sunlight shoot off its blade like a torch aflame with victory. "Fear nothing. And nothing can extinguish the light within you."

Movement caught their eye. In the sea, not far offshore, there was a fishing vessel. It held to the place which bordered between the deep and shallow. This was exactly where any fisherman would hold course. Though something was not right.

Slowly, deliberately, Titus aimed the blade of his sword at the vessel. "Is it not hot in this place damned by the gods? This place where only pigs amongst the sand dwell? How then, are fishermen in search for fish at this midday hour, with the sun so upon our backs?" He ventured into the water, his men following. "No, the fish, cleverer than the Jew, stay to the deep at this hour. They do not dwell for food in the shallows, not now."

As he pressed further into the water, holding his sword high, he turned to his men. "See, I speak of fear. And there, those men are drowning in it. Fish do not drive them. It is fear. Oh, this is the typical Jew you see before you there. They mock you, pretending only to be fishermen, to evade their fate. These rebels disguised as fishermen, they think you, brothers, no wiser than fish."

The rebels in the boat, seeing Titus and his men draw closer, quickened their oars.

Titus slashed at the open air with his sword, thrusting in an almost gleeful way. "They take to the sea to run from the will of Rome. Show them, brothers, show them! We are the true fishermen. Fishers of men!" He coursed through the water faster, faster, leading his men, with the desire for blood thickening. "By their skins, we hook their bodies. Fillet them with our blades. They are not men, but fish! My brothers, give them the same regard you would a fish!"

The waterline here in the fishing towns of Galilee was shallow for a great distance, and Titus's men waded swiftly. And swimming the last few feet, Titus easily caught the fishing boat. Capsizing, the sea consumed it. He and his twelve disciples took the nets now afloat in the water and threw them upon the Jewish rebels disguised as fishermen. Caught and tangled within the fishing nets, they thrashed for escape they'd never find.

"Fishers of men," Mike said, shaking his head, feeling a deep sadness indeed. As the Jews trapped in the nets started to sink, a solemnness as well sank within them as witnesses.

"Even, being the embellished, and clearly, metaphorical version of the battle at Galilee," Ingrid said, "this is a terrible thing to have absorbed into one's memory." The cries of the Jewish rebels and cheering jeers of the Romans blended with the collapsing of the waves of the sea, mingling into a grim melody.

"This is dark," Howie said.

"History is men killing men," Mike responded, and perhaps more jaded than he meant.

"*That's* dark," Tom said.

As Titus returned to shore, his face had begun to morph. Though the change wasn't a vast one as Titus was Italian, and the man he transitioned into was also Italian, at least having always been visually depicted so.

"Jesus. Christ," said Tom....

Jesus

*B*eneath the shade of the same humble tree along the banks of the sea was Jesus, transitioned from Titus right before their eyes. The colors in all things richened. All signs of poverty and struggle had erased. Within this pastoral scene, the air was free of any air of war.

All around, the native Jews of Judaea were without weapons, without their many scars of battle, without worry. It was a world without resistance to oppression, because there was none. And the few Roman soldiers present were a welcomed sight, guardians for the natives.

It was picture-perfect, absent of desire for rebellion against the Roman's colonialism and imperialism. There was no need amongst such tranquility. Though, for their team of five, having witnessed the real fall of Galilee, they saw this realm was an illusion within a lie. Even the impossibly lush green of the land was insincere to the harsh reality they knew to be true.

"Feel like I just exited a painting by Goya and now am in a Kinkade," Mike said.

"Who?" Ingrid asked.

"Never mind," he answered.

"In a way," Tom said, "this version's more disturbing."

"Think it falls under the category of egregious defilement of history," said Howie.

"Doesn't stop people from believing this version true though," Mike said. "Being what we have here. The Gospels, this New Testament depiction."

"Mike, in that case," said Howie, "then tell me, ex-Bible scholar, how do people adhere to the belief that, if, according to the Church, the Gospels, as they insist to claim, was written in the first century Middle East, by guys named Mathew, Mark, Luke..."

"John," Ingrid added. "Logically speaking..."

"Just as your ancestor, Ameci, told the Flavians," Mike answered, "faith is the replacement of logic with emotion. Facts, *especially* historical ones, get denied by the Church."

"Since we're on the whole name thing," Howie said, "Jesus, his name in Aramaic, translates to Yeshua. The literal meaning for which into English, is Joshua. Not Jesus."

"Why exactly then do people call him Jesus?" asked Tom. Before he'd given anyone a chance to answer, he realized Camorra was missing. "Where's our Vatican chaperone?"

With the lapping of the waves, the shoreline of sand and smooth pebbles, perpetually coated with water so clear, sparkled in the afternoon sun. This song of the sea blended with a man's words, carried by the breeze. Their eyes came to rest on Jesus beneath the little tree.

"There," Ingrid said, pointing. Camorra, amongst the twelve disciples, sat cross-legged directly before Jesus.

"Life's unpredictable," Tom said.

"And then some," said Howie.

Invisibly so, they joined, taking a place close. The sea breeze caught Jesus's long Italian hair in its grasp, gently caressing it. His skin was tanned, having grown so over time from exposure to the sun. He, like they, stood in stark contrast to the natives' richly beautiful, naturally so, and much deeper complexion. Neither, were the features of this Italian Jesus anything like those of the surrounding people of Galilee.

"As true to form an Italian painting," said Howie. "Blue eyes and all, long and fair-haired, exactly how the Church claims him to be."

"Yes, yes," said Mike, "the fingerprints of authorship remain clear to this day." Feeling Camorra's glare from where he sat intently before the feet of Jesus, Mike realized they could be entirely missing the point for being here. "Let's at least listen to what the man has to say."

"Hear me so, my brethren, for it shall be so," Jesus said. His voice was hypnotic, charismatic. More, it was endearing, sincere, and earnest. They couldn't help but be pulled in.

"Do not be afraid. Follow me. And become fishers of men." He drew up his staff, a simple and unassuming stick by his side. "Come, lay down your nets, and be. Be fishers of men." Raising his staff high, he pointed for the sea. There, spread out over the glassy ripples, were the simple fishing vessels of the Galileans. The morning breeze flowed in around them as he spoke not just to them, but into them... Through them.

Jesus then simply left and walked away along the road past the lonely tree. Turning back to his disciples, he said, "Come, my brethren, let us find men to be fished. Let us go forth and catch them." His disciples followed down this path, baked and beaten beneath their feet.

"Well," Mike said, moving into the light of the warm sun. "That was... unique."

"Cool and strange," Ingrid said.

There was a squishy sensation beneath Mike's foot. He brought his eyes down to see his boot had connected with a large pile of some animal's, likely livestock's, dung. "Shit."

Tom patted him on the back. "Certainly."

His own foot had begun to sink, not into the ground, but through it. A ribbon of white light shined up from this tear in the earth. It spread quickly, dissolving to rich white light, ensnaring them all. As they fell into it, the pastoral Galilean countryside disappeared into vaporous nothing, as though only having been a sweet mirage.

"Now for the demons!" Mike shouted.

"Demons?" Tom shouted back, tumbling past, deeper, deeper into the light.

"Oh yes." Mike grinned, freefalling. "A legion of them..."

Devils of Gadara

*H*itting harshly, the five of them landed at a most barren place with the light's end.

Flat upon his back, which, he was starting to realize, had grown nearly too old for such adventures, Mike sized up their new surroundings. "Gadara."

They pulled themselves to their feet, brushing the dust from their bodies, freshly tumbled and tossed.

"Gadara?" Howie asked.

"Directly en route for Titus's march to Jerusalem," answered Mike.

Titus and his entourage were easy to spot. Once again, Titus had chosen the place offering the only shade. They joined him and his twelve disciples, there within the grove of trees near the top of the plateauing cliff, which led to the well-populated community of Gadara.

The voice of Titus, brimmed with authority and patriarchal leadership, filled the hot and dry air. "Listen, I tell you my brothers, the true devils of this world are those who hold a rebellious spirit. I tell you, their bodies are as vessels. As a pitcher."

He took the water pitcher from one of the men near him and drank from it. "Unlike this pitcher, theirs holds no water." He passed the pitcher to his men. "No, theirs holds a rebellious spirit. These spirits of rebellion, I tell you, brothers, are the true devils contained to this world. They exist only to bring rebellion. Against you, the guardians of Rome. And more dire, these..." He wiped away the water still clinging to his chin. "These rebels, devils, they defy Rome herself!"

Camorra, as the others, quite thirsty by now, reached for the pitcher, but it passed right through his hand. Tom offered him a bottled water from his pack, which he accepted.

"Brothers, we are the only ones who can free these poor men captive to these devils inhabiting them. Soon we will be at the walls of Jerusalem, the very den of these swine, these devils. Den of the Jews! We do not hate them. No, we must pity these men, for they, like that pitcher, lack their own resolve. Oh, but they have turned rebellious to their father, our beloved Rome." He banged his fist to his breastplate. "We will strike down their rebellious spirits."

"Love the subtleness of Josephus's symbolism," Tom said.

Camorra gave him a look, and he immediately became silent.

Titus and his twelve disciples drew their swords. A mob of Jewish rebels had gathered not far, along the road near the entrance to Gadara.

"See, my brothers," Titus said, "before us, these devils appear."

Without so much a second's thought to it, Titus charged the mob of rebels, which could have been nearly fifty men. Titus's disciples, swords aimed, gave chase. By the madness alone in Titus's eyes, the rebels began to disperse. He sliced the air wildly though masterfully out in front of him with his sword, forcing the rebels toward the cliffs where Gadara perched upon, overlooking the sea.

Camorra ran to the place, the others following, both wanting and not wanting to see. With his sword raised over his head, Titus leapt at the mob, releasing a spray of crimson with his blade. Chaotic dread seized the rebels, pushed to the cliff's edge....

"Oh god...," Ingrid said, placing her hand over her mouth.

But there was no sign of a god to intervene to save them. The Jewish rebels, all fifty, fell, entangled with arms and legs, fear and frenzied screams, over the cliff. They struck as one, far below into the rock-crested sea.

Titus stepped to the very edge and gazed upon his work. The five of them ventured closer. Not as close as Titus, but it was enough for the view they each loathed to see, but forced themselves to be witness.

Men laid crushed upon the rocks. They were as tiny islands of death within the sea. Others had been impaled on the narrow rocky shards which lined the edge of the cliffs, jutting straight up like vast harpoons.

The rest, who died a little slower, had a moment to release their cries to no one in particular, as the waves bashed them over and over again against the great wall of rock there. One by one, until there was no more, they sank from sight. The ones which remained became lifeless as the dead weeds of the sea caked to the cliff sides, which grimly held their corpses now strewn to it.

Titus returned his sword to its sheath and turned to his men. "The sea has cleansed us of these devils of rebellion." A single sandal was along the edge of the cliff, the only thing which remained from this mob. He kicked it over the side. "These Jewish pigs, they think they can stand against Rome?" His face grew smug. "They cannot even swim," he said, drawing a brief release of bemusement from his men.

Noticing the blood splattered across his muscular and tan forearm, Titus wiped it away, having already started to dry in the desert sun. "Come, let us all have a vat of wine."

He led the soldiers down the road as though the great horror which they'd just committed had never happened. Before the five of them could follow, the cliff face crumbled beneath their feet, leaving them with nothing but a fall of fatal distance to the rocks and waves below....

Pigs

*T*hey dropped for the sea and rocks, awaiting cruelly, snarling up at them. Their fall grew gentle. They drifted softly to the top of the waves, which lapped coolly along their feet.

Camorra took a step onto the water's surface. Then, Ingrid, as she too walked upon it. Doing so, the five of them journeyed across the sea, and around the bend of the cliffside. The cliffs ended, leveling into the land lined with sand.

There on the wet sand, a man, long hair adrift in the sea's breeze, waited. His back was to them, though he was dressed in simple clothes of the first century. Moving closer, they saw it was Jesus, with his long, fair hair, and piercing eyes, vividly blue... *Impossibly* blue.

"Back to the Gospels' portrayal," Mike said.

Another man came into view. Wrapped in rags, not even clothes, he wore scraps tied around himself in a mangled way. Suddenly, he fell. Smoothly, Jesus's palm stopped him, coming to rest flat against the man's forehead, now leaned strangely forward. The man's eyes were vacant. Drool ran from the otherwise dried-out edges of his mouth.

Tom stepped back. "Something's not right with that guy..." The man bit at the wind, chomping, desiring the air as though blood to quench his deep thirst. Not exerting great force, Jesus's palm somehow held him.

Despite the man being completely outside his own mind,

Jesus began to speak to him with the gentlest grace as one would a child. "These devils within you, using you as a pitcher of water, as their vessel, they bring a dire evil, a spirit desiring rebellion. There are many inside. Know now, I tell you, these demons, they wish to infect not just you, but others. A great many."

Continuing to hold him upright, Jesus told him, "Surely, I say to you, they spread their spirit of rebellion. They dare to tempt even me. They've brought you against your mother and your father. Against your leaders of spiritual affairs and those of government. Rebellion against *any* of these, I tell you, is as rebellion against me."

With his hand, he closed the man's vacant eyes. Scooping up damp sand, he placed it to the man's forehead. "Go, now, Legion! And leave my brother free from your vile deeds. From your rebellious intentions. Wickedness be gone! I cast you to the sea to drown this spirit of rebellion. Go!"

Hearing what distinctly sounded as the snort of a pig, they all turned. And there, running across the beach, were a herd of pigs. The man's arm thrust out at the pigs. His eyes suddenly opened, with color returning to his pale face. Collectively, the herd released a blend of squeal and scream. Their lips spread wide upon their grimaced and terrified and snouted faces. Going for the sea, they smashed their bodies into the crash of the waves, continuing deeper, deeper, drowning themselves. The man, free of his legion of demons, ran to Jesus. The glaring sunlight radiated down its beams like a crown of thorns. Without warning, from the universe or beyond, a total eclipse blackened all....

Joseph Bar Mathias

*T*he moon, full and swelled to monstrous scale, passed directly between the sun and the earth. And there she sat, denying the daylight now darkened. Not black, but silverly, this sphere from above filled the sea's flat surface. For, the sea was as glass, without waves nor wind.

Jesus and the man possessed were no more, gone from their place upon the sand. Lightning split the darkness, searing the cloudless sky. They saw something even rarer to be seen. The largest of the white and purple and burning yellow bolts, branching outwards on either side, held the shape of a cross.

These electrified fractures of light didn't fade away. Instead, the lighting kept its stance gripping the night, ablaze. Two more bolts shot down the sky before them, and along both sides of this cross of lighting. They too remained afire, frozen, as the smaller crosses they were.

The sand and the sea were gone. Their group of five now found themselves on a broad road of stone. With a world all around veiled in darkness, nothing could be seen or known. Then, as easily as a cloud adrift, the moon passed away, ending this total eclipse.

In the light of what seemed to be early morning, there were palms, tall leafless trees, and long grass. The three crosses of lighting dissolved, leaving in their place actual crosses. Perched upon the knoll along the road, beams of wood fashioned these crosses. On each hung a person. They could not tell if life still clung to any the three souls.

Dust billowed before them as Titus and his disciples came down the road on horseback, stopping at the crosses. Josephus, with them, climbed down from his horse. They hurried to the place, awaiting to see what would happen. The slender shadows of the crosses fell across their faces and bodies in the rising of the sun. Straps of thick leather bound the men, securing them to the beams at their wrists and ankles.

"No spikes?" asked Tom.

"No spikes," said Mike. "Even as crass as the Romans could be, they *never* used spikes for crucifixion. One, metal, you see, was strictly used for critical necessities. Weapons, building materials, and the like. Two, real-life logistics. Imagine if you were a soldier on crucifixion detail. Given the option, which is easier, removing a body nailed with giant spikes? Or leather straps?"

"Fair enough," Tom said, never really having thought about it logically before.

Camorra turned to them while they watched Josephus, clearly distraught, circling around the crucified men. "The body would tear free almost immediately by its own weight, if nailed by spikes through the wrists and ankles."

Camorra's words gave them all a shiver, as he seemed to speak from experience. But Ingrid, she cared not for these overlooked accuracies of history. The horror of seeing it in person was what tore, deeply so. She looked away from these men, hanging, with their despair seized so on their ashen faces.

"Great Titus," Josephus said, "I beg of you, have I not done all, and more than you have required of me? Have I not served you in the interests of Rome over my own people? Bear mercy now, I ask humbly. These men, they are my friends. Lifelong, they are as brothers, of the same blood as my own. You and you alone, great Titus, son of the emperor of Rome, father of all soldiers of the Empire, can spare their lives."

Titus, who looked as though on the brink of falling asleep there upon his horse, after hearing this earful of Josephus's groveling, simply raised his pinky. Two of his disciples dismounted from their horses, and swiftly cut down the men from the crosses. Josephus went to his three friends, now on the dusty ground. Two were gone, though the other remained with some life.

"Alas, Alas! My friends have died. But one still breathes. My gratitude unto you, great Titus! You, Titus, father of the legions of Rome. Savior of the people, even to those who defy your will! Your will knows no limits, Titus, Son of Man!"

Titus yawned, snapped his reins, and led his horse down the road toward Jerusalem.

An earthquake began. The road tore down its center. The sky became grim, cast amongst clouds which shadowed out the sun. The convulsing of the earth continued, bringing them to their knees before the crosses.

The knoll rose up, tearing from the ground, pushing high into a hilltop of rock-laden earth. All that was green withered, dried up, becoming dead. Something wet and warm fell upon Howie. He looked up at the center cross directly above him. Jesus, or at least his earthly body, hung there. It held no life....

Joseph of Arimathea

*A*t the places pierced by the crude crown of thorns adorning Jesus's head, droplets of dark, very dark blood escaped, gently sprinkling down as though baptizing each of them. Jesus was not alone, for a man hung from the crosses on either side of him.

A gruff voice came from behind. "You."

Their group of five turned. Thick muscle-bound legs of a glistening black horse, with armor, stood at eye level. Towering above them on the horse was a Roman officer.

"A centurion," Mike said.

The horse stepped aside, revealing the man there blocked from view, who had more than an uncanny resemblance to Josephus. His features were nearly the same. He was more distinguished, younger, a touch better-looking in this idealized version of himself.

"Your pleadings bore me," said the centurion. "Who are you to make such a request?"

"Joseph of Arimathea," said the man. He offered up to him a brass token slightly larger than that of a coin. "From Governor Pilate, so you'd know my request has been rendered by him."

The centurion took the token, eyeing it suspiciously. He gave a dismissive but agreeable wave of his hand toward Jesus, hung there upon the cross. "Go, and remove that slain lamb, the King of the Jews, and do what you will."

In humble clothing, women and men stepped from the shadows and helped remove Jesus's body. Mike, about to open his mouth to explain his realization, stopped. Seeing Howie had the same realization, he'd let the moment instead be his.

"Our resident turncoat," Howie said, "Mr. Josephus, was a clever fellow. I'll give him that. Being that we now know Josephus to be the same author for the paralleling accounts of

Titus Flavius's campaign against the Jews, as well the ministry of Jesus we've seen thus far. Incredible coincidence too, being the same author for these *only* two accounts of the first century allowed to survive Rome's wrath against Jewish history."

"Which are?" Tom asked.

"Josephus is the author of the *New Testament* and *The War of the Jews*," Howie answered.

"Oh, right," said Tom.

"Josephus's own fictionalized version of himself *is* Joseph of Arimathea," said Howie.

Camorra drew closer to their group. "Now, others—*anyone* can know this as we do."

"Precisely," Mike said, seeing Camorra didn't miss a thing.

"How's that?" Ingrid asked.

"As we're well aware, Joseph Bar Mathias is the given Hebrew name for Flavius Josephus," Mike answered.

"Yeah...," Ingrid said.

"Remember," said Mike, "time and *place*, being the only way to preserve the original and intended context. Josephus was born in Jerusalem. And Jerusalem, being the cultural epicenter for the Jews, Joseph Bar Mathias was the proper and formal spelling of his name." He paused, nodding to Howie.

Howie smiled at his father, and picked up where he'd left off. "See, if Josephus had been born in a less culturally sophisticated place, such as Nazareth of the day, then his name would have been spelled 'Joseph of Arimathea'."

"It's the equivalent of Robert to Bob, by today's standards," Mike offered. "*Deliberate* wordplay on Josephus's part. For those with eyes to see, to see..."

"Josephus's unspoken, though, crystal clear signing of the Gospels," said Camorra.

In front of them, Josephus's own idealized version of himself, Joseph of Arimathea, led the others away with Jesus's body, vanishing back into the shadows from which they'd come. A deep rumble began. Something on either side of the crosses started to break through the rocky soil, reaching up into the pale air. As these things broke free, rising from the ground, they saw them to be two more crosses.

"Have a bad feeling about this," said Tom.

"*Really* bad," Ingrid said.

Before them stood five crosses now. Their bodies lifted, ascending higher, higher until the five of them were each level with a cross of their own. By forces unseen, their bodies were forced to turn, aligning their backs to the wooden beams awaiting them.

"No," Tom said, "no, no, no..."

Sucked backwards, they drew flush to the crosses. And there they were, bound by nothing, held by all. Suffocating... A cross was truly an unbearable thing. At least those men, whom they'd witnessed hung here, had warning before finding themselves in such a position without hope. The five of them had no warning. Powerless and forsaken, they hung....

The Ninth Gate of Jerusalem

*R*apidly, the ground grew further away. Or maybe it had been that the crosses binding them became taller. Whatever the cause for their climb upwards held to those angelic devices of death, they found themselves twenty, thirty, then forty feet high.

The sunlight, nearly gone, with only the faintest echo of its being, lingered in an illumination most broken. This too dimmed, becoming long golden shadows as the horizon swallowed the sun, melting so into dusty hills. Birds unknown flowed forth their songs with this ending of the day.

Camorra somehow had broken loose one of his wrists, and removing a knife, sliced his remaining bonds before dropping down off his cross to the stone walkway beneath. He threw the knife, sinking its tip skillfully close to Howie's bound wrist where he hung from his own cross. His fingers took hold, working the knife free by its handle.

Ingrid closed her eyes. Within her mind, she envisioned her shackles to be no more. And it was so. The leather dissolved, and for all of them. Dropping hard to the stone beneath the crosses, they realized they now stood upon the legendary four-story-tall wall of Jerusalem.

Light from fires and torches and lanterns formed a patchwork glow which sprawled out before them. Amidst the landscape, surprisingly green as it was, the Romans had made camp. Legion upon legion upon legion, tens of thousands of soldiers and auxiliary personnel came into focus.

In the low and varied breeze of deepening dusk, the vexillum, the banner of the Roman army, waved, as though beckoning them. Alongside it, the Flavian banner stood outside what could only by Titus's immense tent. Ingrid turned to Howie, smiled, then climbed up over the ledge of the wall. She stood on its cusp, with nothing except open air between her and the rocky ground forty feet below.

"She knows what's she doing, right?" asked Tom.

"Do any of us," said Howie.

The four of them watched her, their hearts constricting with awe and apprehension. Teetering, she closed her eyes. Her arms raised out at her sides, wing-like. For them, she seemed there in the setting twilight of the night as a beautiful and suicidal angel. They each needed to know the answer... *Was she to plummet or take flight?* She let her body fall forward off the legendary wall of Jerusalem....

It was neither, and perhaps, both. For she was not free of gravity's will, though the invisible force that it was, guided her down, doing so with a graceful mercy. As if gliding through the layers of cushioned air designated for songbirds, she floated softly to the earth. Her feet found the grass and sandy soil. She stood within a great grove of fruit trees there which occupied the shadowed expanse between Jerusalem's wall and Titus's army.

Camorra, not bothering to close his eyes nor raise his arms to his sides, simply leaped off the edge. The others dredged up a combination of will and faith to do the same. Each, in their own way, made the leap. They drifted down to the open place amongst the fruit trees.

"Strangely pleasant," Howie said, surveying the easy enough looking route to Titus's tent.

Ingrid led across the grove of fruit trees to the sea of flicking flames, a mosaic of campfires, lanterns, and torches. Invisibly, they slipped past the guards and entered Titus's tent. Only Titus and Josephus were present, seated upon stools around a table of average size.

They moved in closer, silently invading the space of these two men, deep in discussion for their plans. Directly overhead, a large and square section of the tent's roof pulled back, providing a starry view above. The constellation Virgo was crisply clear, for reasons untold, at least for *now.*

By starlight and torchlight, Titus filled his goblet upon the simple and wooden table. "We've arrived early to these walls of Jerusalem, as Passover hasn't begun. Many Jews still have yet to enter the city for its celebration. So, we will wait before building our blockade around the city. Tell me, Josephus, what shall we do, in waiting?"

Josephus's lips perched, hesitant, as though divided within himself to speak, or not. "There is a ninth gate..."

"A ninth gate? My scouts have surveyed and surveyed well. It's as you said. Thirty-four watchtowers. And eight gates. Tell me, Josephus, where is this ninth gate?" His fingers danced along the edges of his goblet, eager, not as a man for war, but one anticipating great pleasure. "Come now, tell of this ninth gate."

"Hidden. Only accessible to heads of state. And guardians of the Temple." Josephus revealed a key. "For those with a key. As the neck of a bottle, narrow and small, this passage is designed for one and only one man to pass at a time."

"What of sentries?" Titus asked, draining his goblet.

Josephus nodded. "A handful on the other side. We will need a distraction to slip through."

"Distraction..." After a moment, a smile released from Titus's deeply tanned face. "Tell me, Josephus, what do you know of building a tower...?"

Cut it Down

*T*rance-like, Ingrid reached out for Howie's hand. Camorra took hold instead, and she led from the tent. They followed. Hit by the full light of day, she returned them to the grove of fruit trees. Jesus was there, beneath a tree, with his disciples.

"Back to the world of the Gospels," said Mike.

"Which one of you who is going to build a tower for war, doesn't first sit down and think about the cost? For is not the cost of war great for a city, just as it is for a single household?" Jesus asked.

He peeled a piece of bark from the tree and held it out to his disciples. "This tree. It is healthy, without sickness. Strong to the wind and rain. But if a piece of its foundation is broken away as I've done with this bark, it will start to whither, and it will fall."

Camorra got as close as he could to Jesus. Tom nudged Howie, quietly smiling at this.

"Brethren, all war is from the hearts of man. Their hearts, hardened by the devil's spirit of rebellion. I tell you, rebellion is a lust for war, and like a wall with no foundation, it will always fall. The foundation of a man must be free of rebellion. His foundation is his father and his mother. And their foundation is those who govern over them. There cannot be walls within a family. A house divided is as a city divided. It will fall, I tell you."

He stood, turning to Jerusalem. "This great wall to our backs, is as vulnerable, is it not? This wall, it is as a mountain. As a tower. It is a titan among men. But it will fall. Be as this tree providing us shade. It stands firm, yet it is not so tall. Be as the grass at men's feet. Quiet and yielding to all things. Let titans be titans. And you, my brethren, remain small. Be not as lions, for their mouths become filled with blood. No, I tell you, be as lambs. As lambs, you forever will know the comfort of a shepherd leading your wills. Then, your heart will hold no walls to bring division within you. You will be free from war. Free from rebellion. I command it so unto you, brethren."

"Despite everything," Ingrid said invisibly, alongside Jesus beneath the fruit tree, "this deception by the Roman political establishment, and truly disheartening betrayal of the Jews by Josephus, Josephus, the man, he really could write."

"Could've given Shakespeare a run for his money," Howie said, a bit bitterly.

Mike frowned at the idea, the crude comparison... "Let's not get carried away."

Jesus crumpled the bark in his hand, letting it fall to the sandy soil and thin grass. "Just as a man, soured within himself by a rebellious spirit, his actions will not reap good fruit. This tree, here now, if it does not bear good fruit, then cut it down. In this way, my brethren, do the same with any evil desires. Any temptation to rebel against your leaders... Cut it down! I tell you, your leaders *are* your father and your mother. They are as a husband to a wife. A wife always must honor the will of her husband, for he, as they, are your leaders. I tell you, brethren, be small, bending to the wind, be quiet to all things. Not as a lion. As a lamb."

Jesus began walking toward Jerusalem's wall. His disciples, and his five invisible, though entirely immersed guests, followed.

Reaching the wall, Jesus set his hand upon it. "Brethren, if the devil has already placed a spirit of rebellion within your heart, then I tell you, be as a king. Send out a delegation to those you've wronged with your devil-filled hearts. I tell you, beg for terms of peace. Beg as a child would to his father and to his mother. Lastly, I tell you, be as a servant, forever unto them."

A shadow fell on them. Jesus and his disciples sank away, vanishing into the shadow. They looked up, seeing a great tower, even taller than the wall. The top of the tower brimmed with Roman soldiers, and they knew they'd returned to the realm of Titus and his campaign against the Jews.

As the walkway atop the wall flooded with the fierce soldiers of Jerusalem, the Romans and the Jews stood nearly face to face. The Jews proudly wore the armor of their warrior ancestors, for they were true lions of war. The Romans were a relentless machine tailored for battle, knowing no end. This culmination of combat was within a sword's reach....

Things Fall

*W*ith dusk nearly on the land, torchlight cast along the wall. They saw now the tower was built from the wood of the fruit trees, *all* the fruit trees. Thousands of sad splintered stumps remained as the only evidence the great grove, lush and beautiful, ever existed. Beneath the tower's shadow, Titus joined Josephus. They drew closer to hear.

"What news does our delegate return with?" asked Titus. "What did the Jewish rebels have to say of the Great Titus's terms for peace?" He grinned darkly. "Do they abide to declare themselves the pigs they are?"

Josephus silently shook his head and moved away from Titus, far away. Before Titus could call after him, an argument erupted between the Jewish soldiers and the Jewish sentries, both stationed on the wall closest to the tower.

Titus turned to his legions before him in wait. "Our enemy is divided! They will not stand!" He slammed his right fist to his breastplate. "They have already fallen and we... We have already claimed our victory!"

Relishing his moment, he realized his men's eyes weren't on *him*. His own voice no longer filling his ears, he heard it now... The burst of flames to his back... The unmistakable chorus of a mighty fire. He spun around. All eyes were on his tower, aflame. Camorra looked to Mike. Then the others did, silently asking for this answer of history.

Mike shrugged. "No one knows how."

Josephus crept back into the light, meekly approaching Titus. "Shall we wait to enter the ninth gate?"

Titus exhaled deeply. "Obviously. Now go."

"Go where, Great Titus?"

"Out of my sight."

As seamlessly as he'd appeared, Josephus slipped into the darkness, away from the fire before them all. With a thunderous snap, the tower split in two. They, along with Titus, ran as the tower, swirling in fire, came hurling down. Titus dove, landing in a pile of horse dung.

"Nice to see hubris finally show itself," said Howie.

Titus leaped to his feet, drawing his sword, and proclaimed, "My men, Passover is on this eve! We've allowed many Jews entry into the city for their celebration. Now let us build our blockade to ensnare all within. Let their great wall be their noose."

Brushing himself off, he closed in on his legions in perfect formation, row after row of trained killers, all under his will. Strutting back and forth before them, he waved his sword. "Let us swell pangs of desperation in the belly of Jerusalem. The den of swine. And once they've drunk their wine..." He thrust his sword straight into the air. "The world will remember the Passover of Titus to be greater than that of the god of the Hebrews. For the Great Titus alone is divine!"

Ingrid glanced at Howie. "You were saying something about hubris."

"Yeah, well, some men take longer to fall, is all," Howie responded.

Night fell away, and dawn reclaimed the sky. Upon this sudden shift from the darkness to light, Camorra led for Jerusalem's great wall. Reaching the wall, they came to rest.

Mike studied the flawless masonry. Being right up close to it, it was a true marvel. Nearly forty feet high and eight feet thick, it wasn't just its scale that was awe-inspiring. It was its historical importance... Its *role*.

He rested his palm to the wall's almost hot surface. The sun's perpetual kiss upon the precision-cut stones, nearly perfect in every way, brought such heat. This was only a detail one would know if they had themselves been there—here, alive in the first century. Otherwise, it was long lost to the tides of time. Realizing he was entirely zoned out, staring at the wall, he placed his focus on what the others already had. Jesus, enveloped by his disciples, sat cross-legged in the shadow of the wall.

"Brethren, accept your plight. Accept your struggle. Be as the mule who stays silent within the storm of great burdens placed onto his back each day. Accept these things into your hearts. To be with me is to be as the salt of the earth. Be as the meek, for that is the mortar which binds these stones here as one. Listen, for I tell you the truth, to be free, you cannot be as a single lamb unto itself. Surrender your hearts to the shepherds of the world, those who lead over you. Be of his flock, under his care. Do as he, your leaders, command."

Jesus stood, and leading his disciples and them, moved along the wall. He set his hand on the very place Mike had done not so long ago.

"To be as a lamb unto a flock will serve you greater than this wall. I tell you, brethren, even a city of God can fall. Fall to temptation. To rebellion. I tell you, in your very lifetimes these events will occur. Now know my words, for I reveal their meaning. It will pass that Jerusalem will be encircled with a wall from a great enemy of her people. None shall pass through. And all shall know the pangs of hunger."

He pulled away from the wall, facing them directly now, as though looking specifically at their group of five. "Jerusalem's mighty wall will fall. The Temple will be razed. It too will fall. This is true. Do not doubt my words. Not one stone, I tell you, will be left to remain upon another. *Only then*, brethren, will the Son of Man come to be amongst you. Now come, do not dwell on the future. Let us enter the city. Our people await for celebration."

By impulse, they began to follow through the front gate. Ingrid set her hand on Howie's shoulder, turning him around. "No, this way..."

Impact

*B*ack in the realm of war, they passed the charred remains of Titus's tower. At each of Jerusalem's gates, stood hundreds of Roman soldiers. Titus had sealed off the city from entry or exit. The breeze shifted, bringing them immediately to grip their noses and mouths.

What tore now at their senses, clawing raw their very humanity, was a great stench, impacting all. This repugnance that leached into everything, and refused to leave once there, was a horror unto itself. The Jews upon the walkway along their wall were perpetually dropping something over the side. What this was, they couldn't quite determine, though now realized there were vast piles all along the outer perimeter of the wall.

There was Titus, perched proudly on a rock which protruded up from the dusty earth as though a pedestal meant just for him. With a thrust of his sword toward Jerusalem, his archers, with arrows ignited, launched an inferno across the dawn-kissed sky. Striking these piles, fires bloomed forth, encircling the city. Pillars of unnaturally dark smoke clung to the air. This smoke pulled itself in thick, filthy plumes high into the sky.

"Bodies," Howie said. "They're all bodies."

Mike knew the grim history of Rome's annihilation of the Jews... Of so many dead. He'd known to dread this moment. Though, he'd hoped, very much so, to spare them... *But what good was history if its truths were sanitized for modernity's convenience?*

"Sometimes, the facts *are* gratuitous," he said with a heart most heavy. "Sometimes the wrongdoers get away with the worst of things imaginable... Passover placed a tremendous strain upon Jerusalem's food and water supply. Titus, tyrant that he was, but brilliant tactician, capitalized on this. Both denying anyone within the city from leaving while preventing any supplies to enter, was, well, beyond warfare. It was extermination."

He turned away, feeling his eyes, then insides, well up. "Perhaps, the real travesty is that this crime against the Jews, against humanity, has all but been pushed out of the history books. And Titus's, or I should say the conspirators' denouement, their ultimate insult to injury is blaming the Jews for Jesus's death, a figure who never even existed. Thus, branding them with a seal of mistrust and hate down through the generations to come... Forever after haunted by the flames of humanity's own ignorance."

Ingrid's eyes agaze, reflected this horrid blaze before them. "How many? How many here died?"

Camorra, resting a hand on Mike's arm, let him know he'd take over. And Mike readily accepted.

"Not counting the combatants...," Camorra said, "well over a million Jews, just from thirst and hunger."

Ingrid's eyes shifted to him, those coldly blue eyes, searing in, demanding the full account of the damage brought on by her ancestors.

"And loss of life from the actual conflict," Camorra started to say.

"No more," said Mike, cutting him off. "Let us speak of this no more. Please. At least, not now." He couldn't, simply couldn't stomach this place wrought with such rot. It was soul-deadening. He needed his remaining strength to get through to the end of things... Past this darkness of their present which had burned itself into history long ago.

Consumed by the disgust of this calculated and deliberate act, Ingrid abandoned them. Hating who she was, the very blood within her veins, she raced away, away into the land with dust and rock and unbearable pain. Alone, she leaned against a stone. Legs and mind weary, she let her body slide down, settling to the dusty earth.

The only solace she could find was that she hadn't chosen her DNA, that crimson chain linking her to her ancestors... To those architects of horror. Of... *This.* She brought her eyes up from the ground to face the reality casting its thick smoke most darkly. She was not them, not those which she'd come from. She could—would change this course. That would be *her* legacy. Her creation—a vast, thunderous jolt impacted the land. In the distance, a billowing cloud of dust plumed out from a large swath of Jerusalem's wall, having just fallen. An unwelcomed image flashed within her mind of the fatal tunnel collapse in Malta. She thrust it away.

Thousands of Roman soldiers converged, swarming through the wall's great cavity. Swords and spears and all manner of weapons to bring harm and death in their fists raised high, they flooded the city. And at the place with the hidden ninth gate, Josephus silently unlocked the passage there. Unnoticed, he slipped through. Inside, he quickly released the main gate, pushing open its great doors to the thousands more Romans soldiers in wait.

Titus, having taken a rare act to let his men spearhead this charge of glory, now mounted his horse and galloped. With sword high, he raced for the open gate. The beat of his heart drew louder, blending with the pounding of his horse's hooves as this most holy city wholly welcomed him with screams and flames....

Render

*T*itus, flanked by his disciples of twelve, tore past on their horses, past Howie and his group of now four. For, they'd lost sight of Ingrid to the wilderness at their backs. Upon entering through Jerusalem's main gate, Titus transitioned into Jesus. His horse became a donkey. And Titus's twelve disciples were Jesus's own.

Doing the only thing they knew, they followed Jesus into Jerusalem. The people of the city lined the streets, in celebration of Passover. They deeply welcomed this savior unto them, who spoke of his famous message of peace, of freedom through servitude. These people of simple means and hands worn by the toil of the day, placed palm branches onto the street.

Close behind Jesus and his disciples, their group of four headed down the center of the street of stone with the uneven squish of the palm branches beneath their feet. They soon came to a cluster of fig trees, offering shade. Each lowered himself to the grass underneath.

Jesus sat cross-legged, facing them. "Render unto Caesar what is Caesar's. Bend to the will of your leaders as these fig trees do to the wind." He reached up to the tree he sat beneath and snapped a small twig from its slender trunk. "To not bend to the will of that which is greater than you, is to break oneself." He took the twig between his fingers and broke it. "Honor your leaders, I say unto you. Are the Romans not as your father? As your mother? Yes, I tell each of you these things again, as it is so."

Pulling figs from the tree, he passed them around until all of his disciples had tasted the ripe flesh. "The Romans, brethren, I tell you, they are your protectors. Are they not? Even now, guarding the city of Jerusalem. The city of God's own. And are you not God's chosen? Ask yourselves, why has God allowed the Romans to be here now, if not to guard you from the wills of men with all manner of evil within their hearts?"

He stood, and they did the same, following along the road, leading deeper into the city, this city of both legend and truth. "I tell you, then, brethren, pay your dues to them, to your guardians. For they stand guard over Jerusalem by God's will alone. To know freedom is to surrender your hearts to your Roman protectors, to the will of Caesar. It is God's will. It is my will. It is your father's. It is what is and what is meant to be. Your hearts are as coins. To be paid for Caesar's many services to you. Only then, I tell you, will you truly know freedom."

The Temple on its mount broke into view in the distance, there at the end of the road. Glorious, in its prime, it was angelic, or nearly so. Quickening their pace toward it, they hung on every word Jesus released unto them.

"If you are not as children in need of a shepherd, then why do you follow me now? As lambs in need of a protector, free from your own wills, that is the natural way of man. Is it not? Man is lost by his own mind, by his own will alone. To be free is to serve. Now lay down your fears. Lay down your hearts unto your protectors, for they are here for your own protection. As a child unto his father. To hold rebellion against your master, is to hold evil within your hearts. It is to defy God. It is to defy me. Now, I tell you, the time of the Son of Man is nearly upon you. It will be he who delivers Jerusalem from all who hold a spirit of rebellion within their hearts. His will is my will. He will seize all nations unto him. Brethren, know my words, and know what is locked away, hidden within them. And you will know the *truth*..."

Jesus ended his ministry, stepping aside, letting everyone's focus immerse into the glory of the Temple behind him. Releasing a smile, Jesus's Italian features seamlessly transitioned back into Titus's own. The Temple faded to rubble, absolutely so, in every sense and way.

Titus stood, with sword stretched to the dark sky, thick with flame and smoke, and of death. The ranks of the Roman army were before him. He wiped away the blood, half dried, half moist, on the blade of his sword. Blood caked to him, clung to his jawline and neck.

As he began to speak, this dried blood peeled away in flakes. "I razed the Temple. I destroyed this so-called god of the Jews. Alas, where is he now? Perhaps..." He turned to the broken wall of the city offering a view of the land beyond. "He's found a nice cave to dwell within instead?" Pointing his sword, he grinned. "Somewhere out there, amongst mice and fowl?"

His men roared with laughter. Their faces were streaked in dirt. The thin paths of sweat running down their skin left the only areas free of filth. Splattered in the blood of their enemies and of themselves, they watched Titus, their leader, their father in all things, with admiration.

"Not one stone," Titus proclaimed, wielding his sword. He scooped up a shattered piece of the Temple slightly larger than his own fist. "Not one stone has been left upon another. I, Great Titus, Son of Man, have rendered it unto you! I have delivered Jerusalem."

He hurled the broken stone toward the heap of what was, but no more, the Temple of the Jews. Following the stone, their group of four now saw, at the center of the rubble, within a cushion of space all her own, Ameci. Tranquil amidst this destruction, in lotus pose, her eyes were closed.

A tree came to be, sprouting forth beside her. It was the strangest thing. With leaves on fire, or perhaps, *of* fire, its flames did not devour. A fire free from its will to bestow destruction was a thing to see, to know, unequalled in beauty.

Plucking, then cupping a leaf aflame within her palm, she balled it up gently. Pulsing soothingly, it was now an orb of crimson perched upon her perfect skin. With a kiss, her lips solidified the flame, rendering it to sweet flesh, ruby agleam... Of this apple which called to all of them most desiringly...

Standing, she faced the tree. A triangle of fire grew out from the center of its trunk, large as a doorway. While holding the apple in her left hand, she placed her right palm flush to the fire. It frosted over. Then, shedding its icy veneer, became as a mirror, reflecting her, and them smoothly back within its triangle-shaped space. A thin ribbon of flame around this mirror ignited, both framing and illuminating. With eyes steadfast, she sent a glance, an offer to follow, then let her body swallow into the doorway of mirror and glass....

Darkness at Bay

*T*he four of them accepted, entering. Light and color faded, hardening to shadow. Blackness with golden specks drifted around them as everything else seemed to rotate upside down, though their feet held them in place. A stillness came to be, and Howie led, continuing on into the darkness.

Outlines, then shapes took form. With the return of the light, they found themselves back in the chamber beneath the Vatican. The soft glow of the mossy film along the walls bathed all. At the chamber's center, the sphere upon the crystal table was dark, silent, and unmoving.

"We're back," Tom said.

"Perhaps we never left," said Mike.

"Perhaps," Ameci said, making herself known.

"How are you with us?" asked Mike.

"I am," she answered.

"But how—how, with our space and time being so different than your own?" he asked.

With a twinkle in her eye, she clasped her palms around his. "Is time and space really that *different* from each other, Michael?" She released his hands, leaving him to accept not all answers were answers in themselves.

"What of Ingrid?" asked Howie.

"She is free of physical harm," Ameci answered.

Howie stepped toward her. "Where is she?"

Ameci smiled softly. "Close. Close indeed." She closed her palm, then opened it again. The apple she'd fashioned from the leaf aflame rested within. "For you humans, is it not so that on one day, you reap sour fruit. And on another, good. Is that not what makes you humans... Interesting?"

Moving to the table, she gazed upon the sphere there as though a crystal ball containing the answers, any and all, swirling within. "Hmmm. A quest for truth. Facts. And freedom." Her eyes returned to their group of four. "Is there not sacrifice for such gifts? Even paradise can be traded away, *if* these are the treasures to be treasured."

Raising the apple, she blew on the red flesh, flawless and lush. It became glassy, then filled with white light, not bright, but beautiful... Something as the breath of an angel. She held out the apple.

Howie's hand started to go for it, but she stepped past him. Then Mike, then Tom, and she ignored them as well. She placed the apple into the hand which didn't reach for it... Camorra now held the apple.

"May it serve you well," Ameci said to him. "And you, it."

"Why does the bad guy get the magic apple?" Tom asked.

"Oh, Thomas, this is not to eat," she answered.

"Is that a trick?" asked Tom.

She cocked her head at him.

"I mean, does that mean we're *supposed* to eat it?" he pressed.

"It means don't eat the apple," she answered.

Mike went to her. "Why? Why bring such suffering to the world through manipulating history? Instead of making things better? Good?"

"My, direct aren't you... Sometimes, Michael, the darkest path is the only one with light at its end. Good, bad, these are but limits in perspective. You're looking at things as a human. As linear. Know better. For you know history. Is it chance of such a swift death for Vespasian after becoming emperor? Or, Titus's own death within two years of becoming emperor himself? Or the soon following annihilation of Rome by the Great Fire of the year eighty as well the complete destruction from Vesuvius? No, Michael, that it is not chance. That is craftsmanship. That, is *design.*"

"You know of these events," he said, "though they have yet to take place within your place and time... *How?*"

"Knowing something is not contingent upon having witnessed it firsthand. Your concept of time, it is no different. Things having happened or not having done so is but perception. Perception is context. And context, you know, Michael, you all do, is relative."

She clasped his hand once more. "There are things I cannot speak on. But I can this, without manipulating, as you say..." Her eyes trailed off into the shadows, dwelling on things none of them would or should ever know. "If all of these things hadn't taken place in the way they had, in the order they had, and at the time they hand, then your present world would be in a much... darker state of being than you know it to be. For you all."

Releasing his hand, her face grew solemn. "You all must know, this darkness that's been held at bay, has returned. You will each face it head-on. Not in this time nor place, but in your *own.*"

"When?" asked Howie.

She was extremely delicate in her words, as she dared not reveal too much. "It won't be in *this* quest. It will be in your next one. Now I must leave."

"Wait," Howie said, "where do we go from here?"

The twinkle returned to her eyes. "Oh, dear Howard, heart of a man, spirit of a boy, all the answers are before you... You really should listen to your father more. Now, if you truly wish to understand, here is a quote from a friend... 'Think in terms of energy, frequency and vibration.'"

"A *friend?*" Howie asked, recognizing the words.

"Complete this quest, dear Howard. For, it's no longer your collective of five's alone. The fate of the world, and more, deeply more, is at a crossroads. A place dire. Entirely terminal."

She pivoted, and quickly headed for the shadows awaiting at the end of the chamber, to a place with no apparent door. She stopped at the wall, keeping her face obscured from their view. Howie went to her, reaching for her, to turn her around. As he did, he saw the transition...

Her eyes closed. Then, her eyelids drew back, opening. His eyes met hers, unyielding, unapologetic, blue. The eyes remained the same. But her face was Ingrid's own. Where Ameci had gone, he knew not, for Ingrid now stood in her place. She pulled away from the wall. And more than a bit disorientated, he helped steady her.

"Ingrid!" Mike shouted, thoroughly relieved. "But... where'd Ameci go?"

Realizing his back must have blocked their view of what exactly had just occurred, Howie kept it to himself. And perhaps, from Ingrid herself, who seemed as unaware of what had happened as they.

"How are you?" he asked, letting such a cliché question slip from his lips before thinking.

"I need, time," she said.

He held her. "To debate the moral value of the L' Entita's... value to humanity?"

She looked up at him, studying his eyes, their warmth. "Yeah. Something like that."

"Well," he said, leading her to the table at the chamber's center, "any consolation, I think they knew what they were doing."

"You think?" she asked.

Stopping at the table next to Tom and Mike, Howie rested his fingertips on its crystal surface. "Looking at the events shown us here, as well those shown by history, to unite a full context... What I think, I don't think they left anything to chance." He slid his hand onto hers. "*Anything.*"

Leaving her right hand beneath his, she set her left onto

the sphere awaiting on the table. It glowed to life, immediately beginning to spin. A beam streamed straight up and out the hole at the top of the sphere. With a deep resonance, it radiated a vivid three-dimensional projection, flooding before her. Without waiting for the others, she stepped into this energy field. And she was no more, raptured away....

The Dead Shall Rise

A rich emerald luminescence pulsated out from the sphere, washing over them and the chamber in electric-green. They were absorbed into the light, and Ingrid returned to their sight. The soft glow of the moss along the walls ceased to be. The walls themselves grew smokey, fading, then transparent.

The emerald light spread far past the chamber, passing through the rock beyond and all around now nearly see-through as well. The floor and the ceiling became the same. They could see the city of the dead, that great sprawling necropolis in the near distance which surrounded.

Mausoleums and tombs and graves of stone and marble, it did not matter, they all could be gazed on and through, leaving a thin and ghostly outline. Encased for as far as their eyes could see, though wished not to, were remains most skeletal. Each was unique in their own yellowed and decayed way, grimacing and grinning.

From above, the ground grew translucent, then it too became entirely transparent. Daylight flooded in as a wave, blinding them, though for only a moment. With pupils acclimating, they saw the Vatican Necropolis overhead. It was a truly and strangely unique perspective on the remains contained there.

Layered beyond this, the Vatican Grottoes and the bones of the dead sealed and stacked within grimly took form. A tunnel of light, a bright eye staring down on them, opened, leading to a view up into Saint Peter's Basilica. They could see this wasn't the basilica from their time, but from another.

"The first Saint Peter's Basilica," said Mike.

The closest of the countless skeletons distinctly moved. Mere yards away, it unfolded its crumpled and mangled self as it began to crawl upwards toward the tunnel of light at the center of all things. Both ghastly and fascinatingly, as it crawled, its hollow insides manifested organs. Then, a complete circulatory system birthed within this mobilized vessel of death. Blood flooded throughout its frame, while blossoming tissue, solidifying with sinew-laced muscle.

From the inside out, a time-lapse reversing of death, releasing from their poses of demise, the skeletons surrounding them from every direction did the same. Now lacking only skin and eyes, these creatures without sight, crawled, crawled for the light. By their fingers of bone, they pawed and clawed up through the earth, tearing their way along the soil and stone. Saint Peter's rested steepled above, upon them all, as a lone and great mausoleum for this city of the dead now undead.

"*Now* I really want to go home," said Tom.

"It's like... something out of Revelations," Howie said.

"Isaiah," said Mike, the words coming into his mind. "'Your dead shall live; their bodies shall rise. You who dwell in the dust, awake and sing for joy! For your dew is a dew of light, and the earth will give birth to the dead.'"

"If that don't turn you green," said Howie.

Tom shook his head. "Hell of a thing... Skeletons dressed as humans."

Camorra wandered off toward a cluster of these creatures, entangled upon each other, having become a knotted thing quite unnatural.

"Hey! Leave the living dead alone," shouted Tom.

Howie leaned close to Tom, whispering, "Not like we need him around."

Not knowing how she'd heard him, she had, and Ingrid looked him dead in the eyes with her own, crisp and serious. "Like it or not, he, just as each of us, is here for a *specific* purpose—" The tunnel of light began to spiral into a vortex, sucking them upwards. Spinning and churning, they were mixed with these living dead, vacuumed up into the daylight. With solid ground returning beneath their feet, the creatures were no more. Neither was the basilica, or any sign of Vatican City.

The sweet smell of wild grass and flowers filled their lungs. Sun and cobalt sky, wispy clouds and unseen birds whispering brought some normalcy. They stood atop a vast hill.

"Vatican Hill," said Mike. "I mean, before the layers of earth and tombs and everything else piled up to a point of burying the actual hill onto a plateau of marble and pavement."

Directly in their view of this place undisturbed, a man stepped. Turned, his profile wasn't quite visible. Then he shifted, revealing his face....

"Is that...," Howie began to ask.

"Yes," said Mike. "Yes, it is..."

Lap through Time

"Constantine," Ingrid said.

Before Constantine, lavishly adorned in the royal purple robe reserved for Roman emperors, that he was, and before them, another time-lapse occurred. Though, this one free of skeletons, or perhaps not so much, showed the genesis of that opulent structure known the world over as Saint Peter's Basilica, shifting into existence, to perch gleamingly upon the many dead that laid beneath. Complete, the basilica stood as though it'd always been.

The sun radiated overhead, melting in brilliant pinks and burning reds and endless shades of orange along the skyline. A vast crowd awaited. Elevated nearly twenty feet above the crowd, Constantine proudly posed upon a marble platform.

Arms outstretched, head tilted to the Italian sky, afire in color, he then faced his people. With a voice fit for an emperor of Rome, he announced his decree. "As both a god and emperor, direct descendant of the immortal and eternally divine Flavian bloodline, I, Emperor Constantine, by this authority, proclaim Christianity, and Christianity alone, from this day and all days forward, to be the one religion known to the empire of Rome. And you, you loyal citizens, shall be practitioners of Rome's Christianity. All shall be unto it. The Roman Empire, *our* empire, shall be united, indivisible, as one, by it. She shall be eternal! You, my people, the people of Rome and her provinces, by divine right, I here now deliver this universal religion unto you." With a sweeping bow, he gracefully tipped his head and broad shoulders, caped in his royal robe, to his people, to the people of Rome.

The lapse through time began to accelerate again. As the constellations and moon and sun transitioned across the sky, centuries drifted by in the span of seconds. Torn down, a more elaborate version of Saint Peter's Basilica replaced itself. All sight of Vatican Hill disappeared with its evolution, birthing forth Vatican City.

Time became as the rate of what they knew, as humans knew. Approaching dusk, modern traffic, congested and a bit chaotically so, coursed along Vatican City of the twenty-first century. All had become bigger, more ornate depictions of itself in this place. Only the ancient Egyptian obelisk remained unchanged, towering at the heart of Vatican Square. Electricity, not torchlight, cast its shadow upon the face of Saint Peter's Basilica.

High above, a jetliner faintly rumbled by, caressing the near-evening sky with a trail of white. On every street, sidewalk, and corridor, a swirling blend of people from all nationalities flowed. It was a truly universal spectacle. All headed for somewhere, filled with a buzzing urgency to arrive. The surfaces of the grand marble and domes, both hard and silky, glowed in the setting sun of the Italian skyline.

Everything, from the kitten there on the sidewalk, to the shrinking sun, to the rising moon, went completely dark....

Delusions of Comfort

*T*heir team of five stood before the crystal table at the chamber's center beneath the Vatican. The sphere's spinning came to a stop upon the table. Its light and projection died, evaporating away to a place no more. The mossy film on the walls came aglow.

Ingrid removed her hands from the sphere's cool surface, then stumbled back. Howie reached to catch her, but Camorra was faster, now holding her in his embrace. He set her onto the table, then gave her a bottle of water.

"Why would the L' Entita show us, but provide no tangible proof for us to give the rest of the world?" asked Tom.

Ingrid set aside the now empty water bottle. "Maybe we're just not seeing it."

"Not seeing it," Howie quickly responded. "The irrefutable proof is within the historical texts themselves. One needs just read."

"Kid, I'm a former Bible scholar, in addition to having sincerely searched for the truth all my life, and I didn't even see it. Not until now anyway, being shown all this," Mike said. "How do you expect others to, when they don't *want* to?"

"We have this," Howie said, rapping his knuckles upon the sphere's dark surface. A sharp, resonating echo released throughout the chamber.

Camorra watched silently from along the wall, biding his time.

"Suffice to say, Howie, I just don't think the Vatican's going to let us set up shop in their basement," Ingrid said.

"Why not? It's perfect," Tom said, framing the envisioning of it with his hands out in front of him. "We can have a line alongside entrance to the Sistine Chapel. But... Instead of our sign saying, 'Come be enchanted by our multi-billion-dollar religious complex to celebrate your immortal status as one of god's best friends because you lived a life exempt from materialism, and your reward for not being materialistic is to live forever and ever in a magical kingdom in the sky made of gold and giant jewels, happy as a clam, while knowing your loved ones, who were materialistic, burn in hell forever and ever'..."

He turned to Howie. "*Our* sign can say, 'Enter at your own risk. Your bubble will be burst'. Can't you just see it now, we'll put good ol' Saint Peter's out of business in no time. No. I think not. Howie, she's right. They have a better sales pitch, despite false advertising. The whole surprise—your personal relationship with the son of god is a lie devised for social control, like Santa Claus for adults bit is a bit lackluster. Better luck next time! But, oh, wait! Wait—there is no next time. Shucks."

He lowered his hands and shook his head. "That's not going to happen." Leaning close to Howie, he whispered, "*That's* sarcasm."

A heavy solemnness filled the air, forcing a quiet within them. *Were they to accept defeat from the myth that solidified itself as fact for far too long? If not... Then how were they to stand up to it... To such a thing as blind belief?* Caught within this trap without physical release inside his mind, Howie watched Camorra, stationary, though somehow adrift in the shadows there at the edge of the chamber, who seemed to be waiting for something... Pivoting, Howie watched Ingrid and wondered... *How do you stare a thing in the eyes that holds no face of its own?*

For Camorra, a relief began to fill him brought on by this

Tom, this Irishman's words of jest, though truth. It felt increasingly so now he wouldn't have to spill more blood in order to achieve his task at hand. This whole situation, incited by the earthquake in Malta, just might be negated after all... And simply so by people's refusal to let go of the comforting convenience of the lies which they lived by. Truly, it was true... People *didn't* want to know the facts... Even when presented clear as day, undeniably before their very eyes.

Maybe Domenico had overacted too. But that was his job, his duty to. There was no reasoning with that man. But still... *Maybe.*

Howie broke their long moment of silence. "Tom."

"Yeah?"

"You're a *bit* much sometimes."

"Just sometimes? I'll try harder."

Camorra stepped between them. "Enough."

"I need some space to think," Ingrid said. Still regaining her senses, she moved away from the others, to the far wall. Noticing for the first time this was the only wall which wasn't covered in the glowing moss-like substance, she rested her head against it. Her exhausted eyes closed. Swiftly, she lost herself in thought... *I just... wish we had something more... something to hold. To show the world. Something...* A click. She opened her eye. "Did you hear..."

A few inches down, along from where she stood, a large section of the wall in the shape of an inverted triangle had begun to slide out. Vertically so, it was nearly the height of the chamber, reaching from the ceiling down to the floor. Light escaped from the other side of it as it continued to slide out by a full couple of feet, revealing its immensity.

Seeing this, and knowing something of great importance awaited them behind this heavy and hidden door, Camorra's belief abruptly shattered in not having to bring them any harm in order to complete his objective....

Held Within the Threshold

*T*he section, having pulled itself free, rotated, sliding flush along the wall. Now out of the way, an open doorway remained, shaped as an inverted triangle. As shallow as paper is thin, beneath the skin of the doorway, amongst glittering crystalized patches, entangled bolts of electricity smoothly flowed within. Agitated or enthralled by its exposure to increased oxygen from their side of the chamber, or perhaps to the five of them, these illuminated webs of liquified light ignited brighter.

A hum followed, deeply, swiftly, becoming a thickly vibrant vibration. Its light intensified, glowing in breaths, as though alive. Along the ceiling over the doorway, this electric heartbeat, thumping deeper, most heartily, dislodged rocks, pebble, gravel-like, to egg-size.

Ingrid started to enter. Compelled to shield her from harm, Howie passed. He stopped, framed within this threshold, doorway agleam, pulsing with its perpetual drizzle of small rocks. The webbed veins of energy began to tear from their crystal skin. Rising up, these entangled bolts, opaque and snake-like, hissed, connecting with the open air. Swishing, swaying before him, they glistened quite charmingly in their own white light.

Stretching longer, continuing to pull away from the doorway with tremendous longing, they reached out like the feelers of energy they were. And with his back obscuring the others' view, he saw what they did not. One of the littlest of the rocks, a touch smaller than a human eye, as it fell from ceiling to floor, caught within a vein of energy, altering the respective physics of its course in a most disrespecting way.

"Move or go," Ingrid said at his back, voice brimming with impatience.

"A second. This could be important," he said, as quietly as he could beneath his breath. The rock continued for the floor, but much too slow by gravity's will alone. How ever it was happening, there was an energy field within the doorway causing the rock to drift, not fall. As it did so, its path wasn't straight down, though pulled to the left.

Needing to preserve his dignity in front of her, he decided the fact this electrified threshold hadn't turned the rock to sizzling mush, was good enough. He poked his finger through, penetrating the field. It felt as pressing oneself into a brook of enthusiastic current. A few degrees cooler than the air of the chamber, it was rather refreshing.

While keeping his eye on the rock, still making its way slowly down, he pushed into the energy field. The little rock finally reached the floor, though a good six inches to left of its original trajectory. With his body inside the field, it very much felt as fighting against a water's current, as this invisible membrane of energy filled the doorway.

The electric snaking bolts were the only visible parts, a frame of strange sorts. Something warm coiled around him. Enveloped, he felt himself growing energized. The brightness of the electrified feelers increased tenfold, illuminating the space beyond, revealing what awaited....

Separated Through Connection

*B*y no means grand in its scale, the space was no larger than a generous walk-in closet. The walls within, with speckled facets afire in the light, were crystal or crystal-like. There were other things which mingled with the crystalized sparkles of these glossy and glassy walls. More of the electrical bolts were there. These seemed to swim of their own accord and awareness, skimming beneath the crystal skin.

Ingrid joined him. Without a word, she set her left palm flush to the wall. Its surface became as glass, leaving no gleam of crystal or pulse of electricity to be seen. What became within their sight was clear, that seal of the L' Entita sealed thinly within the wall. Vastly tall, the Praesidio Autem Veritas spanned from the ceiling to the stone floor. A triangular keyhole awaited at the center of the cross within this archaic symbol, sublime and timeless.

"Your key," he said.

As she turned, he spoke lowly, lower than she'd ever heard him. "Whatever happens, it's okay."

Not certain what he meant, she pushed through the energy field and headed back for the table. Passing Camorra there, she noticed his hand was concealed under the edge of his coat. His gun likely waited there, lingering for the opportunity to take what tangible secrets were to be discovered... Then do with those untold mysteries and answers most veiled whatever dark will he desired.

Upon reaching the table, its crystal surface began to change. It liquidized as a purée of diamonds, then parted down its center, providing her access to the compass piece resting beneath within the table's cavity. The sphere descended, sinking, and coming to set deeply so next to the compass piece.

Before she could unlock it, a hairline beam of crimson shot up from the capstone atop the compass piece. An unexpected, as well *final* inscription to illuminate their way to the L' Entita's cherished library, bloomed vividly, projecting before them all. The lush letters in crimson transitioned to fiery gold....

Meant to profit the return, the eternal fall among giants and man
At last, the inhospitable see, heal the brimmed of life when golden
is the son
Moved by order, within the stone within a gate, the truth awaits
upon this span
A crusade's theater rings in blood, swallowed by an enemy never
thought one
Circle the walls holy, while the book was taken, hidden as the sun

"Remove it. Now," Camorra ordered, his mind having already photographed the lines of cryptic text entwined with layered context and allure through and through thoroughly sub rosa.

Hating to, she did as he desired, removing the compass piece from within the table's cavity, then hurried back to the energy field. She started to step through the field, but Howie stopped her, placing his hand out, blocking her path. As he did, his other hand harshly yanked away the compass piece.

When the compass piece made contact with the field, the membrane filling within became visible. Lightly flowing, churning, it was a very pale crimson, as watery blood. Through this rose-colored lens, grimly beautiful, his eyes spoke silently.

They said what he'd already told her, that it'd be okay...

Despite what would happen. As a piece of rock broke free, swallowing into the membrane, she saw as he had. The speed of its fall slowed rapidly. Its course veered to the left as it now drifted down. The pale crimson swirled around it, rippling quietly amongst the electric hum of the serpentine energy. This suspended beauty passed. The electrified feelers along the doorway dramatically expanded, swelling wetly, grisly, thrashing violently. Thickening, the membrane became as ruby.

"I'm sorry," he whispered, somehow with such softness seeming to send an eternal echo deep within her. Denying her why, or a goodbye, he pivoted sharply, going for the wall of glass at his back....

Tangible

*I*nserting the compass piece capstone-first into the triangular keyhole, Howie rotated it to the right. With a satisfying click, it locked in. A seam released on the glass wall. Vertically spreading, it opened at its center, revealing a bookcase carved from stone. With his body blocking the others' view, he unlocked the compass piece, sliding it inside his pocket.

"What is it?" Tom shouted from on the other side of the energy field.

It was a treasure. Not the one, precisely, he'd been hoping for, but still, it would do. Scrolls and leather-bound volumes packed the bookcase's shelves. He stepped back, allowing them to see as good as they could through the energy field's ruby membrane.

Tom frowned. "I thought the legendary library of the L' Entita would be... Bigger."

Howie beamed, grabbing the scroll closest to him. He untied the leather strap binding it, then unrolled the scroll. "This isn't their library." Tightly, though carefully, he gripped an end in each hand, holding up the scroll in front of the field for Ingrid to see.

Scanning through the Latin text before her, she beamed as Howie. "No, Tom, this is not their long-lost library." She turned to them all. "These scrolls are the New Testament. The *original* New Testament."

Howie unrolled more scrolls, each written in Latin or Greek. "The Gospels... *Signed* by the hand of the Flavians and Josephus themselves." He showed them the signatures proudly sealed upon the pages. "Yes, the original drafts... Never intended to be seen by anyone outside their inner circle of authorship."

Mike peered through the energy field at the texts. "Because the originals would reveal who, and thus, *why* they'd been written... And as to why they're in Latin and Greek and not Aramaic. Because, simply, they weren't written in the time or place the Church claims."

"Nor by who they claim," Howie added, pouring over the ancient and frail writings which emitted a bit of a stale odor. *How long had it been since these words had been gazed on by human eyes? How long had it been since they'd felt human touch...* "Aside from the actual library, I can't imagine a greater find."

"I can," Tom said. "It's called the HMS *Sussex*. Full of gold."

"No hope for you, Irishman," Mike said, shaking his head. "Ever since the Roman's scourge on the first century Jews, has there been but three accounts to go by. Now, now we have something..."

"Tangible," said Ingrid, smiling at Howie. "Sorry, Mike, you were saying?"

"Just, as we know," he said, "as far as documents that reference Jews at all, during the first century, the public has only ever had three sources to go by."

"Until now," Howie said, standing on his toes and with a single swipe, scooping all the scrolls off the bookcase's top shelf.

"And irrefutably so...," said Mike. The magnitude of what they'd found hit him, and it hit hard. "Think I'm going to be sick." He leaned against the wall, gripping his head in his palms, slumping to the floor.

Needing him fully attentive to the situation, as they all

depended on his expertise, Ingrid tried to get him focused again. "Mike."

"Uh huh?"

"You said there was a third."

"The Dead Sea Scrolls of course," he answered. "Having been deliberately hidden from the Romans within those caves in the middle of nowhere. Being, *until now*, the sole source not adulterated by the hand of the Church. Their historical account of the Jews of the first century is in stark, glaring opposition to the Church's own. And look, despite the Roman's proficiency with wiping out entire cultures when politically convenient, the *only* two records of any kind referencing first century Jews, being the New Testament and Josephus's works, just happen to both outright advocate Rome's rule over the Jews as well promote Christianity in doing so. And, further, they do so unscathed, in mass quantity and circulation the world had never seen before. *That*, my friends, does not happen by accident."

"That's why the Dead Sea Scrolls have been a royal crown of thorns in the Church's side, forever," said Tom. "As it were."

"Well," Mike said, "at least ever since their chance discovery in 1947. Nonetheless, they proved the Jews of the time most certainly weren't the Jews of Roman propaganda, bowing down, cheek turning, complacent pacifists, as Jesus. Theirs was a god of wrath. Hence the egregious rift between the Old Testament's god of hellfire versus the New Testament's god of peace and love. Telling you, there's no greater account of carnage, murder, and glorified horror wrapped in misery than the Old Testament, to be found in all history..."

"And the scrolls?" she asked, having successfully sparked a second wind within him.

Resting his head against the wall, he looked up. "Simply, the Dead Sea Scrolls showed the Jews were survivors of whatever history threw at them. That legacy has not changed to this day, despite the Church having deceived so many to believe the opposite. Those scrolls were without context though. But now we can change that. Give the people the truth."

Camorra watched Howie closely, as he riffled through the scrolls and texts. He listened as well to another of Mike's history lessons. Which... may or may not end up proving of value to his objective here and now. For the moment, it was still not quite right to strike...

Howie approached the energy field. He opened wide the six-inch thick leather-bound text in his grip for them to see. "You know all that dirt the Vatican keeps under lock and laser in their massive archives... Now they don't have the only copy."

The ruby glow of the field illuminated his face, bleeding forebodingly into the blue of his eyes, making his irises appear as blood. "We have the Vatican's little... big black book."

Ingrid scanned down the pages before her, tinged in the red of the light. "The first Pope was Flavian... The first several all were. All positions..." Her focus intensified on the text... "Literally there was no difference between the Flavian family tree and that of the founding of, and subsequent running, of the Roman Catholic Church..." She pulled as close she could to the field surging with hissing bolts of energy. "*Every single position* that could be held, both administratively and symbolically, was done so by a Flavian."

Mike gazed on the words clearly held upon the yellowing pages. "They were, in the truest sense, lobbyists."

Howie flipped through the book. "As you see, the evolution of this dynasty, this out-and-out incest of church and state, leads to the absolute merging of not just the Flavians running the Church as well the government, but that of the Alexanders and Herods too."

He came to stop on the page he'd been searching for. For, there at the book's center, in crisp color, was an actual family tree stretching centuries, coming to fold out tantalizingly, as though a centerfold. "The endgame, their trinity of families became the same bloodline. Running all."

Tom released a long and very Irish whistle as only he could. "And people today complain about there being a revolving door between business and government."

"Government *is* business," said Howie. "Just ask the Flavians."

"They at least should have the morality to be honest about their deception," Tom said. "They should call that place Saint Flavian's. Not Saint Peter's. And, man, the best part for the Church, no one can demand a refund when they're dead."

Camorra chambered a round. They immediately turned. He let his gun rest in the open, at his side. He didn't point it, affording them that dignity. For him, it was a small, yet large gesture.

At his feet were two duffel bags he'd apparently had with him, folded compactly so within the pockets of his jacket. "Ingrid, take these to Howie. Howie, pack the tangible proof inside." He raised his gun, aiming it at the bookcase. "By my calculations, it should all fit. Barely."

What Men Do

"*A*s you command, Mr. Camorra," Howie answered, more than surprisingly to the others.

Mike pointed his finger damningly at Howie. "We've the blueprints and authorship of Christianity in our grasp—"

"Mike," Howie said, nearly shouting, cutting him off, "you cannot negotiate against bullets. It doesn't turn out well for the one not holding a gun."

Camorra tilted his gun at the wall, and Mike and Tom reluctantly went there, out of the way. Ingrid retrieved the bags, taking them to the edge of the energy field as instructed. Her eyes connected with Howie's through the ruby membrane framed by slithering bolts, feeling, pulling toward, then away from her, driftingly so.

Her hand pressed through the field, delivering the bags. His hand met hers, taking hold, eclipsing over her soft skin within this electric threshold. Things unspoken, though felt, passed between them.

He'd made his decision. It was the only logical one to be made. He was right, she knew. And she hated him for making it. Her hand released, drawing back to her side of the field. Filling with an emptiness, she felt certain that was the last time she and he would ever touch.

With the duffel bags now in his grip, his lack of gesture of warmth or closure was a gesture in itself she'd have to accept, settle for. This brief, though fate-changing moment was over much too soon, a shared heartbeat of time between them, to live in memory for a lifetime. She joined Tom and Mike at the wall.

"Camorra," Howie said. There was both an authority and absoluteness in his voice none of them, including himself, had ever known, nor thought possible.

Camorra stepped close to the energy field. The two men watched one another, the flowing, pulsing light casting bloodlike on their faces.

"What happens once I give you these records?" Howie asked.

"What happens is she goes with me," Camorra answered. "She's as vital to all of this as those texts behind you are. More so. And you three go free, alive. That's what happens. *Once* you give over those texts."

"You're going to use her to go after the lost library then," Howie said. "Now that you've seen the final inscription."

"Yes," answered Camorra. "If intact, the library's contents will surely overshadow even what we've found here. The Holy See will have their eye on that now."

"I see," said Howie.

"Do not doubt, if you resist, I will end you. I will end them," Camorra said, glancing back at Tom and Mike. "She's the only one not disposable. That goes for myself too."

"On that part, Mr. Camorra, that she's not disposable, we agree."

Sensing resistance, Camorra raised his gun, aiming it pointblank at Howie's heart. "And for the rest?"

Howie eyed the gun, then Camorra. "You're just going to have to shoot me, Mr. Camorra." Having said it, he gave a final look to his three colleagues, partners, along the wall.

"What the hell are you doing, kid?" Mike yelled. "He's going to kill you..." But he saw, realized the decision his son had made, had been made minutes ago. The causation was in motion, unstoppable. This assassin, in front of his son, had accepted the call to action. There would be no point in pleading further. All that remained were the consequences. "I was wrong. Wrong about a lot of things..."

Howie broke eye contact with his father, returning his focus to Camorra. Beneath the veneer of the red glow upon Camorra, a blankness took hold, negating all emotion. He looked his prey in the eyes. He did not enjoy taking life. Particularly when it was needless, as this was. He'd kill this man. Then, he'd take the texts and continue on his course. The only difference between then and now is this man would be dead.

Needless. But it'd become necessary. Perhaps, even... *Inevitable.*

With only one thing left to do, he aligned his sights. The front sight grew a little fuzzy while holding focus on the rear sight. Things were in perfect alignment with where he knew this man's heart to be, precisely so... Mere inches away.

Though, something vexed at him. There was a bravery in this man that he hadn't calculated for. And it was bravery, not courage, for he could not detect fear. A lack of fear was a rare thing... *Extinct* even by many measures. *Truly vexing...* The hiss and pop of the energy field seemed louder now. "That's electricity. Not a bulletproof vest."

Howie stood there, unwavering, facing him, ready. For the briefest instant, he glanced past Camorra, then returned his eyes to him. Point-blank, Camorra squeezed the trigger.

The Ballistics of Suspended Animation

*H*aving shot, and in no way being able to possibly miss, only then did Camorra turn. He needed to assess what it was that'd caused this man to break eye contact at such a critical moment. There was a blurring glimpse of the others as they slipped through the doorway leading out of the chamber.

She'd never leave without that triangular key to lead to her quest's end. *Unless—*Camorra's heart froze. The immense, ten-foot-thick door started to shut. Its heavy grinding of stone against stone as it began to seal the chamber loudly proclaimed his gross miscalculation... She already *had* the triangular key when she'd left. The door would never close otherwise. Nor open—Camorra bolted for the swiftly shrinking space standing between him and escape. It was closing too fast—shedding his coat, he dove, balling his body, rolled, barely scraping through.

~~ ~~

Just as Howie had believed, Camorra, the Vatican's finest assassin, had aimed and aimed true for the place with maximum efficiency to manifest death... His heart. He knew a man as Camorra, a man skilled, experienced, and most importantly, governed by statistical calculation, would not aim for the head. There were far too many variables when dealing with thick bone, such as the human skull. Especially so, when factoring in such a thing before him now, strange and unknown, as a subterranean energy field membrane.

As with the rocks he'd witnessed, the bullet led off course, its trajectory pulling inches to the left. Breaking through the field, it traveled sluggishly, slowly spiraling. Drearily drifting so, it glistened cold, void of feeling, utterly objective in its single purpose of moving forward until it could no longer.

A few feet from where he stood, it struck the wall. The impact happened in a most delayed and lagging way. The bullet's nose mushroomed, distorting, bending back unto itself, folding almost meekly, artfully. Then, as something suddenly dead, it dropped straight to the floor of stone, plopping to a heavy stillness, laying there as snarled up ball. Joining the bullet, he slid to the floor. His fingers found the piece of lead. It was warm, not hot, but simply warm. He drew in a long breath and held it to his heart.

"Well, Howie, you didn't think this through all the way. Did you."

The path before him was but one with the deadest of ends. The field of energy shut off, fading away. The amber glow of the chamber walls offered the only light.

Tom and Mike were gone. The compass piece, which he'd slipped to her when taking the duffel bags, was gone. And she was gone. She... who he could not stop thinking about, despite his present situation... That strange and striking girl who plagued his mind in a wonderful and dreadful way, was but a shadow now melted seamlessly unto the darkness surrounding him.

Witness Amongst Dark Waters

*A*s Ingrid led Tom and Mike at full sprint, the passageway through the cave widened. The blank walls transitioned to the archaic paintings of Mithraism, with Mithra, its son of god and savior of humankind, exhibited vividly along the dark slates of rock. Then, Camorra broke into view, devouring the darkness which separated him from them.

The relentless strike of his boots against the stone of the cave's floor thumped, drum-like, in their ears as they ran with all their will. At a wholly unnatural pace, he gained, driven by a prehistoric hate through this ancient and holy place. The paintings were as silent witnesses to this pursuit between predator and prey. Surging past Mithra's sacrificial bull evocatively so on the wall, Camorra's silhouette cast across it, then across the cross Mithra was to be crucified upon.

Hearts pulsed, sweat glistened, as the cold fear flowed through their hot lungs and tired legs. And still he gained. Reaching the end, they exited through that beautifully strange inverted triangular doorway, having been formed from the twin pentagrams, and entered the narrow passage beyond.

Around the gentle jog to the right, they faced off with the painfully steep incline there, leading higher and higher. With the sounds of their pursuer growing ever louder, they dared not turn to look. Finding level ground, they fled through the pentagram-shaped doorway at the end of the stone passageway, returning them to the mausoleum of the Flavians, Herods, and Alexanders, withered to bone.

They raced across the marble floor and out the open door, spilling through into the sprawling city of the dead. Ingrid zigzagged along the headstones and collapsed graves and mausoleums of grand and dusty and cracked marble. Having run out of will, fear alone fueled them. And his footsteps were close, much too close....

There was another sound. It too was close. The call of flowing water now led their way. By the beam of Tom's flashlight, they found the river, having carved its tangled path through the subterranean terrain long ago. The water was black, fast and choppy, strangled with currents.

Camorra's deep breathing fell upon them. They needed not look, to know where his gun aimed. For they were the only living prey in such a place filled with death. Ingrid shoved Tom and Mike into the water.

With her back to him as he drew nearer in the thick shadows entwining her to him, she repeated within her mind two simple words... *Not disposable.* She hoped it true and jumped. Camorra, alone, was witness to these dark waters taking her most hauntingly.

Dreams of Poppies

*T*he bullet rested quietly in Howie's hand. There was a weight to it that surpassed its borders. Fate had been persistent to connect them together, to share their beginning forever, during the end. There he laid with this lump of led, alone, trapped, without any ideas, neither clever or less than so, and so he felt certifiably unclever, and far less than.

Then, when darkness felt greatest, the glow of the mossy-film on the walls ceased to be, elongating the shadows. The only illumination came from the crystal surface of the table, milky, with but the strength of a few candles. Golden, it washed over the table's edges, drifting thinly to the floor.

"Come, bullet, if death is what it is, then let's have a say in how comfortable we are before it takes us."

Pocketing the bullet, he pulled himself up. Already having filled the two duffel bags with the ancient texts, he took a bag in each hand. He placed them on the table, then himself. Flat upon his back, the crystal pulsed, shedding its luminescence along his contour.

Perhaps his skeleton would one day be discovered. Some most fortunate seeker of treasure would recover this fortune of writing. That was the least he could offer, by any measure. Not satisfied, but accepting this fatal fate, he settled into fetal pose amongst the golden light.

Sleepy, his eyes and mind drifted to the glow of the crystal fragments adrift beneath the table's thin skin. Swirling and floating through their translucent sky-like plane reminded him of something... Of flying monkeys. *No... That was not it, not quite so anyway... Dorothy.* His eyes closed and the thought of Dorothy, in her blue and white pinafore dress, warmly entered his mind. The dress, it now reminded him of something else... Of a tablecloth one would use for a picnic amongst the grass and flowers... *Amongst the poppies.* In the chamber's silence, a voice echoed salaciously in his mind... *Come, succumb to the sleep of the witch...*

~~ ~~

Outside the Basilica, at the far edge of Saint Peter's Square, bordering the Tourist Office, Camorra slipped on the Ducati's helmet then straddled the sleek bike. The digital display overlaid a city map upon his visor. A blinking green dot was there... The tracking chip he'd placed on the bottom of that triangular key Ingrid now possessed. The Ducati roared to life, tearing down Via Conciliazione. She was not far, not at all... Just on the other side of the bridge dead ahead.

Falling Awake

O n the chamber's table of crystal and stone, deeply asleep, Howie's chest rose and lowered in steady intervals. The glow of the crystals within the skin of the table's surface matched the rhythm of his breathing, pulsating, in and out, in and out. A new movement began, with the table sinking through the floor, to the chamber beneath, unknown.

As it descended, the table's halo, frail, golden, silhouetted shapes within this small space. It came to stop with the kissing of stone to stone, resting with a subtle splash onto the bit squishy, though solid floor. A coolness nibbled at his skin, coaxing him awake. For how long sleep had held him, he could not know. The air tasted fresh. Drowned with dampness, it was earthy and visceral.

Removing his phone, he turned on its light. Water was quickly bubbling up from somewhere near the base of the table, through the floor blanketed in moss. The walls too were covered in this deep-green moss, not entirely normal as he knew moss, but neither glowing. There were mushrooms along the walls and floor of this circular place of rock. Red and white, they were easy to recognize as the Amanita muscaria. His empty stomach churned at the thought of consuming them.

"I think not."

The water, not cold, but peaceful, natural to the body's

embrace, had reached the table's edges, flowing over. Securing the duffel bags to his belt, he zipped them up all the way.

"Well, you two better be water-proof."

Lowering himself off the table, the water's source was obvious, as it coursed out a hole, a coffin's width, from the floor. His apprehension for small spaces crept up.

"Be no more."

Drawing in a deep, deep breath, he dropped, falling far, flowing away into the darkness....

* * * *

He awoke with his face pressed to wet brick. Things smelled of trash. Coldness drenched him. Water trickled beneath and along his body... Toward light—*sunlight* at this tunnel's end.

After a surge of panic, he found the bags safely beside him. He got to his feet, which he did not notice, aside from a single sock, were now bare. Where the tunnel, broad and brick, ended, it drained into the Tiber River. He knew the place, for their hotel was only on the other side. Barefoot, he ran.

The One that Didn't Get Away

*T*om and Mike met him in the hotel's hallway, having received the rather concerned call from the front desk. Ingrid's absence gave Howie his answer. She'd been taken. He collapsed. They rushed to catch him, but it was too late....

* * * *

Howie emerged from sleep on the bed. Bare and clean, he was embraced by soft Italian linens wrapped around his body. He pulled on the cargo shorts waiting for him upon the dresser.

In the other room, Tom and Mike sat on the couch, focused on the laptop's screen. Grabbing a bottled water and handful of fruit from the kitchenette, Howie joined them. Footage played of the chamber beneath the Vatican captured from Tom's hidden cam.

Howie hit the pause button. Frozen on screen was the moment Ingrid reached for the compass piece, and the final inscription projected into the air. Howie's fingertips hovered near her face in frame. "How?"

"How it happened," said Tom.

"Yes, Tom," Howie said. "How did he get her away from you two?"

"Man, Howie, the guy's a ghost. One instant she was with

us, having just crossed the bridge. Second later, he flies past on his motorcycle and she's on the back."

Howie remained silent, locked upon Ingrid's face.

"There was nothing we could've done," Mike said.

"Yeah," Howie answered. His finger struck hard onto the play button, letting the footage resume. His eyes found their notes of paper, scrawled, covering the coffee table. "Walk me through what you two have so far. If anything..."

Tom zoomed in on the inscription on screen, knowing it best to crop Ingrid out of the frame for the time being, pausing once more. "Oh, we have something alright." He grinned, his boyish eagerness welling up. "Don't we, Mike."

"That we do." Mike shared in the sly smile. "That we do..."

Diametric Fact of Life

*H*owie stared blankly, gazing not at the inscription on screen, but *into* it... He needed not only find the lost library. He had to rescue Ingrid, for she'd been taken by a dark knight indeed. This was a creature of a world no longer present amongst the present time.

At the cusp of his quest's end, he now stood, a weaving path woven and carved by the collision of fate and chance. It'd led him through forgotten history to a destiny climaxed in the twilight of mystery. And while divergent in their desires for seeking the truth, that destination was one with Camorra's. Binding them was an invisible string, commanded by a hand of shadow that held all things. This thread of the L' Entita, society of light forever shrouded by night, was a line charted across their souls, wrapped in spiral, through their DNA, a map to—

Tom snapped his fingers in front of Howie's face. "Where the hell were you?"

"Hell if I know," Howie answered, trying to center himself. He returned his eyes to this final message... Their call to destiny emblazoned on the star-kissed fabric of time, against great darkness drenched in light most golden... "So...?"

With the stroke of a key, Mike underlined the first letter of each line for the inscription.

M̲eant to profit the return, the eternal fall among giants and of man

At last, heal the brimmed of fire when golden is the son
Moved by order, within the stone within a gate, truth awaits
upon this span
A ring of blood, wings for land, not the sky, they did run
Circle the walls holy, inhospitable to see the free were taken,
hidden as the sun

"Mamac," Tom said, stating the name formed by the underlined letters.

"Who?" asked Howie.

"First century Roman general," said Mike. "He and his men, about four-hundred and eighty or so, went missing, never reaching their final destination."

"Which was where?" Howie asked.

Mike shrugged. "Unknown. Somewhere within the Roman Empire at the time."

Howie looked incredulous. "That really narrows it down don't it."

"Kid, don't you see," Mike said, "all we got to do now is figure out where Mamac went. *That's* where the final chamber is."

Howie got up from the couch. "That's all?" He went for the minibar. "And here, I thought we had to solve a disappearance that no historian has been able to since, forever."

"While you're over there..." Tom said. "And no, we don't have to solve *all* that, regarding history and historians and what not."

Howie threw a can of Sprite in Tom's direction, more at him than to him. "No?"

Tom narrowly caught it. "No. That answer is within the puzzle."

Howie returned, gulping on a miniature bottle of Jameson.

"Don't you think...?" asked Tom.

"I think..." Howie climbed over the back of the couch, plopping down between them. "That's a reference to Titus's encirclement of Jerusalem's walls." He tapped the line on screen.

Circle the walls holy...

"Yes, I think so too. And look at this," said Mike, underlining three more words.

Meant to profit the return, the eternal fall among giants and of man

At last, heal the brimmed of fire when golden is the son

"Son of Man," said Howie. "Titus. Titan... Among giants."

"Profit, *prophet*," said Tom.

"Yeah," Howie said, "definitely all referencing Titus. But was there historical context between him and this Mamac?"

Mike highlighted the words on screen.

Moved by order...

"'Order'", he said. "General Mamac's select group of soldiers had the official title, *Order* of the Commotoris."

Howie recalled his Latin. "Commotoris, or commotor, meaning... 'Mover'."

"Yep," Mike said. "When there were items of great value, political sensitivity, or high-risk prisoners, these guys were the ones tasked with the transporting."

"Like, *The Transporter*," said Tom.

Howie's eyes narrowed. "Yes. Tom. Exactly like that."

"*Now...*," said Mike, with a click.

At last, heal the brimmed of fire when golden is the son

A ring of blood, wings for land, not the sky, they did run

"The famed symbol of the Order of the Commotoris was a red ring encircling a gold goblet brimming with fire, along with winged feet in mid-sprint. And if I remember right... yeah, with their *heels* aflame."

Thoughts of Ingrid, and admittedly, of the lost library, that treasure which he sought, filled Howie's mind. He reached over, taking the laptop, underlining the single word, now seeming more important than all the rest combined.

Circle walls holy, inhospitable to see the free were taken, hidden as the sun

"Latin, the default language of the first century," he said.

501

"And in it, 'free' translates to liber. Which, in today's context, means 'liberty'. And the Latin root for liberty, of course, is 'liberal', still to this day holding the direct context for '*free*' or 'freedom'. And, for those of us educated in the classics of history, will know that 'liberal' is in itself a variation of the word... *Library*." Ending his realization, another filled him. *God, I sound like my father.*

"Good bet Mamac was transporting the lost library of Alexandria then," Mike said.

"And I'd say," said Howie, "he didn't even know it."

Mike nodded. "That's my instinct too, kid. But the fact they disappeared en route, means Ameci and her L' Entita knew *exactly* what was being transported, if not had orchestrated the whole thing from the beginning, then intercepted the transport."

"Now that we know they had the library," said Howie, "do you see anything else here?"

Upon mention of the word 'see', Tom pointed to it, this simple word they'd overlooked offering dual meaning, cloaked in its own commonness. "See or *sea*?"

"That's it, Tom!" Mike immediately underlined what'd just jumped out at him.

Circle walls holy, <u>inhospitable</u> to <u>see</u> the free were taken, hidden as the sun

"Inhospitable Sea was the first century name for the Black Sea, my friends," he said, leaning back, kicking his legs up on the coffee table, entirely satisfied with himself.

"So...," said Tom, "Mamac's dudes transported the library across the Black Sea."

"*Exactly*," said Mike, "don't you all see—that's *it*!" On the laptop's screen, he brought up a map of the Black Sea.

"No, I don't see," said Howie. "I see a big sea brimmed by a bunch of countries..."

"Where precisely they were headed, kid, does not matter. There was but one port as well one route, a lone road the Romans would and could take when it came to military transport through that most remote and treacherous region of their empire."

He zoomed in on the place that'd held this lost path, a slender swath along the lands once lorded by the barbarians of old, that mysterious country of lore, mythologies and tales of darkness and fears of both the known and unknown. Its name, superimposed upon the map, stared back at them ever imposingly.

Howie, then Tom, turned to Mike, and together, said, "You've got to be kidding..."

A Deal Between Devils

"Why are you telling me this? And what is it I can do for you, Mr. Teresi?"

With just the two of them in the quiet park, on the edge of Rome, Domenico sat across from Rino on one of the benches there under the canopy of trees. Beneath the fractured sun, both men let their shared distrust of one another seep in, filling this moment of mutual silence.

"It's come to happen, Mr. Favignana, Mr. Camorra has fallen out of communication with his business partner. Being, myself. Oh. You didn't know he and I had an arrangement."

Domenico absorbed every inflection in this man's voice, every gesture, no matter how slight, and the pace and tempo of every wheezing and heavy breath, as he sat there upon the bench not designed for a man of his particular stature or size. He knew of this man in the most general of terms, by reputation. Their worlds, that, while both large and both powerful, had never come to overlap, until now.

"You're right, Mr. Teresi, Camorra didn't mention you had an arrangement. Can you elaborate?"

Having let this spy study him, allowing Domenico to establish the necessary baselines in behavioral patterns, speech, and vital signs, so now his spy-mind could determine easily enough if the words he spoke were true, Rino would *now* answer the man. He'd do so with a question. "You want to know how much of Mr. Camorra's mission he'd told me?"

As any good spy knew, a lie was only used to serve an end, and only as the last tool in one's toolbox. The truth was always easier to maintain. It gave the appearance of moral alignment. Which, people, even immoral ones, were more trusting of. "Yes, Mr. Teresi, it's my job to know to what degree things have been compromised. Let us to the point, why exactly am I here, and not in my office?"

"Right, to the point then. Rest assured, I know nothing regarding Mr. Camorra's mission for you. The nature of our business relationship came to be for another reason. Mr. Camorra isn't the only individual you and I hold a common interest in."

"Go on."

In defiance of the shade, sweat bubbled up along Rino's face. Removing his handkerchief from his front suit pocket, he dabbed at the sweat, knowing no end. "Mr. Howard Lyon. He's a business partner of mine too. That in mind, Mr. Favignana, I'm under the impression, if your agency were to locate Mr. Lyon, then it wouldn't be a good day for Mr. Lyon."

"In not so many words, yes. He's not viable to the interests of the Holy See."

"I understand. And please see, Mr. Favignana, unfortunately, Mr. Lyon owes me money. A great deal of it. I admit, Mr. Lyon has caused that debt unto himself. However, he is my business partner, and he is of value to me in that capacity. Now, to the point, if your agency were to cause Mr. Lyon to... have a bad day, he wouldn't be able to pay me. Then, that'd be a bad day for me as well. Bad days are bad business... For *everyone*. So, it's my intention, Mr. Favignana, to resolve this—what's that word?"

"Amicably?"

"Amicably. I simply was looking out for my investment when I hired Mr. Camorra to assist in recovering what Mr. Lyon owes."

"If I may, Mr. Teresi, what compensation did Camorra ask?"

Rino dabbed at his forehead, neck, and chin. Though little good it did. "Land. One of my best villas."

"Sounds like Camorra. If I may again, what is the amount owed by this Lyon?"

"A truly fatal sum."

"Indulge me. Please."

"A hundred and thirteen million. Dollars."

"That's some number. Nonetheless, understand, respectfully, I need this Lyon. As we Italians say, 'the gallows were made for the unlucky'. I tell you now, Mr. Teresi, none can stop the sun rising on that bad day."

"There's no persuading you on that then?"

"No. Compromise is the devil's lipstick. And it's undeniably a fiery shade. What I *can* do for you, Mr. Teresi, whatever the value of your villa you'd agreed to Camorra for his services, I can offer that amount to you in return for your services to *me*, in guaranteeing Lyon, *as well* Camorra, are dually brought into my custody. More alive than dead." He studied the large and sweaty man across from him on the bench. He'd spin this to his own opportunity. Alas, it was impossible to see through Teresi's half-truths willfully eclipsed so fully. "A fair offer, Mr. Teresi?"

"It is, it is, Mr. Favignana. However, a shrewd businessman doesn't settle for fair."

Now he *knew* this Teresi was being forthcoming with him in his reasons for meeting. He'd just revealed his greed. And the predictability of a man's greed could always be trusted, especially one as rich as Mr. Rino Teresi. *Yes... Nothing was more sincere than a rich man's greed.* He relaxed a bit against the park bench. "How's an additional fifteen million euros wired to an account of your choice sound, Mr. Teresi?"

"Twenty sounds like a good day."

"Twenty... Done. *Once* both men are delivered into my custody."

Rino refolded his handkerchief before sopping up along his glistening forehead. "One more item, if it's in your realm of things possible."

Domenico gave a slight rise of his hand.

"I got this nephew who would be a great addition to the sainthood. I mean, if that's something you dabble in."

The mention of sainthood from the lips of this man birthed the beginnings of what would prove to be a considerable and long-lasting headache. Though he smiled, and he held his smile. "Even men such as ourselves are with limitation." Gracefully, he released his smile. "In parting, I must know. How do you plan to locate a man as Camorra?"

"Here's something I'm certain you can appreciate, Mr. Favignana. To the point once more, as a prudent businessman, through various and... creative means, I maintain a substantial amount of surveillance on those I partake in business with."

"You know where Camorra and this Lyon are right now?"

"I can offer better than that, Mr. Favignana." Rino neatly tucked the handkerchief back inside his front suite pocket. "I can tell you where they're *going* to be..."

Bound for Romania

*T*he rather soothing hum of the private jet's engines flowed thinly through the exceptionally comfortable cabin. Howie awoke, shoeless, nested within the large and plush chair, with both the headrest and footrest extended.

"Feeling better after some real sleep?" Tom asked, seated between him and Mike in front of the cabin's glossy walnut table.

"Being better," Howie answered. "There is a difference, Tom." He saw that the laptop was closed on the table. "You guys give it a stab while I was out?"

"Nope. Think we all needed some distance from it, mentally and emotionally, for the sake of clearer objectivity, as it were."

Mike opened the laptop, revealing the inscription. And using the touchpad, he underlined the line they had yet to unlock.

Meant to profit the return, the eternal fall among giants and of man
At last, heal the brimmed of fire when golden is the son
<u>*Moved by order, within the stone within a gate, truth awaits*</u>
<u>*upon this span*</u>
A ring of blood, wings for land, not the sky, they did run
Circle the walls holy, inhospitable to see the free were taken,
hidden as the sun

"Was thinking," said Tom, "that since we've changed arenas, right, different country and all, that we should look at context through the lens of historical Romania."

"Sounds like a plan," Howie said. "And watching for words with dual meaning as markers, as locks needing unlocked."

"*And*," Mike said, "we're looking for a location. Being a noun, indicted by something specific geographically. Physical features—description."

"'Stone', 'gate', and 'span'," Tom said, quickly listing them off.

"Using the lens through the eyes of ancient Romania," said Mike, "or, I should say, Dacia, as it was known, this Germanic lens changes the context of 'order'."

"Entirely so," Howie said, seeing clearly where his father was leading.

"So show us what you got, kid," Mike said.

"I will then," said Howie. "One of the most famous orders of knights. The... Order of..." He turned to his father.

"Order of the Brothers of the German House of Saint Mary in Jerusalem," Mike recited from memory. "Later becoming known as—"

"The Teutonic Knights," said Howie.

Tom raised his hand. "Who?"

"Getting there, Tom," Howie said. "Catholic military order headquartered in what'd we know as Israel and Palestine. Essentially, a state sponsored Roman Gestapo used to hunt down, torture and kill strategically valuable Jewish rebels. These knights, as, over time they'd become known as, were instrumental in the Roman's establishing of Christianity in Judaea and elsewhere."

Mike nodded, impressed by his son's historical aptitude.

"But what do these guys have to do with Romania?" asked Howie.

"With Rome's destruction of Jewish society at large," Mike answered, "the purpose and role of this Roman... Gestapo was no longer needed in Judaea. The little there is of historical record states the order was then dispatched to the region of the Roman empire in most need of their skill sets. To a land wrought with barbarians and lawlessness."

"First century Romania," Tom said, quietly typing away on the laptop before him. "Which, is where the new headquarters were established for the Teutonic Order."

"How do you know that?" asked Howie.

Tom turned the screen, revealing he was online, using the inflight WI-FI.

"Of course," Mike said, striking a palm against his thigh. "That explains why Mamac's men just happened to be transporting the library to Romania at the exact time the Teutonic Order was relocated there as well."

"Who better to guard the library once there, than the Teutonic Order," Howie said. " *Where* their headquarters was specifically, is the question."

"I don't know," answered Mike.

Howie's mouth dropped open. "Hear that, Tom. He doesn't know."

Tom finished his search and spun the laptop around. "Dietrichstein."

Mike grinned, knowing what they soon too were to know. "A stronghold in Transylvania. Or, once was, before being leveled."

"That's disappointing," Howie said.

Mike took back the laptop, bringing up the line in the inscription.

Moved by the order, within the stone within a gate, truth awaits upon this span

"Throughout history, Transylvania has been a prize for Turkey. And '*gate*' in Turkish quite literally translates to 'Bran'. And, wait for it... 'Dietrichstein' was the name of the original structure upon which Bran Castle *now* stands."

"Fitting," said Howie.

"Like a glove," Mike said.

"And the bit about 'span'?" Howie asked.

Tom entered his search, reading off the screen. "Bran Castle, like Fort Dietrichstein, the stronghold preceding it, shared its location upon the cliff of Bran, directly along the traditional borders of Wallachia and Transylvania... Uh, okay, skipping to... This placement upon the cliff was not just for its tactical advantage. It had been built there, as directly above the castle, is where the sun sets. Thus, the setting sun aligns perfectly with the castle each evening. Overtime, this alignment became known as the *span*, for the castle on the cliff bridges the space between Wallachia and Transylvania, in the light of morning. For this reason, the castle has long stood as a beacon, a symbol of this light for the people of Transylvania... *The Bearer of Light unto the People.*" Tom looked up from the screen. "Enchanting really."

"Quite," said Howie. "From Rome to Romania. And if one is to do Romania, then Transylvania is the only way. And what is more Transylvanian than Bran Castle..."

Bran Castle

*T*he trio exited the rideshare car parked along the narrow and curved street. This medieval village had been immortalized, holding its form from many lifetimes into the present. Though bitten with hints of modernisms, these shined thinly through. Here, it was fragile, and grim, of grace. There was never a place in the world where twilight looked so ominous and beautiful, tender yet menacing.

Their eyes lifted, magnetically drawn high within the darkening sky. The structure which they sought, its famous profile outlined, was ignited by infinite layers of pinks and indigos and golds. They had to pause and admire it, not just the sight of it, but the *feel* of it. In the shadowy canopy of hardwoods afire in their fall-time shades, with the legendary Bran Castle perched upon its cliff face, their hearts were humbled, beating thirstily with the tempo for adventure.

Heading to their left, across the empty and slender street, oddly bent as it was, they made their way through the corridor of souvenir shops and restaurants offering authentic cuisine and drink and things less than genuine. Clustered and disjointed, this realm held along the foot of the hillside where the castle towered above. Providing ticket vouchers at the booth, they passed through the gate painted flat brown, entering the castle grounds.

The centerpiece of this park, with its enchanted oaks and maples, full of bloom, color, and desire, was the large pond reflecting the castle amongst these hardwoods with their branches, interwoven and heavy. The pond's surface, glassy, still, silently screamed with ravished charm, blending these hues of nature and humans, speckled with the lights, near and distant, of the village of Bran.

"Truly, there is a spell holding this place," said Tom, low on his breath. "Dark or lovely, or both, it is thick."

Turning the spires and towers to shadowed outlines, the sun drifted down, liquifying into the hills behind the castle. The pinks and indigoes and golds deepened, filling the curves and bends of the sky framed against these hallowed hills. Serene blues, richly royal, engraved by steely grays now remained, hollowing in crimson for night to complete this scene.

Much seclusion existed here, with the tall stone wall severing the castle grounds from the surrounding village. The cool swiftness of the dark dispersed the tourists and locals back out the brown gate and into the narrow village streets in search of warmer surroundings. There were stragglers who wandered, aimlessly, taking a final picture, simply lost to the measurements of time, captive to this forested space of myth, and perhaps, peace.

A green light blinked on Howie's watch. "Castle's officially closed." He guided Mike and Tom, passing the cottage on their right, with its simple sign stating, '*The Tea House of Queen Marie*'. Alone, it sat neatly within its nook beside the pond. Continuing on to the left, they pressed up the steep slope for the castle wall. Close now, the face of the castle glared down, gripped upon the cliff's rocks that protruded tall and fang-like. The three of them reached the summit, beside the tree there. Great and proud, it wasn't a hardwood, but a pine. Howie's eyes scanned up the castle's wall. A second-floor window awaited.

"Why that one?" Mike asked.

"Second-floor, no alarms," Howie answered.

Tom patted Mike on the back. "No one's ever been crazy

enough to try to climb it."

Using a grappling gun of his own design, Howie shot a bolt linked to a cable to the wooden overhang above the window. Then, as quickly, he secured a bolt to the rocky ground at their feet. Linking the cable's end through the bolt, he slid on his gloves and climbed swiftly.

From the ground, Tom and Mike watched as he snapped on a respirator over his head and carefully held an aerosol can as far away as possible. Thoroughly soaking the caulking around the double-pane window, he then popped the glass out and gently set it on a broad branch of the towering pine beside him. Now free to enter, he squeezed through. Tom and Mike climbed as fast as they could, joining him.

Inside, Howie brought up the castle's layout on his phone. "Watch your head. Ceiling's entirely uneven." By the light of his phone, he led down the spiraling stairs and narrow passages of stone and wood, racing ever-lower through the castle's center. Past the roped off rooms and museum exhibits, they ran until reaching the final staircase's end. Here, they faced a very old door of maple with a sign proclaiming, 'No Access'. Howie took hold of the door's thick iron padlock. Not secure, it fell off, clunking to the floor.

"Think they—that Camorra and her unlocked it?" Tom asked. "That they beat us here?"

"Maybe," Howie answered, considering the complications either way. He pushed and the door slowly creaked open, revealing a large and oddly shaped room. Now safe to do so, away from any windows, they turned on their flashlights. The space was cramped with stacks and piles of dusty furniture.

"Lowest point of the castle on any known map," Howie said. "Mike, what'd you find with that memoir of Queen Marie's?"

"Actually," Mike said, "it's her daughter, Princess Ileana. Did find one reference to a room that could indicate a basement of some kind, despite this place being upon solid rock. Reference wasn't much... 'Underfoot with the vines'."

"Vines as in tree roots?" asked Tom.

"If you'd let me finish, Tom," Mike said. "When Romania was pinned between the Russians and the Germans during World War Two, Princess Ileana worked for the Red Cross. She had a stash room beneath the castle for supplies, so that both the Russians and the Germans wouldn't simply loot the Red Cross supplies all for themselves."

"Safe to assume," asked Howie, "being a secret room, the memoir didn't give a map pinpointing its location?"

"Safe to say," answered Mike. "Wish there *was* an 'X'."

Just as he'd said so, a rat of ungodly proportions bolted from behind a stack of wooden chairs to the center of the room. There, it stood on its disturbingly large back legs. It twitched its nose fiercely, released something between a squeak and a piercing snarl, then dropped to all fours. Apparently satisfied with its own spectacle, it sauntered to the largest piece of furniture, a truly antique armoire sitting not flush, but within a few inches along one of the uneven walls of stone.

"Jesus," Tom said.

Their beams aligned on the rat, who wedged its nose between the wall and back of the armoire. Stuffing its opossum-sized body behind the armoire, it appeared to disappear. They ventured closer.

Howie held his flashlight on the darkness. "Tom, crouch down and see where that fella went."

"The hell I am."

"Over here," Mike said from the other side of the armoire.

Shedding his backpack, Howie had just enough space to pass, leading through into the arched doorway there. His flashlight beam found the end of the surprisingly short passageway fifteen feet beyond. They stopped at the passageway's end, facing the cold rock wall. A clink came from behind them. They turned. Camorra stood there, with Ingrid, quite seemingly of her own accord, by his side.

Camorra flipped on his flashlight in Howie's face. "Let's go."

A Place of Secrets

*S*eeing Ingrid was free of harm, a much-delayed relief spread over Howie. Catching her eyes, it was something neither need express in words. They felt it. And that was enough.

"Where?" he asked Camorra.

Camorra nodded to the slightest of a bend along the wall. Veiled in shadow, the passageway did endure. United as five in their collectively divided way once more, Howie led through the dark corridor.

Coldness immediately lurched at their skin. This damp frigidness was old, permanent and perpetual. Goosebumps drew out upon their bodies by primal wonder adrift within this air most chilling.

Flashlight beams struck the door before them. Terribly decomposed, it soggily clung, limply so by a single hinge. By nothing more than a nudge, Howie brought it its release, collapsing with a mushy shudder at their feet.

Entering the small room, what this place was, had been, was obvious. Some of the wine racks, bolted to the rock walls, still held. Most had tipped onto each other, splintered and sunken with rot. A few of the wine barrels, within various stages of decay, remained.

"Underfoot with the *vines*," Tom said.

"What is it you know?" Camorra demanded.

"From my understanding," said Mike, "the royal family,

they didn't drink alcohol. None of them did. See, they had a rare blood disease, preventing them from it."

A noise came from one of the collapsed racks along the wall.

Howie's flashlight illuminated the rat there in its nest. "Your friend, Tom."

They drew closer. The rat lazily lifted one eyelid and stretched. Rising its swelled body, it strutted back down the passageway for the room rich in dust and abandoned furniture. Passing Tom, it bared its teeth, crooked and yellow, hissing as it went.

Tearing away the rotted wood, Camorra exposed the shelf, unlike the others, of metal built into the wall. Pressing his ear, he could hear the drip of water from... *behind*. Hastily searching the wine cellar, they looked for a lever of any kind.

Going to the only thing still fully intact, Ingrid tried to move the barrel against the far wall. Not lifting from the floor, but titling on end, it triggered a mechanism unseen. With a click, the metal shelf slid out along the wall.

Ten-foot by ten-foot or so with walls of rough rock, the space beyond was modest. With paint peeling, the Red Cross symbol on the crate there was distinct. The small and splintering table against the wall had but one chair for companion. Maps of Bran, of Brasov, and of Romania hung on the coarse rock. Before the table, as well, hung a black-and-white photo of Princess Ileana's mother, Queen Marie.

Upon the table, withered and wrinkled, laid an invoice for medical supplies, handwritten, elegant and faded. Ingrid stood where she, the unsung princess, hero of Romania, savior of her people, would have stood. There was an unspoken sadness here. It wrapped around her bones, inside her heart, in her mind.

Wanting to settle into the chair, she dared not. It'd surely collapse. Then, with her eyes adrift, she spotted it. How had she not seen it first, but last, she couldn't explain. She pointed, bringing their eyes to the little triangular-shaped keyhole in the seamless slab of rock directly above the queen's photo. Beside this, a 'question mark' had been carved.

Ingrid ran her fingertip along the question mark, branded wonderingly into the rock. *If only you'd known, sweet Princess.* She smiled softly. *We each hold our secrets. Our acts, both selfless and selfish...*

Without looking, she held her hand out behind her. Camorra removed the compass piece from his pocket, setting it on her palm. Smoothly, she sank its tip into the triangular keyhole, releasing a long-lasting pressure binding this unseen doorway before them. Seams appeared on the rock's seamless face, forming a perfect triangle of six feet tall. A hissing of air came next as the section drifted in floating fashion inward eight inches before coming to a silent stop.

Unlocking the compass piece, she placed it into her own pocket. Peering in, she shined her flashlight. Far beyond anything she'd witnessed before, it was... *Angelic... If* heaven were heaven. The overwhelming beauty of what laid before her wasn't the final chamber. But they were close. *Very close...*

Enchantment

*S*he stole a few more seconds for herself before allowing the others a view. There was a sloping path. It was something not quite a staircase, not quite a ramp, with its small and slender steps smoothly tapered. Their flashlight beams danced across its faceted crystal surface. The light fed the crystal, igniting pastel flames to flow as smoke within its glassy skin. This liquidly fire, shades for the lightest of sunrises, spread as fireflies riding wisps of airless wind.

Where the crystal path ended twenty feet down, there was a different light. Opening into a tremendous subterranean cavity, it was an amazement of polychromasia, a charismatic symphony of illumination from a place churning of life, entirely free of the world above. Things there, plants or plant-like, glowed lush in hues foreign to any flora they knew. Of mellow iridescences, whispering currents, what it was, was harmony, wholly undisturbed.

Each step they made upon the path of crystal, toward this sea of meadowed forest, wrapped within its gully of prismatic enchantment, the pastel fire of the crystal skin rippled out and down, all around. At the bottom, their boots left the crystal, finding the kaleidoscope of colliding color, a blanketing tapestry of thick moss. Affectionately, it tugged at their feet, sucking them a few inches down to the bedrock, firm and uneven.

One by one, their flashlights clicked off, not needing them, for the natural light of the life encompassing them was as the sun. With the touch of their bodies, the various vegetation shifted in pinks, reds, bled to burgundies, plums, purples, then softened to lilacs. There were ribbons of rich blue that laid veinlike, four or more inches across, crisscrossing the meadow, possibly roots, pulsing with a misty radiance, as they carefully crossed over these strangely beautiful things. And if ferns could be opal-like, then there were hundreds, perhaps more than that even, swaying in uneven heights, shyly ricocheting their essence of luminescence throughout this meadow without sky.

Waterfalls, slim and dribbling, some vast and hearty, some squat and wide, as that of great tree trunks, and others, healthy and weaving, each came to connect through pools linked by sleek streams. The air was the purest their lungs had tasted. Then there were the flowers. The flowers, throughout, everywhere, were not like any species they'd seen. They had a single petal, fused with complex complexions and tones, from virgin snow to royal purple, gleaming orange and silken cream. Blades jutting from their centers sparkled hypnotically with spiraling vapor. Bringing them to wrinkle their noses, it seemed as pollen. But who could truly know of such things.

There were things, other things beneath the water. Spirits afire, they shined, swimming. Joining Ingrid, Howie crouched at the pool clearer than any he thought possible. Peeling up his sleeve, he plunged his arm in, not deep. With his skin now touching them, they became still, as frozen flames of pearl. Beginning to draw one from the pool, she stopped him.

Her hand set on his, pushing his arm down, returning this thing to its rightful place. "Leave it be."

Letting go the creature, being, or maybe something more, it was as it'd been, and darted away.

"Over here," Camorra ordered, severing their shared moment of solitude.

Making their way down to the base of what could have

been the tallest of the waterfalls, the others waited for them at a large, though shallow pool. Its symmetry was not possible to occur in nature. For, precise and sharp, it was a triangle, with tip pointed toward the falling water.

Great and pale white rocks protruded halfway up the waterfall, stabbing through, as though the fangs of some monstrous beast now extinct or of myth. These rocks split the water, dividing its path all the way down to the pool. Here were twin arched doors framed by the split streams of the water. These streams continued, cascading, joining as one once more, flowing into the pool coolly as a liquid carpet, coursing and pure.

Together, the doors spanned about twenty feet. Emblazoned upon them was the Praesidio Autem Veritas, with the narrow seam between each dividing perfectly down the symbol's center. Inlaid within the dual arches above the doors was the L' Entita's encoded language crafted from their metal of mystery. A large ring, two feet across, hung from each door. These rings, yellow, shimmered, despite resting in shadow. They could only be of gold.

"As above so below," Ingrid stated clearly, translating the markings.

She nodded to Howie, then took a step forward, positioning herself squarely in front of the gold ring on the left door. He took his place before the right door, seeing the triangular keyhole awaiting him. She removed the compass piece from her pocket. Releasing the capstone from it, she passed it to him. She held out the compass piece, and he, the capstone.

Nodding once more, she said, "Now."

In tandem, they sank their keys into their respective locks. Together, they turned them clockwise. Then, following her lead, he brought his hand to the ring of gold hanging at his door.

"Now," she repeated.

Pushing upon them, firmly so, these far from normal doors

swung inward at the speed of any normal door. Now facing them was what they'd sought, fought, and searched for across the globe, a journey that'd tested their beings, encircling their hearts, to forever change their souls—harshly, Camorra shoved past them, going through.

Howie's eyes met Mike's. Mike's met Tom's. And Ingrid saw the promise, a pact these three had made in her absence... Forged by a masculine affinity for violence, a pledge to deny Camorra closure to his mission. In this moment, she too recognized the certain doom it would bring them *all*. For Camorra's will was not something that *could* be stopped. Being the last of his kind, as she was hers, she knew this truth. If his deviousness were to be deviated, it'd be her sacrifice alone.

With a heavy breath, she entered....

The Romanian Chamber

*T*he chamber was about that of the Pantheon. And like the Pantheon, circular, this too had a great dome for a ceiling. The air was rich, swollen with aromas of the neighboring meadow. Its walls, floor, and ceiling blended together, glossy and black.

All surfaces were smooth and there was but one object to be seen. For the first time on their quest, there wasn't a table at the center. There was a pulpit. It was in size and form as any to be found in the confines of a church. However, not likely to be found in church, this was fashioned from a single shard of clearest crystal.

Ingrid unlocked the keys from the doors, keeping the capstone for herself and slipping Howie the compass piece. While their team pulled to the center, focusing upon the pulpit's simple elegance, clean, without markings, the chamber's doors closed silently, unnoticed. Placing her hand on the surface, a golden halo radiated from the pulpit, swallowing it and her in this aura of heavenly light. Without a how or why, it repelled the others, pressing them back. Then it grew, becoming bubble-like.

"Howie," she said, offering her hand.

Taking it, he stepped toward the golden bubble. As though accepting him because she'd willed it so, he found himself within. He did as she, setting his hand along the pulpit.

A softest of hums began flowing into them from the

crystal's lukewarm surface. They aligned their keys to their respective keyholes, awaiting them on the pulpit's face. As one, they locked in their keys. The hum deepened, bleeding fiercely, lowly into them. It felt natural, meant to be. There was a beguiling rhythm in it, seductively unifying it to them, and they to each other.

Their senses became sharper. Their tiredness erased. Anxiety of the unknown was no more. A knowing settled in. It echoed through them, not in words, but in feeling that it'd be okay. This song of vibration awoke something deeper, gleaming in dreams from its endless slumber from somewhere within their DNA.

A slot opened on the pulpit's crystal face. An object of twelve inches slid out, rising up. She took hold of this thing, glossy and black as that of the chamber. It was a cross. There was a slender point at its top where it sleekly ended as such. At its center was an indentation. And within was the pattern of a thumbprint.

Setting her thumb inside, it fit exact... *Perfect.* Puncturing her skin on the cross's point, she returned her thumb to the indentation, letting her blood coat over the thumbprint pattern. Inserting the cross back in its slot, it descended into the pulpit.

All at once, the vast dome overhead became as a planetarium. Crystals, alight as stars, drew out along its black surface. Glittering, there they rested at various depths and scales, a precise recreation of the night sky.

At the dome's center, a beam of gilded light birthed forth. Extending straight down, it was a crystal shard, slender and translucent. It came to meet the bubble encapsulating Ingrid and Howie, piercing it. The bubble popped in a most congenial way, gradually melting away.

An apple-sized droplet aglow dripped from the shard's tip, now hanging over them and the pulpit. Wetly, it expanded to that of a globe. Not slowly and not swiftly, this ball of liquified light solidified. Without warning, it spread dramatically, rapidly growing in size, immersing the entire chamber.

The five of them, inside, watched in awe as all surfaces came to be as the night sky, flooding the space around them with these stars of crystal. There were no more walls, ceiling, or floor. They were as though afloat in this holographic sea of celestial wonder. What was up and what was down no longer was certain. In seeming of infinite depth, the seamless skin of the chamber pulsed with every star known and unknown, every body of cosmic thing.

A colossus of a sun manifested directly before their faces. Its liquid inferno reflected in their eyes as its convex field of swirling gas gurgled and glowed. Thick magma-like bubbles swelled, pushing from its churning surface, popping and bursting into hissing plasma ablaze. Snarling flames danced, stretching into solar flares, reaching for them.

Its power amongst the void of darkness was truly divine. Powerless to its will, they could only gaze upon this terrifically terrifying spherical hell. The utter absence of its heat was the only thing affording them from seeking a retreat. Though, they still had yet to realize they were locked in, with the chamber's doors sealed as stone within stone.

Holes of blackest black tore upon the sun's surface. They contorted, each morphing into individual symbols. As they developed, these symbols formed something larger than themselves, something which connected one to the next. Completing, what now stood superimposed against the towering surface of the sun was the Cross of the Zodiac.

The sun deflated, shrinking smaller than this symbol. Fading through, it came to sit at the center of the Zodiac, aligned within the symbol's crosshairs. Locked there as a prisoner, it rotated around and around, brightly burning. Above, across the star-kissed palette of darkness, drawn by an invisible finger, appeared a message blazing in fiery crimson, 'As Above So Below'.

Unrealized to her, her thumb continued to bleed, feeding the pulpit's crystal surface. Hungrily, it absorbed her blood, quietly devouring her life force. As it drank her DNA, it spread as thin veins, deeply into the pulpit of crystal.

She, as they, watched the sun held hostage unto the Cross of the Zodiac, and wondered what her ancestors' endgame truly was. *One of hellfire? Or redemption...*

Written by the Stars

*F*rom the pulpit started a resonance unlike any they'd heard before. It rumbled low and weightless as tender whiffs through a trombone. The pulpit of crystal greedily drained her blood, accessing humanity's earliest memories. A sprawling three-dimensional projection blossomed.

Before them, a double helix of her DNA Illuminated in ice-blue, idly spun, towering imposingly. At rushing speed, they zoomed in on a single point of this most elegant lattice of existence. An outline of Africa took form. Opening into a doorway, the starry sky of night framed within beckoned.

Ingrid stepped toward it, letting it envelop her. The others followed. Sand was beneath their feet and firelight softened the darkness. As invisible witnesses, searchers of truth, their team of five encircled the modest fire, joining what appeared to be the earliest of humans. One of these, a leader she seemed, spoke in words they could not know.

They sat below the night sky. They watched as she, this teller of stories, pointed her hand to the darkness above. Her finger painted a picture in rich cerise on this black canvas, linking one star to the next.

A multitude of fires populated across the ancient land cast in shadow. Each, with their own storyteller, drew in this lushest of red, using the sky of night, the greatest of pages, to write their stories for all forever to see. Countless constellations filled this infinite palette until its inkiness softened with a sea of firelight from below, and an interlocking collage of crimson from above.

Shadows fashioned from the firelight hypnotically danced across Ingrid's face, eyes, and mind. She rose, turning to the horizon. There, the Pyramids of Giza came to be. Encased in their white granite, crowned with capstones of purest gold, now told their team of five the present time was thousands of years from long past.

Behind the pyramids arose a silvery moon, enormous and timeless. With it, the eternal whisper of the desert wind, hoarsely laced with sand, began. It lapped at their faces, coarsely so. Swiftly, with their first step, they found themselves at the base of the Great Pyramid.

It was both foreign and familiar standing there, having known this monument of the ages in how it'd come to be, and now seeing it in how it'd been. As the wind blew, swirling, circling them with building speed, a realization set in. This hand, unseen, had indeed brought them full circle.

Time flowed faster. The moon cycled over the sky, sinking from view into the dunes. With the death of darkness, the sun came to rise, born again, baptizing the earth with life most eternal. And below the plateau, within the shadows of the pyramids, was the bustling metropolis of ancient Giza.

Voices came from behind them. They pivoted to see an old man in whitest linen, remarkably tall, and remarkably thin. As though a flock, a group of children were with him. Ingrid closed her eyes, shifting all words revealed in this place to those of English.

"I am Revelare," he said to the children.

"Privileged class's class time," Tom said.

"With their fine clothes and jewelry," said Mike, "yeah, these are little ones of the elite."

Revelare turned to the sky. The passing of the hours were as seconds. Gradients of blushing coral rippled ripely to purples, flirting with the birth of twilight. The sun was no more, and the moon returned.

Revelare's arm stretched for the dark heavens. He aligned a long and bony finger with the moon. Using his finger, he drew upon it. The moon's silvery face transitioned to a humanoid figure.

Completing its anthropomorphic transformation, the moon self-importantly stood in the sky. Cloaked brightly in red, with the face of a jackal and the brawny physique of a man, he emanated power and mystery. His eyes were sharp, his foxlike ears alert, and his short though sharp claws were at his ready. His wolfish teeth shined silvery as that of the moon's surface. He held a great and slender scepter of the same silver, agleam. Etched across the scepter was the distinct shape of a 'D'. And there was no doubt this creature commanded all which touched the dark.

"Say hello to Set," Mike said. "The Egyptian god of darkness. Among other things."

Revelare drew with his finger, leading Set over the canvas of night. Following the very same path the moon had taken across the sky, Set marched along the stars, toward the east, to the gray line there on the horizon marking the pending sunrise. With dawn igniting the east, Set raised his silvery scepter. With it, he took aim at the light that now bled away the darkness. The sun awoke from its nightly death, entombed by the dark no more.

"Rising in the east, with his crown of thorns, was he who brought life eternal," said Revelare to his students.

Set readied his scepter. Its end began to glow red. From it, long and slender tines extended out, transforming into something as a pitchfork. His foxlike eyes, inflamed by the light, narrowed at the glory of the rising run. His muscle-bound arm tensed, contracting, posed on the cusp of launching his scepter. Then, his eyes too turned red. His sharply pointed tail flicked out from beneath his crimson cloak.

"Correct me if I'm wrong, Mike," Howie said, "but the

Egyptians equated red with evil, right?"

"Correct," answered Mike.

The sun, with its rays upon its brow, brilliantly crowning as thorns along this golden halo, faced off with Set. Its fiery thorns of flame burned away what little darkness remained. Set thrust his scepter into the sun, piercing its side as though a spear.

The scepter sank, its tip penetrating, tearing deep inside, gushing blood. As they gazed upon this ever-reoccurring and epic battle between light and darkness, the sun of the heavens lording over all, birthed forth into a man. With his falcon-head, he stood now just as regal as his villainous enemy, Set.

"Horus," said Ingrid.

Mike nodded. "Quite right, Ingrid."

Horus, taut with muscle, was of equal proportions to his red-cloaked adversary. The lower half of his body was wrapped in a robe of fierce royal purple. Around his head was a sun disc, that iconic and ancient symbol of the rising sun. And upon his head, he wore a bronze crown of thorns. He wielded a scepter identical to Set's. Though, instead of emblazoned with a 'D', this one had across it, 'O'.

In one cruelly swift motion, Horus plunged his scepter into Set's heart. Set fell from his high and proud perch in the heavens. As he plummeted toward earth, Horus shot flames through his crown of thorns, igniting Set. Illuminated as the sole and soulless morning star, he burned across the sky, falling.

Revelare, with his finger, traced the arching trajectory toward the horizon. "The morning star was swallowed deeply into the earth, to its center filled with fire." Revelare then drew upon the sky a large and burning 'O'.

"Anyone know that hieroglyph?" asked Mike, his eyes shifting to Howie, Ingrid, Tom, then even to Camorra.

It came to Howie, recalling from some class lecture long ago. "The first hieroglyph in the name of Horus is 'O'.

"Yep, kid, with Horus being the Egyptian god of the sun

here before us," Mike said. "Ingrid, please, if you will."

And willing it, Ingrid closed her eyes, bringing the 'O' hieroglyph of ancient Egypt, burning in the morning sky upon the palette of dawn, to morph. It became a single word, inflamed in purple most royal, 'Good'.

"Good work, Ingrid," said Mike, "as 'good' is the literal English translation for Horus."

Ingrid's eyes drew closed. A large 'D', richly red, appeared in the sky. After a moment, it shifted to 'Evil', aflame, directly beside 'Good'.

Mike glanced at Howie.

"The first hieroglyph in Set's name is 'D'," said Howie.

"And, 'Evil' is the literal translation of Set's name from ancient Egyptian into English," Mike said.

Unexpectedly so, Camorra reached up at the sky. Stretching his finger to the heavens, he wiped away an 'O' in 'Good'. Then, he added a 'D' in front of 'Evil'.

Burning before them now in the sky....

God
Devil

Mike grinned at Camorra. "Very... *good*, Camorra. Devilishly so. And, for those who don't know, thus, the origins of where these two concepts, good, god, evil, devil, came from."

In the background, as Revelare continued to share these same secrets of the cosmos reserved for his young pupils, the elite class, the passage of time accelerated. The sky of day gave way to darkness. Set broke free from the hell from which he'd been banished. Ascending from his fiery tomb, he rode a chariot of flame across the dark heavens.

He pressed back Horus toward the west. Surrounding him in shadow, he pushed Horus deeper down, crushing him into the horizon. Standing over his enemy, Set raised his scepter, electrified in red. Its tines slid out, returning to its pitchfork form. He struck Horus through the heart. Horus collapsed, consumed by the dunes at the line of the horizon, becoming no more.

Stars of night gleamed. Revelare pointed to the east, toward the thousands of lights of flame and torch and fire from the metropolis of Giza. His finger rested upon a most impoverished place, the poorest section of the city. A great shard of light stretched down from the brightest star in the sky, from the star of the east. Radiating brilliantly, the beam met the spot where his finger aimed.

Ingrid stepped forward. Suddenly, they all were brought to the modest location within the city. Together, they stood before a doorstep illuminated by this brightest star above.

Surely, it was humble, for it was a stable....

As Only a Mother Could

*T*wilight cut by the starlight which shined upon this poorest of streets, had only the shadows to pass along its barren path. Quietly, they followed Revelare and his students into the stable. It was not a small space, as one may picture a stable to be, but as a stable would be in the time and place that it was.

And like any stable of this time, it was square, with a generous and open courtyard at its center. Its coarse wooden walls which formed individual stalls held sheep, pigs, and horses. There was one even with a lone plump little donkey, shiny and gray.

The brightest star, the star in the east, pierced down its single beam, striking the heart of the open courtyard. Bathed in its light was the central feeding trough, or as one would call it in contemporary terms, a manger. What it contained, they could not see.

But now in their sight stepped a creature of tremendous beauty. She was equally intimidating and gentle. Flawless, she was a stunning Egyptian woman, with features fit for a goddess. Moving into the starlight, to the manger, the thing which transcended her from human to perhaps an actual goddess were her angelic wings.

With a span of eight or more feet, they were perfect in shape, broad of feathers, full and long. Unlike the plain white of angels' wings, hers sequenced in rows of rich color. From the top layer along her shoulders, they began in teal, and the layer beneath in turquoise, then aqua, with the last layer holding the most vivid shade of celeste.

She watched down on her child they were certain was there, though still could not gain sight of. Her gaze held a complexity and simplicity as only a mother could. Alongside her, Revelare and his students remained unnoticed, apparently as invisible as their team of five were in this place. With his hand directed at the brightest star, Revelare painted in gold upon the canvas of night. Seamlessly translating by Ingrid's will....

Three Thousand B.C., December Twenty Fifth

Camorra pushed past everyone, peering into the manger. They ventured close. Nestled there within, in traditional Egyptian swaddling clothes, was a newborn. Complete with sun disk framing his little falcon-shaped head, rested baby Horus.

Mike set his hands against the edge of the manger crafted of sandalwood. "The lady in wings here is Isis. The virgin mother of Horus."

Tom stuck his finger in at the baby Horus.

Howie swatted it away. "No poking at the sun god."

There was a noise from just outside the stable. Wings folding back, eyes alert, Isis quickly went to the door. There, three men, each with skin of a unique shade, awaited. Their clothes and jewelry silently proclaimed both their status and wealth.

They held up their offerings. Seeing their sincerity, Isis granted them passage within. One at a time, they laid their gifts before the manger.

The first opened a bag made from silk, releasing the rich and rare scent of frankincense. The next unrolled a sheepskin, revealing a fist-sized ball of gold. The final man placed a jar filled with dark and uneven lumps.

"What's that?" asked Tom. "Looks like goat droppings."

"Myrrh," answered Mike. "And, yeah, that's how it looks."

Tom frowned. "What exactly does one do with myrrh?"

"Embalming oil," said Camorra, quite bluntly.

Mike nodded. "Key ingredient in the Egyptian's mummification process."

"That's disturbing to give a baby," Tom said, reaching for the jar.

Howie stopped him. "Questions never asked in Sunday school."

Ingrid smiled, admiring Tom's protectiveness. "You're right, Tom, it would be for a human baby, but for the baby Horus, an Egyptian sun god, Egyptian embalming oil was just the thing he used to vanquish his enemies." She slid her finger across her throat, as though slicing.

"Don't think I want to know," Tom said.

Mike leaned over the manger, watching the newborn Horus. "It's true, but mummies weren't the only thing myrrh was used for. It was also the centerpiece to the Egyptian's ritual of the Seven Sacraments of the Sun."

"Like the Catholic's seven sacraments?" asked Tom.

"*Quite* like," Mike said. "Though, the Egyptians carried out their ritual once a week, every week, in reverence to their sun god, Horus, their savior, born of a virgin."

"The real kicker though," said Howie, "the best part, the day on which they did so, they called it *Sun*-day. 3000 B.C."

Tom joined beside Mike, studying this infant, this baby Horus. He was a god, yes, but he still appeared helpless... Deity or not.

"Don't worry," Ingrid told him. "Horus turns out alright. *All things* considered..."

Isis approached. They moved back, not needing to, but feeling it the right thing, the honest thing to do. They were in her space and place, after all. In simple and satisfied silence, they observed this original nativity. Isis spread her wings, shielding this baby within the manger as an angel would.... *As only a mother could...*

The Baptist

*T*hey followed Revelare and his students out of the stable. Sunlight hit them, finding themselves on the soft shore of the Nile. Knee-deep within the river stood a man crudely clothed in animal skins. His eyes held something wild, something impassioned, with purpose. A long line of commoners, the working-class of Egypt, awaited him.

"I, Anup the Baptist," he said, "baptize you today with water. But the one of whom I speak will baptize with the spirit."

Tom glanced at Howie.

"Answers never given in Sunday school," said Howie.

Mike shrugged. "All this is in any book on Egyptian mythology. A library card away..."

The next in line was an elderly woman, weathered deeply by the hardships of poverty. Anup lowered her into the water, to its saving grace she believed it to be.

Returning her to the surface, Anup looked upon her tenderly. "Go and be at peace with all. Welcome struggle. It cleanses us. I am your servant. And you are life's."

"Give you one guess what 'Anup' translated into English is," said Mike.

"John," Ingrid answered. "And Anup loses his head."

"That what you'd call topography?" asked Tom.

"That's what I'd call topography," answered Mike.

The tall grass along the riverbank parted, revealing Horus, fully grown.

Anup held out both arms, welcoming him. "This is the one I speak of. He has arrived among us. Mark this day within your heads and on your hearts."

Revelare wrote on the waters of the Nile, painting words in gold.

Horus, upon his thirtieth year, began his ministry

"Who am I to baptize you?" Anup asked. "It is you who should baptize me."

Revelare continued to write across the water.

Horus went on to perform a multitude of miracles, gaining   a great following

The Nile parted, exposing a doorway of liquid and light....

Universal

*I*mmersing themselves, they passed into a place of dry earth and rock. Grand and soaring columns were all around. Revelare guided through this extensive complex. Entering gates of nearly forty feet high, they found Horus. He had companions, simply dressed, and by their count, twelve in number.

"Let me guess," said Tom, "Horus's twelve disciples."

"Astute you are," said Howie. "Where are we anyway?"

Mike studied the expansive columns. "I'd say... Thebes."

"Luxor then," Ingrid said.

"What would become it, yeah," Mike answered. "Predates even the pyramids."

Camorra brushed past, following Horus. In the distance, they could hear the cheers of the people of this city welcoming Horus and his twelve disciples. Catching up, they came to the street lined with the working-class citizens of Thebes. Palm branches, vibrant and green, covered this path.

Quite quickly, it brought them to a mount, and upon it sat the famous temple of Thebes. Stretching exactly sixty feet into the blue sky, it towered over all things. Hieroglyphs, each six feet tall, covered the front of the temple. And centered before the temple was a golden ankh standing two stories high.

Mike pointed to the temple. "Ingrid, if you would. Please."

Not closing her eyes, but keeping her gaze deep and intensely so upon the temple's face, she willed its giant hieroglyphs into English. Spanning the nearly sixty feet of the temple from top to bottom, came to be the Ten Commandments. As Revelare and Horus dually shared these archaic words of universal wisdom with their students and disciples, their team of five pulled closer.

The sun was bright, and Ingrid closed her eyes, bringing the commandments to illuminate vividly in gold. Tom sighed.

Mike patted him on the back. "Come now, religion is but the recycling of mythologies. Howie?"

Howie drew his eyes away from Camorra in the distance, seated quite peacefully, cross-legged, amongst Horus and his disciples. "Oh. Yeah. The... Egyptian's *Book of the Dead*, their equivalent to the Bible, spelled out the Ten Commandments thousands of years before the Old Testament was written."

"*Book of the Dead?*" asked Tom.

"Actually," said Ingrid, "the title's direct translation is, *Book of Emerging Forth into the Light*. In ancient Egyptian, that carries the exact equivalent to, Sun Book, or, as we in contemporary times know it to be called, the Bible. So, Tom, yes, the Egyptian's holy book of long ago has the very same name as the Bible has come to have. Less than coincidently."

"And interestingly," Mike said, "the Vatican has virtually every original copy in existence, locked away in their secure vault, far from inquisitive eyes."

"And the temple," Tom pressed.

"Still stands to this day, I mean, present day—you know what I mean," said Mike. "As well, do these very hieroglyphs here, listing the Ten Commandments far predating Christianity."

Howie wandered to the golden ankh. Ingrid, then the others, joined him.

He rested a hand on its gleaming and warm surface. "Since it's staring us in the face, this is actually where the word 'Catholic' derives from."

"Ankh?" Ingrid asked.

"Yeah," he said. "Catholic, from the Greek 'Katholikos', comes directly from the Egyptian word 'ankh'. Meaning, universal, rebirth, and life eternal."

"Also," said Mike, "the ankh itself was the original symbol to depict Horus." He took Ingrid's hand, guiding her touch along it. "How the ankh there looks, well, as a cross with a circle, or head positioned at its top. It's literally Horus upon the cross, when he was crucified."

"The Egyptians practiced crucifixion?" asked Tom.

"Where do you think the Romans picked it up from," answered Mike. "Back to the ankh though. See, in how it's formed by a composite of two hieroglyphs. The top of the symbol, being the circle or 'O' shape, was the Egyptian's most fundamental symbol for the sun. And the cross symbol itself, was, well, the way in which the god sun, Horus, was killed, before he was resurrected."

Chaos abruptly broke out at the temple's entrance. They turned, seeing Horus striking down three men at a booth there, throwing them to the ground of tightly fitted stone. Coins flew, clattering in every direction.

"Well," said Tom, "can always count on the tax collectors to make an appearance."

Camorra positioned himself into the center of it all, savoring the scene of combat, as guards now rushed Horus, drawing their blades. Horus struck them down as well. Realizing what he'd done, he fled. And Revelare, gathering his young students, wrote upon the temple wall in fierce crimson....

Horus, the voice for the people, became feared by the oppressors of the people

The sun fell, plummeting from the sky, sending dusk's rapid descension onto them. The moon rose. Revelare touched his thumb to it, pressing hard. The moon, full and swelled, bled, eclipsing its own silvery glow, becoming as blood....

Iscariot Judas

*T*he temple faded away. Dusk became night. There was a new moon, a crescent, bright and pale. With grass beneath their feet and song birds hidden along distant trees, they joined Revelare and his students in a courtyard. Horus, with his disciples, stood at the courtyard's center, a garden aglow in the moonlight. Revelare drew gilded words on the night.

Typhon, one of Horus's own disciples, brought betrayal

"Let me guess what Typhon translates to," Tom said.

"Actually," said Mike, "it's not Judas."

"It's Iscariot," Ingrid said. "Literal translation for which is 'traitor'."

"Clever girl," said Mike.

"Grandfather, in fact, had a library card. A well-used one." One of the disciples placed a kiss on Horus's cheek. The courtyard flooded with soldiers, seizing Horus. Beneath the silvery moon, Revelare wrote onto the sky.

Horus was charged and convicted for blasphemy

A punishment remedied only by crucifixion

The moon bloomed, spreading out, transitioning into a sky of day filled with clouds, grim and gray. Their surroundings shifted, stripping away the courtyard's serenity. The heavy clouds repelled the sun unseen above. Erect, atop the hill now staring dead in front of them, was a cross. Fashioned from splintered beams and yellowed rope, truly, it was a vulgar device devised only for misery. Bound with the same yellowed rope, Horus hung, drained of all life.

Mike averted his eyes. "Now, is where the term 'judas' comes from. "'Judas', in its earliest form, Judacrux, in ancient Egyptian, means—"

"Crucifixion," Camorra stated, coolly, coldly, with his eyes reflecting something personal... Something intimate with this darkest of words... Horus's mother passed by, up the hill. Her great, beautiful wings dragged along the earth most barren as she approached her son's lifeless body. Revelare turned, bringing them all to face the tomb at their backs. Of sallow and pallid rocks, it was not much, just enough to conceal something as unwanted and unsightly as death.

Swiftly, time cycled through three days. With a rumble, an earthquake tumbled away the stone sealing the tomb. Horus, wrapped in snow-white linens, appeared from within. A handful of his disciples now were present. Revelare and his students, and their team of five moved aside. Before his disciples could greet him, Horus smiled, briefly bowing, then ascended into the sky of wispy clouds and soft blue—an aftershock split the ground, tearing open the earth beneath them, to an angry whirling, rolling with grinding and crushing stones. They fell, obliterated into this abyss of darkness....

Sun of God

*L*anding hard, though free from harm, they returned to the chamber they possibly never had left. The crystal pulpit pulsated with waves of light, graceful and white. Gliding thinly, rippling across their bodies, it lured them with the ease of the moon pulling the tide.

First Ingrid, then they each placed their palms to the pulpit's silky surface. With the light deepening, these luminous waves folded, wrapping until bending themselves into a single bubble which filled the chamber. In three-dimensional depth and radiance most golden, words listed upon the air, flowing as satin.

Born of a virgin on December twenty-fifth
Star in the East
Twelve disciples
Crucified upon the cross
Dead for three days
After which, arises

This golden text became wetly crimson. A smaller bubble, of eight or ten feet, birthed from the face of the pulpit, dripping up, and off of it. Tethered invisibly, it floated in place, aligning beneath the crimson list.

The bubble misted over with the mystic charm as a great crystal ball, manifesting Horus within. The iconic events of his life played in lush imagery. With the passing of each scene, the corresponding event along the list in crimson highlighted, becoming as gold as it cycled through. Equally as gilded, text came to emblaze above....

Three Thousand B.C. ~ Horus of Egypt

A second droplet, rising upwards from the crystal pulpit, materialized, lifting into the air. It too hung stationary beside Horus's own illuminated sphere. Crowing this bubble, words etched....

Seventeen Hundred B.C. ~ Thulis of Egypt

Thulis, this mythical figure's life events unveiled, syncing perfectly with Horus's own. For, their story was the very same. Coming to be, arching elegantly in open space....

Twelve Hundred B.C. ~ Krishna of India

A third bubble of equal size revealed, centering itself underneath. The images inside, sequencing the tale of Krishna, as well synchronized, matching this savior mythology. As the list bleeding in crimson shined high overhead, cycling these events, another, and another, and another bubble arose.

Faster and faster they came, dramatically populating all around until the chamber no longer could contain anymore. Each adorned with title and date, each more and more recent with their inception into the world, perfectly paralleled one another. A bit dizzied from the spectacle, their team of five could only gaze, mesmerized, as now, there were far more than two thousand solar messiahs.

The borders of these bubbles faded away. The echoed tale they contained, merged, blending to a single sphere as big as the chamber. Only Horus remained. Painted within, at his journey's end, he ascended through the clouds, for that glittering sun in the sky.

Though, his course changed, sending him to drift back to earth. Rapidly, his life reversed, rewinding to his naivety. In his traditional Egyptian swaddling clothes, he rested, innocent, in the manger. Seamlessly, crisply, clearly so, before their very eyes, the baby Horus transitioned into the baby Jesus, the newest addition to this epic line of solar messiahs.

Four B.C. ~ Jesus of Nazareth

In identical fashion to each of the preceding god suns, ever personified, Jesus's life transcribed in impassioned imagery, recycling so in its sphere, circled on itself, forever cycling. Around it went, reaching its fabled end, a star-crossed ending upon the cross. After three days, death escaped him, sending him afloat in the sky, radiantly agleam, as though the sun itself. The light fizzled away.... The veneer, and once magical glow of the bubble went dull, strikingly dull. It was but an empty shell now, no longer hallow. Just... Hollow. And all at once, the bubble popped, resoundingly, undeniably, forever, gone. Into nothingness it absorbed, with the abruptness as nothing more than a cheap illusion.

Filled with darkness once more, the chamber awoke, igniting its countless crystals resting in its glossy skin. At the chamber's center, their team of five awaited, enveloped now by this planetarium of crystal and mystery. Within the eye of the dome, the largest of the crystals extended down. From it, a stream of ghostly light glistened, wraith-like....

You shall know the truth.

And it will set you free...

It shifted from its vaporish form, to no more. Then, more formed....

The truth is...

Context is a Mother

*A*S Above So Below

"Get to it already!" Tom shouted, with only these words aglow in front of them, torturingly tantalizing their resolution.

As if nailed to the star-speckled darkness, the list authored in wet crimson hung. Beneath, a star shined brighter than all the others. Precisely so, it faced east. Illustrious, in pure and lustful white, entwined with a thorny aura of sapphire, fiercely it flared. Beams spread from its center, cutting far and long into the night. Camorra, then Ingrid, then the others turned to Mike.

Who, in turn, turned to Howie. "Believe stars are the one subject you're more familiar with than I, kid."

"Thanks..." Being a searcher of things lost across the Seven Seas, Howie knew well his astronomy. "That's Sirius, that, from earth's vantage point, is brightest."

"And before Sirius was called Sirius," Ingrid said, "it was actually known to all, as the Star of the East. Given, that's the place it points to."

A horizon line took shape before them, richly, holographically, within the chamber's generous expanse. Orion's Belt, where it sat in the sky, ever slightly up and to the right of Sirius, began to glow in red. In a breathtaking blend of blue and purple, dually royal, words ignited upon the canvas of night.

December Twenty-Fourth

With the changing of the day in the sky of night, Orion's Belt lowered by a few degrees and toward Sirius. From their point of view, looking up, this brought the three brightest stars within Orion's Belt into perfect alignment with Sirius. Now in line, these four brightest stars all pointed to the east.

Howie stepped in front of the crystal pulpit, subconsciously doing so, and gestured to Orion's Belt. "Those three brightest in Orion there, they're called the Three Kings."

Ingrid moved beside him, equally so at the chamber's pulpit of crystal. "Going hand in hand, this configuration of stars we just observed, is known as the Precession of the Three Kings." She glanced at Howie. "Grandfather insisted on me knowing all about the constellations."

"But of course he did," Howie said.

'Twenty-Fourth' transitioned in the night sky....

December Twenty-Fifth

Darkness faded to sunrise, erasing the stars from their view. This was true for all, except the four brightest. The Three Kings, following the Star of the East, appeared as if in journey toward the sun. Captive, their team of five witnessed as the sun became the fifth star in this sequence of brightest stars, queuing itself before the others.

"And *this* alignment," said Howie, "only happens once a year. Being, December twenty-fifth."

"The Three Kings followed the Star of the East to the birth of the sun," Tom said.

"Context...," said Mike.

"It's *everything*," Ingrid said.

"And then some," said Howie.

Camorra directed their attention back to the sky. On the pale dawn, another constellation took hold, redly alight. Immaculately geometric, as if crafted by the square of a carpenter, it sat squarely above the sun, while right below the Star of the East.

"Again," Howie said, "that only happens on December twenty-fifth."

"Constellation Virgo," said Mike.

With the Three Kings following close behind, the Star of the East pierced a shard of light into the horizon. There, a stable, angelically illumined. The stable's doors parted, luring them. Accepting, they entered. The virgin, known as Mary, awaited. Sleeping in the manger was the baby Jesus.

"Mike," Howie said, "you're better at articulating, when it comes to the whole evolution of language thing."

"Alright," answered Mike. "But rather simple, really, Virgo in Latin means 'virgin'."

Ingrid rested her hand along the white cloak Mary wore. "And 'virgin', in its initial Latin, directly translates to 'House of Bread'."

"End of summer, harvest time, as it were," said Tom.

"Right," Mike said. "Bringing us full circle, to the base root for the actual word 'Mary'. And, quite interestingly, this is true for *each* of the ancient languages it can translate from... 'Mary', in point of fact, means 'virgin'."

The sky went black. Then, warmly, the chamber's countless crystals awoke, shedding their starlight. Slicing the dark sky, thickly red, appeared, 'M'. Coming to connect to it was a fish of the Christian style, forming the Zodiac sign for Virgo.

"'M' for Mary," Ingrid said. "Thus, how the Virgo the Virgin symbol was... Conceived."

"I'll do you one better," said Mike, smiling slyly. "The original translation for 'House of Bread', in Latin, is Bethlehem."

"Why do you *think* the Vatican speaks in Latin," said Camorra, leading out of the stable.

A time-lapse began, lapping in reverse. In the blend of royal purple and blue, drew text across the night....

December Twenty-Second

With the dawn of a new day, the time-lapse shifted in

direction, now playing forward as time normally would. And upon this day of December twenty-second, the sun held in place, unmoving. For, despite the flow of the hours passing as seconds, the sun, perched ever low, kissing the horizon, refused to budge. There it remained, as though lashed tightly to something unseen, something yet to be realized....

"So," Howie said, "quite intriguing phenomena during these three final days before reaching the twenty-fifth. For these next three days, the sun doesn't change its perceived position in the sky."

On the palette of night, vividly white, came to gleam a truly unique formation of stars. In the shape of a cross, they appeared, aglitter upon the very place the sun hung. As the time-lapse flowed across the sky, pulling them closer to December twenty-fifth, the sun, as though dead, stayed dead center of this cross-shaped constellation.

Howie jumped a little, feeling Camorra's palm set onto his shoulder, fingers tightening, demanding explanation. Howie wiggled away from his grasp. "This constellation, lady and gentlemen, ever creatively, is called... the Constellation of the Cross. Or, the Crux Constellation."

Completing its cycle of three days, the sky brought dawn. Words of fiery crimson scorched above....

December Twenty-Fifth

After three days upon this cross, the sun arose, ascending into the clouds. As though freed from a spell, or, perhaps, curse, the Constellation of the Cross transitioned from its literal form, formed by stars, into its anthropomorphized form, actualizing into a literal wooden cross, radiating down from the heavens. There it stood, where the horizon ended and the sky began, framed by the light, most overcast, richly thick with swollen clouds, ashen, cold and sullen. Illuminated by the cross, they watched in bewitched silence as the sun slipped from view.

And just as the sun had slipped so smoothly, so did the words from Ingrid's lips. "So it happened, upon the cross, after three days, the Son arose, reborn, ascending to the heavens."

The glow of the cross dimmed. At its center, a pinpoint of light began to grow. Expanding, it evolved into Horus, tied so to the cross. Gazing up at this crucified solar messiah, he too started to change. Upon completion of its metamorphosis, this anthropomorphic metaphor achieved climax. For, there on the cross, was Jesus. And adorning like thorns, was a sun disk crowing his head.

Mike, keeping his eyes on this sight, knew they'd all but reached the tail end of their tale's end. Though, he didn't know, as neither did they, its ending... Just yet. "Tom, remember when you'd asked why Jesus is called Jesus, even though the original translation of his name in the Bible, Yeshua, when converted to English, is Joshua, not Jesus?"

"Yeah...," Tom answered.

Breaking from the enchantment of the cross, Mike turned, facing Tom, facing them all. "In ancient Egyptian, 'Jesus', translates literally to 'Horus'."

"*Three thousand B.C.*," Howie added.

Mike looked to him. "What they don't tell you in Sunday school."

An incredible empathy seized Ingrid, for the deceived... For those who'd believed, told to by well-meaning loved ones, sold to it, enslaved to its servitude, shackling their minds to a lie. And she knew, this understanding, it didn't shackle her to some elevated air, to something superior. Quite the opposite, for a great weight hit her, dragging her down, far down, to a feeling of something inferior.

She pulled in a deep breath, and attempted to appear confident, not for herself, but for them, her team, and now, friends. She understood, and largely so to the DNA coursing through her veins. Her ancestors, the L' Entita, those invisible architects, hadn't just revealed the *how*, the blueprints to this deception. Much more importantly, they'd exposed *why*.

The words flowed, channeling through her. And not that

they weren't from her. Just... they were equally of *them*. The L' Entita's voice collectively echoed out of her blood... "The human subconscious is shown the story every day. With each sunrise and sunset, nature paints it with a brush of many colors on the sky. This eternal dance of darkness and of the light, of providence, how deeply, deeply, it's been ingrained within humanity's watching eye..."

As Above So Below

*T*he cross began its own transformation, with a ring encircling at its midpoint, leaving a cross-haired design of the ancient and Celtic style. Jesus's body faded away, with only his head remaining, framed within these cross hairs. And no longer of wood, the cross appeared as gilded stone.

Against the palette of night, lines of heavenly white light drew out from the cross, forming a vast spoke-like radius. Fashioned before them was a blank template for the Cross of the Zodiac. Aglow, its centerpiece was the face of Jesus.

Drawn with all the beauty and grace of a Renaissance master, each of these twelve empty sections filled in with a disciple of Jesus. Etching golden, their names appeared across their sections, respectively. Spellbound, bound in wonderment, deeply wondering where this was all heading, it hit them head-on.... The names for the twelve disciples of Jesus, every one of them, all at once, morphed, translating to Latin. Then, each, in Latin, translated to ancient Egyptian.

"How'd I ever... *Ever* miss that?" Mike asked, demanding an answer to the unanswerable. "I mean, the line between mythology and astrology is one intertwined, but this is..."

Unable to find their voices, they read the names with a silence most immutable. These no longer were names of individuals. They were the twelve titles for each of the twelve signs of the Zodiac.

"What the hell." Tom shook his head. "I mean, *what the hell?*"

"Yeah...," said Howie. "Not to repeat what we're seeing. But to repeat it, to say it for *our* ears, now that our eyes have seen... Starting in their original Latin form, each one... *All* twelve names of the disciples translate... *Perfectly* so in ancient Egyptian to the precise names of the Zodiac signs."

Tom leaned against the crystal pulpit, with his brain certifiably hurting. "What are the chances of that? Howie, man?"

"Impossibly improbable," Howie answered.

"Oh, no," said Ingrid. "This was destiny. This... was a sure thing."

"Fitting, I guess," Howie said. "Jesus, or whichever solar messiah, take your pick, being the metaphorical sun, to always be surrounded by his twelve disciples, dually representing the twelve signs of the Zodiac, as well the months of the year."

The surface of the Zodiac Cross iced over with a silken film richly reflective. Enticed from within herself, Ingrid set a single fingertip to it. Rippling as liquid glass, the renditions of the twelve disciples bled away. Solidifying in their place were the twelve signs of the Zodiac.

"All that's left," said Ingrid, "is for the sun..." She stepped deeper into this hologram most graphic, and rested her hand along Jesus's brow. With her touch, he ignited. Consumed to flames, he became the sun held at the center of the Zodiac Cross. Complete in its evolution, it appeared as any Cross of the Zodiac they'd ever seen or known.

Breaking away from the projection, she joined beside Howie at the pulpit. Her hand found his. And together, they watched as this Cross of the Zodiac too faded from their view. All that was left was the actual cross. Its golden veneer melted away, leaving the coarse stone of itself beneath. Stripped down to its most basic form, in the ancient style, with the circle at its cross-haired center, this Zodiac Cross was identical to those steepled upon the earliest of churches.

"Jesus H. Christ," Tom said.

Howie sighed. "No wonder the Church is so insistent their followers never learn about astrology."

The cross burst into fire, then was no more, thinly drifting away as a knot of smoke. By a hand invisible, or by *their* hand, hued with a swirl of fierce purple and sensual blue, drew across the shadowy palette of night....

As Above So Below

"I get it now," Ingrid said.

"Believe... We all do," said Camorra, stepping from his quiet place within the dark. "The stories we believe, we conceived by the sky above."

"But...," Tom asked, "how do we—so many, not see the truth of it all?"

"Tom, that's just it," said Mike. "One has to *want* to see. It takes a heart driven by sincerity."

They took a long pause to absorb this realization... This fact, both most convenient and inconvenient.

"Man's own fabled tales have come full circle, encircling us," said Mike. "Reining over us."

"Time for man to hand over the reins to women then," Ingrid said.

"Where did that come from?" Camorra asked. Collectively, they turned to see what he was pointing at.... The place where the entrance to the chamber had been, but no longer was, had been replaced by something different, something grander....

Beyond the Vortex of the Aurora Borealis

*T*he passage from which they'd entered was now on the opposite side of the chamber. In its place was a large and arched double doorway. Camorra led. Ingrid unlocked the compass piece and capstone from the face of the crystal pulpit. Catching up, she joined them.

Howie rested a palm on one of the doors. "Chamber walls must've slowly rotated all the way around, to bring this about."

"What's it made from?" Tom asked.

"Don't know," answered Howie, "but the keyholes are obvious enough."

Ingrid passed Howie the compass piece. "On one... One." And as one, they locked in their keys to the doors before them. Whatever these doors were, began to glow of emerald. Camorra held out his hand. Ingrid removed the capstone and compass piece, and securing the capstone onto the tip of the compass piece, gave them over.

Parting without a sound, the double doors slid away from another, swallowing into the walls to somewhere unseen. Very much seen, the open doorway left no doubt what was contained on the other side. There, was the L' Entita's library of legend. Countless rows and shelves held untold knowledge, records, and documents, lost, now found. The space itself could only be described as hanger-like. Seeing it in its full and flawless form, they knew it to be more than a library. Collectively, it was an unadulterated account of human history. It was... Pure.

Camorra stepped forward. The section of floor around the doorway melted away. To their best account of what it did next, simply, it changed. To what, water. Its state of being, no one, at least, no *human*, had ever seen. Liquid, frozen, and gas, it was all three simultaneously.

Camorra stood at the center of this pool, or pool-like section of but a few inches in depth. Pushing past, Ingrid entered the doorway—an eruption of blending colors shot up, streaming in a broad ribbon, swirling, churning, rising forth from the pool. Utterly and rapturously, it consumed, filling the doorway. Both raw in beauty and power, it was as though a tornado had wrapped itself in the aurora borealis.

Illuminated by its elegance most sheer, and colors, shifting, spiraling, she knew, as though being told by forces unknown, this was not her frontier to enter. Or, at least, she wasn't meant to be first to cross its threshold, to acquire its intimacy. She turned to Camorra.

Seeing in her eyes an understanding he himself did not understand, Camorra moved aside. Looking to Howie, and holding out her hand, he took it, stepping into the pool. She too removed herself from his path.

In that moment, he wouldn't have traded places with Neil Armstrong himself. Ingrid, beside Camorra, smiled deeply, darkly, placing her hand along Camorra's shoulder. Without hesitation, Howie entered—his body was immediately devoured by the vortex of the aurora borealis, atoms shattering, ripped to vapor, no more.

Not as Expected

*U*nbeknown to him, from their perspective, he'd been wholly removed from existence. Here, in this sanctuary of secrets, cathedral for the enlightened mind, place most holy, the air was as clean as that of the meadow. All surfaces were of crystal. Though of many colors, these crystals were cut and fitted as stained glass.

As a pilgrim reaching the sum of his progress, his feet found the epicenter of this place. As a lush and vast seal of stained glass, it was the Praesidio Autem Veritas. And he, upon it, the seeker of truth who'd penetrated its realm, stood.

He tilted his head toward the vaulted ceiling of so many shades of natural wonder. His eyes closed—the sound of Tom clearing his throat brought him to spin around. Within the doorway, where that terrifyingly wonderful aurora no longer was, the others watched.

"How long—," he started to ask.

"Not long," said Ingrid.

Taking her place beside him, she gazed across the many rows of books and texts and records, and so very much more. "Say this exceeds what the Library of Alexandria contained."

Howie slowly nodded. "Say so." He smiled briefly at her. "Well, we've reached that point."

"Yeah," she said. "It's been... something else."

Giving her hand a quick squeeze, he glanced at Camorra looming directly behind them. His stomach immediately knotted. *No better time than the present, Howie.* Forcing himself, he pivoted, facing off with Camorra. Keeping his eyes locked upon him, he pushed Ingrid to the side, out of alignment with himself, and that which he'd been dreading.

"Camorra," he said, directly, soberly, "there's a responsibility, socially, to make whatever knowledge held here public. *Then,* if people ignore—deny its truths, that's their choice. Free will. But we—I, at least, must give the people the choice."

Camorra's fingers, then hand, slid beneath his coat, taking hold of that familiar object, cold and metal, and full of power. Concealed there, he'd hold it for a little longer. He'd allow Howie a few words before bringing closure. He could afford that.

The pounding of Howie's heart felt as though it was beating inside his ears. He clenched his hands into fists, not in anger, but to keep them from shaking. "And if that means I'm forcing you into a choice of your own, then, then..." He swallowed. "Then so be it."

Though Camorra had made his decision. Like the trapdoor of the gallows already having released, both the mechanism and consequences were in motion. It was unstoppable. And certainly, the words of this man, this *idealist,* Howard Lyon, could never change that. He pulled his hand from beneath his coat, gripping tightly the metal object full of power....

"Just like that?" asked Howie.

"Yes." Camorra took one look around at the enormity of what surrounded them. "I surely don't want the responsibility. Besides, blind allegiance to authority never ends well. For anyone."

Howie's hand met Camorra's, accepting the compass piece. Camorra's gesture, it wasn't just the passage of this key to unlocking mystery. It was the passage of the responsibility of this place. He'd be its caretaker. It'd be his mission, and his alone to be as *they,* those invisible watchmen. This was something without limit, without measure. It was his burden, as well treasure...

"I'm going with him." Ingrid said, suddenly.

She held out her hand, offering her open palm. "It is the best thing. The logical thing, given, well... Everything."

Embracing that which he could not change, he took her hand. He shook it professionally as he could. He released.

Without a second look, she turned and nodded ever briefly to Tom, then Mike. She departed with Camorra.

Penance

*T*he afternoon sun thawed, diffusing to dusk, casting an elongated shadow of Bran Castle on the giant oaks at the bottom of the hill. There, nestled under the trees, was the moss-clung structure among the emerald grass known as the *Tea House of Queen Marie*. Behind the teahouse, cloaked in the dying light, a gloved hand fitted a suppressor to a Heckler and Koch Mark 23 handgun.

Rubber moccasin-like shoes skillfully avoided the dry leaves as the silhouetted figure came to stop at the teahouse's backdoor. The gloved hand ran a rather simple-in-appearance electronic device, a touch smaller than a cellphone, over the door's handle. On screen, the device scanned, then found the frequency for the door's alarm. Shutting off the alarm, the screen glowed green. In perfect silence, the gloved hand turned the handle of the door.

Inside the rustic-style teahouse, Brahms Symphony Number One played rather loudly, and ever ominously. Howie held an empty coffee cup and got up from the café-style table. Without a care, though with many, he went to the kitchen and began to prepare a fresh pot of coffee.

The symphony flowed out from his laptop on the kitchen counter. Pausing the music, he checked his phone there charging beside the laptop. He had thirty-three missed calls, all from Tom. His finger hovered over the call button.

Gun-sights aligned with the back of his head. With accent

guised, a voice broke the short silence. "Hands flat on the counter, Mr. Lyon."

Howie forced himself to maintain calm, as his mind scrambled to determine who the voice could belong to. Whoever it was, was clearly skilled... Having gotten this close without setting off the new security system he'd just installed at the castle grounds. Which meant, this man wasn't just a man now likely holding a gun, but was one who also held a well-crafted skill set in taking life.

With no choice, Howie slowly breathed in, then exhaled. He placed his hands on the counter as told. He sensed this man grow closer. Though only an eerie silence filled the gap where footsteps, even the softest, should have been when crossing the old wooden floor.

"Where's the girl?" the voice, now directly behind him, asked.

"Not here."

"Turn, Mr. Lyon. Slowly."

Howie turned to face a man he'd never seen. Though there weren't many men who'd go through the trouble to be here now. "Mr. Favignana."

Domenico maintained a few feet of distance, just enough to discourage any attempt to disarm the gun. "Call me Domenico." He glanced at the digital watch on his wrist. "*Let's get this over with.* Shall we? Before your friend, Tom, it is, yes, returns from the neighboring town of Brasov." He pivoted slightly toward the dining area. "Let's take a seat at the table over there, the same one where you'd finished your coffee not long ago."

Howie knew he was powerless to change this ending. It was a consequence of the choice he'd made. This was his responsibility to own, now being caretaker of the library. It'd inescapably led to this moment of intersection. That was okay. For he'd made the right choice.

What *was* next was certain. There was a singular nature, purpose, for the suppressor attached to the gun now staring him dead in the face. And it silently proclaimed his situation's absoluteness.

"Walk to the table, Mr. Lyon. And keep your palms pressed firmly together."

Howie did.

"Sit."

Howie had begun to take his place at the table.

"No—the chair opposite that one."

Howie did as commanded. His back was now to the front door of the teahouse. Domenico took the chair across from him, giving himself a direct view of the door. He held his gun at retention, a technique only a seasoned marksman as he would do, ever close and in line with his own body. He let his elbow rest on the table, holding his aim perfectly steady. "Best to do these things sitting down. There's an unspoken dignity in the small comforts. Don't you agree, Mr. Lyon."

"Whatever you say, Domenico. You do know, you'll need the key to unlock the chamber."

"*Keys.* Plural, Mr. Lyon. And I know. You doubt my ability to find them?"

"Just trying to be helpful."

Domenico again glanced at his watch. "Your timing couldn't be worse on that field, Mr. Lyon."

Howie's hands had begun to drift away from the tabletop. "Please."

Howie stopped and held his palms flatly so on the cool metal surface of the table. "Now?"

"Soon, Mr. Lyon, as you know, your friend, Tom, will pass through that front door, the one that your back is to, and then, well, you know..."

"One thing..."

"Yes, the door's locked? And Tom doesn't have the key. Only you do. Isn't that right, Mr. Lyon? Isn't that what you were going to say?"

"You've thought of everything, haven't you."

"Yes. I've unlocked it. There's something I just don't

understand."

"Yeah?"

"With your intimacy with history, Mr. Lyon, you should have known there's ever only one end for social revolutionaries."

Howie stared back at Domenico. And maybe not with the dark intimidation this man projected, but with the same coldness. "Just because I'm afraid, which I am, Domenico, if I'm emotionally honest here, doesn't change the fact I'm not going to do what you want me to."

"Spoken like a true martyr."

"We each do what we do best. You, the adversary. Me, the hero, and thanks to *you*, Domenico, I now am elevated to martyr."

Domenico frowned. "Mr. Lyon, this isn't a thing defined by terms of morality. If the world is truly anything, it's a place filled with gray. Who's the adversary, who's the hero, is only a matter of perspective—" The glass on the front door exploded as a shoebox-sized rock sailed through it. Almost at the same time, the door kicked open, and Tom leaped in, adorned with a Dracula cape.

Not many things, and in fact, in that fraction of a moment, Domenico could not think of anything, not one which had successfully caused a delay in his reflexes to pull a trigger, *ever*. But that had done it. Be it a nanosecond of time, it was nonetheless long enough—Howie's laptop slammed at incredible speed against the side of Domenico's face, lifting him completely off the chair. Pieces of laptop splintered, showering in every direction.

Camorra stepped into view. He kicked away Domenico's gun and stood over him where he laid on the hardwood floor. "How's that for perspective." He dropped what little was left of the very much broken laptop next to the now very much unconscious Domenico.

"Damn, man," said Tom, "you hit him with that MacBook like it was a Mack truck."

Camorra crouched down and made sure Domenico was indeed out. He retrieved the gun. Howie, still seated, and his palms still glued flatly to the table's surface, struggled to process what had just happened.

"Say thank you, Mr. Camorra," Tom told him.

"Thank you," Howie meekly said. He silently pointed to the cape.

Tom pulled it off. "Worked, didn't it."

Camorra patted down Domenico. He found only the coin which he'd given him during their first meeting within the Vatican Gardens. He returned the coin to his own pocket, then tightly secured a pair of handcuffs to Domenico's wrists.

What'd actually happened began to set in for Howie. "If you're *here*, Camorra, then you had to have been here..." He looked to the window. "Lurking out there somewhere, waiting for Domenico to show up." He got up from the table, starting to feel his heart return to a more normal pace, as well place within his body. He shifted to Tom. "You guys used me as bait..." He pointed at Tom, then Camorra. "You *used* me as bait."

Tom slapped him across the back. "Okay, yes, bait. But our man, Camorra, here, caught the shark, now didn't he."

"By using a bigger shark!" Howie turned to Camorra. "No offense."

"What can I say," said Tom, "sometimes, you need a bigger shark."

Howie glanced at Tom, lacking the energy to respond... "Now what?" he asked, not sure if the complacent numbness flowing through him was the product of exhaustion or trauma.

"There's only one thing to do with a man like Domenico," Camorra answered, lifting Domenico's unconscious body.

With Domenico over his shoulder, he started for the broken door. The shattered glass crunched under his boots like shark teeth upon bone. Or that's what Howie and Tom envisioned it sounded, as it popped violently, grinding along the floor's wooden planks.

Camorra quickened his pace out of the little teahouse. He had a plane to catch. The Teresi brothers were not individuals one wanted to be late to meet, not even for someone like himself...

The Assassin and the Spy Part II:
A Sicilian Baptism

*D*omenico awoke to the roll of the ship swaying back and forth in the waves. There was a patchwork of cobalt sky and ashen clouds of earliest morning. A seagull flew across his field of vision. Adapting to his surroundings, he realized he was on the top deck of what looked to be a container ship. Just, this massive and rusty place which he laid upon, had no containers.

A single question entered his mind. *Where the hell was he?* He pulled himself up. Pain rushed to the side of his face. Touching the spot, dried blood rubbed off.

There, not far, was something peculiar. Crudely formed from two wooden beams, badly splintered at their ends, it was lashed together by a knotted, rust-soaked chain. There was no doubt within his mind who had fashioned this thing... This cross. Camorra emerged from behind the creaking door of the ship's bridge, gripping Domenico's gun.

"What're you doing with my gun?"

"Bilge rats." Camorra closed the space, though maintained a prudent distance. With his other hand, he held up the coin. "Contract's reached dissolution."

"All this over a woman?"

"Told you, Domenico, at the beginning, my oath has always been to the Rite of the Camorra. Not to you." He glanced at the seagull, having just landed on the railing.

"And *my* duty is to preserve the Vatican's legacy."

"So it is, Domenico. Now, we're on opposite sides. It happens."

The wind blew one of the feathers loose from the perched seagull, who seemed a curious spectator. The feather floated along an invisible path of cool and salty air.

"Should know, Domenico, the Church's legacy holds about as much value as that feather there, with all I've seen."

"You found something of significance then?"

The feather swirled within the space separating them.

"Yes. The greatest adversary... Truth." Camorra pointed the gun at the cross.

Leading to it, for the first time in his life, Domenico was without power. The seagull watched as the feather, no longer its own, glided away. This feather followed these two men, who were not quite friends, not quite enemies, but damned to a place between.

At the cross, Domenico stopped. "What truth?"

Before it could escape, Camorra snatched the feather from the air. "How about the fact our lives have been a sick irony? Your beloved Santa Alleanza, it was founded by the L' Entita. It was their creation, when they first established Christianity. To be its guardian angels—did you know?"

"Yes." Domenico focused on the ocean before them. "Of course I did. The snake which eats its own tail. So goes the tale."

Camorra's free hand imprisoned the feather. It was a fragile thing, just as life. In one minute, connected, part of something alive, bigger than itself. Then, in the next instant, and for no reason other than the whim of the wind, torn away, adrift, alone, forever disconnected, becoming... Dead. But there was reason now. He did not enjoy it, but it was his path, his way. "That coil of rope next to the cross."

Domenico stared at him, defiant.

"You can do it shot, Domenico, bleeding out for the sharks

down there. Or without."

Domenico knew better than any, Camorra's iron will had been forged by fires not known to many men, and few indeed, as it could not be bent, twisted, or challenged. He laid his body to the cross and did his best to secure himself with the rope. Camorra leaned down, tucking the feather into Domenico's jacket pocket.

He did something to absolve any guilt that could haunt him. He removed a small but sharp knife from his own pocket. First cutting halfway through the rope binding Domenico's right wrist to the cross, he then tucked the knife into Domenico's belt.

"Warrior's death," Domenico said, squinting up at him.

"Warrior's death."

"Until that day, Camorra."

"Until that day, Domenico." Camorra stood and waved toward the ship's bridge.

Rino and Richie exited through the bridge's creaky door. Camorra handed the gun to Rino. With Richie's help, Camorra hefted up Domenico tied to the cross. Camorra paused, giving Domenico a few seconds more.

Domenico watched the rising sun along the horizon. It was a beautiful thing... The sunrise. Such a simple thing. *Why hadn't he watched more of these?* He nodded to Camorra. The cross, with him upon it, dropped over the side of the container ship. Camorra refused to watch, turning away.

Rino returned Domenico's gun to Camorra. "Nothing quite like a Sicilian Baptism. Oh, here. Deeds done reap deeds under the sun." He gave Camorra the deed to his Monaco villa.

Loose Ends Ending Naught

*T*he uniquely glorious North African sunrise of Casablanca, Morocco, painted itself across the skyline behind the mother and father and boy as they stood there, more than a bit bewildered before the brand-new bicycle, brand-new scooter, and brand-new motorcycle neatly aligned at their doorstep on their modest lawn. An equally new chain, wrapped and locked around all three, secured them from any would-be thieves, or even, from well-meaning men in a frantic situation.

In a simple paper bag, the father found a key to the locked chain. The key was threaded upon a perfect bow, tied to a stack of ten thousand dollars. There was no note. The boy's parents had no clue for such unclaimed generosity. But the boy knew.

˜ *Once Domenico's Office - Vatican City* ˜

"Congratulations on your new position, Prefect Vaccaro," said the well-dressed man holding a box of Domenico's personal items.

"Yes, thank you," Lucia said. "This direct merger between the Santa Alleanza and Roman Curia should have happened years ago."

She took a seat in the empty chair behind the desk in what had been Domenico's office, now hers. Her eyes drifted to Domenico's family coat of arms on the wall. Open, it hung there by its hinges, revealing the safe behind it. The safe was also open.

"See that they remove that," she said, nodding to the coat of arms.

"Certainly. And what of Favignana?"

"MIA," she answered, smoothly, coldly.

"The field, it can be a dangerous place, even for men with instincts as his, for the fiercest of predators."

"You know what they say." She leaned back in the chair. "In the mouth of the wolf..."

"May the wolf die."

Upon his exit, she used her phone, now programmed to do so, to seal the office's double doors. Setting aside her phone, she opened the rather ordinary looking wooden case on the desk. Inside, a chill wafted up from the book nested within. Removing it, she shivered.

Reading the title aloud, a curse incarnate, the fateful words escaped her lips in a most eternally damning way. "*Nascita Dalla Morte.*"

From her purse, her hand took the antique and gilded contact lens case. It was quite old. In fact, the oldest in existence, when it came to cases for lens involving the eyes. And her lens had been on her eyes for a long time, far, far too long. She removed her contacts, and ever carefully placed them within in the case.

Her fingers came to rest on the Praesidio Autem Veritas at the center of the book's cover. Gilded, like her lens case, the golden symbol on the decaying leather began to transition, turning glassy and perfectly reflective. She stared at herself in its now mirrored surface. Her impossibly blue eyes reflected back.

Slipping the lens case containing her brown colored contacts, which concealed her true identity, into her purse, she reached for the *Nascita Dalla Morte.* Something caught her deeply pale sapphire eyes. And mid-reach, she stopped, and instead took hold the DNA scanner on the desk.

Yes... The simple technologies of humans. *They* placed far too much faith in such things. Religion offered answers it knew not to be true, while science lacked the context to answer anything. That'd been Domenico's undoing. He hadn't a chance... Faith in science, in order to preserve religion... A venture dually doomed.

Though, it couldn't have been more sublime, masterfully so, this masterpiece she'd planned. Domenico's descent to those dark waters was her ascension. He couldn't walk across the sea most holy after all. It'd wholly swallowed him. And reciprocity had spoken, having the final word. *Finally.*

And finally, the clandestine knights of the Holy See, guardians of the headquarters for Christianity, the Santa Alleanza, were once more under the control of the L' Entita. Since its inception, Christianity had always been the L' Entita's creation. And, of course, with the helping hand of the Flavians, Herods, and Alexanders... Though these bloodlines, most powerful, they were still just mere tools to an end... *The* end.

Not even the Santa Alleanza had ever recognized the truth to this end. Unlike the Holy See, and to be fair, any institution regarding religion, the L' Entita never cared about establishing Christianity or other systems of belief. Nor did they of the consequence of making that trinity of first century families incredibly powerful throughout history ever after. Simply, all this was a pretext, a ticket most golden. It'd been the perfect means to collect and acquirer the necessary blood samples— DNA of a *very select* group of lineages.

"As above so below."

The true meaning of the L' Entita's motto had yet to be revealed. She opened the *Nascita Dalla Morte.* By a divine union of fate intersecting with chance, out of all the hundreds of pages it contained, the one page she sought rested before her. *Soon. The end would arrive. After all...* She smiled. *It'd already begun...*

~ *Somewhere Off the Moroccan Coast* ~

On the deck of the old container ship, Rino, Richie, and Howie stood along the railing. They watched the sunset. Fully bloomed, burning fiercely across the sky, it began to settle into the ocean.

"The small things," Rino said.

"The big things," answered Richie.

"Both," said Howie.

Rino tucked in his tie as the sea breeze tugged playfully at it. "Howard, can't believe you've already spent your cut of the money from all that gold we pulled up."

"Yeah, you should've bought a new pirate ship," said Richie. "This one, what's the word, Rino?"

"Sucks," Rino answered, attempting to wipe away the rusty dust coating his expensive Italian shoes.

Howie's blue eyes sparkled in the ocean sunlight. "Well, not all, but a chunk of the money, yes. And naw, I'm happy with my castle. Even if it's not exactly new." His sparkling eyes wandered to the fragmented pieces of decayed metal and rotted wood heaped in a pile before them.

"Oh, Howard, almost forgot," Rino said. "Atop all that junk there is something we Teresi brothers found for you."

"Being business partners, and all," said Richie.

Scooping it up, Howie held the brass nameplate. He read aloud its name. "HMS *Sussex.*" Pocketing it, he smiled at them. "Thank you. In my younger days, I'd have mailed it to the Spanish Government." He started digging through the heap of junk, sifting for things needing discovery. "Wish I could've been there when you'd brought up all that gold."

"You didn't miss nothing special," Rino said. "Just a big, big pile of moldy-looking metal. Green and smelly."

Howie wiped the sweat from his brow, streaking his skin with the muck now clung to his hands. "Hey, only the movies claim treasure hunting to be glamorous."

Epilogue
~ A Very Romanian Reunion ~

*S*now silently cascaded onto Bran Castle. Huddled inside the master living room, Howie, Ingrid, Tom, and Mike drew warmth from the lively flames of the large fireplace. Resting above it was the sword Howie had found in Malta.

"Really did keep that old thing didn't you," said Ingrid.

"Sometimes a sword makes it play before it's displayed on the mantle," Howie answered. "Think I'll leave it there when the castle reopens in spring for the tourists."

"Cost ninety million bucks to buy and you don't even get to live here," said Tom.

"Was a steal," Howie said. "Considering the contents of the wine cellar." He held up his glass of wine. "Thank you all for coming on such short notice."

"Sure thing, kid, always up for crossing the Romanian countryside in the dead heat of a blizzard." Mike said. "So, where's this map?"

Sliding it from his pocket, Howie unfolded the eight-by-eleven leather map, giving it to Ingrid. She ran her fingers across the ancient symbols only she knew, and along the grid-like pattern covering this map of the world. "Well, Howie, you've found yourself a chart showing the hidden locations for each of the L' Entita's chambers, for the entire planet."

"There's other chambers than what we've already seen?" Tom asked.

"Oh yes," she answered, holding it up. "See these lines. Those represent an energy grid not yet quantified by science, but make no mistake, it's there."

"What do they have to do with the chambers?" Howie asked.

"Everything." She set her finger on a point on the map. "For every place where those lines intersect with each other, like where this castle sits, there's an energy anomaly."

"And those are the locations where your ancestors built their chambers," said Mike.

"Exactly," she said, handing back the map to Howie. "According to this map, that energy grid is the actual power source for the chambers themselves."

Before she could pull her hand away, Howie took hold of her wrist. Their eyes met in the crackle of the firelight. He leaned close, severing the distance between his lips and hers. Her heart beat quicker, harder. Tom and Mike shared a glance as Howie drew closer, making his advance....

There was something cool to her touch. Her eyes shifted from him to the crystal tablet he'd just placed in her hand. Leaning back, he finished his wine and smiled.

Remarkable in dimensions to that of a VHS tape, she read silently the symbols carved into it. Not certain she'd translated correctly, she read it to herself again. Her fleeting feelings of romance withered. In their place sprang up a twisting knot of awe and fear. She looked up. "Howie... Where did you find this?" The shift in her demeanor was sharp, demanding.

"It is important then," he said. "In the same section as the map. I'm guessing that area is the L' Entita's own library, and that crystal tablet there was at the center of it all."

"I see," she said. Her gaze returned to the symbols carved elegantly into the tablet. The magnitude for what it claimed to be, greatly challenged the edges of her mind. The scale of what it offered... Was nearly too much. *Nearly*. For... *How could anyone believe there could an adventure greater than the one they'd so recently taken...*

"Ingrid," Tom said, "you're killing us here. What is it?"

Setting the tablet down, she pushed it away, giving herself some distance. "There's no direct translation, but what this proclaims to be, is... Well, an actual video of the history of *everything*."

Tom's eyes grew bigger than any of them had ever seen. He grabbed the tablet. "Like a videotape of the history of the planet that's—that's been recording since the beginning of the earth?"

"Like a videotaped recording of the *universe* since its inception," she answered.

"But how is that possible?" asked Mike. "I mean—not that we haven't witnessed shock and wonder thus far, but, but you're talking about, the comprehensive record of human evolution. Of the planet. Of... *Everything*."

"Hey, I'm just the interpreter," she said. "And, yes, absolutely, I admit, I don't have the answers. Though I know this much, guys, I know without a doubt the L' Entita's ability to unlock the recorded information within DNA wasn't *exclusive* to human beings. It couldn't be." She gestured to the tablet. "Clearly, they held that ability for all species. And perhaps, for life... other than how we know it. How else can we explain how they've constructed this recording? This comprehensive record of life itself... Of all things experienced..."

Still clutching the tablet in one hand, Tom took the wine bottle from the table and topped off Mike's glass. "Looks like you're going to be out of a job, *old* man."

Mike grinned. "You two might be as well." He ignored the wine and jumped to his feet. "Let's go—let's go play it!"

Howie rose from the large and antique chair he'd grown surprisingly comfortable in, joining his father. "Shall we?"

Ingrid turned to Tom, who reluctantly gave over the tablet. She studied hard this tablet of crystal glossily sparkling, staring back at her. Her ancestors had placed her and these three men on a path to its discovery, creating this moment of intersection with it, here and now. That, was design. That... was deliberate. *Why?* She had to know.

* * * *

Beneath Bran Castle, past the Romanian princess's secret passage, beyond the lush and luminous meadow of enchantment, at the heart of this mountain of legend, the chamber's crystal-laden skin breathed waves of light, various and vibrant. The four of them settled into the soft embrace of the plush theater-style chairs now installed there, encircling the pulpit. On the pulpit, the crystal tablet rested, fitting perfectly between the compass piece and capstone.

Thin ribbons of glowing gold spiraled up from the tablet. These electrified slivers drifted, spreading as if seeds of a great gilded dandelion. In their seats of modern luxury, surrounded by this archaic technology, a desire built, a truest need for what secrets it could whisper into their souls. This call to adventure bled into them, staining itself, wrapping tightly, with bonds unbreakable to their blood, blending to their very DNA. In this way, they offered their bodies as vessels, to be filled with its magic, to be engraved with the mystery.

Full and steady, the hum did come, funneling out the crystal pulpit. The hiss of things cloaked in enigma slithered as silk through their ears, teasingly. Bubbling from the pulpit began a hazy membrane coated with colors gnawing across its veneer. Taking the shape of a sphere, it manifested a cosmic jungle within. Swallowing them, galaxies unknown swirled all around, around and around.

Bringing them with, this cosmos burst out far and away, an explosion adrift. Blurring by, they saw each galaxy to be as unique and plentiful as snowflakes. With every heartbeat, new perspective abounded them, assaulting their minds to a subdued peace. They accepted their inability to not understand the things revealed to them. And that was the closest they could achieve to understanding.

What they did know now, through, and through it, space was not how humans believed it to be, perceived it to be. It was not separate unto earth. The most distant celestial bodies were no more detached from their home planet than the sand was from the ocean or land beyond its shores. Size did not denote importance. This place of space filled with certain death, saturated in life, in not how they knew it to be, didn't belong to them. Its scale was meant for things other than themselves.

Barely catching their breath, they zoomed in, racing toward a specific planet. It was their home planet. Piercing its atmosphere, breaking through to the clouds, the layout of the land and water was unfamiliar. It was of an earth before humans, of a time before continental drift in how they were familiar, and before a great many cycles of ice and drought had sculpted it. Still, this place, the most beautiful in all the cosmos, was undeniably earth. In full flight, as things took shape beneath the clouds, they shared a single question... *Had life started on earth, or ended up here from somewhere else?*

As if answering their call, a voice known only to Ingrid, for it was her grandfather's, floated out from the pulpit of crystal. "How life began on planet earth..."

A prehistoric landscape appeared. As the wings of eagles singing across the sky, they sailed away and beyond this desert of volcanos most volatile. As the Atlantic, an expanse of sapphire waves blanketed beneath. Gliding down, they closed in on one of the green islands speckled across its rich blue.

An overlay of a new earth, of the earth they knew, displayed onto this place of another time, of their time. With its broken crescent shape, windingly graceful coastlines, distinct beaches of pink sand, this was Bermuda. Flying overhead, they saw the town of Mount Pleasant, then Hamilton, to the obscured and entirely charming, Flatts Village. Skirting its outskirts, beneath the foliage thickly gripping the jagged labyrinth of rocks which bordered between ocean and land, steeply steeped in the exotic, was a cave, entirely hidden.

Sailing down through it, they found themselves within an underground vault of rose-hued rock and sand, smooth and snowy. At the center of this place, known only in dreams, was a pool, clearly deep and deeply clear. Broken beams of slender sunlight streamed in from somewhere above unseen. Ignited, delicately so, by one of these beams, something shimmered at the bottom of this pool. Taken beneath the water's surface, to this object which sparkled, they saw it be a box, triangular in shape. The size of a suitcase, it was metal, beautiful and brilliant. Seared into its face was the Praesidio Autem Veritas.

The voice of her grandfather came to be once more, all around them. "In the beginning, life began—" Everything shut off, with the projection going completely black, vanishing.

"Oh come on!" Tom yelled.

Stepping from her chair, Ingrid went to the pulpit, placing her palms flush to its crystal surface. Her eyes closed. A single phrase projected out....

Enter the Word Key

Tom slumped in his chair. "They want a bloody password before they'll tell us the history to our *own* bloody planet— to our own bloody species?"

Howie turned to Mike, sharing a mutual scream in silence. Then Howie's eyes met Ingrid's. He realized those things unfinished, those things never given a chance between her and him, those things could have both a beginning and resolution... *If* they shared another adventure... A grander adventure. He jumped from his chair, then yanked Tom up. "Get the tickets for Bermuda." With Tom staring blankly at him, he grabbed him by the collar, shaking him. "Tom—there's no snow in Bermuda."

Tom's face lit up. He took off out of the chamber. Mike chased after.

Removing the compass piece and capstone, Howie stepped close to Ingrid. He set these keys into her hand. "Ready. For this quest… *Quest for Life*."

"What of Camorra's apple?" she asked.

"If it's to be needed, then we haven't seen the last of him."

Hand in hand, they departed on their *Quest for Life*….

ABOUT THE AUTHOR

JC Damien is the author of *The Quest Series*, featuring Howie Lyon. The second book in the series is *Quest for Life*. JC Damien has written six feature-length screenplays, each registered with the WGAW. He earned his MFA in Screenwriting from CSU Northridge, his Professional Certification in Screenwriting from UCLA's School of Theater, Film and Television, and his Bachelor of Arts in Creative Writing from UC Riverside. When he's not traveling for "research", he spends his days writing screenplays, novels, and poetry. After the sun succumbs to twilight, you can find him with a captivating book or movie. He resides in the San Diego area.

www.jcdamien.com

www.biblequestthenovel.com

www.thequestnovelseries.com